Happy Mother's Day
Mom,

Thank you for all
you have done for
us.

All our love!
Marge John

WHAT
SHE LEFT
BEHIND

**Center Point
Large Print**

Also by Ellen Marie Wiseman and available from
Center Point Large Print:

The Plum Tree

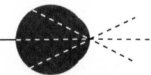

**This Large Print Book carries the
Seal of Approval of N.A.V.H.**

WHAT SHE LEFT BEHIND

Ellen Marie Wiseman

CENTER POINT LARGE PRINT
THORNDIKE, MAINE

This Center Point Large Print edition is
published in the year 2014 by arrangement with
Kensington Publishing Corp.

The text of this Large Print edition is unabridged.
In other aspects, this book may vary
from the original edition.
Printed in the United States of America
on permanent paper.
Set in 16-point Times New Roman type.

ISBN: 978-1-62899-065-2

Library of Congress Cataloging-in-Publication Data

Wiseman, Ellen Marie.
 What she left behind / Ellen Marie Wiseman. — Center Point Large
Print edition.
 pages cm
 ISBN 978-1-62899-065-2 (Library binding : alk. paper)
 1. Psychiatric hospitals—Fiction.
   2. Self-actualization (Psychology) in adolescence—Fiction.
   3. Psychological fiction. 4. Large type books. I. Title.
 PS3623.I833W43 2014
 813′.6—dc23
                                                    2014001488

For my husband, Bill—
who believes in me always

ACKNOWLEDGMENTS

Once again, it is with great joy that I honor the people who helped, supported, and believed in me throughout this amazing journey.

First and foremost, this novel would not have come to fruition if not for the work of Darby Penney and Peter Stastny, authors of *The Lives They Left Behind: Suitcases from a State Hospital Attic.* It was your book that inspired the idea and opened my eyes to the often heartbreaking world of the insane asylums of the past. I'm especially indebted to Darby Penney for taking the time to answer my questions about Willard State and what it might have been like for female patients in the 1930s. I hope you'll forgive any historical inaccuracies and creative licenses I've taken.

For answering my questions about women in prison, I thank Deborah Jiang Stein, author and founder of The unPrison Project. Thank you also to Andrew Thompson for sharing his knowledge of correction officers.

Thank you to my family and friends for understanding my crazy schedule, for forgiving me when I had to say no, and for allowing me the time and space I needed to make my deadlines. I'm forever grateful for your belief in me, for your patience and understanding during this sometimes-bumpy ride, and most of all, your steadfast love.

To say that I'm grateful to my author posse at BP is an understatement. I can't imagine experiencing this crazy, exhilarating ride without your friendship and brilliant advice. Together, we're conquering the world, one book at a time!

It is with great pleasure that I send my love and gratitude out to my friend and cosmic sister, Barbara Titterington. Thank you for being one of my biggest cheerleaders and for reading an early draft of the manuscript. It helps knowing that in your eyes, I always sparkle.

Again, I'm eternally indebted to my wonderful editor, John Scognamiglio, for his faith in me, and to my patient and insightful agent, Michael Carr. I can't thank you enough for your unwavering support, your great advice, and for helping me make this story stronger. Thank you also to my publicist, Vida Engstrand, for getting the word out about my novels, and to Meryl Earl, Director of Sub Rights, for securing foreign rights for my books. Thank you also to Kristine Mills-Noble for your gorgeous cover designs. And again, a thousand thanks to the rest of the Kensington team for all the hard work you do behind the scenes.

I cannot write a note of thanks without a shout-out to the people who live in and around my community. Whether you are a librarian who invited me to do a presentation, a journalist who did a story on me, a member of a book club who invited me into your home, an online supporter, or someone who read my work and made sure to tell me you enjoyed it, I can't begin to tell you how much your encouragement and thoughtfulness has meant to me. Seeing your smiling, excited faces has filled my eyes with tears and my heart with pride. It truly has been one of the highlights of this experience and I will remember it always.

As ever, thank you from the bottom of my heart to my beloved mother, Sigrid, for being my rock, and my dear husband, Bill, for seeing me through. Words cannot express how much you mean to me. Lastly and most importantly, I want to express my immense love and gratitude to my children, Ben, Jessica, and Shanae, and my beautiful grand-children, Rylee, Harper, and Lincoln. You are my greatest accomplishment, and I love you with everything that I am. You, alone, make life worth living.

CHAPTER 1

ISABELLE

Willard State Asylum
1995

Within minutes of setting foot on the grounds of the shuttered Willard State Asylum, seventeen-year-old Isabelle Stone knew it was a mistake. If anyone saw her standing on the cracked and pot-holed main road of the vast, tree-lined property, they would have no clue of the horror festering inside her head.

On that hazy Saturday in late August, the warm breeze smelled of cattails and seaweed, occasional gusts rustling the grove of pines to the left of the open yard. Heat rose in shimmery vapors from the sunbaked earth and cicadas buzzed in the long grass near the woods, a droning, live thermometer that grew higher pitched and more insistent with every rising degree. Willard's manicured lawns sloped away from the main buildings, gently rolling downward toward the rocky shoreline of Seneca Lake. Sailboats bobbed across the waves and a long pier stretched like an invitation into the sparkling waters.

Isabelle—her father used to call her Izzy—should have been enjoying the warm sunshine and beautiful view. Instead, she grit her teeth and struggled to push the image of a bleeding hole in her father's skull from her mind. She felt like she was trapped in purgatory. Would she ever find peace, or would she always be that seven-year-old girl, reliving the horrible night her father was murdered?

Izzy stepped out of the shadow of Chapin Hall, the institution's massive main building, and faced the sun, eyes closed, trying to repress all thought. But when she turned to look up at the three-story brick Victorian with cathedral windows, the snarl of grief and fear returned. An enormous two-story cupola with porthole windows towered above a black mansard roof sprouting numerous attic dormers, turrets, and chimneys. A stone portico with disintegrating pillars protected the giant double doors of the main entrance. Black bars covered the tall, multipaned windows, nearly all of which were boarded up from the inside, except for the dormers in the attic and the round, porthole windows in the cupola. It looked more like a haunted mansion than a place designed to help people.

Izzy wondered what horrors the hulking building had witnessed. What dreadful memories had attached themselves to the bricks and mortar and clouded glass, forever part of the structure, mortared and sealed with blood and tears? Just as pain and anguish would always be part of who she was, the memories of thousands of tortured souls would live on in Chapin Hall and the surrounding buildings of Willard State. How could this place ever be anything but a miserable reminder of lives and loved ones lost?

She swallowed and turned toward the water, one hand shielding the sun from her eyes. She wondered if passing boaters looked over at the asylum and assumed the cluster of brick buildings and pastoral grounds belonged to a country club or college. From a distance, it looked orderly and genteel. But she knew better. She imagined the former patients in the yard, sitting in wheelchairs or shuffling across the grass, hospital gowns hanging from thin frames, eyes glazed over. She imagined being one of them, looking out over the blue lake. Did the patients realize that other people were taking boat trips, cooking dinner, falling in love and having children in the small communities across the bay? Did they wonder if they would ever be released, allowed to rejoin the "normal" world? Or were they completely unaware of the lives they were missing?

Izzy's stomach cramped as another memory flickered in her mind: her mother, Joyce, sprawled across a bed at the Elmira Psychiatric Center, eyes glazed over, staring blankly at the ceiling, hair sticking out in all directions. It had been a sultry day just like this one, and Izzy remembered her mother's mascara and eyeliner, melted and running down her pale cheeks, like a clown left out in the rain. She remembered burying her face in her grandmother's skirt, begging to go home. She'd never forget the endless white halls of the psych ward, the smell of urine and bleach, the dim rooms, the patients in wheelchairs and beds surrounded by rubber walls. After that visit, she had nightmares for years. She asked her grand-mother not to make her go back and, thankfully, her grandmother agreed.

Izzy wrapped her arms around herself and moved along the broken pavement of Willard's main road, wondering how she found herself here, exploring a giant replica of that creepy hospital ward. She could have claimed a headache or a queasy stomach, anything to get out of coming. There were other museum employees who could have come in her place. But she didn't want to disappoint her new foster mother, Peg, the museum curator. For the first time since she was ten, after her grandmother died, Izzy had foster parents who seemed to care.

Sure, she was going to turn eighteen in less than a year. She'd been in the system long enough to know that eighteenth birthdays weren't marked by celebrations. When the checks stopped coming, she'd be on her own. "Aging out" of foster care meant becoming homeless. She'd heard stories of kids ending up in jail and hospital emergency rooms, selling drugs, living on welfare and food stamps. How desperate did a person have to become before they broke the law to survive? For now, things were good, and she didn't want to mess that up.

Earlier, Peg had asked her to come to the old asylum to help safeguard anything that might be worth keeping before the buildings were condemned. Without a word about her reservations, Izzy had agreed. She was relieved when Peg let her explore outside first, instead of making her go inside with the others, clambering into basements, wandering through the morgue, touring the dozens of abandoned patient wards. But she wondered what Peg would think if she knew that just being near Willard made her nauseous.

She crossed a wooden bridge over a dry creek bed, then followed the one-lane road toward the grove of pines. To her left, a flock of Canada geese foraged in an overgrown field, their heads curved above the goldenrod like black canes. A few feet from the edge of the road, three grayish-yellow goslings lay cradled in a nest of timothy and chickweed, their necks stretched out in the grass. Izzy stopped to watch, motionless. The babies' eyes were open, but they weren't moving. She edged closer, keeping one eye on the adults in the field. No matter how close she drew, the goslings stayed in the same spot, still as river stones. Izzy swallowed, her throat burning. The goslings were either dead or dying.

She knelt and picked one up, turning its soft, limp body over in her hands, feeling beneath its wings and stomach for wounds. She moved its legs and neck, checking for broken bones. There was no sign of trauma, and the bird's fuzzy down was still warm. Then the gosling blinked. It was still alive. Maybe they were sick, poisoned by improperly disposed chemicals or psychiatric medicines from Willard. Izzy picked up the other two goslings, found no sign of injury, and laid them back down.

Briefly, she wondered if Peg would allow her to bring them home, to nurse them back to health. Then she remembered that wild animals were better off being left alone. Maybe their mother would return and recognize what was wrong. Izzy straightened and continued down the road, her eyes brimming with tears. She watched over her shoulder, hoping the goslings' parents would appear. Hopefully, nothing had happened to them. Then, all of a sudden, the goslings jumped up and scurried into the field, their mother honking and rushing toward them through the grass. Izzy grinned and wiped her eyes, surprised that geese would play dead.

Breathing a sigh of relief, she continued toward the pine grove. On one side of the road, a leaning four-story building sat in the middle of a field, its shattered windows covered with iron bars, its roof collapsed, the green tiles and broken wood covered in black mold. It looked as if it had been dropped from the sky, like a ship pulled from the sea and tossed a thousand miles from shore. On the other side of the road, rows of cast iron grave markers lined a scraggly meadow, tilting left and right like crooked, gray teeth. A bitter taste filled Izzy's throat. It was Willard's cemetery. She spun around and hurried back to the main structure, toward the staggered rows of brick, factory-sized buildings connected to Chapin Hall—the patient wards.

The wards' fire escapes were inside wire cages, and the dirty windows were covered with thick bars, the rotting sills oozing a black sludge that ran down the brick walls. Most of the doors and windows had been boarded up from the inside, as if the memories of what had happened there should never again see the light of day. Izzy shivered. How many patients had suffered and died in this awful place?

Just then, someone called her name, pulling her from her thoughts. She turned to see Peg trotting along the road in her direction, a wide smile on her face. From the moment Izzy met her new foster mother, she was reminded of a sixties hippie. Today was no exception. Peg wore denim overalls and a flowery gypsy top, her hair a free-flowing mess of wild curls.

"Isn't this place amazing?" Peg said. "I didn't know it was this huge!"

"It's big, that's for sure," Izzy said, trying to sound agreeable.

"Did you see the boathouse and the dock?" Peg said. "That's where Willard Asylum's first patient arrived by steamboat in October 1869. Her name was Mary Rote and she was a deformed, demented woman who had been chained without a bed or clothing in a cell in the Columbia County almshouse for ten years. Three male patients arrived at the dock that day too, all in irons. One of them was inside what looked like a chicken crate."

Izzy looked toward the pier. To the right of the dock sat a two-story boathouse with broken windows and missing shingles, like a bruised face with drooping eyelids. "That sounds barbaric!" she said.

"It was," Peg said. "But that's why Willard was built. It was supposed to be a place for the incurably mad who were taking up space in poorhouses and jails. Within days of their arrival at the new asylum, the new patients were bathed, dressed, fed, and—usually—resting quietly on the wards."

"So people were treated well here?"

Peg's face went dark. "At first, I think so, yes. But through the years, Willard got overcrowded and conditions deteriorated. Unfortunately, nearly half of Willard's fifty thousand patients died here."

Izzy bit down on the inside of her cheek, wondering how to ask if she could go wait in the car. Then Peg grinned and grabbed Izzy's hand.

"Come on!" she said, her eyes lighting up. "One of the former employees wants to show us something in the shuttered workshop. I think it's going to be an important find and I don't want you to miss it!"

Izzy groaned inside and followed her foster mother along the main road toward the workshop, trying to come up with an excuse not to go inside. Nothing came to her. Nothing that didn't sound stupid or crazy anyway. And she didn't want Peg to think she was crazy. This past summer, when she first arrived at Peg and Harry's, she was certain they'd be like the rest of her foster parents, taking kids in for the money and free labor. Harry was the art director of the state museum, and Izzy got the feeling that between the two of them, they didn't make a lot of money. But thankfully, finally, this time she was wrong. Her new foster parents were actually decent people, willing to give her the space, both physically and emotionally, a young woman needed. Back at Peg and Harry's three-story house in Interlaken, she had her own room that looked out over the lake, with a TV, DVD player, and a personal computer. They said it was up to her to keep their trust. It was the first time anyone had ever put the ball in her court, without judging her first. And now, for the first time in a long time, Izzy felt like she was part of something "normal."

And yet, sometimes her new situation seemed too good to be true. In the back of her mind, she knew something or someone would come along and screw it up. That's just the way her life worked. Then she remembered that her first day at her new school was in two days and her stomach twisted. Being the new kid was always hard.

The closer they got to the workshop, the hotter Izzy's neck and chest grew. Like her mother, she had silver-blue eyes, black hair, and a bone white complexion. When she got nervous, red, blotchy patches broke out over her neck and chest. She could feel her skin welting up now. Being outside on the lawns of the asylum was one thing. But now she was going inside one of the buildings. The urge to flee swelled in her mind, making her heart race. *It's just part of my job,* she told herself. *It has nothing to do with me, or my mother. Besides, it's time to put away childish fears.*

She pulled her long hair up on top of her head and tied it in a knot, letting the breeze cool her neck.

"Aren't you hot in that long-sleeved shirt?" Peg said.

"No," Izzy said, pulling the edges of her sleeves down and holding them inside her fists. "It's pretty thin."

"I noticed when I was folding your laundry that you don't have any short-sleeved shirts," Peg said. "Maybe we can go shopping and get you some new clothes."

Izzy tried to smile. "Thanks," she said. "But I like long sleeves. And you don't have to do my laundry."

"I don't mind," Peg said, smiling. "I just can't understand why anyone would want to wear long sleeves in this weather."

Izzy shrugged. "I'm a little self-conscious about my arms," she said. "They're so skinny and pale."

"Most girls would love to have long, slender arms and legs like yours," Peg said, laughing.

Not if they could see the scars, Izzy thought.

She looked toward the lake and saw groups of people gathered near the shoreline, sitting at picnic tables, walking, playing softball and badminton. Most were in worn, faded clothing, shuffling along as if dazed by medication. She stopped. "Who are they?" she asked Peg.

Peg shielded her eyes from the sun and squinted toward the shore. "They're probably from the nearby Elmira Psychiatric Center," Peg said. "There's a campground down by the lake. Sometimes the staff bring the patients here for outings."

Izzy's eyes filled and she started walking again, staring at the ground.

Peg followed. "What's wrong?" she said.

"That's where my mother was," Izzy said. "In Elmira."

Peg put a hand on Izzy's shoulder. "I'm sorry. I didn't know."

Izzy lifted her head and tried to muster a smile. "It's okay. It was a long time ago."

"I hope you know I'm willing to listen if you ever need to talk."

"I know," Izzy said. "Thanks." *But no thanks,* she thought. All the talking in the world wouldn't change the fact that people were damaged goods. Before Izzy's grandmother passed away seven years ago, Izzy had seen three different doctors, trying to find relief for her recurring nightmares. Nothing helped. Besides, doctors don't know anything. A roomful of them had insisted Izzy's mother was of sound mind and body and could stand trial. Now she was in jail, instead of getting the help she needed. But Izzy knew madness was the only explanation for her mother shooting her father while he slept.

When they reached the shuttered workshop, a former employee unlocked the door and led Izzy, Peg, and two other museum employees inside.

"This was where the patients packed pens and glued paper bags," the former employee said cheerfully, as if she were showing them a display of quilts at a county fair.

Inside the building, workshop tables stood empty in barren rooms. Curling calendars and old fire extinguishers hung on cracked and peeling walls. The old freight elevator had been out of service for years, so Izzy and the others had to take a steep, narrow staircase up three flights to the attic, stepping over broken stair treads and chunks of old plaster, brushing aside cobwebs. When they reached the top, the former employee unlocked the attic door and leaned against it, trying to force it open. The door wouldn't budge. Peg stepped up to help, pushing on the wood with both hands. Finally the door gave, hinges screeching. The stale, dusty air inside the stairway whooshed upward, as if the attic was taking a giant gasp. The employee led them inside.

The attic was stifling hot and airless, filled with the smell of old wood, dust, and bird droppings. Dead leaves dappled the wooden floor here and there, blown in over the years through a broken pane in one of the windows. A dingy lab coat hung from a nail, and several gutted suitcases spilled their contents onto the attic floorboards. House keys and photographs, earrings and belts, blouses and leather shoes mingled with dirt and dead leaves, like disintegrating belongings dug from a grave. In the center of the vast room sat a doctor's bag and what looked like a torn map, both covered with a thick layer of dried pigeon droppings.

Beneath the attic rafters, rows of wooden racks took up nearly the entire floor. Labeled "Men" and "Women" and lettered A through Z on each side, the oversized shelves sat perpendicular to the high walls, a long corridor running down the center, like the main aisle in a grocery store or library. But instead of canned goods or books, the shelves were stacked with hundreds of dust-covered suitcases, crates, wardrobes, and steamer trunks.

"What is all this?" Peg asked, her voice filled with awe.

"It's where they kept the luggage," the former employee said. "All these suitcases and crates were left behind by patients who checked into the institution but never checked out. They haven't been touched since their owners packed them decades ago, before entering the asylum."

Izzy bit down on her lip, blinking against the tears in her eyes. She pictured her mother's open travel case on the table at the foot of her hospital bed, underwear, bras, and nightgown in a jumble. She would never forget the first time she entered her parents' bedroom after her father was shot. Her grandmother needed help finding and packing her mother's things, and Izzy had opened her parents' dresser drawers in slow motion, the familiar smell of her mother's perfume on her camisoles and slips wafting out to remind her of all she had lost. At the time, Izzy could still smell her father's blood and a hint of gunpowder in the air. She remembered staring at her parents' bed, the headboard, footboard, and railing taken apart and leaning against the bedroom walls as if they were finally moving to the bigger house her mother always wanted. Now, it was all she could do not to run out of the asylum attic and down the stairs, toward fresh air, away from the reminders of lost and ruined lives.

"This is an absolute treasure trove," Peg said. She walked along the aisles, gentle fingers touching the leather handles of Saratoga trunks and upright wardrobes, squinting to read name tags and faded monograms. Then she spun around and looked at the former employee, her eyes wide. "What are they going to do with these?"

The employee shrugged. "They'll send them to the dump, I suppose," she said.

"Oh no," Peg said. "We can't let that happen. We have to take them to the museum warehouse."

"All of them?" one of the museum employees said.

"Yes," Peg said. "Don't you see? These suitcases are just as important as an archeological dig or a set of old paintings. These people never had the chance to tell their stories outside of the confines of a mental hospital. But we can try to understand what happened to them by looking at their personal belongings. We have the rare opportunity to try to re-create their lives before they came to Willard!" She looked at Izzy. "Doesn't that sound exciting?"

Izzy did her best to muster a smile, a cold slab of dread pressing against her chest.

CHAPTER 2

CLARA

Upper West Side, NYC
October 1929

Eighteen-year-old Clara Elizabeth Cartwright stood on the thick Persian rug outside her father's study, holding her breath and leaning slightly forward, trying to hear her parents' conversation through the carved oak door. When she was younger, the opulent decor of her parents' mansion—the paneled hallway, the gleaming wood floors, the framed portraits and gilded mirrors, the silver tea set on the cherry hutch— made her feel like a princess living in a castle. Now, the thick woodwork and heavy damask curtains made her feel like an inmate being kept in a prison. And not just because she hadn't been allowed to leave in three weeks. The house felt like a museum filled with old furniture and out-of-date decorations, reeking with dated ideas and archaic beliefs. It reminded her of a mausoleum, a final resting place for the dead and dying. And she had no intention on being next.

She exhaled and tried to relax. Her plan for

escape had been tried before, but it was all she had left. The rotten wood smell of her father's cigar filtered beneath the door frame and intermingled with the lemony scent of furniture polish, reminding her of the hours she'd spent in this very spot, waiting with her older brother, William, for their daily "consultation" with their father, Henry Earl Cartwright. For as long as she could remember, every Friday after school, after homework and a walk in the park, they'd waited outside his office until dinner, careful to amuse each other quietly so they wouldn't disturb him. Then, when their father was ready, he called them in one at a time to hear their reports about school, to nip behavioral problems in the bud, to explain what he expected from them at their respective ages. She and William were required to stand on the other side of his oversized desk, chin up and eyes straight ahead, listening without fidgeting until their father nodded and lit his cigar, the signal that they were dismissed.

Their mother, Ruth, had made it clear that conversations about discipline and school performance were too taxing on her delicate sensibilities. She took her afternoon nap at the same time every day, while her husband took care of the unpleasant business of rearing their children. It wasn't until the last few years, as Clara blossomed into young womanhood, vulnerable to the ploys and desires of young men, that Henry insisted Ruth get involved. Ruth had made a halfhearted effort, but it wasn't until three weeks ago that she decided to take her job seriously. Clara wondered what William would say about their parents keeping her locked up like a common criminal.

Thinking of her older brother, Clara's eyes filled and her heart turned to lead. William's body had been pulled from the Hudson River a year and a half ago. It felt like yesterday. She remembered seeing her father's face when he heard the news, his jaw working in and out, his cheeks red as he processed the fact that his eldest child was dead. And yet, his eyes had remained dry. Clara remembered fighting the urge to pound her fists on his chest, to scream that it was his fault. But he would never believe her. His mind was a closed and locked book, with only his version of "the way the world should work" written inside. She hadn't hugged him, or her mother, instead suffering silently while they played the part of grieving parents. Now, if nothing else, she was determined not to be the next victim of Henry Cartwright's iron fist.

If it weren't for Saturday nights at the Cotton Club, when she could be herself, laughing and dancing with her friends, she was certain she'd have lost her mind months ago. But the last time she'd gone out with her friends was three weeks ago. It felt like a decade.

As a young girl, she'd done her best to please

her parents, getting perfect grades in school, keeping her room spotless, never interrupting, and—most importantly—never mouthing back. Then, as she got older, she realized her parents felt that she and her brother should be seen and not heard. The adults of the household provided food and shelter for their children, nothing more. Over the last two years, ever since William first disappeared, it had become easier and easier for Clara to lie, to say she was going to the library when she was really going to the afternoon matinee with her girlfriends to watch a Charlie Chaplin movie, or to Central Park to watch boys play at the SkeeBall Parlor or Shooting Gallery. At first, she was surprised when she returned home and her mother wasn't waiting by the door with her hands on her hips, ready to call Henry to inflict whatever punishment he deemed suitable. Clara could hear Henry's deep voice in her head, his words rattled by fury.

"Your place is here, at home, learning how to cook and care for children, not out gallivanting all over the city! What were you thinking? You're a Cartwright, goddamn it! And you'd better start acting like one, or you'll find yourself out on the street!"

Eventually she realized her parents never knew she was gone. At first, she thought they were too busy worrying about William, wondering if something had happened to him or if he had decided to cut ties for good after his fight with Henry. She started to wonder if maybe her mother had a heart after all, that she really was overly sensitive, that maybe worrying about two children was too much. But then she realized that, while her son was missing and her daughter was doing as she pleased, Ruth was having ladies over for tea, talking to caterers and florists about her next party, looking through magazines and drinking bootleg whiskey, ordering new dresses, jewelry, and furs.

After William's body was found, Ruth stopped planning parties. But she kept drinking whiskey to the point of passing out almost every night. She claimed the alcohol soothed her nerves, and Henry, who spent his days conducting business, only coming out of his office to eat and sleep, made sure his grief-stricken wife had a never-ending supply. It became obvious to Clara that her parents were relieved to have her out of their hair, as long as she was home for supper by five-thirty sharp, in which case, if she was late, she'd better be dead or dying.

Every week for the past seven months, she'd told her parents the same story—she was going to a show with Julia, Mary, and Lillian. Afterward, they would spend the night at Lillian's. Ruth barely knew Lillian, but she approved of Clara spending time with her and the other girls, based solely on the fact that their mothers were members of the women's league and went to Ruth's church. In Ruth's mind, it came to reason that if Julia and Mary were allowed to spend the night at Lillian's, it must be all right.

Except, instead of going to the theater, the girls met at Lillian's house to finger wave each other's hair and change into their beaded, fringed flapper dresses. They rolled their stockings down to their knees to show they weren't wearing corsets, put on strappy, high-heeled shoes, and wore long strings of pearls hanging between their breasts. Then, at ten o'clock, Lillian's boyfriend picked them up in his Bentley and drove them downtown, her brother's Rolls-Royce full of friends close behind.

Their favorite place, the Cotton Club, was a hip meeting spot on the corner of 142nd Street and Lenox Avenue in central Harlem, otherwise known as the playground for the rich. In the dark, smoky interior of the club, Clara and her friends drank bootleg gin, ate chocolate-covered cherries, smoked cigarettes, and did the Charleston and the tango. They listened to jazz by Louis Armstrong and got too juiced to stand up straight.

And most importantly, the Cotton Club was where Clara met Bruno. He was born in Italy, the son of a shoemaker, and had come to America alone. He wasn't used to the glitz of a New York club. Even so, the first time she saw him, threading his way through the crowd in a white vest and tie, a black coat and tails, he looked like he fit right in. He brushed past the girls asking him to dance, showing no interest in the caviar and trays of martinis, and made his way across the room, his smoldering eyes locked on Clara. At the time, she was waltzing with Lillian's brother, Joe, who was smashed and blathering on about his job at the New York Stock Exchange and how he had the means to lavish a woman with whatever she dreamed.

When Clara saw Bruno making his way toward them, her heart hammered in her chest. He looked incensed, as if someone was making moves on his girl. Wondering if he had mistaken her for someone else, she steeled herself, ready to defend poor, drunken Joe. Then Joe leaned in to kiss her and she turned away, letting go of his clammy hands. Before she knew what was happening, Bruno stepped in and whisked her across the floor, leaving Joe dazed and teetering in the middle of the room.

Bruno gazed down at her as they danced, his eyes serious, a heavy hand pressing on the small of her back. Up close, he looked like an Adonis; his black hair slicked back, the skin of his chiseled face smooth and bronze. She lowered her chin, unnerved by the intensity of his stare.

"I hope that wasn't your boyfriend," he said, his voice deep, his accent making every word rich and exotic.

She shook her head, keeping her eyes on the people around them. Lillian and Julia were at the bar, glasses of gin dangling in their hands. Lillian twisted her pearls between her fingers while Julia tickled a handsome man with a feather from her headdress.

"I'm sorry for stealing you away from your dancing partner," he said. "But I was afraid if I asked first, you'd turn me down. Do you forgive me?"

She looked up then, into his ebony eyes, and was lost. She swallowed, unable to draw her gaze away from his. She flashed a smile, trying to look amused and nonchalant. "I suppose so," she said.

"You think I'm being too forward," he said, his full lips parting in a slight grin.

"No," she said. "But I . . ."

Just then, Joe appeared, tapping Bruno on the shoulder. Bruno turned and Joe raised his fist, his red face contorted. "Stop!" Clara cried, putting up her hand.

Joe froze, his fist cocked in the air. "How do you know this guy's not a floater?" he said, spittle flying from his lips. "He looks like a lounge lizard to me."

"It's all right," Clara said. "We're just dancing."

"You sure?" Joe said.

"I'm sure," Clara said. "We'll talk later, when we all go to the diner. Okay?"

Joe considered Bruno, his bloodshot eyes narrow,

then dropped his fist. Bruno smiled, held out a hand, and introduced himself. "I promise to deliver . . ." He touched Clara's wrist with warm fingers. "I'm sorry, I don't even know your name."

"Clara," she said, feeling heat rise in her cheeks.

"I promise to deliver Clara back to her friends in one piece," he said to Joe.

"You better not be smooth talkin' me," Joe said. "Or me and my buddies will turn you out on the street in two seconds flat."

"I assure you," Bruno said, "I'm a man of my word."

Finally, Joe tugged at his tie, shook Bruno's hand, and staggered away. Bruno reached for Clara.

"May I have this dance, Bella Clara?" he said. She nodded and he pulled her close. The beads on her dress pressed against the hard muscles in his chest while the pleats of his trousers brushed across her bare knees. The song "Someone to Watch Over Me" was almost over, but she suddenly felt like she needed to sit down. Her knees felt weak, her insides jittery. She'd danced with dozens of men at the Cotton Club, some who knew her father and were hoping to get her fortune, some who were genuinely interested in getting to know her better. But no man had ever made her feel this way. She gripped his hand tighter, wondering if it was the gin or the musky scent of his cologne that was making her dizzy.

"Are you all right?" he asked. "Do you need some fresh air?"

She shook her head. "I'm fine," she said. "I think the booze might be making me a bit woozy, that's all."

"I won't let you fall," he said. Then he dipped his head and nuzzled her ear, his warm breath sending shivers across her skin. Just then, the song ended and he stopped swaying. Still, he didn't release her.

"Would you like to join me and my friends at the diner?" she said, her voice raspy. "We always go for coffee after . . ."

"I'd like that very much," Bruno said. His hand brushed her jawline and he lifted her chin. "There's just one thing I need to get out of the way first," he said. Then he pressed his mouth to hers, kissing her so hard his teeth nearly cut her lip. At first, she resisted, but then she kissed him back, melting into his arms. The sound of laughter and clinking glasses disappeared and all she could hear was her thundering heart. White lights flashed behind her lids, the warm tug of desire burning inside her pelvis. When they parted, he looked at her, breathless.

"See," he said. "Sometimes it's better not to ask."

She nodded, unable to speak.

Later, at the diner, they sat alone in a booth, drinking coffee and sharing a slice of apple pie.

Lillian, Julia, and the rest of the crew talked and laughed in two oversized booths across the aisle, but Clara and Bruno barely realized they were there. He told her about his family back in Italy and his dreams for a successful life in America. She was surprised to hear herself opening up more than she had with anyone, except William. She confessed her frustrations with her parents, tearing up when she talked about her late, beloved brother. Bruno reached across the table and took her hand, saying he understood difficult family matters. More than anything, he wanted a family of his own, a family who loved each other and always got along, no matter what. She wanted the same thing.

By the end of the night, they couldn't keep their hands off each other, and by the end of the week, they were meeting at his apartment. By the end of the month, Bruno had become part of the gang and even Lillian's brother, Joe, thought he was the cat's pajamas.

Now, standing outside her father's office, Clara could hear her father's low baritone on the other side of the carved oak door, rumbling like a slowing train, her mother whining and sniffing, their hushed exchange of angry words. They weren't arguing with each other. They were talking about Clara, irritated that, for once, she wasn't obediently going along with their plans.

She put a protective hand over her lower

abdomen, blinking against the moisture in her eyes. The engagement party was tomorrow night, complete with a photographer, a caterer, and all her parents' important friends. Her father's business partner, Richard Gallagher, had invited a dozen guests, eager to show off his son's future bride. The invitations had been sent out ten days ago, and only a few responses had returned with a negative reply. James Gallagher, the man Clara was supposed to marry, had sent his late mother's two-carat ring to be cleaned and polished, with instructions to add four extra diamonds for good measure. Ruth had picked out Clara's dress and hired a hair stylist to do her hair before the party. Everything was going along exactly as her parents had planned. The guests would arrive thinking they were there to celebrate Henry and Ruth's anniversary, and then, right before dinner, they'd be surprised by the announcement of James and Clara's engagement.

All at once, the rotten egg stench of fermenting water filled Clara's nostrils and she nearly gagged. It was coming from the vase of flowers on the cherry end table. She stepped away from the door and put a hand over her nose and mouth, trying to calm her churning stomach. If she stood out in the hall much longer, rehearsing her speech, she'd either pass out or throw up. It was now or never.

She knocked on the study door.

"What is it?" her father bellowed.

"It's me," she said, the words catching in her throat. She coughed softly, and then continued. "It's me, Clara. May I come in?"

"Enter!" her father said.

Clara put her hand on the doorknob and began to turn it, then realized her other hand was still on her lower abdomen. Blood rose to her cheeks and she pushed her fists down to her sides. She knew her mother had been watching, scrutinizing the width of her waistline, gauging her appetite in the mornings, counting the number of feminine napkins below the bathroom sink. If Clara walked into her father's study with a protective hand over her stomach, her mother would know in an instant that her worst fears had come true.

Clara took a deep breath and pushed the door open.

Her mother sat on a rose-colored settee next to the brick fireplace, fanning herself with a flowered fan, her feet on a cushioned stool. As usual, her auburn hair was swept up in the Gibson girl style, pinned on top of her head in a loose bun. To Clara's surprise, her mother's floor-length, bustled skirt was pulled up, revealing pale ankles above pointy, lace-up boots. Ruth believed a proper woman should always keep her arms and legs covered, no matter what. *She must be really upset,* Clara thought.

Clara wasn't sure when it happened, but she had

come to despise her mother's Victorian dresses, her out-of-date hairdos, her cameo brooches and rings. Every traditional mannerism and old-fashioned saying reminded Clara of her mother's prudish ways. Just the sound of Ruth's layered skirts rustling along the hallways, her hard shoes clacking along the floors, was enough to make Clara cringe.

Now, Ruth stood and ran her hands along her dress, her swan-billed corset extenuating her tiny waist. Instinctively, Clara put her shoulders back and held in her stomach, hoping her mother wouldn't notice she wasn't wearing a corset.

Clara had been forced into her first corset at the age of six, after her mother measured her waist and said it was horribly thick and clumsy. Ruth had proclaimed that if preventive measures weren't taken right away, Clara's posture and health would suffer, and no man in his right mind would marry a romping girl with a waist measuring more than seventeen inches. That night, her mother laced her into heavily boned stays, insisting they come off only in times of illness, and to bathe. A week later, Clara undid the straps in the middle of the night so she could sleep. The next morning, Ruth found the corset lying on the floor next to Clara's bed and yanked Clara out of a sound sleep to properly spank her. After that, every night for the next two weeks, she tied Clara's wrists together with a silk handkerchief to keep her hands out of mischief. As Clara grew older, her corsets were drawn in tighter and tighter by the muscular arms of a sturdy, waiting maid. At eighteen, Clara's waist measured seventeen inches, and still her mother scoffed, reminding her repeatedly that hers was sixteen, forgetting that Clara was two inches taller.

Now, in her father's study, Clara glanced in her mother's direction. Ruth would be appalled if she found the bangles, hair feathers, and fringed dresses hidden in the back of Clara's closet, tucked inside her steamer trunk beneath an old wool suit. As if reading Clara's mind, Ruth sniffed and turned her gaze toward the window, pressing her lips into a thin, hard line. Her father raised his eyebrows, tapped a silver lighter on his desk, and chomped down on his cigar. As usual, he was wearing a chalk-striped business suit, his walrus mustache curling over his upper lip.

"What is it?" he said.

Clara released her fists and clasped her hands in front of her waist, trying to keep them from shaking.

"May I speak to you about something?" she said, struggling to keep her voice steady.

Her mother mumbled under her breath and went to the window, her skirts rustling. She pulled back the curtain and pretended to look out.

Henry took the cigar from his mouth. "If this is

about tomorrow night," he said, "the conversation is over. The party is going on as planned."

Clara swallowed, her stomach churning. "Of course!" she said. "As well it should! You and Mother haven't had an anniversary party in years!"

With that, her mother spun away from the window. "You know very well why we're having the party," she said. "It's for you! And James! It's the first time I've wanted to celebrate anything in months!"

Clara grit her teeth, forcing her lips into something she hoped resembled a smile. "I know, Mother," she said. "And I appreciate all your efforts. Really I do, it's just . . ."

"Do you have any idea how lucky you are to have a man like James willing to marry you?" Ruth said.

Willing, Clara thought. *Because I have so many shortcomings and faults no one in their right mind would ever marry me. Then again, maybe you're right, Mother. James is not in his right mind. He's a low-down, abusive womanizer. But what do you care, as long as he takes me off your hands? As long as he keeps me away from Bruno?* Clara stepped toward her father's desk, her cheeks and eyes burning. "But Father," she said. "I'm not ready to get married! Especially to James!"

Henry stood and crushed his cigar out in the ashtray, his thick fingers turning red as he pressed down harder and harder. "Clara," he said. "We've been over this before. Your mother and I have made it clear how we feel—"

"But what about what I feel?" Clara said, her heart about to burst. "What about what I want?"

"You're too young to know what you want," her father said.

"No," Clara said, looking him in the eye. "I'm not. I told you before. I want to go to college." It was the only excuse she could think of to try to get them to call off the engagement. For now, at least. At one time she'd wanted to go to college to get away from her parents, to learn how to be a secretary, or maybe a nurse. She wanted to be able to stand on her own two feet. But now her dreams had changed. For the first time in her life, she knew what it felt like to be loved and cherished. There was nothing she wanted more than to share her life and make a family with Bruno. "Lillian is going to college," she said, knowing it was a weak argument.

"I don't give a damn what your friends are doing!" her father said, his face turning red.

"We're not paying good, hard-earned money to send our daughter off under the guise of higher education so she can smoke, drink, and attend petting parties!" her mother said.

Clara rolled her eyes, an incredulous chuckle escaping her lips. She knew her mother was thinking of the latest ditty that had been circulating:

"She doesn't drink, she doesn't pet, she hasn't been to college yet." *Of course* her mother would think that way.

"That's not why girls go to college, Mother," Clara said.

"This is about that Bruno boy, isn't it?" her mother said. "That immigrant you brought home for dinner a few weeks ago?"

Clara felt heat rise in her cheeks. "I don't know, Mother," she said. "Is it? Is that why you want me to marry James? To keep me away from Bruno?"

The memory of the dreadful night she brought Bruno home to meet her parents played out in Clara's mind, the scenes flipping in her head like photos in the coin-operated machine at the penny arcade. Bruno at the door, smiling, his thick, dark hair slicked back from his chiseled face, his hands in the pockets of his borrowed dinner jacket. Clara thanked him for coming and kissed him once on the cheek, inhaling the clean scent of his soft skin, a pleasant mixture of Barbasol shaving cream and Lifebuoy soap. He had arrived fifteen minutes early, having been warned that Ruth despised late arrivals.

Clara took Bruno's hands from his pockets and straightened his tie, her stomach fluttering. Trying to act calm so he wouldn't be nervous, she told him to take a deep breath, reminded him to shake her father's hand, then led him through the foyer and down the hallway to the parlor. He gaped at the lily-globed chandeliers and framed paintings, no doubt surprised that she lived in such an extravagant home. She had told Bruno that her father was in banking, worried the truth would scare him away. Henry Cartwright was half owner of Swift Bank, the largest bank in Manhattan, with branches in all New York boroughs and several upstate communities. And her mother, Ruth, was the lone heiress of the Bridge Bros. Clothing Emporium.

Clara opened the ivory doors leading into the parlor and motioned Bruno inside. Her parents were taking tea before dinner, her mother sitting next to the fireplace, her father resting one arm on the marble mantel. Henry looked up when Bruno and Clara entered the room, then grunted and checked his pocket watch. At first, Ruth stood, a bright smile on her face. But when she saw Bruno's ill-fitting jacket and scuffed shoes, she sat back down.

Clara clenched her jaw and led Bruno toward her father, hoping he would be impressed by Bruno's story about coming to America alone, to build a new life in the land of the free. After all, Henry's father had done the same thing in 1871, bringing his new bride from England to the USA. But instead of shaking Bruno's outstretched hand, her father checked his pocket watch again, declaring it was time for dinner. Ruth stood and held her delicate fingers in the air, as if allowing

Bruno to touch her hand. Bruno shook her hand and nodded.

"Pleased to meet you, Mrs. Cartwright," he said.

Ruth gave him a thin smile, then took her husband's arm and sauntered into the dining room. Clara patted Bruno's arm and followed, nodding toward her parents and rolling her eyes. Bruno frowned at her, doubt lining his forehead. He took a deep breath and let it out slowly. She mouthed, "I love you," and kissed his cheek. He finally smiled. Without a word, they found their places at the table, her parents on each end, she and Bruno across from each other. To see Bruno, she had to look around one of the ridiculously large vases of flowers her mother insisted on displaying everywhere in the house.

Clara always wondered if the display on the dining table was so Ruth wouldn't have to look at Henry during dinner, no doubt irritated when he slurped his soup or chewed too fast. Henry ate with gusto and greed, shoving in more food before he was finished chewing, talking with his mouth full, taking the last serving of fish or chicken before others had barely started eating. Henry was always the first one finished, and it annoyed Ruth to no end. Clara found her father's bad manners typical of the way he lived, taking what he wanted without consideration or awareness of those around him, plowing forward as if he had every right. Now, Clara stood, lifted the flowers off the

43

table, carried them across the room, and placed them on the buffet. Ruth watched without a word, her mouth hanging open.

While the maid ladled soup into their bowls, Ruth kept her eyes on the dish in front of her. Henry stared at Bruno and Clara, forehead furrowed as he sized up the situation. Clara shifted in her seat, waiting for him to start the conversation. When she caught her father's eye, he looked down, suddenly interested in positioning his napkin in his lap. Normally, Ruth had to remind him to use it.

Clara gripped the edge of the tablecloth and sat up straight. "Father," she said, trying to sound chipper. "Bruno has only been working down on the docks for six months and he's already been promoted to foreman."

Henry grunted, picked up his spoon, and took a mouthful of soup.

"Thank you for inviting me into your home," Bruno said. "It's very kind of you to open your doors to your daughter's friends."

Clara looked at her mother, waiting for a response. While Clara was growing up, Ruth had told her repeatedly that first and foremost, she judged people on their manners. Ruth always said you could tell a lot about a person's upbringing based on their use of please and thank you. Apparently, manners only mattered when they suited Ruth's agenda. At the end of the table, Ruth dipped her spoon in her soup, her eyes on her bowl, as if eating were the most interesting thing she'd ever done. Clara felt blood rise in her cheeks. Normally, when they had guests for dinner, Ruth talked nonstop, opining on artwork, the theater, the most modern electrical appliances, asking questions to the point of being nosy. Even after William died, she put on her best behavior for dinner guests. It was expected, after all.

"Mother?" Clara said. "You always said it was rude to ignore company."

"Oh," Ruth said. "Excuse me." She set down her spoon, wiped her mouth with her napkin, and shifted in her chair. "I didn't realize your guest was talking to me." She considered Bruno, eyebrows raised. "What were you saying, young man?"

"I wanted to thank you for inviting me into your beautiful home," Bruno said.

"You're welcome," Ruth said. Then, without another word, she picked up her spoon and started eating again, her pearl-drop earrings swinging beside her pale neck.

The veins in Clara's neck throbbed as if about to burst. So this was how it was going to be. They were going to take one look at Bruno and make a decision about him. Was it because of his clothes, his job, or his accent and bronzed skin? She clenched her hands in her lap, digging her fingernails into her palms.

Clara had told Bruno that her father would be impressed by his quick climb up the ladder, even if it was only at the local seaport. She thought her father would be surprised that Bruno had already saved enough money to lease an apartment. He was saving toward investments too, hoping to buy into the stock market. She had said Henry would be happy to advise him, to give him tips and possibly the name of a trustworthy investor to steer him in the right direction. Now, she berated herself for being so stupid and blind. What was she thinking, bringing Bruno here?

Her mind raced, trying to come up with a way to escape, to put an early end to this disastrous dinner. She pretended to eat her soup, her stomach churning. She wondered what Bruno was thinking. Could he see that she was distraught? Did he know that if she'd had any idea her parents would react this way, she never would have asked him to come? Or does he think it was all a setup? She could feel her chest and neck getting hotter and hotter, her cheeks starting to burn. Then, suddenly, her father spoke.

"I'm trying to understand something," he said, looking directly at Bruno for the first time. He paused and rested his arm on the table, one finger pointing at Bruno. "What is your last name, by the way?"

"It's Moretti, sir," Bruno said. "Bruno Moretti. I was named after my late father."

"Hmm," Henry said, lifting his chin. "And what did your father do in Italy?"

"He was a shoemaker. A very good one, sir."

"I see," Henry said. "So your father was a shoemaker, and you work down on the docks? Down at the South Street Seaport?"

"Yes, sir," Bruno said, the slightest hint of a smile playing at his lips.

Clara felt her heart lift just the tiniest of degrees. She inhaled, her first deep breath since Bruno had appeared at their door. Her father was talking to Bruno. It was the first step.

"And how much do you make working down on the docks?" Henry said.

"Father!" Clara said. "You always said it's impolite to ask people about their personal finances."

Henry considered Clara, frowning. "I'm assuming Bruno is here because he's interested in courting my daughter," he said. "In which case, I have a right to ask whatever I want."

"It's all right," Bruno said to Clara. He smiled and directed his attention to Henry. "I make enough to have my own apartment, Mr. Cartwright. And I've already been promoted to foreman."

"And where is this apartment?" Henry said.

"On Mulberry Street, sir," Bruno said.

"In Little Italy?" Henry said.

"Yes, sir," Bruno said.

Henry muttered under his breath, then wiped a

hand over his mustache. "My daughter is used to fine things," he said. "Do you really think you'd be able to take care of her properly on a longshoreman's salary?"

"Maybe not yet, sir," Bruno said. "But I'm working my way up and—"

"Working your way up to what? Do you aspire to be a shoemaker like your father? My daughter can't live on my charity forever, you know. I hope that's not what you were counting on."

Clara gaped at Bruno, her heart dropping like an anvil in her chest. Bruno's face fell and he stared at the table, his temples working in and out. But he averted his eyes for only a second. Without missing a beat, he lifted his chin and looked her father in the eye.

"With all due respect, sir, your daughter told me that before you went into the banking business, you sold shoes for a living. Quite possibly the very shoes my father is famous for. Moretti Salvatore?"

To Clara's surprise, her father blanched. He sat back and cleared his throat. "I've never heard the name."

"Could that be because they only sold the lower-end shoes where you worked, sir?" Bruno said. "My father's shoes are only sold in expensive specialty boutiques."

Clara bit down on her lip, trying to suppress her laughter. She'd never seen anyone make her father flustered. But her amusement was short-lived. She should have known no one could embarrass Henry Cartwright and get away with it.

"If your father was a famous shoe designer," Henry said, "what are you doing here, in America, working on the docks for your supper?"

Bruno pressed his lips together, his cheeks turning red. Then he cleared his throat and said, "My father passed away last year. My uncle and older brother took over the business. Unfortunately, there is much truth to the saying that business and family don't mix. My brother and I did not get along. To keep the peace, I left. Besides, I've always dreamed of living in America. I came here to prove myself. I know I can make it on my own because I'm strong and determined, just like my father."

Henry leaned back in his chair, his arms crossed over his barrel chest. "Well then," he said. "I think you should prove it to yourself first, before you try to come here and prove it to me. Because so far, I'm not impressed."

Claire dropped her spoon in her bowl, the heavy silver clanking against the gold-rimmed china. She pushed her chair back and stood. "I'm sorry, Bruno," she said. "Forgive me for putting you through this. I had no idea my parents were this closed-minded. If I had, I never would have tried to introduce you to them. We should have had dinner at your apartment, like we normally do on Friday nights."

Ruth gasped, the color draining from her cheeks. She put a hand to her throat, her lips working like a dying fish.

"It's all right," Bruno said. "I understand. Your father has concerns . . ."

"No," Clara said. "Trust me, it's too late for any kind of understanding. Please, let's just go."

Bruno stood and Clara went around the table to take his hand. Without looking back, she led him out of the dining room. Behind them, Henry shouted and cursed, telling her to turn around and come back that very second. Clara ignored him.

That was nearly a month ago. Three days later, her parents told her about the arranged marriage to James. She hadn't been allowed out of the house since. She had no idea if Bruno had come looking for her, because she hadn't been allowed to answer the door or the phone, and the help had been instructed to not tell her who had come to call. Now, in the study, her mother stared at her.

"Please show me the proper respect," Ruth said. "You know I've always wanted nothing but the best for you. I want you to marry James because he's a good man."

"But he's not! He's—"

"He'll take care of you and keep you fed and clothed, living in a nice house," Ruth said. "He'll give you the kind of life you're accustomed to!"

"Believe it or not, Mother," Clara said, failing

to hide her disgust, "not everyone marries for money. Some people marry for love."

"Do not speak to your mother that way!" Henry said, his jowls shaking.

But it was too late. Something had come undone in Clara's brain. Once she started speaking her mind, she couldn't stop. It was as if years of frustration and anger came boiling out all at once. "That's all you care about, isn't it?" she said to Ruth. "You'd rather have jewelry and a nice house than your family together and happy."

"That's not true!" Ruth said, a wounded look in her eyes. "How can you be so mean and hurtful when you know what I've been through? Your brother would have never spoken to me this way! No wonder he left. He was probably afraid of sharing the business with you."

"He didn't leave because of me!" Clara said. "He left because Father fired him and you didn't stand up for him. I'm sorry, but sometimes I think you'd step over your dead son to pick up a dollar on the street."

Henry charged around the desk, his hands in fists. "You apologize, young lady!" he said, his lips twitching. "You're marrying James in September and that's the end of it!"

Clara felt something shift inside her head, something solid and final, like the closing of a heavy door. For years she'd stood by and let them run her life, from telling her what to wear, to what courses she should take in school. Her mother instructed the maid to perform weekly checks of Clara's room, to make sure she wasn't hiding cigarettes or alcohol. Henry took away "inappropriate" library books and wouldn't allow Clara to take piano lessons because it was improper. He told her how to spend her allowance, returning dresses he didn't approve of. Clara wasn't sure if it was a mother's instinct kicking in or something else, but she couldn't take it anymore.

"Why?" she cried. "Why do you want to marry me off so bad? Is it because James's family is rich and you won't have to support me any longer? Or is it to secure the business, to make sure James's father will always be your partner?"

Henry grabbed her by the shoulders and shook her, his thick fingers digging into her flesh. "You can't talk to me like that!" he said, his eyes blazing with fury. Clara could tell he was struggling, trying not to throw her across the room.

She glared at her mother. "How can you just stand there and let him do this to me?" she said. "How can you choose your husband over your children? I know this is what he did to William! I know he beat up his own son. And you did nothing!"

"Don't you dare bring William into this!" her mother said.

"Why not?" Clara said. "You let Father ruin him, why not me?"

Ruth put her thin wrist to her forehead and fell into the settee. Henry released his grip and rushed over to his wife, kneeling at her side.

"Look what you've done!" he said, giving Clara a scorching look. "You made your mother cry!"

Clara stared at her parents, years of suppressed anger swelling in her chest. "William did everything for you," she said. "He worked day and night, by your side, for years. He gave up everything just to prove himself. But it was never enough, was it? You could never give him your approval because it meant you'd have to give him what he deserved!"

With that, her father stood, charged across the room, and slapped Clara across the face. She reeled sideways, found her footing, and put a hand to her throbbing cheek, blinking through her tears.

"What did he do?" she snarled, holding her father's stare. "What did he do that was so horrible to make you stop loving him?"

"I'm warning you," her father said. "One more word and I'll—"

"Oh, that's right," she said, hot tears spilling down her cheeks. "You thought you owned him because he worked for you. You treated him like a slave while you raked in the money. He finally had enough and stood up for himself. But you couldn't handle it, so you threw him out on the street!" She glared at her mother. "And you let him do it! You never asked William's side of the story. You didn't even bother to find out if he had a place to live, if he had anything to eat!"

"Stop talking, right now!" Henry bellowed. "Before you regret it!"

"I don't regret anything," Clara said. "The only thing I regret is not seeing the truth about you sooner."

Henry hurried back around his desk, picked up the telephone receiver, and dialed. He stared at his crying wife, waiting for the other end to pick up, his face crimson, his jowls trembling. The light from the chandelier reflected in the sweat on his forehead. Clara turned to leave. If she left, she'd be penniless. If she stayed, she'd be trapped. There was no other answer. She put her hand on the door handle.

"Yes, Lieutenant?" her father said into the phone. "This is Henry Cartwright. I need you to send someone over here right away. I'm afraid we have a situation on our hands." Clara paused at the door, waiting to hear what her father said next. "It's my daughter, Clara. We believe she's having some kind of episode."

Clara yanked open the door and ran out of the room.

CHAPTER 3

IZZY

Lakeshore High School

Izzy carried her backpack slung over one shoulder, her thumb hooked through the thick strap, trying to find the senior class homeroom. The hallways of her new school were crowded and the other students hurried past in their haste to get to their lockers, listening to Walkmans, laughing and talking with their friends. Like all schools, the halls smelled like a strange mixture of sweat, bubble gum, and pencil shavings. Lakeshore High was one of the smallest schools she'd ever attended, with only seven hundred and sixty-five students in ninth through twelfth grades. She wondered if a small school would be easier, or harder, to fit into.

That morning, she'd dressed in a black, long-sleeved T-shirt with jean shorts and black Converse. Now, she noticed that nearly all the girls were in ripped jeans and heels, or miniskirts and Doc Marten boots. She looked at the forms in her hand, her stomach in knots. Was she supposed to give the paper with her name and information to her homeroom teacher, or the school nurse? Or maybe the one with her foster parents' names and numbers was supposed to go to the school nurse. And was she supposed to give the one with her class schedule to her teacher or keep it for herself? She couldn't remember.

Finally, she saw the name "Mr. Hudson" on a door and headed toward it, trying not to bump into anyone. Just then, someone shouted and two guys ran through the crowd, one in a Doors T-shirt, the other with braces and red hair. The redhead bumped into her, nearly knocking her into the lockers. She spun around and dropped her information forms, her hair flying over her eyes, her backpack slipping from her shoulder. The redhead laughed, said he was sorry, and hurried away. She pushed her hair out of her face and searched the tiled floor, where her papers were being torn and crumpled beneath sneakers and sandals and heels.

Finally, there was an opening in the crowd. Izzy stepped in front of a group of kids and knelt to snatch the papers from between rushing feet, trying not to get stepped on. When she reached for the last form, someone picked it up. She stood, ready for a chase.

"Hey!" she said.

"Just trying to help," a guy said, handing her the paper. His light blue eyes were nearly silver, his hair the purplish black of a raven.

"Thanks," she said, feeling blood warm her cheeks.

"No problem," he said, smiling. He was hanging on to his girlfriend's hand, even though she was still moving. Then his girlfriend stopped and laughed, glancing over her shoulder to see what he was doing. Her hair was blond and long, her legs smooth and tanned. She looked cool and pretty and amused, the kind of girl, Izzy knew, she herself would never be. Raven Boy's girlfriend glanced at Izzy with little interest, then yanked on his hand, pulling him forward. He shrugged and disappeared into the crowd.

Izzy smoothed the wrinkled papers with her fingers, trying not to smudge the ink. She found the one she needed, shoved the others in her backpack, and followed the other students into homeroom. Stuffed and mounted animal skins lined the walls: beaver, rabbits, a fox, a muskrat, a crow, and a pheasant. Jars filled with pig embryos lined the shelves above the windows, and a faint hint of formaldehyde filled the air. Mr. Hudson sat reading a book at his desk while the students talked and laughed, sitting on desks and the backs of chairs. A group of kids with black hair, black clothes, tattoos, and multiple piercings sat near the rear of the room. The boys who bumped into Izzy earlier were dropping water balloons out the windows. A group of jocks and cheerleaders sat near the windows, their arms draped around each other.

Izzy grit her teeth and walked over to Mr. Hudson's desk, her stomach doing flip-flops. She didn't understand why she was so nervous. She'd been the new kid before. Four times, as a matter of fact. After her mother was put in jail, she moved to another town to live with her grandmother, where she had to start over in a new school. Three years later, after her grandmother died, Izzy was put into foster care and had to change schools going into fifth grade. Two years after that, her foster father put his wife in the hospital after a drunken argument. That night, Izzy was moved to a different foster home. The next day she had to start seventh grade at a new school. When her second set of foster parents moved to another state, she was moved yet again, going into her freshman year, this time to a home with an alcoholic mother. For three years, Izzy did her best to take care of the two other kids, one the biological seven-year-old son, the other a ten-year-old girl in the system. When their foster mother was too drunk to function, Izzy cooked and made sure the other kids had clean clothes to wear to school. The day before Izzy finished her junior year, her foster mother drove the family minivan into a lake and drowned. A week later, Izzy was sent to Peg and Harry's. So, when it came to being the new kid, she knew the drill.

But this year was different for a number of reasons. Fitting in would be tougher than usual because most kids in a senior class have been together since junior high. At least on her first day at her last school, she'd been a new freshman like everyone else. Being the new kid in a senior class felt like crashing a private party.

Now, she held out the form from the office, waiting for Mr. Hudson to look up and take it. She felt the other students glancing curiously toward the front of the room, then nudging each other, pointing and staring. The teacher kept his head down, reading his book. Little by little, the laughing and conversation faded.

"Hey, nice backpack!" a male voice yelled. "You going hiking?"

Everyone laughed. Izzy felt her face growing hot. What was wrong with her backpack? She cleared her throat to get Mr. Hudson's attention. Just then, a wrapped condom hit her in the head and fell to the floor. She looked at her new classmates. A group of girls giggled and turned away. One of the girls was Raven Boy's girlfriend. Raven Boy stared at her, searching her face. Was that coldness or pity in his eyes? It was hard to tell. Izzy put her information on the desk, picked the condom up off the floor, and held it out to the teacher. He finally looked up.

"I think this is for you," Izzy said. Everyone laughed.

"Is this some kind of joke?" Mr. Hudson said, his forehead furrowed.

"No," Izzy said. "I was just standing here waiting to give you my papers, and someone threw this at you. They hit me with it instead."

Mr. Hudson took the condom, threw it in the garbage, and stood. "Okay, everybody," he said. "Settle down and take your seats." He took the paper from Izzy, read it, then addressed the class. "This is Isabelle Stone. Make her feel welcome, please." He looked at Izzy. "Sit wherever you'd like."

Izzy scanned the room for a seat. The only empty desk was in the back corner, on the far end of the classroom. She slid her backpack from her shoulder and headed toward the windows, intending to walk along the edge of the desks instead of through the middle. Then she realized that, to get to the empty seat, she had to walk past Raven Boy and his girlfriend. For a second, she thought about turning around and going the other way. But it would have been too obvious. She kept going. Halfway down the aisle, she passed Raven Boy and his girlfriend. Then, one of the guys put his sneakered foot on the windowsill, blocking her way.

"Excuse me," she said, forcing a smile.

"What's your name again?" the guy said. He was good looking, with clear skin and thick, blond bangs pushed to one side above blue eyes.

"Isabelle," she said, trying to sound friendly. "But everyone calls me Izzy."

"Izzy?" the guy said. "Like Izzy Pop?"

"No," Izzy said. "That's Iggy Pop."

"Mr. Anderson!" Mr. Hudson barked from the front of the room. "Is this how we're going to start the year?"

"I'm just introducing myself," the guy said. "Making Izzy Pop feel welcome, like you said."

Everyone laughed. Izzy felt her neck and chest welting up.

"Don't be a jerk, Luke," someone said behind her.

Izzy turned to see who had spoken. It was Raven Boy.

"Let her by," he said to Luke. Raven Boy's girlfriend slapped his arm, scowling at him. He ignored her.

Luke let his foot drop and winked at Izzy. "If you need someone to show you around," he said, smirking, "I'm your man."

"Thanks," Izzy said, and went to her desk.

This is starting out well, she thought, sliding into her seat. *And I've been here, what, five minutes?*

During roll call, Izzy learned Raven Boy's name was Ethan Black, and his girlfriend's name was Shannon Mackenzie. Izzy surveyed the other kids while Mr. Hudson talked about fund-raisers, prom committees, and class elections. One of the girls sitting next to Shannon—her name was Crystal—glanced back at Izzy, then leaned over and whispered something in Shannon's ear. They looked over their shoulders and laughed. When another girl—if Izzy remembered correctly, her name was Nicole—looked at Shannon with questioning eyes, Shannon whispered in her ear. The three of them stared back at Izzy, grinning as if sharing a private joke.

Izzy dug her nails into her palms, fighting the urge to flip them off. There was always one group in every school—a clique of mean girls who made the other girls' lives a living hell. It didn't take a rocket scientist to figure out who the mean girls were in this school. She knew the best thing to do was ignore them, and hope they never found out her mother was doing time in a maximum-security prison for shooting her father. But it wouldn't be easy in this small class. Just then, a memory came to her: two girls in her last school calling her "psycho" in the hall, asking if she still had her mother's gun. She could almost taste the coppery blood in her mouth from biting her lip to keep herself from clawing their eyes out.

Now, she tugged on her sleeves, making sure they were pulled all the way down. The scars on her forearms were finally getting lighter, and she'd vowed never to cut herself again, no matter what. A month ago she'd thrown away her razor blades, and she wasn't going to let these idiotic girls make her go back on the promise she'd made to herself.

The first time she cut herself, the night after her grandmother died, she'd gone into the bathroom of her grandmother's old farmhouse to get the miniature glass man full of her dead grandfather's razor blades out of the medicine cabinet. She shook a blade out of the glass man's head—a barber with black hair and a blue shirt—then sat on the toilet and made a one-inch incision in her forearm. Then she passed out cold. A few minutes later, she woke up on the bathroom floor and clamped a hand over her arm, unable to look at the fresh wound. That was when she realized physical pain made emotional pain disappear for a few minutes, and the sight of her own blood made her faint. Over the next seven years, she cut herself to erase her anger, frustration, and pain, but she did it without looking.

After moving in with Peg and Harry, she began to realize cutting herself was crazy. And if nothing else, she was determined not to be like her mother. Becoming mentally ill was her greatest fear. If she could just control her emotions, more specifically her anger, maybe she wouldn't snap.

Now, near the front of the classroom, another girl sat at her desk, facing forward, her slick, black hair like a velvet cape down her back. She scribbled in her notebook, oblivious to the chaos around her, except for the occasional quick, cool glance at the other students. Izzy had known girls like her too. She was probably dating a college guy and didn't have time for her classmates' shenanigans. Either that, or she was the leader of the mean-girl pack.

Finally, the bell rang and the students clamored out of their desks, heading toward first-period class. No one else had a backpack. Izzy took her time gathering her things, purposely waiting for everyone else to file out of the room first. When she reached the door, Mr. Hudson called out to her. She turned to face him. "Yes, Mr. Hudson?"

"You gave me the wrong form," he said. "This one is for the nurse."

"Oh." Izzy went to his desk and took the paper, then rummaged around in her backpack for the right one. "Sorry about that."

"Listen," Mr. Hudson said. "This is a small school and this class has been together since junior high. It's been a couple years since they've had a new classmate."

Izzy shrugged. "Okay," she said.

"The best thing to do if anyone tries to egg you on is ignore them."

Easy for you to say, she thought. "Okay," she said again. "Thanks."

After homeroom, the girl with the black hair approached Izzy at her locker.

"Hey," the girl said. "Welcome to hell."

"Thanks," Izzy said, shoving her empty backpack into her locker.

"No one uses a backpack here," the girl said.

"The school is so small everyone goes to their locker between classes."

"I noticed," Izzy said. The girl had a slight lisp, but other than that she looked like she could fit right in with the mean girls—perfect figure, perfect makeup, perfect clothes. What was she doing talking to Izzy?

"My name's Alexandra," the girl said. "Alex for short."

Izzy shut her locker and held her math book to her chest. "Izzy, short for Isabelle."

"I like it," Alex said, smiling. "It fits you. Listen, Shannon and her friends are trouble. The best thing to do is ignore them and try to stay out of their way."

"You're the second person to tell me that."

"Because it's true," Alex said.

Izzy shrugged. "They don't bother me."

Alex smiled. "Okay. But don't say I didn't warn you. I doubt you've dealt with anyone like Shannon before."

"What could she have against me?" Izzy said. "I just got here."

Alex frowned. "Her boyfriend stuck up for you, for one thing," she said. "That's one strike."

"That wasn't my fault," Izzy said.

"I know," she said. "But the last girl Shannon saw as a threat to her and Ethan had to transfer to another school."

"You're not friends with her?"

Alex looked away for a fraction of a second, and just that small movement, that tiny delay when Alex averted her eyes, made Izzy wonder if she was telling the truth. Maybe Alex was a spy for the mean girls, sent to make friends so she could report back.

"We used to be really close," Alex said. "But that changed a while ago."

"What happened?" Izzy knew her question sounded nosy, but she didn't care. She wasn't going to let herself fall into a trap.

"Why don't we get together later?" Alex said. "I can give you a ride home if you want. I've got a '76 Beamer. It's a junk heap, but I bought it myself and it serves the purpose."

Izzy dug her nails into the cover of her math book, uncertainty fluttering in her stomach. "I'm supposed to take the bus home," she said. "My foster parents told me not to ride with anyone they don't know."

"Well, how about if I stop by later then?" Alex said. "I'll introduce myself to your foster parents and maybe we can hang out."

Izzy was just about to agree when Alex glanced down the hall, past Izzy. Alex's face dropped. Then Shannon and her friends were standing beside them, followed by a strong cloud of hairspray and perfume. Shannon beamed at Alex, her eyes twinkling, barely able to contain her exciting news.

"You're still coming tonight, right?" she said. "Dave's parents left for Florida and his fridge is stocked with beer!"

Alex frowned, her forehead knitted. She started to answer, but then Shannon looked at Izzy, as if noticing her for the first time.

"Oh," Shannon said. She glanced back at the other girls, then smiled at Izzy. "You can come too, if you want. I'll introduce you to everyone!"

"I . . ." Izzy started.

"Don't forget," Shannon said to Alex. "You promised to bring some tequila!"

Before Alex could react, Shannon hurried down the hall, laughing with the other girls. Izzy looked at Alex, waiting for an explanation.

"She knows I'm telling you I can't stand her," Alex said. "She did that to make me look like a liar."

"If you say so," Izzy said. "I've got to get to class." She brushed past Alex and started down the hall, thinking it was going to be a long year. "See you around."

CHAPTER 4

CLARA

The Long Island Home for Nervous Invalids
New Year's Day, 1930

Two and a half months after the fight with her parents, Clara stood at the narrow, six-paned window of her third-floor room in Norton Cottage, looking out over the main grounds of the Long Island Home for Nervous Invalids. It was early morning on New Year's Day, gray clouds hanging low and ominous in the winter sky. It had been storming all night, a near blizzard, and everything was cloaked in white. The trees in the cedar grove drooped under the weight of wet snow, and the rushing water in the nearby creek was the color of tombstones. The groundskeeper was shoveling the sidewalks, his back hunched, his red hat bobbing up and down as he heaved the wet snow into higher and higher banks. A low, black truck plowed the wide driveway, its blades raising and lowering like the wings of a giant wasp, the rumble of the engine and the scrape of the plow vibrating through the thin window glass. The wind had finally stopped, but every few minutes the sky opened up again, releasing a slow flurry of thick flakes.

Blinking back tears, Clara wondered where she would be next year on New Year's Day. She pictured herself living with Bruno, raising their child together, finally out from beneath her parents' rule. But first, she had to get out of the Long Island Home. She had to convince Dr. Thorn that she was being needlessly confined. So far, nothing had worked. He was taking her father's word over hers.

If nothing else, she was relieved that the morning walk had been canceled. Not only was she glad that she didn't have to go out in the snow and cold, but she had spent the morning in the bathroom throwing up, her first bout of morning sickness leaving her weak and shaky. She slid her hand down to her abdomen, already feeling protective of the baby growing inside her. Luckily, no one was able to tell she was pregnant just by looking at her, but she could feel the slight, firm swell below her navel. The baby was a girl, she was certain of it. Every night for over a week, she'd dreamed about a toddler in a pink lace dress, Bruno's dark curls and chocolate-colored eyes looking up at her. Now, Clara swallowed the growing lump in her throat, surprised by the overwhelming love she already felt for her unborn child.

It made her think of her mother, Ruth. While

pregnant with her firstborn, had Ruth put a protective hand over her growing belly, vowing to love and protect her baby for the rest of her life no matter what? Or was her burgeoning girth a burden to her fashion sense? Did she long for the day when she could finally hold her newborn in her arms and kiss his tiny, sweet-smelling forehead, or did she want to get her pregnancy over with so she could hand the baby over to a nanny and get on with her life? Clara had to believe it must have been the latter. Otherwise, how could a loving, nurturing mother turn into a selfish woman who didn't give a damn about what happened to her children?

Clara pushed the image of her mother from her mind, knowing that trying to figure out the woman who brought her into this world wouldn't change anything. She turned and sat on the narrow bed, wrapping her sweater around herself, and stared at the unopened letter on her desk. It was from her father, the second she'd received since being admitted to the Long Island Home over two months ago, despite the fact that she'd written every day, begging to be released. The ivory envelope had been sitting there since she'd returned from breakfast an hour ago. She'd picked it up twenty times, thumb poised on the edge of the back flap, then set it back unopened every time.

Henry's first letter, delivered a week after Clara arrived, said her stay in the Long Island Home was for her own good, that it was just temporary, until the doctors could help her. But as the weeks went by with no more word, Clara started to worry that her father had changed his mind and she was going to stay longer than originally thought. Now, her future could be determined by the words inside her father's latest letter, and, for as long as possible, she wanted to hold on to the hope that her parents were going to allow her to come home. When James found out she was carrying another man's baby, the marriage would be called off. Her parents would disown her and kick her out on the street. But anything was better than this. Anything was better than being locked up in a loony bin, even if it was the best money could buy.

The rooms at the Long Island Home were warm and clean, the grounds well maintained. And, for the most part, the staff was pleasant. Patients dined with silver and fancy porcelain, and lounged in parlors on Louis XV sofas. Treatment consisted of rest, relaxation, good food, fresh air, and activities such as bicycling and tennis on the grass. And, of course, therapy sessions. But there was no mistaking that she was being kept against her will. During her first therapy session the day after her arrival, she had asked Dr. Thorn what would happen if she tried to leave.

"Why do you want to leave?" he'd said, looking at her over his round spectacles. He was tall and whippet thin, with an enormous Adam's apple that bobbed up and down in his leathery throat like a fish in a pelican's beak.

"Because I don't need to be here," Clara said. "There's nothing wrong with me."

"I see," Dr. Thorn said, scribbling on his pad. "How then, do you think you came to the Long Island Home?"

Clara sat in a wooden chair, her ankles crossed between the seat, her hands folded in her lap. She dug her fingernails into her palm and tried to look calm. "My father isn't used to me standing up for myself. He thinks women should be seen and not heard. This is his way of silencing me, of trying to prove he can control me. He's trying to force me to do something I don't want to do."

"Isn't it a father's job to do what's best for his children?"

"Yes," she said. "It is. But he's not doing what's best for me! He's trying to force me to marry a lousy, no-good . . ." She paused, stomach churning, worried she was saying too much. "What did my father tell you about me? Why did he send me here?"

"He said you had some kind of breakdown. He's worried that you're not thinking clearly."

"That's absurd," she said. "He just can't handle the truth."

"And what is the truth, Clara?"

"The truth is my parents care more about money and power than their children."

"You seem to have a lot of anger toward them for sending you here."

Clara sat up straighter. "Of course I'm angry!" she said, raising her voice. "Who wouldn't be?"

Dr. Thorn nodded and wrote something down in his notebook. He asked the next question without looking up. "Do you believe your father is plotting against you, Clara?"

Clara stiffened. "No," she said, shaking her head. "Plotting is too strong a word. My father thinks sending me here will teach me a lesson. He doesn't approve of the man I love. He thinks when I go back home I'll go along with his plans."

Dr. Thorn set down his pen. He took off his glasses and rubbed his eyes, then folded his hands on the desk and gazed at Clara, searching her face. "Sometimes," he said in a quiet voice, "when we get anxious or upset, we imagine things. Your father says you accused him of killing your brother."

"That's not true!" she said. "My brother committed suicide because he thought he had nothing to live for. My father ruined him and my mother let it happen."

"Do you hold your parents responsible for your brother's death?"

"They could have handled things differently," she said. "Instead they went to extremes like they always do. Instead of talking things through like normal parents, they got rid of him!"

"And now you think they're trying to get rid of you too."

"That's not what I . . ." Clara stopped talking and tried to slow her thundering heart, suddenly realizing her words could be twisted around and used against her.

"Is something wrong?" Dr. Thorn said, lifting his eyebrows.

She shook her head.

"Why don't you finish what you were saying?" he said.

She looked down at her hands, feeling her eyes flood. "You're not listening to me," she said. "You're only hearing what you want to hear. You're twisting my words and making it sound like I'm unstable."

"You seem to be very suspicious of people," he said. "Your parents, the man they want you to marry. Even me."

"How would you feel if the tables were turned, Doctor? Wouldn't you try to explain yourself and ask to be released if you were perfectly sane?"

Dr. Thorn closed his writing pad and put his glasses back on. "The patients here at the Long Island Home are only allowed to leave with a release from me, or at the request of the admitting party, in this case, your father."

"So what would happen if I just packed up my suitcase and left? What if I just walked down the driveway and out the front gate?"

Dr. Thorn smiled and sniffed, as if suppressing a laugh. "I suppose you could try," he said. "But the Long Island Home consists of fourteen acres and it's quite a walk to the front gate. We'd stop you before you got very far. Besides, the gate is locked and I've seen the size of the trunk you brought with you. I can't imagine you'd have a very easy time of carrying it out of your room, much less down the stairs and across the lawns."

Clara's face grew warm. She was about to tell him she didn't give a damn about her steamer trunk. She'd leave without it if she had to. But then she realized he might take her anger as something else, as part of her "condition."

Her first mistake the day she argued with her father was taking the time to pack a bag. She should have left the study, grabbed her coat, and run out of the house that very instant. She should have fled the minute she heard her father telling the lieutenant to bring a doctor. Instead, she'd hurried to her room and started packing her steamer trunk, forgetting that she'd have to carry the oversized chest down the stairs by herself, that the butler and driver would not be called upon to carry her luggage out to the car. After all, she was running away, not going on another overseas voyage. But she hadn't been thinking clearly, her panicked mind unable to string two coherent thoughts together. All she knew was that she needed to take as much as possible, because, when she left, the clothes in the trunk and the dress on her back would be all she owned in the world.

Thinking about it now, she berated herself for being so stupid. She knew the police could be at her house within minutes because Ruth had called them numerous times—when she couldn't find her string of pearls, when the candlesticks from the parlor went missing, when her favorite English tea set had disappeared. Every time, the police arrived and talked calmly to Ruth while she paced and wailed, convinced that the help was stealing. Then, like common criminals, the maids and butlers and limo drivers were lined up and questioned. Eventually, a logical explanation came to light; Ruth's necklace had slipped behind her dressing table, the candlesticks were in the pantry waiting to be polished, the tea set had been returned to the wrong cupboard. After Ruth realized her precious things were no longer missing, she thanked the police for coming so quickly. Meanwhile, Clara did her best to apologize to the help.

If only Clara had remembered the speed at which the police could arrive, instead of being like Ruth and worrying about her "things," she might have had the chance to slip away. When her father brought the lieutenant, two policemen, and a doctor up to her room, her steamer trunk was nearly full and the possibility of escape no longer existed. Henry ordered the men to close the trunk and take it away, along with his only daughter.

She could still picture her father's red face and wild eyes, his arms gesturing as if he were ordering a criminal taken out of his house.

"What seems to be the problem?" the lieutenant said.

"She was spouting all kinds of horrible accusations," Henry said, shaking his head. "I'm afraid she's imagining things."

"It's not true!" Clara said. "I just . . ."

Henry looked at the doctor, his eyes pleading. "Can you help her?"

Clara ran toward the door and a policeman grabbed her wrist. She struggled to break free but it was no use. "Let me go," she cried. "You can't do this! I didn't do anything!"

"Has Clara suffered any emotional trauma recently?" the doctor asked Henry.

"She lost her brother," Henry said. "And somehow she's got it in her mind that I . . ." Henry hung his head, his clenched fists to his forehead, as if it was too much to bear.

"That's not why I . . ." Clara cried. The policeman tightened his grip on her arm. "No, let me go!"

The lieutenant directed his attention to the doctor, letting him make the final call. The doctor nodded. Before Clara could protest further, the policemen grabbed her by the arms and led her out of the bedroom, down the stairs and outside, where she was shoved into the back of the doctor's black Buick, her jacket and winter boots tossed onto the backseat beside her, her luggage thrown into the trunk. She remembered looking out the car window at the stone entrance of her parents' house, the familiar granite balustrade and carved fleur-de-lis above the doorway. She wasn't sure why she looked; maybe a small, hopeful part of her expected her mother to be crying on the steps, upset that her only daughter was being taken away. But the only thing she saw was the hem of her father's smoking jacket as it disappeared through the entryway, the brass knocker bouncing with the slam of the door.

Now, Clara chewed on the inside of her cheek, trying to think of a way to convince Dr. Thorn to let her go.

"I'm sorry," the doctor said. "But I'm afraid our time is up."

"But I . . ." Clara said.

The doctor stood and went around the desk. "We're finished for today, Clara."

Clara stood. "That's it?" she said, throwing up her hands. "You're going to make decisions based on a twenty-minute conversation?"

"We'll talk more at your next appointment," he said, opening the door.

"When?" she said. "Tomorrow?"

Dr. Thorn smiled and shook his head. "I'm afraid I have to see some of my other patients tomorrow. We'll meet again next week."

Clara's stomach dropped. *Next week?* The thought of staying a full week nearly caused her to cry out. Surely her father didn't mean for her to stay that long.

Out in the hall, a young nurse waited to take Clara back to her room. Clara walked down the hall with her arms crossed over her middle, trying to keep herself from falling apart. It wouldn't do any good to appear emotionally unstable in front of the nurse, even if the woman had smiled at her when she came out of the office, her soft blue eyes filled with pity.

A block of fear settled in Clara's stomach and her skin prickled with goose bumps. The corridors seemed to stretch on forever, the red and green carpet and crystal sconces reminding her of being inside the Funhouse on Coney Island, where patrons were harassed by a clown with an electric wand through crooked rooms and dark corridors with tilting floors and moving walls. She'd always hated the Funhouse, remembering her panic when an air jet burst across her ankles. After turning and clawing her way past the other patrons to get back outside, she vowed never to go inside again, no matter how much her friends made fun of her. The Long Island Home was a thousand times worse. Here, there was no way out, no exit, no way back to sunshine and corn dogs and laughing friends.

When Clara reached her room, she stood at the door waiting for the nurse to let her in. She stared at the floor for what felt like a full minute before realizing the nurse had stopped a few steps behind her. The young nurse looked at Clara with a furrowed brow, as if trying to make a decision.

"Have you been out on the grounds yet?" the nurse said.

Clara shook her head. "I just got here."

"I know when you arrived," the nurse said. "I was with Nurse McCarn when she led you to your room last night. I helped unpack your things."

"I'm sorry," Clara said. "I don't remember. I . . ."

"It's all right," the nurse said, smiling. "Would you like to go outside for a little while? We've got a little time before lunch and it might be one of the last warm days before winter comes. The lawns are beautiful." The nurse looked up and down the hall, as if worried someone might hear.

Clara shook her head. "I just want to be left alone for a little while."

"Are you sure?" the nurse said. "The sun is shining and it's so warm you don't even need a sweater. Tomorrow it's supposed to start getting cold and . . ."

Clara sighed and let her shoulders drop. If nothing else, maybe she could learn her way around the Long Island Home and find a way out. She nodded and they started back down the hall, then turned to enter a stairwell. The nurse started down first, then stopped on the fourth step. Nurse McCarn was coming up the stairs.

"Oh," the nurse said to Clara. "Never mind. Maybe some other time." She turned and hurried back up the steps. Clara followed.

"Nurse Yott!" Nurse McCarn called behind them, her footsteps pounding up the steps. Nurse Yott's shoulders dropped. She stopped and waited, frowning. Nurse McCarn reached them and put one hand on her hip, her forehead furrowed. "Where were you going? Your instructions were to deliver this patient to her room."

"I was taking Clara outside," Nurse Yott said. "To get a little fresh air."

Nurse McCarn glared at Nurse Yott, her jaw working in and out. "It's not up to you to make decisions about what's best for a patient," she said. "Take her back to her room this very instant."

Nurse Yott dropped her eyes. "Yes, ma'am."

"Try to remember you're not a doctor," Nurse McCarn said. "You might do well to learn from my example. I've been at the Long Island Home for over twenty years and always follow the doctor's orders to the letter!"

"I'm sorry," Nurse Yott said, her face turning red.

Nurse McCarn shook her head and clucked her tongue. "This is the second time I've had to speak to you about something. You'd better watch your step, Nurse Yott."

Clara swallowed and stepped forward. "Dr. Thorn instructed her to take me outside," she said.

"I told him I was feeling a little cooped up and he asked if going outside for a few minutes would help."

Nurse McCarn stared at Clara, her mouth pinched. Clara held her gaze. Finally, Nurse McCarn looked at Nurse Yott. "Is this true?" she said.

Nurse Yott nodded.

Nurse McCarn pressed her lips together, a blue vein popping out on her forehead. She was struggling, trying not to lose her temper. "Carry on," she said, waving a hand toward the stairwell. "You've got ten minutes before lunch. Make sure the patient is in the cafeteria on time. If she's late, I'll hold you responsible." She shook her head in disgust and marched down the hallway.

Nurse Yott smiled at Clara. "Thank you," she said. "I swear she's got it out for me."

That was ten weeks ago. It felt like ten years.

Now, Clara reached out for the letter on her desk. When she first saw it that morning, her heart leapt in her chest, hoping it was from Bruno. At long last, he had answered her daily letters. Then she saw Henry's formal script on the front of the envelope and fell back on the bed, her hands over her face. She couldn't imagine why Bruno hadn't written back. At first, she worried her letters had been intercepted somehow. But that didn't make sense. She took them down to the front desk and dropped them in the locked mailbox herself. After the first month went by with no word, she started waking up in a cold sweat, panicked that something bad had happened. Her father was a power-hungry tyrant, to be sure. But he wouldn't go as far as getting rid of Bruno, would he? Briefly, the thought crossed her mind that Bruno forgot about her. Maybe their love affair had meant nothing to him. Maybe she was just one woman in a long line of women. But no. It had been more than that. Much more. She was certain of it. Still, she preferred picturing Bruno with another woman to the image that assaulted her mind every night: Bruno floating beside her brother, William, faceup in the Hudson River.

She took a step back from the desk and put her fingers over her mouth, suddenly sick to her stomach again, even though eating dry toast at breakfast had helped her nausea. Her father wasn't writing to say hello after nearly three months of silence. Christmas and New Year's had come and gone and there hadn't been so much as a card. Was she finally getting out of this place, or was she being forced to stay longer?

She took a deep breath and picked up the letter again, vowing to open it this time. She bit down on her lip and slid her thumbnail beneath the back flap, then tore it open. Her fingers trembled as she unfolded the single sheet of her father's ivory stationery. She let the envelope fall to the floor and held the letter with shaking hands.

Dear Clara,

Your mother and I hope you are well and getting the help you need. It's unfortunate that your life has taken this turn. Dr. Thorn has reassured me that, sometimes, no matter how hard we try, parents cannot determine the outcome of their children's upbringing. But that is neither here nor there. What's done is done. Your mother and I have done our best and that is all we can ask of ourselves. I'm writing to let you know that things have changed since the stock market crash in September. Due to our losses, and in an attempt to keep our home and the lifestyle to which your mother and I are accustomed, I regret to say that I can no longer afford to pay for your care at the Long Island Home. Dr. Thorn and I have talked at length about your condition, and what we both feel should be the necessary next step. Dr. Thorn will explain what we have agreed upon. Try to remember that your mother and I only want what's best for you.

Warm regards,
Father

Clara stared at the letter, the words blurring on the paper, a hard lump forming in her throat. What did it mean? What was the necessary next step?

Was she going to be released? Was she going to be let go, to be on her own? She dropped the letter on the floor and paced the small room, shivering. Her appointment with Dr. Thorn wasn't until eleven. It was only nine-thirty. She stopped pacing and took several deep breaths, trying to slow her hammering heart. Emotional distress wasn't good for the baby. She needed to calm down. After a minute, she lay on the bed and closed her eyes, pulling the thin blanket over her trembling shoulders.

Then she sat up with a start, realizing there was something she had to do. She needed to write to Bruno. If things were going to change, if she was being released or sent home, he needed to know. Even though she had no idea if he was getting her letters, she had to try to let him know what was going on. She got up, opened the desk drawer, and yanked out the stationery provided by the Long Island Home. She pulled out the desk chair and sat, pen poised over the paper, then realized she had no idea what to say. How could she tell Bruno what was happening when she didn't know herself? The letter would have to wait until after her appointment with Dr. Thorn. Maybe Dr. Thorn would see her sooner. Maybe she could ask Nurse McCarn if the schedule could be changed. She got up and went to the door, then heard male voices in the hall.

She hurried back to the desk and shoved the

stationery in the drawer, then looked around the room for something to make it look like she was busy. Nurse McCarn said idle hands were the devil's playground, and if a patient had nothing to do, there were floors to be swept and toilets to be scrubbed. Clara pulled the institution-provided Bible from the shelf above her desk, sat on the bed, and opened the book to a random page. A light-headed, shaky feeling came over her, as if she hadn't eaten in days.

Just then, there was a soft rap on the door. Dr. Thorn and a man she didn't recognize entered the small room, Nurse McCarn on their heels. A layer of snow sat on the shoulders of the stranger's wool coat and filled the cuffs of his trousers, puddles of melting condensation already forming on the floor around his galoshes.

"Good morning, Clara," Dr. Thorn said. "How are you feeling today?"

She forced herself to smile, closing the Bible on her lap. "I'm fine, thank you. And yourself?"

Dr. Thorn glanced at the other man. "As I told you," he said. "She's always pleasant. She shouldn't give you any trouble." The man raised a gloved hand to his derby and tipped it in Clara's direction. She gave him a half nod, her lips twitching as she attempted to smile. Dr. Thorn glanced at the letter on Clara's desk. "I see you've read your father's letter?"

"Yes," she said, trying to keep her voice steady.

"He said you would explain what was going on."

"Well, yes," Dr. Thorn said. "That's what I'm here for." He gestured toward the man in the wool coat. "This is Mr. Glen. He's from Ovid, a small town next to Seneca Lake." Nurse McCarn took a step forward to stand beside Dr. Thorn, keeping her arm straight and slightly behind the side seam of her white skirt. Clara caught a glimpse of something long and silver in her hand. It looked like a syringe. Ice filled Clara's esophagus, making it hard to breathe. She stood. The Bible slid from her lap, slamming on the floor with a loud bang. Then she saw two orderlies and a nurse in a blue cape waiting in the hall.

Dr. Thorn held up a hand, as if to stop Clara from bolting. Nurse McCarn moved closer, her eyes wide and bright, as if on high alert. "Mr. Glen and a nurse are here to take you to Willard."

"Willard?" Clara managed. She swallowed. Her tongue felt like stone.

"It's a state-run hospital for the insane," Dr. Thorn said. "Your father wants to make sure you get the help you need. Unfortunately, he can no longer afford your stay here."

Clara stepped backward, her hands clutching her sweater. "But I don't understand," she said, sweat breaking out on her forehead. "My father said this was just temporary. I don't need help. I just want to go home!"

Nurse McCarn stepped forward, bringing the

syringe out of hiding. Dr. Thorn put up a hand to stop her. "I understand, Clara," he said. "But you need to get better first. Go ahead and pack up your things. Mr. Glen has the car waiting outside."

"But the weather," Clara said, searching for any reason to delay.

"It's clearing up," Mr. Glen said. "We'll be fine as long as we leave in the next few hours. We'll be back at Willard by nightfall."

"There's no reason to be afraid," Dr. Thorn said. "You'll be taken good care of at Willard."

Clara collapsed on the bed, her legs suddenly weak, her arms useless. It took all her strength not to fall in a heap on the floor. She searched for something to say to make them understand she was perfectly sane, that her only offense was arguing with her parents. She was being punished for standing up for herself, for standing strong for what was right and true. Words escaped her.

"Nurse McCarn," Dr. Thorn said. "Have one of your nurses come help Clara pack while you show Mr. Glen and his nurse to the cafeteria. I'm sure they could use a hot meal before the long drive back to Willard. And bring Clara some hot tea and something to eat before she goes."

Nurse McCarn and Mr. Glen left the room while Dr. Thorn remained in the entrance, one hand on the doorknob. "You'll be all right," he said to Clara. "You're an intelligent young woman with a bright future ahead of you. You just need a little help figuring out the right direction for your life. If you cooperate, there should be no reason to fear going to Willard." Then he closed the door and left, leaving Clara numb and staring at the wooden floor.

In what felt like slow motion, she got up and pulled her journal from beneath her bed. She sat at the desk and opened to her last entry, the words a blur on the page. She'd written in the journal every day since her arrival, but had not mentioned anything about the baby. For some reason, she was afraid she might jinx her pregnancy, or the doctors would find the journal and tell her father. If Henry found out she was going to have Bruno's baby, there was no telling what he might do. He would probably send her away forever.

She wiped her eyes and picked up a pen, trying to think of a way to convey the feeling of being thrown away like a piece of trash, of being locked up like a criminal. She remembered hearing stories of parents who kept their children from public view; deformed limbs, uncontrollable tempers, slow intelligence, and cleft lips being put into hiding, locked away behind a doorway on the highest floor of the family home, or secreted away in a dark attic. Is that what her father was doing? Was he so ashamed that his daughter loved someone who didn't meet his approval that he wanted to hide her away? Or did he truly believe that a doctor could make her see the error of her ways, that she could be forced to marry a man she didn't love? Or did he really think she was sick? She put the pen to paper and wrote in her journal.

> My father is getting rid of me, sending me away. I'm not sure what he thinks this will accomplish. It only makes me more determined, when I'm released, to live my life the way I wish and to get away from him. My father is sending me to Willard. I wonder if I should be afraid?

A few minutes later, Nurse Yott came into her room. She smiled at Clara and looked her in the eye, unlike the rest of the doctors and nurses who always seemed to look through her. Clara thought about telling the nurse she was being sent away, but knew there was no point. There was nothing the young nurse could do. She watched Nurse Yott pull the steamer trunk from the closet and lay it sideways on the floor. Nurse Yott turned on her toes as she went around to open the lid, her white-stocking legs and pale hands moving slowly and purposefully, like a ballerina doing a choreographed dance. Clara guessed that they were close in age, Nurse Yott being two to three years older. She pictured Nurse Yott's parents, smiling and proud at her graduation from nursing school. Tears filled her eyes and she looked at Nurse Yott's fingers to see if she was married.

There was an engagement ring on her left hand.

Suddenly, Clara felt weighed down, like she was trapped beneath a giant boulder. Her chest constricted, the agony of grief pulling her shoulders down. She was certain she heard her heart break. All at once, she knew she was going to be sick. She stood, hurried to the wastebasket, and fell to her knees. The toast she'd eaten earlier came up, stinging her throat, and then there was nothing but pain and acid. She spit into the basket over and over, then stood on trembling legs. Nurse Yott came over and put a hand on her shoulder, concern written on her face.

"Are you all right?" she said.

Clara wiped her mouth with the back of her hand. "No," she said. "I'm not all right."

"Are you sick? Do you want me to get the doctor?"

Clara pulled her sweater around her middle and sat on the bed. "I'm not sick," she said, her voice catching. "I'm pregnant."

Nurse Yott gasped. Clara put her face in her hands and sat forward, her elbows on her knees. Her shoulders convulsed, her breath coming in short, shallow gasps.

Nurse Yott knelt beside her, one hand rubbing Clara's back. "There, there," she said. "Every-thing's going to be all right."

"No," Clara said. "Everything is not going to be all right. The doctors here are supposed to help me, but how can they help me when they won't listen?" She lay down on the bed and curled up on the blanket. Nurse Yott pulled the chair away from the desk and sat down, facing Clara.

"I'm so sorry," she said. "Is there anything I can do for you?"

"Unless you can get me out of this place before they send me to Willard, then no. There's nothing you can do."

"Forgive me for asking," Nurse Yott said. "But what about the baby's father? Does he know? Are you together?"

Clara sat up, a crazy half-laugh, half-wail escaping her lips. "Yes," she said, spittle flying from her mouth. She knew it wasn't Nurse Yott's fault, but she couldn't control her anger. "We're together. Didn't you see him picking me up for a date the other night? He's tall, dark, and handsome and was wearing his best suit. You couldn't miss him!" Her voice was high and tight, and for a moment she wondered if she was losing her mind after all.

The young nurse folded her hands on her lap and looked down for a minute before speaking. When she looked up, her eyes were filled with tears.

"Listen," she said in a soft voice. "I've only been working here for about six months. It's not my ideal place of employment, but it's the only job I could find. My fiancé and I want to get married as soon as possible, but he's been out of work and . . ." She paused and chewed on her lower lip, as if wondering if she should go on. "I could tell the first time I saw you that you weren't crazy. I don't know how, but I just knew. Please don't tell anyone, but I listened to some of your sessions with Dr. Thorn to find out if my hunch was right. I heard you say your father sent you here because you wouldn't marry the person he wanted you to marry. I know how that is. My father doesn't approve of my fiancé. That's why I need this job. I'm trying to save enough money to get married and out of the house as soon as I can. Your father sent you here because you're in love with someone else, right? Bruno Moretti?"

Clara sat up and swung her legs over the side of the bed. "How do you know his name?" she said. "I never told Dr. Thorn his name!"

Nurse Yott's breathing grew shallow, her chest rising and falling faster and faster. "You have to promise me you won't breathe a word of this to anyone," she whispered. "I'll lose my job if anyone finds out."

"I promise," Clara said, feeling dizzy. "Just tell me how you know his name! Was he here? Did he come looking for me?"

Nurse Yott glanced at the door, then sat forward. "I saw the letters," she whispered. "The letters you wrote to Bruno."

Clara shook her head, confused. "What are you talking about? How could you have seen them?

After I wrote them I put them in the mailbox down by the front desk!"

Nurse Yott pressed her lips together and stood. She paced the room, then gripped the back of the chair and looked at Clara, her knuckles turning white. "The letters were never mailed," she whispered. "Nurse McCarn made me go through the outgoing mail to take them out. She said it was doctor's orders. I suspect it was really your father's orders."

All of a sudden, Clara couldn't breathe. Her neck and face felt on fire, a burning lump in her throat cutting off her words. No wonder Bruno never answered her letters! Her father had made sure he'd never received them! She stood and shoved the chair toward the desk, her knees quaking. She sat, pulled the stationery from the drawer, grabbed a pen and started writing, her fingers shaking as she tried to form coherent words.

"You have to mail this letter for me," she said, talking and writing as fast as possible. "Bruno doesn't know where I am, or where I'm going. Promise me you'll mail this to him." She finished the short letter, folded it and shoved it into an envelope, then looked at Nurse Yott, waiting for her to agree.

Nurse Yott wrung her hands, her thin shoulders hunched, her eyes watery. "I don't know," she said. "What if I get caught?"

"Hide the letter," Clara said. "In your brassiere or your underwear. I don't care where. Somewhere no one will look. When you get home, mail it from there." She sealed the envelope, scribbled Bruno's address on the front, and held it out to the nurse.

Nurse Yott looked at the letter, chewing on the corner of her lip. Suddenly, there were voices in the hall. Clara stood and shoved the letter into the nurse's hands. The nurse unbuttoned the top button of her uniform and pushed the envelope inside her brassiere. Just then, the door to the room opened and Nurse McCarn entered with a tray of food. She stopped in her tracks and looked at the open trunk on the floor.

"What's going on here?" she said. "Why haven't you finished helping Clara pack?"

Nurse Yott turned and smiled. "Clara was upset and I was trying to help by telling her how nice the doctors and nurses are at Willard. I think she feels better now. Right, Clara?"

The nurses looked at Clara, waiting. Clara nodded. "Yes," she said. "Thank you." She went to the dresser and starting removing her clothes, carrying them in neat piles over to the steamer trunk. Her legs felt like water, ready to dissolve into a puddle on the floor. She knelt and laid her blouses in the trunk, trying to keep her hands steady.

Nurse McCarn let out a loud sigh. "Nurse Yott,"

she said. "Your job was to help the patient pack her things. You're not a doctor, remember? Please stick to your job description or I'll be forced to write you up for noncompliance."

"Yes, ma'am," Nurse Yott said, taking the tray of food. She set the food on the desk and turned to face Nurse McCarn. "I'll see that the patient finishes packing and eats a little bit before she leaves."

Nurse McCarn watched Clara kneeling at her suitcase, her lips pursed, her eyes narrow. Clara looked up, giving her a weak smile. Finally, Nurse McCarn turned to leave.

"Don't be long," she said. "Mr. Glen and Nurse May are finishing their meals, then Mr. Glen will be going out to start the car. You've got less than half an hour to get ready."

"Very good," Nurse Yott said. "I'll make sure Clara is down at the front entrance shortly."

As soon as Nurse McCarn left the room, Nurse Yott hurried to the door. "I'll be right back," she said.

"Where are you going?" Clara said, her skin prickling with fear. What if she was going to give the letter to Dr. Thorn? What if the whole thing was a setup?

"Just hurry up and finish packing," Nurse Yott said. "When you're done, put on your coat and boots, but don't shut the trunk. We'll close it when I get back." And then she left Clara alone.

After the last of her garments were in the steamer trunk, Clara pulled on her boots and shoved her arms into her coat. She went to the window and craned her neck to look toward the front entrance. The snow had stopped and she could see Mr. Glen in the driveway, smoking next to the running DeSoto. The smoke from his cigarette and the exhaust from the car billowed about his dark silhouette, reminding her of a scene in a movie. But this was no movie. And Mr. Glen was no hero coming to save the day.

Clara jumped when Nurse Yott burst into the room, an extra blanket held to her chest.

"Here," Nurse Yott said, hurrying toward the steamer trunk. "I told Nurse McCarn you might need a warm blanket for the drive." She knelt and unfolded the blanket. Clara's letters to Bruno spilled out over the contents of the trunk. "I thought you would want these."

Clara gasped and picked up one of the envelopes. Nurse Yott snatched it away and shoved it, along with the rest of the letters, beneath the clothes in Clara's trunk. "There's no time for that," she said, breathing hard. She pulled the trunk closed, latched it, and pulled it upright. "Maybe someone at Willard will mail them for you."

Clara threw her arms around Nurse Yott. "Thank you so much," she said, choking back tears. Nurse Yott pulled away and led Clara to the door, but not before Clara saw tears welling up in her eyes.

CHAPTER 5

Izzy

The Saturday after Izzy's first week of school was hot and humid, the balmy breeze moving only the highest branches of the trees. Nearer the ground, the air was breathless. Izzy walked along a shaded sidewalk on her way to work, running her fingers through the birch leaves above her head. It was early, and a layer of dew still clung to the foliage, leaving the leaves wet and cool. Peg and Harry had left earlier than usual because Peg could hardly wait to start opening the Willard suitcases. Izzy had asked to walk the two miles to the museum warehouse instead of riding with them in the car. Now she was glad she did, grateful for the few minutes to herself. Between school, homework, and meals with her foster parents, the week had flown by. And it had been a rough one.

During those first few days, while Izzy was learning her way around the school, she was late for nearly every class. On the few occasions she asked for help finding her classrooms, a couple of the students gave her the wrong directions. It seemed like they did it on purpose and she couldn't understand why. She hadn't done anything to them. She tried to ignore the way they were treating her, wondering if it was the way they treated all the new kids, or if she should take it personally. Either way, it stung.

On her first day of gym, after she finally figured out that the gymnasium was in a separate building connected to the cafeteria through a long corridor, there was a sign on the girls' locker room door saying it was closed temporarily due to a plumbing problem. When she heard distant shouting and the squeak of sneakers on a wooden floor echoing from elsewhere in the building, her stomach dropped. She was already late. She sighed, turned the corner, and nearly ran over a friend of Shannon's, who was kneeling to tie her sneaker outside the boys' locker room.

"Watch it!" the girl said, catching herself with one hand.

"I'm sorry," Izzy said. "I didn't see you." She reached out to help the girl up, but the girl ignored her and finished tying her sneaker. *What was her name again?* Izzy thought. *Crystal? Nicole? Tina?*

The girl stood. "What's the rush?" she said. She brushed off her knees and shorts, then ran her fingers through her highlighted bangs. Like Shannon's and a dozen other girls' at the school, her hairstyle was sleek and layered, curling under around the edges—the Rachel haircut from the TV show *Friends*. Her white gym shorts were skintight, and the letter C glittered on the front of her short, oversized T-shirt. *Crystal, that was her name.*

"I was going to change for gym, but . . ." Izzy said.

"We have to use the boys' locker room until they get the plumbing fixed in ours," Crystal said. "You'd better hurry up. Miss Southard makes us do laps for every minute we're late."

"But what about . . ." Izzy said.

Crystal waved a dismissive hand in the air. "Don't worry," she said. "The plumbing breaks all the time, at least once a month. The boys don't have gym until after lunch."

Izzy stayed rooted to the floor, trying to figure out what to do. "How much trouble will I get in if I wear flip-flops and jeans to gym?" she said.

Crystal laughed and rolled her eyes. "Trust me," she said. "That's worse than being late." She grabbed Izzy's arm and pulled her toward the locker room door. "Come on. It's girls only. I'll show you."

Izzy let Crystal lead her toward the boys' locker room, then stopped outside the entrance, unsure. Crystal pushed open the door and stood against it, holding it open and smiling. Izzy didn't move.

"Oh my God!" Crystal said. "Don't be such a chicken! I'll go with you!"

Izzy took a deep breath. If Crystal was willing to go in, maybe it was okay. She followed her into a ceiling-less entrance hall that led to a second door. The stench of sweat and old urine stung Izzy's nostrils, and the sound of lockers banging, showers running, and people talking echoed in the cement space. But the voices were male. Izzy stopped in her tracks. Before she could turn and run, Crystal grabbed her wrist and yanked open the second door. Shannon and Nicole waited on the other side. The three girls grabbed Izzy and dragged her into the boys' locker room, pulling on her clothes and hair, their manicured nails digging into her arms. The steamy room was full of naked and half-dressed boys. When they saw the girls, they laughed and catcalled, throwing their wet towels in the air and dancing on top of the benches. Izzy kept her head down and tried to get away, but it was no use. In her struggle, she lost one of her flip-flops and dropped her bag of gym clothes.

The girls pulled Izzy through the changing area and pushed her toward the shower room. Then they shoved her forward, into the showers, and turned and ran. Izzy's bare foot slipped on the wet floor and she nearly fell. A damp hand grabbed her wrist to keep her upright. She looked up to see Ethan standing there, his dripping hair plastered against his forehead, his bare chest covered in lather. She stared at his face, like a deer caught in headlights, then turned and stumbled out of the shower.

Cheeks burning, she made her way back through the locker room, picking up her flip-flop and gym clothes, trying to keep her eyes on the floor. The boys hooted and hollered, asking if she saw anything she liked. When a soggy jock strap hit her in the middle of the chest, she stopped and glared at them.

"I've seen bigger penises on the toddlers I babysit," she said, trying to sound tough. The guys laughed and waved her away.

When she came out of the locker room, one leg of her jeans soaked, her shirt torn at the sleeve, Shannon and her friends were waiting in the hall. Izzy bunched her hands into fists and stormed away, wanting to punch them in the face, knowing they weren't worth the trouble.

"Don't be mad," Shannon called after her. "It was just a joke. We do it to all the new girls!"

Cursing under her breath and berating herself for trusting Crystal, Izzy kept going until she reached the principal's office. The principal said he would have the health teacher prepare a lecture on bullying for the next assembly, and if Izzy ever felt threatened she could go to the school nurse. But when he asked for the names of the perpetrators, Izzy refused to give them to him. If the principal questioned Shannon and her friends, there would be hell to pay. Izzy wanted him to be aware of what was going on in his school, but she wasn't ready to be labeled a snitch so he could do his job. Later that night, it was all she could do not to sneak into Harry and Peg's bathroom and look for a razor blade.

As if the boys' room incident wasn't bad enough, yesterday she caught Shannon and Crystal gluing ketchup-smeared Kotex to the outside of her locker. When the girls saw Izzy coming, they ran in the other direction, where Ethan waited for them at the end of the hall, his forehead furrowed, his mouth in a hard, thin line. When he saw Izzy, a look of shame flashed across his face. But when Shannon and Crystal reached him, he turned and fled, an empty bottle of ketchup in one hand. Apparently, he was just as bad as the rest of them. Granted, he had barely said two words to her, but something about his smile and the way he'd stopped her from falling in the shower made her think he wasn't that kind of guy. For reasons she couldn't put her finger on, it made her irritated and sad to discover she was wrong.

Thinking about it now, her heart raced and she could feel angry pressure building beneath her jaw. She had to do something to put an end to Shannon's bullying, but what? And how? It was obvious that Shannon ruled the school. No one had the nerve to stand up to her. Izzy saw other girls fall behind Shannon's group in the halls, walking a safe distance away, even if they were late for class. Some of the girls turned and walked the other way if the halls were crowded and there was no way to avoid Shannon's path. The guys who weren't laughing and cheering when Shannon and her girlfriends pulled a prank on someone would avert their eyes, or look embarrassed instead of standing up for the victims. Izzy couldn't imagine one person having that kind of power over everyone else. It made her sick.

Going to her foster parents wasn't an option. One too many times, she'd seen the results of getting parents involved with bullying problems. The parents, furious that someone was picking on their child, would run to the teachers and school board, spouting threats to anyone who would listen. The teachers and school board, afraid of a lawsuit for singling out one child for bullying, would do nothing. Then, without fail, the bullied child would pay the price for getting the grown-ups involved. Bullies find a way to target their victims, no matter what. If she told her foster parents and they went to the principal, the bullying would only get worse. She'd have to figure out what to do about Shannon on her own. Besides, she'd been relying on herself since she was ten. She wasn't about to start relying on anyone else now.

Izzy slowed on the sidewalk. Thinking about Shannon made something hard and vile push against her ribs, like a beast clawing at its cage. She hated the knot in her stomach, the hard, tight ache in her jaw. The world reeled in front of her and she stopped walking, reminding herself to breathe. She had to get rid of her anger and frustration before she lost control, like her mother had. She took a deep breath, looking around to make sure no one had seen her stop in the middle of the sidewalk for no reason, certain she looked like a crazy person.

Then she saw the drugstore across the road. She dug her nails into her palms, fighting the urge to run over and buy a box of razor blades. She put one foot in front of the other and continued walking, unfurling her fists and counting to ten. She pushed negative thoughts from her mind, determined not to let anyone send her backward, toward that dark, lonely place where her only release was more pain.

Finally, Izzy reached the warehouse. She found Peg waiting, wide-eyed and talking a hundred miles a minute. With her curly brown hair pinned in a wild mess on top of her head, Peg was wearing sandals, a long floral skirt, and one of Harry's sleeveless tees. On the other end of the warehouse, Harry gestured and smiled, talking to a group of men and women.

Peg showed Izzy the 427 Willard suitcases and trunks, lined up on tables and waiting to be opened, their contents finally revealed. Nearly breathless with excitement, she handed Izzy a thick, leather-bound notebook.

"I need you to write down the suitcase owners' names," Peg said. "Then I'll open the suitcases and tell you what's inside. We have to record everything, right down to the smallest detail."

"Okay," Izzy said. "Sounds easy enough."

"We'll do half, and Harry and his crew will do half." Just then, Harry came toward them with two other people. A tall, wiry man with thinning blond hair and silver-rimmed glasses, Harry was, as usual, impeccably dressed in a pinstriped shirt and black dress slacks. Beside him, a massive, gray-bearded man lumbered down the aisle, making Harry look like a child. Izzy gaped at the height and width of the giant walking toward her, his wide, red face, his tree trunk–sized legs. She'd never seen such a large human being. The camera in his hand looked like a doll's toy. Then, for the first time, she noticed the person walking next to the giant. He was carrying bags and a tripod, his hair the color of a raven. Izzy felt blood rise in her cheeks.

It was Ethan.

"This is our friend Peter and his son, Ethan," Harry said to Izzy. "They're here to take pictures."

"And this is my assistant, Isabelle," Peg said. "We call her Izzy."

Peter smiled and grabbed Izzy's hand, her slender fingers disappearing inside his enormous mitt. Ethan shook Peg's hand, then smiled and said hi to Izzy. She nodded in his direction, then glanced down at her shabby sneakers and too-loose jeans. Peg had told her to wear work clothes, any old garments she wouldn't care about ruining. Now she groaned inside, wishing she'd worn a plain-colored shirt instead of the New Kids on the Block long-sleeved tee with "I love Jordan" written across the chest. She'd had the shirt since tenth grade and usually wore it to bed. Not only were her clothes ugly and outdated, but she'd decided not to shower before work. Her dirty hair was in a ponytail, greasy strands hanging in her makeup-less eyes. She could hear the taunts in school now.

Peter and Ethan walked beside Peg and Izzy toward one end of the warehouse while Harry returned to the other. Thankfully, Peter's goliath frame was like a barrier between Izzy and Ethan. She could almost pretend Ethan wasn't there. She used those few moments to take slow, deep breaths, willing her reddening neck and face to return to its normal, welt-free color.

When they reached the first piece of luggage—a deteriorating leather suitcase with a brown handle and metal clasp—Ethan set up a tripod and pulled a handheld light out of a duffel bag. Peg and Izzy stood back while Peter snapped a few pictures. Izzy silently berated herself, unable to keep her eyes from wandering toward Ethan's muscular frame. He was wearing black dress shoes and tight jeans, his wide biceps stretching the rolled-up sleeves of his white button-up shirt. An image flashed in her mind: his tanned, muscular body, naked and dripping in the boys' shower room. *Why does he have to be here?* she thought. *And why does he have to be so damn good looking?* Then she pictured him holding a ketchup bottle, running away with his girlfriend, like a preschooler caught putting a cat in a toilet. No matter how beautiful he was on the outside, he was ugly on the inside. All the muscles and chiseled chins in the world couldn't change that.

Finally, Peg went over to the suitcase and read the luggage tag out loud, spelling the first and last name so Izzy could write it down—*Madeline Small*. Then Peg took a deep breath, pulled on a pair of plastic gloves and, with slow, careful hands, undid the clasp and pulled the suitcase open. Peter moved closer to take pictures before the contents were disturbed, leaving Izzy and Ethan standing side by side. Out of the corner of her eye, Izzy saw Ethan looking at her. She kept her eyes straight ahead.

With careful, reverent fingers, Peg took the dry, fragile contents one by one out of the suitcase while Izzy wrote the items down.

One Bible with three black-and-white photographs tucked inside; one of a young boy in a white shirt and dark pants, written in pencil on back: "Charles—1919," one of a young girl in a ruffled dress and flowered bonnet, written in pencil on back: "Esther—1921," one of an older woman standing on a porch in an apron, written in pencil on back: "Mother—Saratoga Cabin 1927." Four pieces of silver flatware. Two knitted baby caps, one with pink ribbon ties, one with blue ribbon ties. Condition: some yellowing and staining. One pair baby booties with white embroidery. Condition: good.

Izzy waited for Peg to keep going, but there was nothing else inside the suitcase, no clothes or nightgown, no letters or other personal items.

"That's it," Peg said, her eyes glistening. She shrugged and looked at Izzy, Peter, and Ethan.

"Why would anyone bring baby clothes to an insane asylum?" Izzy said.

"I don't know," Peg said. "Maybe they were her babies' bonnets and booties. Maybe they were the only things she cared about. But, don't you see? That's why we're doing this! We're trying to find out more about the people who left these suitcases behind."

"But how?" Ethan said. "How much can you find out just from looking inside these suitcases?"

"We're hoping to get access to some of the medical records too," Peg said. "Right now they're sealed, but we're going to pick the most compelling cases and ask the Office of Mental Health for permission to let us find out more."

"Do you want the items photographed individually or in a group?" Peter asked.

Peg stood with her hands on her hips, thinking. "I guess it's going to depend on how many things are inside each suitcase. For this one, I think we can shoot them together."

Ethan pulled a black cloth from his bag and laid it out in front of the suitcase, then set up another tripod for a second light. Peg gave Izzy a pair of plastic gloves and asked her to help rearrange the bonnets, pictures, and silverware on the cloth. Izzy was thankful for the gloves, carefully picking up the fragile items. She wished she had one of the paper masks Peg always wore while restoring paintings or scrubbing dirt from an old artifact. It was probably foolish, but she didn't want to breathe in the decades-old dust or smell the arid odor of decay radiating from the insides of the suitcase and the yellowing baby clothes. The dry, pungent aroma and bitter tang of death reminded her of old graves, and her parents' sealed bedroom.

At least in the museum the antiques were on display pedestals or behind glass. You weren't supposed to touch them. This was different. Now, like one of the first archeologists on a dig, she was handling things that hadn't been touched by another human in decades. She was helping unearth buried secrets, coming in direct contact with items once owned by people who were now nothing more than a pile of rotting bones in the ground. Not to mention the fact that the owner of these items was insane. She knew it was crazy, but she pictured microscopic particles wafting up from the baby bonnets and silverware, floating through the air and entering her lungs and bloodstream, starting a psychotic chain reaction that, when the tainted molecules reached her brain, would seal her to her mother's fate. She felt light-headed and tried not to take deep breaths, hoping the day would fly by, so she could go home and shower.

Peg and Izzy finished rearranging the items, then Peter and Ethan took pictures. Izzy and Peg stood back, waiting for Peter to tell them if the items needed to be repositioned. Together, the four of them worked in silence, hovering over the baby bonnets, silverware, photographs, and Bible like a group of surgeons and nurses over an operating table. Once Peg was satisfied with Peter's pictures, she and Izzy gently returned the contents to the suitcase, closed the lid, and moved on to the next piece of luggage.

While the process was repeated over the next four suitcases, Izzy became aware of every breath and movement; every position of her hands and legs. She felt Ethan watching and could smell his masculine cologne, the woodsy, spiced fragrance reminding her that they were young and a long way from death. She wanted to stay near him, to breathe in his scent instead of the bone-dry stench coming from the suitcases. Sometimes, she accidentally brushed his arm or got in his way, and he smiled at her, a wide, white grin. She ignored him and looked away, irritated that her face was turning red. What was it about him that made her feel so vulnerable, shaky, and exposed?

The butterflies in her stomach reminded her of the way she used to feel talking to her caseworker. But this was different. It didn't make sense. Ethan didn't know anything about her. He didn't know about her past, her present, her trials and journeys, her hopes and dreams. And he never would. He was a spoiled bully, just like his girlfriend. Izzy didn't want anything to do with him. She needed to pull herself together, especially since they had to go through two hundred more suitcases. Between having Ethan in such close proximity and the discomfort of handling the personal belongings of long-dead, mentally ill people, her thoughts were disjointed and scattered. Every movement took all her concentration.

The suitcases held letters and photographs, silverware and Bibles, suspenders and alarm clocks, buttons and shoes, embroidered handker-chiefs and shaving mugs, a small statue of a dog and a porcelain teacup, a homemade quilt. Izzy wrote every item down, frequently blinking against the moisture in her eyes. She couldn't help but imagine the parents and spouses and children of the suitcase owners, confused and mourning their loved ones' absence, even though they were physically still of this earth. How difficult it must have been to question what went wrong, to stay awake night after night, wondering if there was something they could have done. She wondered if the Willard inmates' loved ones were sideswiped by their family members' descent into madness, or if they had seen it coming all along. Either way, the thought of entire lives lost—family celebrations, Christmases and birthdays, love affairs and bedtime stories, weddings and high school graduations—because of a misfire or unexplained chaos inside a person's brain, made her chest constrict. It wasn't fair.

By noon, they'd only gone through fifteen suitcases, and Izzy was beginning to realize that the project was going to take a lot longer than she thought. At this rate, she'd be spending six or seven days working beside Ethan. Would it be too obvious if she asked to help Harry instead? And yet, if she was being honest, the thought of spending more time with Ethan sent a flutter of excitement across her stomach. Being this close to him made her feel as if she hadn't slept or eaten in days. Her legs felt weak, her head woozy. It was exhausting, irritating, and wonderful all at the same time. *What the hell is wrong with me?* she thought.

Thankfully, when it came time to take a break, Peg asked Izzy if she wanted to sit outside for lunch. She'd packed a cooler with sandwiches and they could eat in the shade beneath the oak trees, in the wide swath of grass next to the parking lot. Peter, Ethan, and the rest of the guys were going to drive to the nearest McDonald's to get Quarter Pounders and milk shakes. Normally, Izzy would have wanted to go too, because eating out while in foster homes was a rare treat, even if it was a fast-food place. But this time Izzy was relieved to stay behind, to get some peace and quiet, some space and time away from Ethan. Then she heard Peg talking to the others and her stomach tightened.

"Oh no!" Peg said. "I've packed enough food for everyone! I've got ham and cheese sandwiches, macaroni salad, hummus and pita bread, potato chips, watermelon, iced tea, and lemonade. There are extra blankets and folding chairs in the trunk of the car. Come on, it'll be fun!"

"Sorry, guys," Harry said, grinning. "My wife has a thing about feeding people."

Peter and the other men laughed and agreed to stay. They headed to Peg's car to unload the chairs. Peg turned to Izzy.

"Can you give me a hand with the food?" she said.

"Sure," Izzy said, groaning inside. *Leave it to Peg to take care of everyone,* she thought. *Working with Ethan was one thing, now she had to have lunch with him?* The last few minutes before it was time to take a break she'd been starting to get hungry, her stomach growling so loud she was sure everyone heard it. Now, her stomach roiled with a strange mixture of elation and dread.

Everyone gathered beneath a row of thick-trunked oak trees, the men setting up folding chairs, Peg and Izzy spreading out a blanket and organizing the food on a foldout table. The men formed a line and Peg poured drinks and scooped macaroni salad onto paper plates while Izzy pulled sandwiches out of the cooler and handed out snack-sized bags of chips. When she saw Ethan next in line, she kept her eyes on her work, hoping he was going to sit far away. She held out a sandwich, pretending to search in a grocery sack for a bag of chips, and felt his fingers brush hers. At first, she ignored it. Then she handed him a bag of chips and he grabbed her hand and the bag at the same time, crushing the chips between their fingers. She looked up.

"Oh, sorry," he said, grinning. "It's hard to see when you're not looking." She tried to pull away but he wouldn't let go. "Thank you for the sandwich," he said, "and the chips."

She rolled her eyes. "Can I have my hand back?" she said.

"Thank you for the service with a smile."

"You're holding up the line."

"Can you say, 'please move along'?" he said.

She pinched the skin on the back of his hand. "Please move," she said, her voice dripping with sarcasm. He let go and took the chips.

"How about, 'you're welcome'?" he said.

Izzy ignored him and smiled at the next man in line.

"How come he gets a smile and I don't?" Ethan said. Izzy forced a thin smile so he'd leave her alone. "That's better," he said. "Now I can enjoy my lunch."

After Ethan walked away, Izzy sighed and tried to focus on the rest of the men in line, her chest welting up. She'd never met anyone so arrogant! She couldn't believe she let herself get nervous around him.

Later, after everyone was done eating, Izzy sat cross-legged on the blanket beneath an oak tree, nibbling on a pita chip while Peg refilled everyone's drinks. Ethan was sitting on a folding chair a few yards away, talking and laughing with Peter and Harry. Every now and then, he glanced over and caught her looking at him. Each time she vowed not to look again, but her eyes were drawn to the sound of his deep voice and his contagious laughter. She wished she'd brought her journal or a book to read, anything to make it look like she was doing something besides just sitting there. She'd already spent way too much time in the bathroom after she was done handing out food, washing her hands and fixing her hair, hoping everyone would be finished eating when she came back out. Instead, Peg was offering them seconds, laughing and pleading with them to eat more because she didn't want the food to go to waste.

While Peg finished doling out the last of the iced tea and lemonade, Izzy kneeled on the blanket and started packing up the empty Tupperware and extra napkins, doing what she could to get this awkward picnic over with. Then Peg came back and sat down, leaning against the gnarled bark of a wide oak tree. She sighed and wiped a wrist across her brow.

"This was nice," she said. "I love picnics, don't you?"

"Uh-huh," Izzy said.

"My word, he's a handsome boy," Peg said. "Don't you think?"

Izzy reached for the empty plastic pitchers. "Who?"

Peg laughed. "You know who. Ethan."

Izzy shrugged and put the pitchers in the basket. "I guess."

"We've known his parents for years," Peg said. "They're two of the nicest people you could ever meet."

"Too bad their son is a jerk," Izzy said, gathering her and Peg's empty potato chip bags and shoving them into a trash bag.

"Whose son is a jerk?" a deep voice said above them. Izzy turned to see Ethan standing over them, one hand gripping a branch above his head, the other in the pocket of his jeans. He winked at her. She wanted to stand up and wipe the self-confident smirk off his face.

Peg offered Ethan a spot on the blanket. "Here," she said, patting the empty space between her and Izzy. "Sit down. We've got a few more minutes before we have to go back to work."

Izzy stuffed a fistful of dirty napkins into the trash bag. *What the hell?* she thought. *Just because you like Ethan's parents doesn't mean I have to be friends with him.*

"That's okay, Mrs. Barrows," Ethan said. "I get the feeling I'm interrupting something."

Mrs. Barrows? Izzy thought. *Ugh. What a brown-noser.*

"Oh no, you're fine," Peg said. "I was just telling Izzy what nice people your parents are. I told her that they're good friends of ours."

"Guess that makes me the jerk then," Ethan said, laughing.

"Oh no." Peg sat up, eyes wide, hands waving as if she could erase her comment from the air. "That's not what I . . ."

"It's okay," Izzy said to Peg. "You don't have to protect me." She grabbed the dirty forks and the watermelon knife, wrapped them in a paper towel, and shoved them in the picnic basket between the Tupperware and plastic pitchers. The pain was instant and sharp as the watermelon knife sliced through her index finger. She yanked her hand out of the basket, looked at the inch-long cut, and her knees went weak. She put her finger between her lips, the coppery taste of blood filling her mouth, then sat back on the blanket and closed her eyes, waiting for the dizzy, whirling sensation to subside.

"What's wrong?" Peg said. "Did you cut yourself?"

Izzy nodded and grabbed a fistful of blanket with her other hand, looking for something to hold on to while the world spun around her. Then she felt someone touch her wrist and she opened her eyes. Ethan was kneeling beside her, gently pulling her finger out of her mouth.

"Let me have a look," he said. Too woozy to object, Izzy let him. His fingers and palm felt warm and silky smooth, like the soft, bare belly of a sleeping puppy. The reeling sensation inside her head seemed to slow, and her heart returned to its normal rhythm. "It's deep," he said. "But it's nothing serious." He looked at Peg. "Do you have a Band-Aid or some gauze?"

"I'll get the first aid kit," Peg said, scrambling to her feet.

"I'm fine," Izzy said, pulling her hand away. "Really." But it was too late. Peg was halfway across the lawn, her flowery skirt billowing behind her as she ran.

"You don't look fine," Ethan said. He pulled a

clean paper towel from the roll. "You're white as a sheet."

"That's my normal color," she said, holding her fist against her stomach.

"Could have fooled me," Ethan said. "I thought your normal color was fury red." He reached for her hand again and she yanked it away.

"Ha ha," she said. "Very funny."

"Put this around your finger to stop the bleeding," he said, handing her the paper towel. She took the towel and did as she was told, wishing he would go away. He was too close, too clean smelling, too warm, too unbelievably handsome. She scooted backward on the blanket and got to her feet. He laughed, looking up at her. "I'm not going to bite, you know."

"No," she said. "I don't know." She picked up the wicker picnic basket and started toward Peg's car.

He stood and followed her. "So you think I'm a jerk, huh?" She could hear amusement in his voice. It made her stomach turn.

"I don't think anything," she said. "I don't know you." She walked faster. He kept up.

"That's right, you don't. So maybe you shouldn't call me names."

"Oh!" she said, rolling her eyes. "I see how it works. You can dish it out, but you can't take it!"

"Dish what out?"

She stopped and turned on him. "I called you a

jerk and you got upset, but it's okay for you and your little girlfriend to play mean tricks on people. Is that it?"

The smile on his face disappeared and he gazed at her, his brows knitted. "I didn't know it was your locker."

"It doesn't matter whose locker it was! It was horrible and mean."

"You're right, it was," he said. "But Shannon . . ."

"Shannon tells you and everyone else what to do, and you just follow along like a bunch of mindless idiots!"

"No, that's not it. It's . . . she . . ."

Just then, Izzy saw Peg hurrying across the parking lot toward them, a white and blue first aid kit in her hand. Harry followed close at hand, his forehead lined with worry.

Izzy shook her head. "That's exactly it. But I don't want to talk about it right now. You and I have to work together until we're finished going through all those suitcases. Let's just agree to disagree, okay?"

Ethan followed her gaze and saw Peg and Harry closing in on them. "Can we talk about it some other time then?" he said. "Some other place?"

Izzy gripped the wicker basket in both hands, pressing her fresh cut against the wooden handle. The sharp pain mirrored the twisting sensation in her heart and mind as conflicting emotions fought to gain the upper hand. Every instinct told her to stay away from Ethan, that he would cause her nothing but trouble. At the same time, she couldn't deny being drawn to him. Her stomach clenched with fury.

"Why?" she said.

Just then, Peg and Harry reached them.

Ethan took the first aid kit. "I've got this," he said. "It's my fault."

"Are you sure?" Peg asked. "She doesn't need stitches or anything?"

Ethan chuckled. "She doesn't need stitches. It's just a small cut."

"Okay, if you say so. You're the future doctor, after all. We'll get the picnic mess cleaned up while you take care of Izzy."

Before Izzy could protest, Peg and Harry left them alone again, going back beneath the trees to pick up the chairs and coolers. Ethan opened the passenger door of Peg's car and ordered Izzy to sit. She did as she was told, sitting sideways on the warm leather seat, her long legs hanging out the open door. Ethan kneeled on the pavement in front of her and set the first aid kit on the ground. Then he took her hand and gently unwrapped the blood-soaked paper towel from around her finger. Izzy cringed and looked away.

"Don't be such a baby," he said. "It's not any worse than a paper cut. The bleeding has already stopped."

"I thought you said it was deep."

"It is, but it's small. You'll be fine, I promise."

She felt his warm, silky fingers glide around her hand, pulling it toward him so he could dress her wound. She wondered what he would think if he knew she used to cut herself on purpose. *He'd probably think I'm crazy,* she thought. *And he'd probably be right.* "Oh, that's right," she said, trying to distract herself by making small talk. "You're the future doctor."

"My parents want me to be a doctor," Ethan said. He opened up the first aid kit and rummaged through it. "I'd rather be an EMT."

"I could never do that," she said. She watched Peg and Harry through the dusty car windshield, trying not to look at her finger. In the shade beneath the trees, Harry gave Peg a quick peck on the lips before taking a cooler out of her hands. Peg smiled and ruffled his hair. The scene reminded Izzy of being at the beach with her parents; her mother and father laughing and chasing each other through the sand, her father grabbing her mother around the waist, kissing her and carrying her into the waves. Izzy remembered smiling as she watched them, feeling safe and content, her perfect world full of happy people who loved each other, just as it should be. Then she was assaulted by the image of her father on his stomach in her parents' bed, the sheets covered with blood, an oozing black hole in his head. She saw her mother crouched in the corner of the bedroom, staring straight ahead, the hunting rifle at her blood-covered feet. Izzy's stomach twisted. In the end, all the smiles at the beach, all the happy Christmas mornings and kisses good-bye, all the jokes at the dinner table; it was nothing but an illusion. She wondered what perfect-world-destroying secrets Peg and Harry were keeping from each other.

"Obviously," Ethan said, laughing. "You're at a bit of a disadvantage if you can't take the sight of blood."

"Umm . . . what?" she said, jarred from her thoughts.

"You okay?" he said, looking up at her, his forehead furrowed.

"Yeah," she said. "Sorry. My mind was somewhere else." She dared to watch as he poured iodine over her finger, waiting for a sting that never came.

"We were talking about what a horrible EMT you'd make," he said.

"Yeah," Izzy said, returning her gaze to Peg and Harry. "When I was little I wanted to be a veterinarian. But I can't stand seeing animals suffer. I wouldn't be able to operate on them, even if it meant saving their lives." She heard herself opening up and cringed. As usual her mouth worked faster than her brain. Maybe she was still woozy from slicing her finger.

"Me either," Ethan said. "Last year my yellow

Lab was hit by a car and I cried for days. I couldn't even go to school. It was pretty pathetic."

"But it wouldn't bother you to be an EMT? To see people suffer?"

"That's different."

"How is it different?" she said.

He shrugged. "I don't know. It just is. Animals are innocent. People are . . . well, they're not innocent. Animals are better than humans."

She looked down at the top of his raven-colored head, his wide shoulders, his tanned neck, and forgot all about her bleeding finger. He held a piece of thick gauze around her fingertip and opened the roll of first aid tape, every movement slow and gentle. Could there be a heart and brain beneath all that bravado and brawn? Or was this another one of his tricks? She thought about the overly polite way he'd addressed Peg—"Mrs. Barrows"—reminding herself that any teenage boy she'd ever met who was that courteous to grown-ups was usually up to no good. His polite manners didn't ring true. And yet, somehow, she felt that right now, for the first time, she was seeing the real Ethan.

"What was your dog's name?" she said.

"Lucy," he said. "She was a girl."

"I'm sorry about Lucy," she said.

"Thanks. My parents bought me another dog last year, another yellow Lab. We named her Lucy Two."

He wrapped two pieces of tape around the gauze, then smiled up at her, his eyes blue as the ocean, deep as the sea. When she realized she was staring, she stood up fast, nearly knocking him over. He caught himself on the door.

Just then, Harry and Peter appeared at the car, coolers and chairs in hand.

"I see she's already knocked you off your feet," Harry said, laughing.

Ethan closed the first aid kit and stood. "I lost my balance," he said, his face flushing.

"Sure you did," Peter said, grinning. "Open the trunk, will you?"

While Ethan helped the men load up the picnic gear, Izzy picked up the first aid kit and started toward the warehouse. She glanced over her shoulder and saw Ethan lifting a stack of chairs into the trunk of the car, watching her walk away.

Back in the warehouse, the next suitcase Peg opened belonged to a man named Lawrence Lawrence. While Peg recited the sparse contents of the deteriorating leather bag—*one pair of men's black leather shoes, one pair of elastic suspenders with white buttons, a blue and white shaving mug, one shaving brush with brittle, yellow bristles*—Izzy was thankful for an excuse to keep her eyes on the notebook. She concentrated on writing everything down in careful script, trying not to think about Ethan. When it came time to set up the suitcase contents to be photographed, Ethan picked up Izzy's plastic gloves and held one open, offering to help put it on over her injured finger.

She felt her face grow warm, took the gloves, and said, "Thanks, I can handle it."

After she finished helping Peg rearrange the suitcase contents, she took off the gloves and set them down again. Ethan picked them up and put them in his pocket. The next time she needed the gloves she had to ask him for them. When she saw him pick them up a second time, she excused herself to get another pair.

Over the next three hours they went through ten more suitcases. One contained Philippine newspaper clippings, a class picture from the Bryant Preparatory Academy in Salt Lake City, a small booklet belonging to Roberto Torres entitled, "My School Memories in America," and an old sailor uniform complete with a navy wool cap. Izzy flipped through the booklet. One entry read: *At the Walbash Public School I studied the following: English, Grammar, Arithmetic, Geography, Hygiene, Music, Spelling, and Carpentry. Here I obtained some knowledge of the works of Henry W. Longfellow. There are five Oriental students including myself.* The last page of the booklet ended midsentence. *I have no definite knowledge of when I shall regain my freedom. I wish to write . . .*

"I wonder if this was his father," Peg said, holding up a newspaper clipping featuring a stern-looking Asian man. "He must have been a banker or a politician or something."

Izzy looked at one of the many photos in the suitcase. In it, a young Asian man held a book in his hands, his handsome face calm and studious. On the back was a name in pencil: *Roberto Torres.* She couldn't imagine the long, complicated journey Roberto must have taken from the Philippines to end up in an insane asylum in New York State.

Another suitcase contained a Bible, votive cards, hymnals, a prayer book, and a letter from a nun to a bishop. An old doctor's bag made of fake alligator skin held a nursing diploma and a carefully wrapped collection of teacups with matching saucers. One large trunk contained pots and pans, a lamp, a set of canisters made of green Depression glass, and a pair of ice skates.

The last suitcase of the day was a massive steamer trunk covered with faded travel stickers; one picturing a black ocean liner with the words "Cunard—Boston to Europe" in red, another with "France" in bold letters across a pink Eiffel Tower, even more stickers from Zurich, Italy, Maine, Cairo, London, and Bremerhaven. Peg, Izzy, Ethan, and Peter gathered around the trunk, each lost in their own thoughts as they examined the teak trim, brass hardware, and faded baggage claim stamps. It was the largest of all the suitcases, a monolith among a sea of ordinary-sized baggage.

Izzy tried to imagine the owner of the steamer trunk. She pictured an old man, perhaps a writer or professor, traveling the world in search of firsthand knowledge of native cultures and traditional customs. Perhaps he was a scientist or an archeologist, who, after exploring Egyptian tombs and ancient ruins, eventually suffered the ravages of old age and lost his mind due to dementia or Alzheimer's. Somehow, he was sent to Willard, with no family to claim him.

After Peter took pictures of the trunk from all angles, he and Ethan set it upright. When Peg read the name on the handle tag, Izzy was surprised. The owner of the steamer trunk was a woman— *Clara Elizabeth Cartwright.* Izzy wrote the name down while Peg released the brass lock and snapped open the draw bolts. Peg took a deep breath and pulled the trunk open. When the insides were revealed, Peg and Izzy gasped. Peter started snapping pictures.

Peeking out from paisley-patterned drawers with leather handles were feathers and silk ribbons, pearls and pastel-colored chemises, sheet music and the scalloped edges of old photographs. Hanging from a clothes bar were ruffled blouses, pleated skirts, beaded flapper dresses, silk stockings, a cardigan jacket with satin bows, and an evening gown with a sleeveless bodice made of gold metallic cloth. Tucked in the suitcase corners were two faded cloches—bowl-shaped women's hats—a beaded handbag, several books, and a pair of high-heeled shoes. In the middle of it all was a haphazard pile of unopened letters.

"We're going to need more room to lay this out," Peg said, her voice high with excitement. "Ethan, will you go ask Harry to help bring over one of the extra tables?"

Ethan did as he was told. Within minutes, he and Harry set a large table beside the steamer trunk.

"I've got more black cloth in the truck," Ethan said, heading outside.

"Grab another roll of film while you're out there," Peter shouted.

While Ethan went to the truck to get more cloth and a fresh roll of film, Peter used the opportunity to visit the restroom. Peg began opening the drawers while Izzy started writing everything down.

One copy of *The Great Gatsby*, by F. Scott Fitzgerald—condition: excellent. One copy of *Lady Chatterley's Lover*, by D. H. Lawrence—condition: excellent. One paper folder of sheet music. Postcards from Germany, Spain, and France—condition: good. One pink feather boa. Three pearl necklaces. Four silver and semiprecious stone bracelets. One black-and-white photograph of a young woman in a flapper dress sitting at a round table, four flapper girls smiling behind her chair—written on the back: "18th birthday—The Cotton Club." One photograph of the same young woman and a young man in a tuxedo with a high collar, written on the back: "Bruno and me—July 1929." One photograph of the same woman with an older man in a fedora and wool coat, and an older woman in a fur wrap and feathered hat, written on the back: "Mother and Father—Christmas 1928." One green, leather-bound journal, condition: good.

In every photograph, the young woman, Clara, was beaming, her bobbed, finger-waved hair loose, or tucked neatly beneath a cloche. She was pretty enough to be a movie star, with large, round eyes, long lashes, high cheekbones, and dark, full lips. In the picture of Clara and her parents, her father's mouth was turned down beneath a walrus mustache. Clara's mother was a tiny, pinched-face woman, looking off to the right of the picture, as if planning an escape as soon as the photographer was finished. They looked unhappy.

While Peg began organizing the contents of the steamer trunk, Izzy picked up the picture of Clara and Bruno to examine more closely. Bruno had dark hair, a wide, square jaw, and flawless skin. His arm was around Clara and he was turned slightly toward her, as if about to kiss her cheek.

Clara was looking at the camera, her eyes soft, her smile content. Izzy stared at the picture, wondering if either of them had any inkling that their lives were not going to turn out the way they'd hoped. If anyone had stumbled upon this picture someplace besides the attic of an old insane asylum, it would have been easy to imagine the two of them married in a lavish ceremony, driven away in a black limousine, to live in a big house with a gaggle of perfectly beautiful children. It would have been easy to imagine that they had grown old together and died happy, after living a contented, normal life.

When Izzy looked at Clara's happy face, a hollow draft of sadness swept through her. Did Clara have any idea she was going to lose her mind? Did she have any idea her life was going to take such a horrible turn? Izzy looked at Bruno, goose bumps prickling the skin on her arms. And what had become of him? Did he have any idea that he'd fallen in love with a crazy person? Hopefully, he'd gotten out of the relationship unscathed.

When Peg gathered the letters and shuffled through them, her head down, something ugly and dark writhed in Izzy's stomach. This was not what she'd expected when she agreed to help with the suitcases. Everywhere she looked was a reminder of the unfathomable turn her own life had taken. Now, the piles of unopened letters reminded her of the manila envelope hidden in the back of her dresser drawer, its sides bulging with letters, birthday and Christmas cards—correspondence from her mother that, to this day, Izzy refused to read.

She had told her caseworker she refused to read the letters because she hated her mother. But that was a lie. No matter how angry she was with her mother, no matter how sorry she felt for her, or how much she feared ending up like her, she didn't hate her. If she was being honest, she missed her mother as much as, if not more than, her father. She still remembered her mother baking cookies in a sunlit kitchen, planting pansies around the front porch, braiding her hair with pink ribbon. The woman Izzy loved and missed was not the same one who shot her father. Something had changed inside her mother's brain and turned her into someone else. It was the only thing that made sense. The thought of her mother losing her mind was terrifying, but it didn't fill Izzy with hate. It filled her with sadness and fear. She had to believe her mother had no choice in the matter.

The caseworker would think Izzy was crazy if she told her the truth—that she didn't want to read the letters because she was scared that the envelopes felt tainted somehow. What if the letters were filled with the insane ramblings of a crazy woman? What if her mother's words influenced her in some way, edging her down the slippery slope toward madness? The easiest thing to do, the easiest way to put one foot in front of the other and try to carry on, was pretend the letters didn't exist. Sure, she took the manila envelope full of letters from one foster home to the other, adding the newest ones when they arrived. But she'd gotten good at reacting to them the same way she reacted to the framed picture of her father that she kept in the outside zippered compartment of her suitcase. The letters and photograph were just her belongings, what little bit of property she owned, like her underwear or a pair of jeans, all things not worth mentioning.

But there was one major difference between Clara's letters and Izzy's. The envelopes found in Clara's trunk were missing stamps and post office marks because they were never mailed.

"They're all addressed to the same person," Peg said, looking at the last envelope.

"Bruno?" Izzy said.

Peg raised her eyebrows. "Yes! Bruno Moretti! How did you know?"

Izzy held up the picture of Clara and Bruno. Squinting, Peg looked at the photo. "Oh my," she said. "What a beautiful couple."

"I wonder what happened," Izzy said, looking at the photo again. "She looks so normal. And happy."

Peg shrugged. "Hopefully we'll be able to figure that out."

"Maybe this will tell us something," Izzy said, reaching for the journal. The green leather cover was stamped with fleur-de-lis, its spine wrapped in black patent. She opened the small book and began reading out loud. "January 1925. Dear Diary, Right now I'm in Switzerland. Mother bought this journal for me in a beautiful gift shop in Engleberg. I wish I could live here. William and I have such a grand time exploring. I love the mountains and the chalets. Mother and Father seem happy here too. But we have to go home tomorrow."

Izzy stopped reading and flipped to the last pages. She skimmed over the long paragraphs and read the last entry. "My father is sending me to Willard. I wonder if I should be afraid?" Izzy looked at Peg, trying to swallow the growing lump in her throat. What catastrophic event had befallen this young woman to land her in a place like Willard? If not some terrible happenstance, then what underlying, inexplicable condition had caused her mind to go around the bend? Why would her own father send her to an insane asylum? Had she seemed normal one minute, out of her mind the next? Had something happened to her, or to Bruno? Had Clara shot the love of her life in a fit of madness or jealous rage?

Just then, Ethan and Peter returned, more black cloth and a fresh roll of film in their hands. Izzy put down the journal and went back to rearranging the photographs and postcards, trying to hide her flooding eyes. She swore under her breath when her nose started running, wiping it away and hoping no one would notice. When she looked at Ethan, he was watching her, his forehead furrowed.

CHAPTER 6

CLARA

In the backseat of the rumbling DeSoto, Clara leaned against the door and stared out the window, the blanket from Nurse Yott draped over her legs. The setting sun illuminated the thinning clouds, filling the sky with feathery shades of pink and lavender. The distant buildings and trees were growing darker and darker, becoming silhouettes against the pastel-colored sky. It was the one time of day when Clara imagined a person could actually see the earthly version of heaven and hell, light and dark, good and evil. The earth and everything on it was cast black for those last few minutes of daylight, as if evil ruled the world for that short period of time, before the stars and moon came out to illuminate the night sky and remind everyone and everything that there really was lightness and goodness in the universe, that there really was hope and heaven. Now, as the world was on the verge of being cloaked in complete darkness, Clara imagined Mr. Glen was going to keep driving and driving, until they were swallowed by the night. She searched the pale sky for the first star and breathed a sign of relief when she saw a pinprick of light twinkling above the bare branches of a black tree.

After six hours of near silence in the car, Mr. Glen finally announced that they were arriving on Willard Asylum grounds. Nurse May sat stiff as a board beside Clara, her hands in her lap and her face pinched, looking straight ahead. Three hours earlier, after they'd left the Long Island Home, Clara had begged Mr. Glen to stop at a gas station or roadside diner so she could use the restroom. She'd been hoping for a chance to escape, maybe through the back door of a restaurant or the window of a ladies' powder room. But the nurse never let her out of her sight, going as far as entering the gas station restroom behind her, standing stiff and silent while Clara relieved herself.

Clara even looked around the toilet room as she washed her hands, searching desperately for something to hit Nurse May over the head with. But the only thing she could find was a wicker wastebasket. It was too lightweight to do any damage. Besides, Clara wasn't sure she'd be able to hurt the woman anyway, even to save herself.

When Clara caught sight of herself in the restroom mirror, a stranger looked back at her. Until that moment, when she saw her weary features and disheveled hair, she felt like the last few hours were happening to someone else. She felt disconnected, certain it would all come to an end, like a nightmare or a practical joke. Someone or something would save her, she was sure of it. After all, she was Clara Elizabeth Cartwright, daughter of the lone heiress of the Bridge Bros. Clothing Emporium and the owner of Swift Bank. She loved Teaberry chewing gum, dalmatian dogs, cherry-flavored lipstick, and dancing the Charleston. Things like this didn't happen to people like her.

But then she saw her hollow eyes and pale skin, and realized that, indeed, this was happening to her. Somehow, she was being sent to an asylum. This was the course her life had taken. Now, it was impossible to imagine that her lips were the same lips Bruno used to kiss, that her cheeks were the same cheeks he lovingly caressed. She wondered what the doctors and nurses saw when they looked at her.

After stopping at the gas station, they rode in silence, except for Mr. Glen's occasional whistling of a Broadway or jazz tune. Rain hammered the metal roof and wind screamed through every seam in the car, like angry spirits from the empty fields, desperate to get inside.

Now, the rain had stopped and it was still light enough that Clara could make out several barns and what looked like orchards and crop fields. Here, the ground was bare, and she could see sheared rows of brown cornstalks and yellow wheat, like embroidery in the soil. Outside the barns, pigs and cows foraged in pens and a small herd of horses grazed in a fenced pasture. Farther along the road were chicken coops, a blacksmith shop, and several industrial-style buildings. She jumped when Mr. Glen suddenly started talking.

"Willard Asylum opened in 1869 and has grown into a sizeable village," he said. "Patients work on the farm and the railroad, and our bakery and kitchens provide most of the food for inmates and staff. We have our own orchards and grow our own crops, and our shops produce clothing, shoes, even the pine coffins used to bury patients in Willard's cemetery."

The hair on Clara's neck stood up. She never imagined people *dying* at Willard. She only pictured them getting help and being sent home. Why would an insane asylum need a cemetery?

"What happened to the patients who died?" she said in a small voice.

"All sorts of things," Mr. Glen said. "Tuberculosis, typhoid, cholera, old age."

"Old age?" Clara said.

"Sure," Mr. Glen said. "Some patients spend decades at Willard."

"There's no need to discuss such things, Mr. Glen," Nurse May said, her voice stern.

Clara swallowed the lump in her throat and pulled the blanket over her shoulders.

After they passed a railroad yard lit up with oil lanterns, where a dozen men pushed wheelbarrows full of coal toward a power plant, she saw the dark silhouettes of factory-sized buildings in the distance, attached to an enormous central structure that looked like a mammoth four-story mansion. As they drove closer to the buildings, she saw lights coming on behind tall, curtain-less windows, figures moving, walking, bending, standing motionless near the glass. The windows were covered with bars. Clara's stomach twisted.

Just then, Mr. Glen started whistling "Someone to Watch Over Me" and Clara's heart seized in her chest, her throat on fire. When Nurse May started humming along, Clara felt like screaming. *Had they chosen the song on purpose? Was this the first step in their plan to drive her insane?* She dug her fingernails into her palms, certain she must be asleep, hoping pain would force her awake. But this was no nightmare. It was real life, her life. Soon she would be on the other side of those windows, looking out, with no one to watch over her. A surge of homesickness roiled through her, so strong it nearly caused her to cry out.

Outside the car window, the three-story buildings went on and on, massive wing after massive wing connected at the far corners, like sideways steps leading to the central house. She tried to imagine how many poor souls were suffering behind Willard's brick walls. If the number of buildings and windows was any indication, the number was high. The twinge of panic that had tightened her throat earlier turned into a swirling mass in the pit of her stomach.

The DeSoto bumped along the rutted road, then turned left to move across the front of the colossal structure. Out the car window to her right, the land sloped slightly downward. But it was getting too dark to see much more. In the distance, what looked like a bank of low clouds lay nestled in a deep valley, then the land rose again. Then she saw lights reflected in the valley and realized she was looking at a body of water.

Mr. Glen stopped the car in front of a mammoth brick Victorian. It was the main building, with a dozen wings leading off each side. A double staircase curved up to the front door and electric lights shone behind the windows. One of the oversized doors opened and a man in a dark suit stepped out onto the stone portico. Mr. Glen turned off the car and got out.

"Wait for me to come around and get you," Nurse May said to Clara.

Clara swallowed the sour taste of fear in the back of her throat, her arms and legs shaking. Beads of sweat broke out on her upper lip. Despite the fact that she was suddenly roasting, she buttoned every button on her coat, reinforcing her only layer of protection. Mr. Glen retrieved Clara's luggage from the trunk of the DeSoto, then came around the side of the car and opened the rear passenger door. Nurse May appeared and Clara stepped out of the vehicle, her eyes locked on the monolithic building before her. A carved marble sign above the stone portico read "Chapin Hall." Looking up at the cathedral-style windows, the attic dormers, the massive chimneys and the three-story cupola, Clara's mouth went dry. It was a castle, a fortress, a prison with no escape. And she was being taken inside.

The man on the portico followed the curved balustrade down the stone steps and met them at the end of the sidewalk.

"How was the drive?" he said to Mr. Glen. He nodded hello to Nurse May, then looked Clara up and down, his hands behind his back. He was a small, wiry man with a precisely trimmed goatee and low eyebrows, his dark hair slicked away from his tanned face. His navy suit fit like a glove, the high collar ghostly white, his leather shoes reflecting the gas porch lamps.

"The roads were somewhat treacherous for the first hour," Mr. Glen said. "But we drove out of the weather."

"Good, good," the man said. "And this must be Clara?"

"This is Clara Elizabeth Cartwright, Dr. Roach," Nurse May said. "Aged eighteen and in good physical condition."

"No need for isolation?"

"Dr. Thorn assured us she hasn't been sick," Nurse May said. Nurse May kept her eyes locked on the doctor, as if waiting for some kind of recognition.

"Did she give you any trouble?" Dr. Roach said to Mr. Glen, ignoring the nurse's stare.

"No, sir," Mr. Glen said. "She was quiet as a mouse."

"Fine, fine," Dr. Roach said. "Bring her inside and we'll get her settled."

Clara tightened her jaw, a growing ache throbbing beneath her skull. They were talking about her as if she wasn't there, as if she were a lesser human being who couldn't hear or feel or speak. She extended her hand, hoping the doctor would recognize she didn't belong there.

"Nice to meet you, Dr. Roach," she said, forcing a smile.

Dr. Roach stiffened and looked at her out-stretched hand, his arms still behind his back. Nurse May shoved Clara's hand back to her side, her lips curling in disgust.

"Keep to yourself," she said.

Dr. Roach turned and started inside. Mr. Glen gestured for the women to follow. Clara stood rooted to the sidewalk, wondering if she should make a run for it. She might be able to outrun Nurse May, but she was fairly certain Mr. Glen would catch her posthaste. Nurse May poked her in the back, urging her to move. Clara glared at her, then started up the walkway toward Chapin Hall.

Dr. Roach held one of the double doors open and waited for them to enter, narrowed eyes watching Clara, as if worried she'd try to touch him again. Inside, Mr. Glen and Nurse May took off their coats and hung them on an iron coat rack. Clara made no move to remove hers.

"She can leave her coat on for now," Dr. Roach said to no one in particular, his voice echoing in the vast, stone foyer. "We'll be taking her to Women's Ward B. Mr. Glen, please bring her luggage."

The doctor strolled across the foyer, his hands behind his back, his hard shoes clacking along the white marble floors. A nurse sitting behind a desk looked up briefly, her pale face illuminated by the light from the desk lamp, its triangular beam like a beacon in the dim room. The ceilings were at least twenty feet high, with a stained glass dome in the center flanked by unlit gasoliers with brass leaves and etched globes. A marble chair railing stretched around the entire room, and images of pastoral farmlands and snow-covered Alps lined the olive green walls. A couch and several over-stuffed chairs formed a seating area near the ceiling-to-floor windows to one side of the front door and, to the rear of the foyer, a grand mahogany staircase led to the second floor. The decor reminded Clara of her parents' mansion, but on a much larger scale. Her knees vibrated and she started to tremble, her legs about to give out.

Dr. Roach led them across the foyer into a short hallway with several doors, stopping in front of the first door on the right.

"Nurse May," he said, keeping his eyes on Clara. "Please take Clara inside and help her choose a sensible pair of shoes, undergarments, and three everyday dresses from her trunk. No stockings. We'll provide her with nightwear and put the rest of her belongings in storage. Be sure to leave out her winter coat and boots for outdoor activities."

"Yes, Dr. Roach," Nurse May said, her voice clipped. She opened the door and led Clara into a changing room, mumbling something under her breath. Mr. Glen followed, lifted the steamer trunk onto a long table with a heavy grunt, then left the two women alone.

"You heard the doctor," Nurse May said. She shut the door and sat in a chair against the opposite wall, her arms crossed. "Hurry it along."

Clara took a deep breath and snapped open the trunk's latches, hoping her letters to Bruno wouldn't come spilling out. She stood close to the table, trying to block Nurse May's view, and opened the lid. She wasn't sure if she should take out a few letters and hide them in her pocket, or hope she'd have access to the trunk later, in case she convinced someone to mail them. But what if Nurse May caught her and took the letters? For some reason, the nurse's mood had darkened considerably since they arrived. What if she decided to take out her frustration on Clara? Clara decided not to risk it. For now, she'd leave the letters in the trunk.

Inside the trunk, an envelope with Bruno's name sat on top of her silk chemise. She put a hand over it, folded the chemise, and shoved it farther inside the piles of clothes. She pulled her brown walking shoes out of a drawer and set them on the table, then carefully searched for her undergarments and three sensible dresses, trying not to disturb the rest of the trunk's contents. When she saw the peach fringed dress she was wearing the night she met Bruno, her throat tightened. Would she ever dance with him again?

At last, she found what she was looking for: a blue cotton dress with a round embroidered collar, a straight, brown skirt and pink blouse that tied at the neck, and a plain yellow housedress. She pulled them out of the suitcase and laid them on the table. Just then, Nurse May stood. Clara slammed the trunk closed, secured the brass clasps, picked up the dresses, and turned, draping the outfits over her arm.

"Will these do?" she said.

146

Nurse May briefly examined the dresses, then took them from Clara. "They'll do," she said, her mouth twisted in an angry pucker.

Nurse May tossed the dresses on the table, opened the door and led Clara back into the hall, where Mr. Glen and Dr. Roach, now wearing a white lab coat, waited. Another nurse stood beside them, a tall, heavyset woman with broad shoulders and curly red hair. Her neck was thick and her cheeks looked bloated, extending past her mouth like overblown balloons. Her narrow eyes sat back in her chubby face and her lipstick stood out against her pale skin, like blood on snow. Although her facial features were those of an obese person, she wasn't fat. Muscle made up the substantial girth of her arms and legs. The giant nurse held a square of white cloth under one arm.

"Mr. Glen," Dr. Roach said, his hands in the pockets of his lab coat. "Please remove Clara's trunk to the foyer. We'll take care of it in the morning."

"Yes, sir," Mr. Glen said. He went into the changing room to retrieve Clara's luggage, then made his way toward the foyer.

"Nurse May," Dr. Roach said. "You can return to the nurses' residence." For the first time since they arrived, he looked Nurse May in the eye. Nurse May smiled at him, but he quickly looked away, his jaw working. "Nurse Trench will take over from here."

"Should I return to my usual room, Dr. Roach?" Nurse May said, her eyes bright with anticipation.

"You can stay in whichever room you choose," Dr. Roach said. He finally smiled at her, a smug, self-righteous grin cloaked in refinement.

Nurse May nodded, her cheeks flushing. She beamed at Dr. Roach longer than necessary, a silent agreement passing between them. The giant nurse cleared her throat. Nurse May dropped her eyes and followed Mr. Glen down the hall.

"We'll get Clara settled in for the night," Dr. Roach said to Nurse Trench. "Then take care of the paperwork tomorrow. It's almost time for lights out and we don't want to upset the schedule."

"Yes, Doctor," Nurse Trench said.

Dr. Roach gestured to Clara and started down the hall. "Come this way," he said.

Clara bit down on the inside of her cheek and followed the doctor, every nerve vibrating like an electric current, her arms and legs quivering as if she'd stuck her finger in a light socket and held it there. Where were they taking her? Would she be in a room with another patient, or would she have her own? It was bad enough being sent here, not knowing what was going to happen, or how long she was going to stay, but what if she was forced to share a room with a stranger who might be violent or disturbed? The thought was almost more than she could bear.

She walked faster, trying to keep up with Dr.

Roach and Nurse Trench, her fists in her coat pockets. At the end of the hall they turned left, then stopped at a riveted iron door with a small, caged window in the center. Dr. Roach stepped aside while Nurse Trench unlocked and opened the door, iron hinges screeching. Dr. Roach gestured for Clara to enter, then followed her into the chilly hallway.

The sharp odor of urine and bleach filled Clara's nose and she gagged, putting a hand over her nose and mouth. She trailed behind Dr. Roach and Nurse Trench, wishing she'd made a run for it while she could. Escaping Mr. Glen was doubtful, but she should have tried. Anything would have been better than letting them take her inside this awful place.

The long hallway looked wide enough to fit two trains side by side, countless doorways lining the high walls. Every Willard building seemed designed to house giants, and Clara couldn't understand why. Halfway down the hall, a door flew open and two orderlies dragged a woman into the corridor, her stringy hair flying over her contorted face, the lower half of her wet nightgown clinging to her bare legs. A nurse rushed out of the room and followed the orderlies as they half carried, half dragged the woman in the opposite direction. The woman screamed, her bare feet unable to catch traction on the floor, and Clara stopped moving, her heart thundering in her chest. Dr. Roach hesitated and glanced back at her. Without missing a beat, Nurse Trench turned, clamped an oversized hand around Clara's upper arm, and pulled her forward.

"Come along," she said, her voice firm.

Clara tried yanking out of Nurse Trench's grasp, but it was no use. Nurse Trench plowed forward, unfazed by Clara's struggle, her face calm and even, as if she were taking a poodle for a stroll. Through an open door on the left, patients called out from what looked like oversized cribs with padlocked lids. Clara felt like she was going to throw up.

At the end of the hall they turned left again and went through another locked iron door, into another hallway exactly like the first. At the fourth door on the right, they stopped. Nurse Trench let go of Clara's arm.

"Give me your coat," she said. With trembling fingers, Clara unbuttoned her coat and removed it. Luckily, she'd put on a sweater before leaving the Long Island Home, unaware that Willard would be so cold. "And your boots."

Again, Clara did as she was told, slipping her stocking feet from her boots, the floor like ice on her soles.

"Bring her to my office for an examination tomorrow morning," Dr. Roach said.

"Yes, Doctor," Nurse Trench said. "She'll be there."

"Very good," Dr. Roach said. He looked at Clara. "We're here to help you, just remember that. There's nothing to be afraid of." Then he gave Clara a quick nod and hurried down the hall.

Nurse Trench watched him walk away, her tongue clicking. She pressed her lips together and shook her head, a flash of pain crossing her bloated face. Then she unlocked the door and entered the room. Clara's stomach tightened. Nurse Trench held the door open, waiting. Clara slowly edged inside, her hands crossed over her galloping heart.

The odor of feces and urine was as thick as the pale green paint on the enamel walls. Clara pulled the sleeve of her sweater over her hand and held it over her mouth. The frigid room contained fifty metal beds bolted to the floor in rows, all with grimy pillows, sheets, and horsehair mattresses. Female patients sat on the beds or moved around the room, wearing thin nightgowns with no under-garments, the sagging shapes of their unbound breasts fully visible. Some wore sweaters and socks, but most were barefoot. Several wore straitjackets. One sat in a corner with a tattered doll in her arms, rocking and singing a lullaby. Two women stood at the tall, barred windows, one staring out into the night, the other bashing her head against the wire mesh protecting the glass. A thin film of ice edged the windowpanes.

"Lights out!" Nurse Trench shouted. The

151

women scrambled toward their beds. The woman with the baby doll stood on thin, crooked legs and shuffled toward the nearest cot, the doll shoved inside her worn sweater. Nurse Trench stood in silence, watching and waiting. When all of the women were sitting or lying on a bed, there was one empty cot left. It was next to the woman with the baby doll. The linens looked as if someone had already been sleeping there, the discolored sheets and pillow askew and crumpled. Nurse Trench took the folded piece of cloth from beneath her arm and held it out to Clara. It was a nightgown.

"Put this on," Nurse Trench said.

Clara's breath caught in her chest. "Here?"

"The first rule at Willard is 'Do as you're told,'" Nurse Trench said. "Obey that and we'll get along just fine."

"Is there a water closet nearby?" Clara said. "Somewhere I can change in private?"

Nurse Trench smiled, one corner of her painted red lips lifting higher than the other. "The second rule of Willard is 'Don't question me.'"

Clara dropped her eyes and turned away from the patients, her legs and arms quivering. She took off her stockings and sweater, then pulled her dress over her head and let it fall to the floor. Then she turned to take the nightgown from Nurse Trench.

"Everything off," Nurse Trench said. "Best not to test me, girl."

Clara removed her slip and brassiere, holding one arm over her bare breasts, then reached for the nightgown again. This time, Nurse Trench gave it to her. Clara slipped the thin garment over her head and stepped out of her underwear. She started to bend over to pick her sweater off the floor, then stopped. Shivering, she looked at Nurse Trench.

"May I?" she said, pointing at the sweater.

"I'm not heartless," Nurse Trench said.

Clara scooped up her sweater and put her arms in the sleeves, grateful that the wool was still warm.

"Just remember what Dr. Roach said," Nurse Trench said. "We're here to help." She gestured toward the empty cot. "It's hard to help someone if they don't follow the rules."

Clara started toward the bed, her stomach churning. She swallowed over and over, trying not to be sick. The woman in the opposite bed rocked back and forth, making a soft, high-pitched noise that sounded like "Uh-oh, uh-oh, uh-oh." Another pulled at her long, filthy hair, laughing and yanking out several strands at once. Clara reached the bed and sat down, still holding the edge of her sweater over her nose.

"Lights out!" Nurse Trench shouted again. The women lay down and pulled up their blankets. Clara did the same, cringing when she touched the dirty linens. She lay on her back, loathing the

153

thought of putting her cheek on the pillow. "And stay in bed tonight, Charlotte!" Nurse Trench yelled.

Then the room went dark.

Nurse Trench opened the door and exited, a rectangle of weak light silhouetting her mammoth frame. Then the door slammed with a final thud and the room was pitched into blackness again. The key turned in the dead bolt. And then, all around Clara, the women started making noises—whimpering, coughing, singing, humming, mumbling, sobbing. Clara heard the creak of bedsprings beside her and felt someone brush past her arm. Someone stood at the foot of her bed, breathing hard. Clara pulled the dirty blanket over her head and curled into a fetal position. She covered her wet face with trembling hands and sobbed, praying for morning.

CHAPTER 7

IZZY

The night after opening the first batch of Willard suitcases, Izzy stretched out on her bed in a T-shirt and underwear, trying to shut off her mind by watching music videos on MTV. It was no use. Every young, kissing couple reminded her of Clara and Bruno. And Ethan. And her parents. Her finger throbbed beneath the first aid gauze, reminding her of Ethan on his knees at her feet. She remembered his soft touch and dark hair, his smile flashing when he looked up at her. *He has a girlfriend,* she told herself. *And even if he didn't, he's better off with someone else. Besides, he's an arrogant ass, remember? He helps his girlfriend bully people. Why are you even thinking about him?*

At midnight she switched off the TV and turned over on her stomach, hoping to drift off into the blissful ignorance of sleep. But despite her exhaustion, Ethan's face floated behind her closed lids, his raven hair, his silver eyes. Then Ethan's face morphed into her father's, his dead eyes staring, his head bleeding. Izzy got out of bed and opened the window to let in some fresh air. *Is this how it starts?* she thought. *Is this how a person slowly becomes mentally ill? The same images and thoughts enter their brain over and over and they can't shut them off? What's wrong with me?*

She went into the bathroom, brushed her teeth a second time, drank a glass of water, and looked in the mirror. Her eyes were puffy and bloodshot, no doubt from the tears she shed earlier. Willard, the suitcases, Clara. It all hit too close to home. If she'd known the suitcase project was going to remind her of all the terrible things she was trying to forget, she would have tried harder to get out of helping. And yet, she didn't want to disappoint Peg and Harry, no matter the cost to herself.

It surprised her that, after all this time, the memory of her parents and the horrible images of what happened that night still held so much power. She was nearly eighteen years old. She should have been able to put it behind her by now, to shelve it with the rest of her past and move on. And yet, every time she thought about her mother and father, she felt seven years old again—like a terrified, confused, and abandoned little girl. And then there was the fear that she could end up like her mother, spending the rest of her life alone and locked up, either in a mental ward or a prison. That, she reasoned, was what really made her cry.

How would she ever have a normal life with those nightmarish genes floating around inside her brain, waiting to make their appearance? How could she ever hope to have a relationship or get married, knowing she might be putting someone else in danger? How could she ever become a mother, knowing she might abandon her children without warning?

She ran her fingers over the scars on her forearms, fighting the urge to dig her nails into her skin. *No,* she thought, squeezing the tears from her eyes. *I've come too far to go back now.* She gripped the edge of the sink, her knuckles turning white. *I'm not going to give in. I'm not going to let my past determine my future. I'm not my mother.*

She took a deep breath and rinsed her face, then went back to bed, letting the cool nighttime breeze drift over her bare legs, her hair pulled up over the back of her pillow. She shut off the light, closed her eyes, and started counting backward, knowing it was foolish but trying anything to keep the constant barrage of thoughts and images from popping into her mind.

Then something hit her window. She opened her eyes. It sounded like fingernails tapping on the glass and scraping down the screen. It happened again and she sat up. Something tumbled along the siding. She swung her legs over the bed and held her breath, listening. Two more taps—*clink, clink*—on the upper pane. She turned on the light.

"Izzy?" a male voice hissed from outside.

She turned off the light again and stood. Wrapping a blanket around herself, she edged toward the window. Another loud *clink* made her jump.

"Izzy!" the voice said again, more insistent.

She peered over the window ledge, trying to make out a figure on the dark lawn. A full moon cast long shadows over the grass and five human-shaped forms stood in a row near the clothesline, their shirts and pants billowing in the breeze, their long, scraggly hair flapping like a string of black flags. Izzy's heart seized in her chest. Her first thought was that a gang of zombie pirates from

157

John Carpenter's film *The Fog* was staring up at her. Then she realized she was looking at the dark silhouettes of branches and leaves, twitching and fluttering on the tree outside her room. She breathed a sigh of relief and wrapped the blanket tighter around her shoulders.

"Down here!" the voice called. Izzy moved closer to the window and checked the length of the gravel driveway. Ethan looked up at her from the corner of the garage, his face a white mask in the gloom. When he saw her, he dropped the pebbles in his hand, picked up a flashlight and held it beneath his chin. "Surprise!" he said in a loud whisper. He grinned, the light casting shadows beneath his eyes and nose, like the black and white visage of a Halloween ghoul.

Izzy leaned out the window. "What are you doing here?" she said, trying to ignore the flutter of her heart.

"I brought you a present," Ethan said. He held up something flat and square, about the size of a paperback novel.

"It's the middle of the night!" Izzy whispered. "Are you crazy?" *Oh, wait,* she thought, *never mind. That's me.*

"Come down!" Ethan said.

"No!" Izzy said. "You're going to get me in trouble!"

Just then a car turned a corner out on the street, headlights sweeping over the lawn and driveway.

Ethan ducked behind the garage. When the car was gone, he came out of hiding.

"Come on," he said. "It will only take a minute. I promise."

Izzy bit her lip. What was he doing here? What could he possibly have for her? It was Saturday night. Why wasn't he with Shannon? Her heart started racing. What if it was a trick? What if Shannon was down there too, waiting to pull another prank?

"I'm not coming down," she said. "You should leave."

"Seriously?" he said, his voice full of disbelief. "I came to your window in the middle of the night with a surprise and now you tell me to leave? I thought we were friends." It was on the tip of Izzy's tongue to tell him he could give her the surprise in school when he said, "If you don't come down, I'll ring the doorbell and ask for you."

Izzy sighed. "Give me a minute," she said. She closed the curtains, tossed the blanket on the bed, and pulled on a pair of shorts. She started toward the door, then turned and went back into the bathroom to look in the mirror. Her hair was snarled, her mascara smudged. She licked her finger and did her best to remove the leftover makeup, then ran a brush through her hair and pulled it into a high ponytail. She yanked off her T-shirt and hurried to her dresser to find a sweatshirt.

Down in the kitchen, she grabbed her sandals, then slid through the sliding patio door and tiptoed across the back deck. On the grass, she slipped her sandals on and hurried toward the garage, her shoulders hunched. Thankfully, Peg and Harry's bedroom was on the other side of the house, so they probably hadn't heard anything. Ethan was waiting on the other side of the garage, leaning against the cedar shingles and shining the flashlight at a small, open book in his hand. When he saw her, he closed it and straightened.

"What are you doing here?" she said.

"Hi to you too," he said, smiling.

"What do you want?"

"How's your finger?"

She held out her injured finger, the white gauze glowing like a tiny ghost in the dark. "It's fine," she said. She crossed her arms. "Okay. I came down like you wanted. What's the big surprise?"

He held up the book, shining the flashlight on its cover. The light reflected off the green, fleur-de-lis-stamped leather, shimmering on the black patent spine. Clara's journal.

Izzy tore it from his hands. "What are you doing with this?" she said. "You have no right to it!"

"Relax," he said. "I just borrowed it."

"It's none of your business!" she hissed.

Ethan scowled. "You were reading it. Besides, that crazy woman is long gone . . ."

"It doesn't matter! You shouldn't have taken it."

"I saw you looking at it and thought you wanted to read it."

"Do you know how much trouble you could get in for having this?" she said, surprised by her anger. "This is state-owned property!"

"Jesus," Ethan said, rolling his eyes. "Will you chill out? We can return it when you're done reading it. Just put it back in the trunk next Saturday when we go to the warehouse. No big deal. No one will even know it was gone."

She held out the journal. "You take it back."

"Okay," he said, shrugging. "I'll take it back. Sorry I bothered you." He took the journal and started walking away. "See you around."

She grit her teeth. He was right. For some reason, she wanted to read Clara's journal more than anything. But not like this. Not when she had to worry about getting in trouble for having it. But then again, what if she never got another chance?

"Wait," she said.

He came back, smiling. "Change your mind?"

"Maybe," she said.

He leaned against the garage and handed her the journal. "They say it's haunted, you know," he said.

She frowned, confused. "What's haunted?"

"Willard Asylum."

Izzy looked down at the journal. "Oh," she said, hoping he wouldn't notice her cringe.

"Some of my friends broke in a couple weeks

161

ago and had the shit scared out of them. One of them was scratched on the neck inside the women's ward and they both heard what sounded like moaning in the hospital."

Izzy shivered. "That's gross," she said.

"I think it's awesome," Ethan said, laughing.

"Well, you're weird."

"The journal isn't the only reason I'm here," he said, his voice suddenly serious. "I wanted to apologize for helping Shannon put those . . . those things on your locker. You're right. It was horrible and mean. When you were reading the journal back at the warehouse, I could tell you were crying and . . ."

Izzy stiffened. "Listen," she said. "Things are finally going good for me and I'm not going to mess it up. If Peg and Harry find out I have this journal, they'll probably ask me to leave."

"Read it over the weekend and bring it to school on Monday. I'll take it back. No one will ever know you had it. I promise."

Izzy sighed and ran her fingers over the green leather. All these years she'd wanted nothing more than to get inside her mother's head, to try to figure out what would make a perfectly sane person suddenly lose her mind. She couldn't ask the doctors. They had declared her mother sane. But Izzy knew better. And right now, right here in her hands, could be the answers she'd been looking for. She was just about to ask Ethan if she should give it to him in homeroom when another thought came to her.

"What about Shannon?" she said. "I don't think she'd be very happy to find out you were here." To her surprise, Ethan went quiet, scratching the back of his neck, his eyes on the ground. Then he looked at Izzy and frowned.

"She's not as bad as you think," he said.

"Yes, she is," Izzy said. "First she acted like she wanted to be friends, then she started playing tricks on me. She's horrible."

"It might seem that way when she's around other people, but when it's just us . . ."

"Oh," Izzy said, crossing her arms. "So you don't care how she treats everyone else, as long as she's nice to you."

"No," Ethan said. "That's not it. We've been together since eighth grade and it's just been the last year or so that she started acting . . . I don't know . . . different. I just want you to know that she's been through a lot."

Izzy rolled her eyes. "That's no excuse. She should rise above whatever happened to her, not perpetuate it. I hate it when people blame everyone but themselves for their behavior."

"Her father left, and her mother is an alcoholic."

"That doesn't give her a license to be a bitch!" The minute the words were out of Izzy's mouth, her stomach tightened with regret.

Ethan sighed and dropped his shoulders. "Her

father used to slap her around and beat up her mother. When Shannon was twelve she stepped between them and ended up in the hospital with a concussion and a broken arm. But her mother wouldn't tell the doctors the truth. She lied and said Shannon jumped off the porch roof because she thought she could fly."

Izzy swallowed. She couldn't imagine a father hurting his child. Or a mother failing to protect her child. Granted, Izzy's mother had shot her father, but she had gone mad. Izzy wanted to believe her mother hadn't been thinking about the consequences. Her mother had to be out of her mind not to realize that Izzy would be devastated by the loss of her father, that when the police found out what she'd done, Izzy would lose both parents. Only a mentally ill person wouldn't think it through. The irony was, before that fateful night, Izzy's mother was overprotective, not allowing her to walk to second grade with her friends, even though the school was only a block away, making her wear a life jacket at the beach while the other kids were free to splash in the waves and play in the sand, unencumbered by a thick, orange vest. Izzy's father had doted on her, buying her pretty dresses and taking her to dance lessons, even promising her a pony when she turned ten. Even now, after everything that happened, Izzy couldn't imagine either of her parents intentionally harming her.

"After that," Ethan continued, "Shannon's father cleaned out their bank account and left them with nothing. They haven't heard from him since." Ethan glanced at the ground, then looked up at Izzy with pleading eyes. "Please don't tell anybody I told you. I've said too much already. Everyone already knows about Shannon's parents, but she'd kill me if she found out I'm the one who told you. I just want you to understand where she's coming from."

Izzy sighed. "Listen," she said. "I feel bad for her. Really, I do. But honestly? Knowing all that just confuses me even more. I don't understand why she wants to hurt people when she knows how it feels."

"I think she's so afraid of being hurt she makes sure no one messes with her. She thinks there's a grand hierarchy or something and she needs to stay on top to protect herself."

"Do you really believe that?"

"Yes," Ethan said. "I've been trying to talk to her, trying to make her see that she doesn't have to be . . ." He looked away, pain flashing over his face. "I feel like I'm all she's got left right now. I'm the only one who understands why she is the way she is. Her mother doesn't give a shit and everyone else is just playing along because they're scared of her."

Oh God, Izzy thought. *He really loves her.* Izzy thought of her father, who had no idea he was marrying a woman who would lose her mind someday. She wanted to tell Ethan to be careful. Instead, she took a deep breath and changed the subject.

"How am I supposed to give you the journal without Shannon finding out? She seemed pretty upset when you stood up for me the other day."

"Yeah," he said. "She gets really jealous, so we need to be careful."

Izzy opened her mouth to say Shannon sounded like a real piece of work but changed her mind.

"Just leave the journal in your locker," Ethan said. "I'll get it between classes."

"Okay. My locker number is . . . Oh. Wait," she said, grinning. "You already know what it is."

Ethan held up his hands. "Guilty as charged."

CHAPTER 8

CLARA

Willard—The Day After Admission

Dust-filled shafts of sunlight came in through the caged floor-to-ceiling windows, cutting through the dim light in the high-ceilinged room but doing little to ward off the chill. Six claw-foot tubs lined one wall, each with a canvas cover strapped to metal pipes that surrounded the bathtub. Drains lined the floor, black mold darkening the cracked tiles. Nurses barked orders and patients argued and screamed and struggled, trying to resist being put into the tubs of icy water.

Clara stood naked in front of one of the bathtubs, one arm across her chest, the other attempting to cover her pubic area. The black and white tiled floor felt like ice on her feet. She shivered, watching a nurse fill the water with ice cubes. Nurse Trench and a muscular patient with a droopy eye stood near the faucets, waiting. In the next tub over, a woman's pale face poked out from a reinforced hole in the canvas, her lips blue. On the other side of the room, two orderlies pulled an unconscious woman from the water and carried her toward an examining table against the far wall.

"Get in," Nurse Trench said to Clara.

"But I . . ." Clara started.

"Do as you're told, remember?" Nurse Trench said. "It's for your own good."

"But I . . ." Clara said, her voice weak.

Nurse Trench moved forward and wrapped her giant mitt around Clara's arm. "We're here to help you," she said, her voice firm. "This will relax you. It will clear your mind."

Before Clara knew what was happening, Nurse Trench picked her up and put her in the tub, shoving her beneath the frigid water. A jolt of pain ripped through Clara's chest as the air was pulled from her lungs. She accidently inhaled, choking on a mouthful of water. She grabbed the edge of the bathtub and pulled herself above the surface, her hands slipping on the wet porcelain. Coughing and trying to breathe, she struggled to stay upright. For a second everything went black and she was certain she was going to pass out. Then the one-eyed patient grabbed her by the shoulder and started scrubbing her face and neck, scraping a rough, discolored cloth over her skin. At last, Clara pulled in lungfuls of air. The patient scrubbed under Clara's arms and between her legs, yanking her limbs out of the way with more force than necessary.

The ice water felt like a thousand knives in Clara's skin. It took everything she had not to push herself up and out of the tub. She let the patient scrub her down, her body shaking violently, hoping the sooner the patient was finished, the sooner she would be let out. Nurse Trench stood watching at the end of the tub, her massive arms crossed over her ample bosom, her crooked red smile contorting the lower half of her bloated face.

"Please," Clara said, looking up at her. "I'm . . ."

"Quiet now," Nurse Trench said, wagging a thick finger in the air. "That posh life over at the Long Island Home has made you soft, that's all."

Clara squeezed her eyes shut, waiting for the patient to finish scouring her hair with lye. When buckets of ice water were poured over her head, she pulled her knees to her chest and wrapped her arms around her legs, nearly hyperventilating, shaking so hard her heart felt on the verge of bursting. Finally, the rough washing ended and the one-eyed patient stood back, panting.

"Step out," Nurse Trench said.

Coughing and spitting, Clara scrambled out of the tub. The one-eyed patient gave her a once-over with a coarse towel.

"Normally, we'd make you stay in there longer," Nurse Trench said. "But you've got your first appointment with Dr. Roach today. Now, do as you're told and we'll get along fine."

The one-eyed patient handed Clara her yellow housedress and undergarments. Clara's teeth chattered uncontrollably, her legs so weak she could barely stand. Somehow, she managed to put on her clothes and tie her shoes. Nurse Trench ordered Clara to follow her, then marched toward the door. Clara did as she was told, her hair dripping down her face and the back of her neck. She used her sweater to mop her brow, then fell in behind Nurse Trench. In the hall, she put her hand on her abdomen. *Would a tiny, unborn baby be able to survive such treatment?* Her eyes filled and her heart slowed, a heavy, black mass weighing it down. If something happened to Bruno's baby, she wasn't sure she'd survive.

Clara followed Nurse Trench across the vast lobby of Chapin Hall, through a double doorway and around a curved hallway to another wing. They passed the telegraph office and the apothecary, then came to a short hallway with a door at the end. Outside Dr. Roach's office, a pale, petite woman in a red wool coat sat in one of three chairs, her head down, her hands on a leather clutch in her lap. She looked up and smiled.

"Good morning, Nurse Trench," the woman said. She looked young, about Clara's age, with high cheekbones, platinum hair, and porcelain skin. When she smiled, her entire face lit up. But there was a trace of sadness in her eyes. Then Clara noticed the woman's bulging stomach. She couldn't imagine what a pregnant girl was doing here, waiting to see Dr. Roach.

"Good morning, Mrs. Roach," Nurse Trench said. "How long have you been waiting?" Clara dropped her eyes, trying to hide her shock. Why would a beautiful, young woman be married to a man twenty years her senior, especially a doctor who worked in an insane asylum?

"Oh, I don't know," Mrs. Roach said. "Not too awfully long."

"Does he know you're here?" Nurse Trench said, one oversized hand on the office door.

Mrs. Roach nodded. "I called before I came, like always," she said. "He said he'd come out and talk to me when he has time."

"You just sit tight," Nurse Trench said, smiling. "I'll see what I can find out."

Nurse Trench pushed open the door and led

Clara inside. An elaborately carved desk sat in the center of the room, a gold-framed portrait of an elderly, bald man wearing a monocle hanging on the wall behind it. Framed medical degrees and black-and-white photos of men in top hats and women in long, bustled dresses posing in front of Chapin Hall surrounded the portrait. The other walls were lined with pictures of the railway, the factories, the orchards, and the apothecary filled with thousands of glass bottles.

At the desk, Dr. Roach smiled around his pipe at Nurse May, who sat perched in a small chair, her white-stocking legs crossed, the hem of her skirt hiked up to mid-thigh. She jumped up when the door opened, her cheeks turning red. Dr. Roach looked up, startled. Nurse Trench led Clara toward the desk.

"How many times have I asked you to knock before entering my office?" Dr. Roach said.

"My apologies, Doctor," Nurse Trench said, her eyes burning. "I guess I'm not used to your new rules yet. Maybe I'd remember if they didn't change every week."

"Just leave the patient," Dr. Roach said, his voice tight. "You're dismissed, Nurse Trench. I'll have Nurse May take her to the cafeteria when we're finished here."

"Your wife is waiting in the hall, Doctor," Nurse Trench said, glaring at Nurse May. "Shall I have her come in?"

Dr. Roach stood. "No," he said. "I'll go out and talk to her."

"Very well," Nurse Trench said. She sniffed and turned, then marched out of the room and slammed the door. Nurse May looked at Dr. Roach, a nervous smile playing on her lips. Dr. Roach motioned toward a glass door to the right of his desk, his forehead furrowed.

"Take the patient into the examination room," he said. "I'll be right there."

Nurse May picked up a chart from the desk and opened the glass door. "This way, Clara," she said, louder than necessary. Clara followed her into the examination room, trying to stop shivering. A cast-iron radiator hissed and clanked beneath an octagon window, filling the room with a moist, even heat. Clara wanted to kneel on the floor and lean up against it.

"Get on the scales, Clara," Nurse May said, still talking loudly, as if Clara were dim-witted, hard of hearing, or unable to understand English.

Nurse May wrote Clara's height and weight down on her chart and took her temperature and blood pressure. Finally, Dr. Roach came into the room and closed the door. Nurse May pulled a small step stool up to the examination table.

"Take off your dress and sit on the table, Clara," she said.

"I know you're talking to me," Clara said. "I know my name."

"Excuse me?" Nurse May said, her penciled eyebrows raised.

"You don't need to shout and keep saying my name," Clara said, unbuttoning her housedress. She took off her sweater and pulled her clothes over her head, draping the garments over her arm. "I speak English and can hear just fine. And I'm not an idiot." Clara climbed onto the paper-covered examination table and sat down.

Scowling, Nurse May snatched the clothes from Clara and tossed them onto a chair. She looked at Dr. Roach with wide eyes, as if expecting him to defend her. Ignoring the exchange, Dr. Roach went to the sink to scrub his hands, put on a pair of rubber gloves, then took his stethoscope from a wall peg and positioned the earpiece in his ears. He placed the cold chest piece above Clara's left breast and listened, his brows knitted. The smell of rubber and Brylcreem filled Clara's nostrils and she nearly gagged. Now that she was warming up, her stomach churned with a sour mix of hunger and nausea.

"I really don't understand why this is necessary, Doctor," Clara said. "I can assure you, there's nothing wrong with me."

"It's just part of the admissions process," Dr. Roach said. He gave her a condescending smile. "Nothing to worry about."

"But I don't need to be admitted," Clara said. "I'm perfectly fine."

"Uh-huh," he said, taking the chart from Nurse May and writing something down. Nurse May stared at him, like a dog waiting for a reward.

"What did she say?" she said.

Dr. Roach scowled at her. "We'll discuss it later," he said, giving her a stern look.

"Please," Clara said. "Just listen to me. I don't need to be here. My father just . . ."

"This is a physical examination," Dr. Roach interrupted. "We'll talk about why you're here another time. For now, let's just cooperate, shall we?"

"When?" Clara said.

"A nurse will get you when it's time," Dr. Roach said.

Clara sighed, clenching her teeth in frustration. Dr. Roach handed the chart back to Nurse May, who took it with both hands, her fingers lingering on his arm for several seconds. Finally, he smiled at her, a knowing look in his eyes. Nurse May's shoulders relaxed. Dr. Roach checked Clara's reflexes with a rubber hammer, then looked in her ears with a magnifying lens. He asked her to step down from the table and bend over so he could check the curvature of her spine. She did as she was told and he ran his fingers along her backbone, then pulled her arms backward and tugged on her wrists.

"Do you have any pain in your back or shoulders?" he asked, pressing his pelvis against her buttocks.

"No," Clara said, wincing. Dr. Roach let go and she straightened, rubbing her wrists. Still behind her, Dr. Roach put his hands on her shoulders and pulled them back. He felt the vertebrae in her neck and pressed his fingers into her scalp, feeling the shape of her skull. He reached around and felt her collarbones, then pushed her arms up and out, instructing her to hold them there while he felt beneath her armpits.

"Nurse May," he said. "Will you be staying at the nurses' residence again tonight?"

"Yes, Dr. Roach," Nurse May said, her voice dripping with sugar.

"And how do you find the accommodations? You know how hard we strive to make our employees comfortable here at Willard."

"The accommodations here at Willard are the best I've ever had," Nurse May said.

Before Clara knew what was happening, Dr. Roach's hands were on her breasts. He squeezed once, twice, then pinched her nipples and let go. It was over so fast it was hard to tell if it was part of the exam or something else. She dropped her arms and crossed them over her breasts, turning to face him, her cheeks burning. Dr. Roach ignored her, removing his gloves. He went to the sink and re-scrubbed his hands, soaping and rinsing them twice, the water so hot it was steaming. He dried his hands on a clean towel, put his gloves back on, then took a wooden tongue depressor from a glass jar on the medicine cabinet.

"Up on the table, Clara," he said. Clara climbed back on the examination table, her arms still over her breasts. "So you really like it here at Willard, Nurse May?"

"Oh yes," Nurse May said, moving closer, as if she needed to look down Clara's throat too. "I enjoy it very much."

Dr. Roach smirked and held up the tongue depressor. "Open your mouth," he said to Clara. "Say ah." Clara did as she was told and Dr. Roach pressed her tongue down with the wooden stick. It was too much. Clara gagged and threw up, vomiting all over Dr. Roach's hand and the front of his lab coat. He recoiled and looked down at his clothes, his arms out, his mouth curling in disgust. Nurse May gasped and dropped Clara's chart on the floor, where it landed upside down in a puddle of vomit. For a second, they stood staring, wide-eyed and frozen.

Finally, Nurse May came to her senses. She opened the doors beneath the medicine cabinet and pulled out a stack of towels, then stepped over the puddle of vomit and began mopping the mess off the front of Dr. Roach's lab coat. Dr. Roach stood stock still, his lips pressed together in a thin, hard line. Nurse May unbuttoned his coat and peeled it off his arms, careful not to let it touch his clothes. Then she removed his gloves, threw them away, and quickly washed her hands. Dr. Roach moved back, carefully stepping over the vomit, then went to the sink and scrubbed his hands with a stiff brush, pressing so hard his skin turned red. Nurse May grabbed Clara by the arm, digging her fingernails into her skin.

"How dare you!" she hissed. "Do you want to be put into isolation? Is that it?"

"It's all right," Dr. Roach said, drying his hands. "I don't think she did it on purpose. Just clean up the mess and we'll get this over with."

Nurse May scowled, retrieving more towels from beneath the cabinet. "Shall I get Nurse Trench to come take care of this?" she said.

"No," Dr. Roach said. "Give Clara a towel to clean herself up and let's finish."

"I'm sorry," Clara said, wiping splatters from her arms and legs. "I didn't mean to. It's just . . ."

"Are you not feeling well?" Dr. Roach said. "Have you been ill?"

"No," Clara said. She drew in a breath and held it, unsure if she should tell him the truth. Maybe she'd be treated better if they knew she was expecting. Maybe they would let her go free. An insane asylum was no place to give birth to a baby. Surely the doctor would agree. She bit down on the inside of her cheek, fighting the urge to throw up again. "I'm not sick. I'm pregnant."

Dr. Roach frowned, his brows knitted together. "Maybe you're just nervous, or ate something that didn't agree with you," he said.

Clara shook her head. "No," she said. "I have a boyfriend and the baby is his."

Dr. Roach lifted his chin, nodding slightly as if having something confirmed. "You can tell me all about it later," he said. "I'm here to help you, remember? Right now you need to go to the cafeteria and get some breakfast."

"But you're a doctor," Clara said. "You can tell if I'm pregnant or not. Surely you agree an asylum is no place for a pregnant woman."

"We have a female physician to do gynecological exams," Dr. Roach said. "But I'm afraid she's not here today."

Clara thought about asking why he felt the need to examine her breasts if they had a female doctor to do those things, but knew it was a waste of time. The most important thing was to make him realize she was going to have a baby. She put a hand on her abdomen. "Look at my stomach," she said. "It's swollen."

Dr. Roach gestured toward Clara's clothes on the chair. "Get dressed," he said. "If you're really pregnant, we'll know soon enough now, won't we? Nurse May, will you take Clara down to the cafeteria, please?"

Nurse May was on her hands and knees cleaning up the floor, her mouth twisted. She pushed herself up and waited by the door while Clara got dressed. "Shall I send Nurse Trench to finish up in here?" she asked again.

Dr. Roach shook his head. "No, she's got other patients to take care of this morning. Get one of the orderlies to help you."

Nurse May's face turned red, her jaw working in and out. Clara buttoned her sweater, thinking that, for now, she'd have to go along with what they wanted. Dr. Roach said they would talk later. She still had a chance to make him understand, to make him see that she didn't need to be institutionalized. She followed Nurse May out of the office, through the lobby of Chapin Hall, to the end of the first wing. An orderly unlocked two iron doors and let them through, the screeching and slamming of metal echoing through the halls. Nurse May led Clara down a narrow staircase to the basement, where they followed a short, stone passageway to the cafeteria.

The cement walls of the cafeteria were a dingy, mottled gray, the upper corners and edges of the room revealing an old coating of white paint. The blue floor was scuffed and pockmarked; circular chunks missing as if someone had gouged the stone out with a spoon. The air smelled like spoiled milk, cabbage, and grease. Dozens of female patients sat and stood at long tables while attendants strolled the perimeter of the dining area, watching them eat. Nurse Trench and two other nurses moved back and forth on the far end of the cafeteria, keeping a row of patients in line. The patients carried trays, picking up their food from workers on the other side of a long counter. Among the women in line were the woman with the baby doll and the woman who constantly rocked back and forth in her bed. Everywhere she looked, Clara saw blank stares, puffy eyes, scowling mouths.

"Time to go to the Sun Room!" one of the orderlies yelled at the patients sitting at the tables. "Clean up your mess!"

The patients stood and picked up their dishes, but a few remained seated, chewing their breakfast in a daze. The orderlies pulled the uncooperative women off their stools, taking the utensils from their hands. One patient tried to climb on the table, her bare foot in the middle of a plate. An orderly reached up and grabbed her arm, swearing as he pulled her down. Finally, the orderlies got everyone to pick up their tableware and file out of the room. Four cafeteria workers picked up the remaining flatware and plates while the women from Clara's ward shuffled over to the tables with their trays. Nurse May led Clara across the room to deliver her to Nurse Trench.

"This patient made a mess in Dr. Roach's examination room," she said to Nurse Trench. "Dr. Roach wants you to bring an orderly over after breakfast and get it cleaned up."

"I don't have time for that," Nurse Trench said, frowning. "You're his head nurse. It's your job to take care of things over there."

"I'm just following orders," Nurse May said, her chin in the air. "He said to send you over." She turned on her heels to leave, then changed her mind. "One more thing." She wiggled a finger at Clara. "This one thinks she's pregnant." This last thing she said in a loud voice, as if making an announcement.

Nurse Trench's eyes went wide. She uncrossed her arms and took a step toward Clara, but it was too late. Half a dozen patients dropped their trays and hurried over, one grabbing at Clara's stomach, another touching her hair, a third wailing and pulling at her face. Clara ducked and put her arms around her head to protect herself. A cluster of dirty fingers touched her mouth and scratched her cheek. Nurse Trench and the orderlies pulled the women away, shouting at them to get away from Clara. Nurse May stepped back to watch, a satisfied smirk on her face.

"Leave her alone!" Nurse Trench yelled at the patients. "Pick up your trays and get over to the table! Right now or you'll be put in isolation!" Most of the women did as they were told. One fell to the floor, howling with her head in her hands. Two orderlies yanked her to her feet and dragged her out of the cafeteria. Nurse Trench looked at Nurse May with fire in her eyes. "I'll be writing you up for that," she said.

Nurse May shrugged. "One other thing," she said. "I'm just wondering. Does Dr. Roach realize what little control you have over your patients?"

"I've been working with Dr. Roach for over fifteen years," Nurse Trench said through clenched teeth. "And I'll be working with him long after you're gone."

Nurse May rolled her eyes and left the cafeteria. Nurse Trench took Clara by the arm and led her over to the counter to get her breakfast. "Whether what she says is true or you're just making it up," she said under her breath, "you better keep quiet about it. Telling everyone won't do a thing to help you. The doctors won't care and the other patients will rip you apart."

She left Clara in line and walked away. Another group of women began filing in the doors at the far end of the room. Clara picked up a tray at the counter and tried to catch her breath, her heart thundering in her chest. The tray held a thick, milky mug filled with what looked like weak tea, and a plate with four prunes and a hard piece of bread. She carried the tray over to a table and found an empty seat. As soon as she sat down, the woman next to her snatched the bread from her plate. Clara hunched over her food and reached for her tea with shaking hands. She had no appetite, but knew she had to eat and drink for her baby. She took a sip of tea. It was barely warm and tasted like urine. She swallowed it anyway. The prunes were hard and dry and it was all she could do not to gag when she put them in her mouth.

The orderlies walked up and down the cafeteria, telling the women to hurry up so the next group could sit down. At the far end of the table, the woman with the baby doll stood and started screaming, pulling at another patient's hands and hair. The other patient slapped at the woman's arms, trying to push her away. The orderlies rushed over to break up the fight.

"My little girl is starving!" the woman screeched, clawing at the slice of bread on the other woman's tray. "Can't you hear her crying? She needs food!"

An orderly grabbed the screaming woman under the arms and yanked her away from the table. The other orderly struck her across the face, then ripped the doll away and threw it across the room. The woman howled and ran after it, her face contorted in agony. She dropped to her knees and picked up the baby doll, cradling it in her arms and crying. The orderlies pulled her upright and led her back to the table, their faces void of emotion. The woman sat down and started singing a lullaby, rocking the doll back and forth, her stringy hair hanging over her face. Everyone went back to eating.

Clara looked at the last shriveled prune on her plate, her stomach growing more and more nauseous. She thought about giving the prune to the woman with the baby doll, then picked it up and put it in her mouth, trying not to throw up as she chewed and swallowed.

CHAPTER 9

IZZY

By Monday afternoon, Clara's journal still sat on the upper shelf of Izzy's locker, resting on top of her math and English books. Unfortunately, the journal hadn't provided Izzy with any answers. Instead, it left her confused. The glimpse into life during the 1920s was fascinating, and Clara's words read like the diary of any normal young woman dealing with the confusion and frustration of being on the verge of adulthood. But there was nothing to suggest that Clara had lost her mind. Nothing at all. Except for what seemed like an overly strict upbringing and her grief over losing her brother, it seemed like Clara's future was destined to be bright. Until she met Bruno. That was when things changed.

Could Clara's fear of not being allowed to be with the man she loved have manifested itself into some kind of mental illness? Could her strict upbringing have caused her to grow nervous, paranoid, or delusional? No, it didn't ring true. Clara's journal read like that of a young woman with a firm grasp on reality. Izzy knew that, back then, doctors didn't fully understand depression or women acting out, but she could barely comprehend Clara's father sending her away because she was in love with a man he considered lower class. Even more unbelievable was that Clara's mother had gone along with her husband's decision! The whole thing was unimaginable. Now, Clara's story haunted Izzy. More than ever, she wanted to find out what happened to her after she was sent to Willard.

During the short break between eighth and ninth periods, Izzy stood at her locker, chewing on her lip and wondering why Ethan hadn't picked up the journal yet. He was in school that day; she'd seen him walking with Shannon in the halls. He had ignored Izzy when she passed, laughing and talking with his friends as if she were invisible. It was all she could do not to walk up to him and ask if he thought she was an idiot. She knew when she was being duped. She yanked her psychology book out from beneath her gym bag and slammed the locker door. What the hell was he up to? He'd had plenty of time to pick up the journal.

The bell rang and she hurried down the hall, her chest tight, thinking she would probably have to take the journal back to the museum herself. She wondered what Peg would do if she caught her with it. Then, halfway to class, she realized she'd left her essay on "Understanding the Criminal Mind" in her other notebook. She turned and rushed through the empty halls, swearing under

185

her breath because she was going to be late. When she got to her locker, Ethan was there, reaching in to get the journal. He jumped when he saw her.

"Finally!" she said. "I was starting to wonder if you were full of shit the other night."

"Sorry," he said, red-faced and out of breath. "Shannon has been acting really weird today. She made me walk her to all her classes, even when it made me late for mine."

"Don't you have psychology with her right now?"

"Yeah," he said. He glanced up and down the hall. "I told her to save me a seat because I was going to the boys' room."

"Why are you acting so paranoid?"

"I think she knows something is up."

"What do you mean?"

"She knows I'm working at the museum with you," Ethan said. "And she's not happy about it."

Izzy rolled her eyes. "So what? That doesn't mean something is up!"

"You don't know Shannon."

She snorted. "Oh, I think I do. How did she find out we were working at the museum together?"

Just then, Ethan looked past Izzy. His face dropped and Izzy turned to look. Shannon was standing near the end of the hall, her arms crossed, watching them.

"Oh shit," Ethan whispered. He shoved the journal into Izzy's hands and hurried toward

Shannon. "Hey, babe," he said, trying to sound casual. "Izzy's locker was stuck. She asked me to get it open."

Shannon stared at him until he reached her, then glared at Izzy. Izzy put the journal back, shut her locker, and started toward them, her textbook against her chest like a bulletproof shield. Shannon watched Izzy walk toward them, frowning, until Ethan took her hand and led her toward psychology class. Izzy followed, hoping she wouldn't have to sit next to them. Shannon kept glancing backward, whispering in Ethan's ear and laughing: a loud, deliberate cackle, as if sharing a private joke. When Shannon and Ethan reached the psychology classroom, they stopped in front of the closed door. Shannon wrapped her arms around Ethan's neck and kissed him with an open mouth. Ethan kissed her back, then pulled away.

"Come on," he said. "We're already late."

Shannon glanced back at Izzy, her lip curled in disgust. "Who cares," she said. "We'll just blame it on Izzy Pop."

Ethan opened the door and pulled Shannon into the classroom. Izzy followed, fighting the urge to tell Shannon the real reason Ethan was at her locker. At the front of the room, Mr. Defoe scribbled on the chalkboard, wet crescents staining the armpits of his blue shirt, his faded jeans tucked into his trademark hiking boots. No matter the season, Mr. Defoe wore his hiking boots. Rumor had it he lived in an apartment above the train station and gave most of his money to charity. He peered over his thick glasses at Ethan, Shannon, and Izzy.

"Nice of you to join us," he said. "Hurry up and take a seat."

To Izzy's relief there was a vacant desk at the back of the room. She hurried toward it while Ethan and Shannon took seats up front.

Mr. Defoe finished what he was writing on the board, then sat at his desk and asked the students to pass their essays forward. When all the essays had been collected, he stood to give his lecture.

"Today we're going to talk about what makes a seemingly normal person suddenly commit a horrendous crime," he said. "Like murdering their spouse or bringing a gun to school to shoot their classmates." He started pacing back and forth, his hiking boots scuffing along the floor. "Every now and then, the news explodes with stories about regular, everyday people who, without warning, do hideous things. They commit crimes that shock those around them, even those who know them extremely well. Everyone is at a loss, trying to understand what happened. When most people learn of the crime, their first thought is that the person they know could not possibly be the perpetrator . . ."

Izzy slouched in her seat, trying to shut out Mr.

Defoe's words. She picked up her pen and drew a square on her notebook, outlining the drawing over and over, pressing down harder and harder, until the point of her pen broke through the cover.

"So the question is," Mr. Defoe said, "are these people acting out of character, or was the tendency to go off the deep end part of their personality all along? What do you think, Miss Stone?"

Izzy looked up. A few of the students had turned in their seats to look at her, eyebrows raised. "Um," she said. "I'm sorry. What was the question again?" Everyone laughed.

"I'd appreciate it if you'd quit doodling and pay attention, Miss Stone," Mr. Defoe said.

Shannon raised her hand and Mr. Defoe pointed at her. "Yes, Miss Mackenzie?"

"I have an idea," Shannon said. "Maybe we can get Izzy's mother to come in and explain the criminal mind to us."

Izzy felt blood rise in her cheeks. No one had ever found out about her mother this fast. She glared at Shannon.

"What do you mean?" Nicole said with phony concern, a lip-glossed smirk on her face. "What did Izzy's mother do?"

"Oh, I'm sorry," Shannon said, feigning surprise. "I thought everyone knew." She frowned and looked at Izzy. "Izzy's mother shot her father while he slept. She's doing life at Bedford."

A collective gasp filled the room. A sea of heads turned toward Izzy. Wide, shocked eyes stared back at her. Girls put their hands over their mouths. Guys high-fived each other, laughing. Everyone started talking at once.

"Is she on death row?" one of the guys said.

"Can you bring her in for show and tell?" Luke said, snorting.

"Is her favorite color orange?" Nicole said.

Mr. Defoe stepped forward. "Okay, settle down," he said, holding up his hands. "Everyone, be quiet!"

No one listened. The girl sitting beside Izzy got up and moved to another seat. Luke stood on his chair and held his hands out as if pointing a gun, his index fingers the barrel of a pistol.

"Bang! Bang!" he said, shooting fake bullets at Izzy. He fired at his friends. Several of them fell out of their seats and onto the floor, moaning and playing dead.

Izzy stood on elastic legs, gathered her books, and started toward the door. Ethan got up and put a hand on her arm, stopping her.

"Wait," he said to her. Then he shouted, "Everyone, shut up! Why don't you grow up and quit being such assholes!" Everyone stopped talking and looked at him, wide-eyed.

"What the hell, Ethan," Luke said. "You got a thing for Izzy Pop?"

"Yeah, Ethan," a red-haired, freckle-faced boy

said. "Does your *girlfriend* know about your infatuation with the new girl?" His voice was high, like a female's, in stark contrast with his brutish size. He wasn't fat, just wide and muscular, like a bull, or a Mac truck. If Izzy remembered correctly, his name was Josh.

Shannon stood and yanked Ethan's hand off Izzy's arm. "What are you doing?" she hissed, her face contorted in anger.

While everyone waited to see what Shannon would do next, the room quieted.

"Everyone, sit down!" Mr. Defoe said, taking over. "One more word out of any of you and you're all getting detention!"

Shannon pulled Ethan away from Izzy and sat down, pouting. Izzy glared at her, eyes burning, then headed toward the exit.

"Please return to your seat, Miss Stone," Mr. Defoe said. "And don't let this bunch of bored juvenile delinquents get the better of you." Izzy stopped in her tracks, facing the door, her heart hammering in her chest. She blinked against the growing flood in her eyes. She wasn't sure if she should stay or leave, not knowing how much trouble she'd get in for walking out. Then Mr. Defoe said, "And, Miss Mackenzie? A week of detention for you."

"What?" Shannon said, whining. "What did I do?"

"What did I do?" a high, mocking voice said

from the back of the room. "As usual, I'm just having a little fun at someone else's expense." Izzy turned to see who had spoken. It was Alex. She was leaning against the windowsill, scowling and talking in a sarcastic tone. "Everyone knows my mommy is an alcoholic and my daddy left. So I can get away with anything I want because I'm just a poor, confused little girl."

"Shut your mouth!" Shannon yelled. She jumped out of her seat and started toward Alex. Ethan held her back.

"Miss Mackenzie!" Mr. Defoe shouted. "Are you trying to get yourself suspended?"

"She's a liar!" Shannon said, struggling to break free from Ethan's grasp.

Some of the other students looked at each other, shaking their heads and rolling their eyes. Others dropped their eyes, as if embarrassed to see Shannon falling apart.

"Calm down," Ethan said to Shannon.

"You're a whore!" Shannon shouted at Alex. "Just like your mother!"

"That's it," Mr. Defoe said. "Ethan and Shannon, go to the office. Right now. Get out of here!"

Ethan grabbed Shannon's wrist and pulled her out of the room, Shannon yelling obscenities the entire way. The students erupted in excited conversation. Izzy stood at the front of the room with her books clamped to her chest, a burning lump in her throat. She couldn't decide if she should go back to her seat or ask to go to the girls' room so she could pull herself together. Mr. Defoe tried to regain control of the class. No one paid attention. Izzy wiped her eyes and went back to her seat. Eventually, everyone quieted and Mr. Defoe finished his lecture. Izzy didn't hear a word.

Afterward, Izzy hurried to her locker, shoved her homework and Clara's journal into her backpack, then went to the girls' room. She could hardly wait for this day to end. Tonight, at home, she'd tell Peg she had the journal. Hopefully, Peg would forgive her and not send her to a different foster home. Izzy pushed open the bathroom door and turned the corner toward the row of stalls, then stopped in her tracks. Shannon was leaning against the radiator, her face red, her eyes swollen. Crystal and Nicole stood on either side, holding Kleenex and rubbing Shannon's shoulders.

"Get the hell out of here!" Shannon shouted. Izzy started to leave, then changed her mind. She turned to face Shannon.

"Listen," she said, staying near the exit. "I don't know why you hate me so much, but I understand what you're going through. It's hard having messed-up parents."

Shannon sniffed and sat up. "You listen to me, shooter," she sneered, tossing a used Kleenex at Izzy. "You don't know anything about me. And you never will."

Izzy chewed on the inside of her cheek, fighting the urge to scream in Shannon's face. More than anything, she wanted to tell her to grow up and stop taking her anger out on everyone else. But she was afraid that once she started yelling, she'd never stop. Besides, it wouldn't do any good. If nothing else, maybe she and Shannon could come to some sort of agreement. At the very least they could be civil to each other until graduation. It was worth a try. Like her grandmother always said, you catch more flies with honey than vinegar.

"Well," she said. "Maybe we could talk sometime? It seemed like you wanted to be friends when I first got here. Maybe we can start over?"

"The only thing you're going to start over is a new job. I don't want you working with my boyfriend anymore."

Izzy shrugged and shook her head. "I'm sorry, but that's not going to happen."

Shannon moved toward her. Crystal and Nicole followed, arms crossed over their chests. "If you know what's good for you, you'll make it happen," Shannon said.

Before Izzy could respond, the girls grabbed her and pushed her up against the wall.

Izzy struggled, trying to get away, twisting her shoulders back and forth. Shannon moved in behind them, blocking any chance for escape. The girls held Izzy by the arms while Shannon tapped a finger on her lips, thinking.

"Hmm," she said. "What should I do to teach you a lesson?"

Just then, someone kicked the door of a stall, a loud, metallic bang echoing like thunder in the high-ceilinged room.

A female voice shouted, "Let her go!"

The girls released Izzy and she stumbled forward. Alex stood next to the sinks, red-faced and breathing hard.

"Really?" Alex yelled at Shannon. "Ganging up on the new girl? Don't you think it's time to grow up?"

"You're pushing your luck today," Shannon said. She shoved Alex backward and Alex lost her footing. Alex scrambled to stay upright, catching the edge of a sink before she fell. Shannon moved toward her and Izzy stepped between them.

"Leave her alone," she said.

Shannon pushed her face toward Izzy's. "And what are you going to do about it?" she snarled. "Go get your mommy's gun and shoot me?"

"No," Izzy said. "I'll just steal your boyfriend. He seemed pretty interested when he came to my house the other night."

Shannon's eyes went wide and her face turned crimson. She screeched and lunged at Izzy, her manicured claws reaching for Izzy's neck. Alex pulled Izzy out of the way and they rushed out of the bathroom, running through the halls until they were outside, heading toward the line of buses.

"Thanks," Izzy said, trying to catch her breath.

"Any time," Alex said. "I told you to watch out for her." She turned to look behind her. "Oh shit."

Izzy looked over her shoulder. Shannon, Crystal, and Nicole were charging across the sidewalk toward them.

"Come on," Alex said, dragging Izzy toward the parking lot. They threaded their way through three rows of cars, dodging opening doors and hurrying around other students. Finally, they reached Alex's vehicle. Alex unlocked the doors and they scrambled inside. She shoved the key into the ignition and started the car. "Put on your seat belt."

"But I have to take the bus home," Izzy said. "I'm not supposed to ride with anyone Peg and Harry don't know, remember?"

"Go ahead," Alex said, gripping the gearshift. She motioned toward the line of buses with her chin. "Let's see if you can make it to the buses before they do."

Izzy looked out the windshield. The buses were on the other side of the parking lot, across the sidewalk and a wide strip of grass. Shannon and her friends were squeezing between two cars, three parking spots away. "Promise you'll come in and introduce yourself sometime?" she asked Alex.

"Yup," Alex said, putting the car into gear. She pulled out of the parking spot, turned left, and tore out of the lot, tires squealing, the peacock feathers hanging from her rearview mirror swinging back and forth. As they drove away, Izzy turned in her seat and saw Shannon, Crystal, and Nicole standing on the sidewalk, their faces red, their hair flying. Shannon stuck her middle finger in the air.

Alex glanced in the rearview mirror. "Oh, man!" she said. "We're forever on her shit list now!"

"Why were you on her shit list to begin with?" Izzy said. Alex reached in her purse and pulled out a pack of cigarettes, offering one to Izzy. "No thanks," Izzy said.

Alex took a cigarette from the pack with her teeth and rummaged in her bag for her lighter. "We used to be best friends," she said, talking around the filter. She lit the cigarette, dropped her lighter back in her purse, and took a long drag. She rolled down her window and blew the smoke out of the car. "Until my mother told her mother what her father was doing to her."

"I thought her mother knew he was hitting her?"

Alex glanced at Izzy, frowning. "How did you know her father used to hit her?"

"Ethan told me."

"He really came to your house?"

"Yeah."

Alex whistled. "I thought you were just saying that to piss Shannon off. How did that happen? I mean, what was he doing there?"

"We work together at the museum," Izzy said.

"He wanted to say he was sorry for playing a trick on me. He wants to be friends."

"Whoa," Alex said. "You're most definitely on the top of Shannon's shit list now!" She laughed and took another drag from her cigarette. "But at least you'll be taking the heat off me."

"Why does she hate you so much?"

Alex stopped at a light and looked at Izzy, as if she could judge her trustworthiness by the color of her eyes. "If I tell you," she said, "you can't tell anyone. Ever."

"Okay," Izzy said.

"It's not that I'm trying to protect Shannon, or feel any loyalty toward her or anything. She's been so rotten to me that I don't owe her anything. I just want to make it through this year with as little drama as possible and blow off this town after graduation. I'm leaving and never looking back."

"I won't tell," Izzy said. "Promise." The light changed and Alex drove the car through the intersection, taking another drag from her cigarette. Izzy waited, holding her breath.

"I'm not talking about Shannon's father hitting her," Alex said, her voice flat. "I'm talking about something worse."

Izzy cringed. It took a moment to form her mind around her next question. She swallowed before speaking. "What did he do to her?"

Alex crushed her cigarette out in the ashtray and

closed the window. "Like I said," she said, "Shannon and I used to be best friends. She always wanted to stay overnight at my house on weekends, but she never wanted me to stay at hers. I didn't think anything about it and was actually kind of relieved because her father always gave me the creeps. I felt like he was always watching me. One day, when we were around twelve, I found her crying in her tree house and knew something was wrong. She told me her father was coming into her bed at night and, you know . . ."

Izzy felt something vile twist in her gut, the angry pressure beneath her jaw releasing, replaced by something hollow and cold. "Oh God," she said. The fiery anger that had been building up in her head like a hot-air balloon deflated in one swift transfer of raw emotion.

"Shannon made me swear not to tell," Alex said. "Ever. For a few days I didn't know what to do. I didn't go to her house, or talk to her in school, anything. I was shocked and just couldn't wrap my head around it, you know? Eventually I knew I couldn't keep it a secret. I had to help Shannon. She was my best friend. So I told my mother and my mother told Shannon's mother. But Shannon's mother already knew."

Izzy recoiled, her stomach turning over. "Shannon's mother knew and didn't do anything? And she admitted it?"

"Yes and no. After my mother confronted her, Shannon's mother finally said something to Shannon's father. They got in a huge fight and it got physical, like it always did. But this time Shannon tried to stop her father from hurting her mother and ended up in the hospital. When I went to see Shannon, she was furious. She said she stepped between her parents because it was the first time her mother had ever tried to protect her. She said her mother knew all along, so me opening my big mouth just made things worse. She told me she never wanted to see me again. I went home crying and my mother called the police."

"Was he arrested?"

"Nope. CPS never had the chance to get involved. That night, he left and never came back. Shannon, her mother, my mother, and I are the only ones who knew what he was doing."

"Holy shit," Izzy said. "Then he got away with it."

"Pretty much."

"But I still don't get it. Why does Shannon hate you?"

"Because I broke my promise. I told my mother what was going on."

"You were trying to help."

Alex glanced at Izzy, her eyes wet. "Would you want anyone to know your father was messing around with you?"

"I don't think I'd let it happen in the first place."

"You don't know that. He started when she was

really young, too young to know any better."

Izzy looked down at her sneakers, feeling like she was going to be sick. "Oh. That's terrible."

"The worst."

"But after all these years, Shannon still can't understand that you only said something because you cared about her?"

"You'd think she'd be glad he left and the truth never got out. I think that's what she was worried about the most, everyone finding out. But it didn't happen. My mother and I never told anyone else. Maybe we should have. Maybe Shannon would have been better off getting away from her mother too. You'd think she'd be able to put it behind her and forgive me. But I broke her trust, just like her parents did. I don't think she'll ever be able to understand someone caring about her. And I don't think she'll ever understand what it feels like to be loved and to love in return. She doesn't know what it's like to be cherished and protected. She's never felt that, not even from her own parents. How could she expect that from me?"

"What about Ethan?"

"Ethan is nothing more than a trophy on Shannon's arm, the handsome jock all the girls wish they had. Shannon is crazy jealous, but she doesn't care about him. She's sleeping with half the football team. She's got the wool pulled over that boy's eyes."

"Does he know what her father did to her?"

"I don't think so. I can't see her ever telling him that."

Izzy dug her fingers into the edge of the leather seat and stared out the windshield. On the one hand, she felt sorry for Shannon. On the other, she still didn't understand why Shannon hurt others to feel better. Izzy understood being angry and wanting to lash out. But she chose to hurt herself instead of someone else. Just because Shannon's father was a monster didn't mean Shannon had to be one.

It made her think of Clara. Her father was a monster in a different way. And her mother had failed to protect her too. Clara and Shannon had both been betrayed by their parents. Izzy couldn't understand it. She thought of her father. He was a good man, the best father a girl could ask for. At least she had that. But he was dead. Her mother had taken him away from her. *Why do people bother having kids if they're just going to mess them up?*

"Just so you know," Alex said, pulling Izzy from her thoughts. "You and I have something else in common. My dad is dead too."

"I'm sorry," Izzy said. "What happened to him?"

"He was killed in a car wreck when I was nine," Alex said.

"So it's just you and your mom?"

Alex shrugged. "Yeah. She's cool, but she works a lot. And when she's not working, she's always going to mediums and having séances. I love all that stuff too, but it's like she's obsessed with trying to talk to my dad."

"Well, at least you know she loved him," Izzy said.

"I guess," Alex said. "Hey, can I ask you something?"

"Sure," Izzy said.

"If you don't want to talk about it, just tell me."

"What?" Izzy said.

"Why did your mother shoot your father?"

Izzy shrugged. "I don't know," she said, tears burning her eyes.

"Oh," Alex said. "Well, that sucks."

"Yeah," Izzy said. "It does."

After Alex dropped her off at Peg and Harry's, Izzy did her homework, took a shower, and put Clara's journal on the kitchen table. Then she waited for Peg and Harry to come home, her heart in her throat.

CHAPTER 10

CLARA

Clara's first winter at Willard was the longest of her life. Nearly every week, furious storms pelted the windows with thick flurries, coating the glass with ice curtains. When every windowpane was packed with wet snow and the only thing Clara could see through the small gaps in the buildup were the ashen clouds in the low sky, she felt trapped inside a giant ice fortress. She imagined she and the other patients were made of ice too, ready to shatter or explode at any second. The ice was made of tears, mixed with mud and blood, and she could taste the salty mixture on her chapped lips.

Like all patients during their first weeks at Willard, she'd been forced to sit in the "Sun Room," eight hours a day, seven days a week. Patients were only allowed to leave the Sun Room for meals and scheduled bathroom breaks. For the rest of the day, until after supper, they were required to sit on hard benches lining the walls, while orderlies watched to make sure they didn't act out or stand up. Clara did her best to shift her weight from one hip to the other, but by the end of the first week her buttocks felt like they were raw and bleeding.

It was a Saturday morning when she stood without permission for the first time, tears of pain burning her eyes, and asked if she could use the bathroom. The orderlies in charge that day, Dan and Richard, sat on folding chairs in the center of the room, playing poker on a card table. The other patients stayed seated, heads hanging, leaning against the walls, sleeping, crying, drooling, singing, or looking around the room as if watching invisible people.

"I think I'm going to be sick," Clara said, holding a hand over her stomach.

Richard put his cards down on the table and stood. He turned to face Clara, his face hard. "Sit down," he said, jerking his stubbled chin toward the bench. "There will be a bathroom break in an hour."

"But I need to go now," she said. "Please."

Richard moved toward her, his chin up, his shoulders back. He stopped a couple feet away. "I told you to sit down."

"You can't do this to people," she said, shaking her head. "It's not right!"

Richard rolled his eyes and stuck out his tongue, mocking her. Clara felt like she was looking at a six-year-old having a fight in the school yard. Then he took a step closer.

"My orders are to keep you sitting down," he said, his upper lip twitching.

Clara moved to go around him, her hand over her mouth, and he grabbed her arm, his fingers like talons on her wrist. She slapped his arm and he yanked her toward the center of the room. She twisted her wrist, trying to wrench free, but it was no use. Richard's grip was too strong. "Let go of me!" she shouted. "You're supposed to be helping people, not torturing them!" Then, unable to stop herself, she bent over and vomited on the floor, just missing Richard's shoes.

The other orderly stood. One of the patients

started screaming and crying, another ran for the door. Another stood, rocking back and forth, while a third paced the floor, nodding his head and wringing his hands. Nurse Trench rushed into the room and made the other patients sit back down.

"Take her to room C!" she shouted.

Richard hauled Clara out of the room and down the hall, dragging her behind him as if she were no bigger than a child. He pushed open a door and, with an angry grunt of disgust, shoved her into a windowless room with a single bed. Then he followed her, closing the door behind him. She stumbled, then found her footing. He moved toward her and she backed away, legs and arms trembling. Then her back was against the wall. Before she realized he'd raised it, Richard's open hand collided with her face in a black bolt of pain. Her neck whipped to the side, her hair flying in her face. She put her hands to her hot, throbbing cheek and glared at him, tears burning her eyes.

He grabbed her by the arms, wrestled her toward the bed in the middle of the room, picked her up, and threw her down on the filthy mattress. Another orderly came into the room and held her down, his hot hands crushing her upper arms. She thrashed on the bed, using every ounce of strength to get away. It was no use. While the other orderly held her down, Richard buckled leather straps around her wrists and ankles, tying her to the bed.

"Why are you doing this?" she screamed. "I just wanted to use the bathroom!"

The door opened and another nurse hurried into the room, a glistening syringe in her hand. She slid between Richard and the edge of the bed, pinched the flesh of Clara's upper arm between her thumb and fingers, and pushed the needle into Clara's skin.

"No!" Clara screamed. "Let me up!"

"This is for your own good," the nurse said.

Richard and the other orderly stepped back and looked down on Clara, their brows shining with sweat, their shoulders heaving.

"Seems like they all have to learn the hard way," Richard said, wiping his hand across his forehead.

"Please," Clara said. "Let me go."

The nurse and the orderlies ignored her and left the room, slamming the iron door behind them. Keys rattled and turned in the lock. A few minutes later, the high-pitched shriek of metal sliding against metal made her cringe as someone opened the square, barred hole in the upper half of the door. She raised her head to look, but could only see part of a forehead and two blinking eyes. Then the window closed and there were muffled voices in the hall. Clara put her head back on the mattress. The ceiling grew fuzzy and dim. She looked at the walls. The corners of the room seemed to curl inward, the lines and moldings pulsating with every beat of her thundering heart.

All of a sudden, she knew she was going to be sick again. She turned her head to one side and threw up, coughing and gagging on her own vomit. Her eyelids felt heavy and she blinked twice, then the world disappeared.

The first thing Clara became aware of was the ache in her stomach and the burning skin around her wrists and ankles. She felt like she'd been in a brawl, every muscle throbbing and sore. She tried to turn on her side, but she was strapped to the bed. The sheet beneath her was cold and wet, the air filled with the stench of vomit and urine. It all came back to her now. She was in isolation.

She lifted her heavy head and looked around the room, blinking and trying to clear her vision. The domed ceiling light filled the room with a hazy, yellow glow. Then the walls started spinning and she put her head back down, waiting for the dizzy sensation to stop. When it felt safe to open her eyes again, she looked down at the end of the bed, toward the door. She started to shout for help, then saw Nurse Trench sitting in a corner, reading a book.

"Can you untie me, please?" Clara said, her voice raspy and weak.

Nurse Trench made a small, startled sound, her head jerking up. To Clara's surprise, the nurse's eyes looked red and watery. Nurse Trench wiped her cheeks and stood, setting the book on the seat of the chair, then came over to stand next to the bed. She looked down at Clara, her forehead furrowed.

"I don't know," she said. "Are you going to behave?"

"Please," Clara said. "I'm freezing and starving."

"Maybe you should have thought of that before you caused such a ruckus in the Sun Room."

"They wouldn't let me use the bathroom and I . . ."

Nurse Trench shook her head. "The rules are in place for a reason," she said. "How are we going to help you if you don't follow them?"

"But I knew I was going to be sick and . . ."

"The orderly said you stood without asking."

"Yes, but . . ."

"Weren't you told to ask before standing?"

Clara nodded.

"That's right," Nurse Trench said. "Now, before I can let you up, you need to tell me you'll remember that."

"I'll remember," Clara said.

"And from now on, you'll do as you're told?"

"Yes."

"You have to say it for me, Clara."

"From now on, I'll do as I'm told."

"Very good!" Nurse Trench said, smiling. "You can sleep in the ward tonight, as long as you don't try anything. Otherwise, you'll just find yourself right back here. Do you understand?"

Clara nodded. "I understand," she said.

Nurse Trench lowered the bed railing, unbuckled the leather straps, then stepped back. Clara sat up and rubbed her wrists, her head pounding. She swung her feet over the side of the mattress and pushed her hair out of her face. It was stiff and smelled like vomit. The room tilted to one side. Closing her eyes and taking a deep breath, she tried to maintain her equilibrium. Finally, the room stopped spinning and she slid down from the mattress, her wet nightclothes clinging to her legs. She wrapped her arms around herself, trying to stop shaking.

"Can I wash up and get a clean nightgown?" she said, her teeth chattering.

"It's too late for that," Nurse Trench said, starting toward the door. "It's almost time for lights out. You'll have to wait until tomorrow."

"But I haven't had anything to eat since this morning," Clara said.

"Yesterday morning," Nurse Trench said. She picked the book up from the chair and turned to face Clara, one arm holding the novel against her ample chest. "You've been asleep for two days."

Clara put a hand on her abdomen. "You're going to make me wait for food until morning?" She opened her mouth to say something about being pregnant, then stopped. Nurse Trench had told her not to mention the baby again.

"I'm sorry," Nurse Trench said, reaching for the

door. "When you break the rules, you get punished."

Clara bit down on her lip. Somehow, she needed to reach this woman, to make her see that she wasn't like the rest of the patients. Nurse Trench had to have a heart, somewhere inside that tough, manly exterior. Clara glanced at the novel in the nurse's hand. On the cover, a woman slouched beneath a tree, her head down, her eyes shut. The book was *The Sun Also Rises*, by Ernest Hemingway. Clara remembered the day she and Nurse Trench walked in on Dr. Roach and Nurse May. Nurse Trench had been angry, disgusted that the doctor would make his wife wait in the hall while he flirted with his mistress. But there had been something else in the nurse's eyes that day; something that looked like the pain of a broken heart.

Clara swallowed, trying to ignore her empty stomach and churning head. "I felt sorry for the main character in that book," she said, nodding toward the novel. "Didn't you?"

Nurse Trench frowned, her brow furrowed. She looked like she was about to say something, to express her feelings about the book, then changed her mind. She pulled herself together, yanked open the door, and jerked her chin toward the hall. "Let's go," she said.

Clara went through the door on watery legs. "It breaks my heart being away from the man I love," she said, trying to sound friendly. "His name is Bruno." Nurse Trench ignored her and trudged down the hall, the novel gripped in one oversized hand. Clara followed. "I can't imagine how much it would hurt to love someone if he didn't return my feelings."

"That's enough talking," Nurse Trench said.

"Especially if he was in love with someone else," Clara said. "And I knew he could never be mine. It would be pure torture."

Nurse Trench stopped and turned to face Clara, her arm out, pointing down the hall. "I can put you back in that room if you'd like," she said, her face crimson.

Clara shook her head and lowered her eyes. Nurse Trench grunted and started moving again, her shoulders hunched, her mouth twisted in frustration.

From that day on, Clara sat on the benches in the Sun Room without a word, trying to picture Bruno's dark hair and sparkling eyes, or silently singing the words to her favorite songs, anything to pull her attention away from her screaming buttocks and numb legs. She did her best to wipe the tears from her eyes before they spilled over her cheeks, trying not to draw attention to herself. Luckily, by the end of the second week, it was determined she could be trusted enough to be put to work. On the day she was sent to peel potatoes in the kitchen, she said a prayer of thanks, her heart breaking for the unfortunate women who would never get the same opportunity.

The main kitchen was housed in a group of large buildings behind Chapin Hall, near the center of the giant, staggered *U* formed by the connected wards. The factory-style structures included the main kitchen, the bakery, the laundry, the boiler room, and the coal house. From the kitchen, food was delivered to the wards through a series of underground tunnels and dumbwaiters.

Every day through the long winter, Clara sat on a wooden stool, peeling potatoes in the sweltering kitchen. The seat of the stool was cracked and hard, and it wobbled back and forth on one too-short leg, but at least Clara was able to stand when she needed a change of position. She couldn't imagine the patients who were never allowed to work and had to spend day after day sitting on benches in the Sun Room. If they weren't insane when they arrived at Willard, they certainly were now. Clara couldn't imagine why the doctors thought that kind of torture would be good for anyone.

No matter the weather, Clara relished her turn at being sent out the back door of the kitchen, to take the potato peelings out to the fenced-in backyard and dump them in the compost pile, where they would be picked up and fed to Willard's chickens and pigs. Even during the winter, when her face felt solid from the frigid air, the bitter wind pushing tears from her eyes, she stayed outside as long as she could, knowing it might be her only escape for days. On mornings when the air was clear and still, she could hear the screech and chug of incoming locomotives, and the deep *thump-thump* of shifting lake ice, like the hollow gulp of a gargantuan drain. Even though she couldn't see the body of water from behind Chapin Hall, she felt a kinship with it, both of them frozen in time, waiting.

By the end of February, she could tell by looking at her boney arms and legs that she was thinner than she'd ever been. Except for a small, protruding bump below her navel, no one could tell she was pregnant. Most of the time, she felt weak and light-headed, as if the baby growing inside her was sapping the strength from her body. But she did her best to eat all the food she was given, even when it was nothing more than a bowl of thin broth or a runny poached egg that made her gag when she tried to swallow it. While working in the kitchen every day, she hid a potato in the pile of peelings, taking bites when no one was looking. The raw potatoes tasted like dirt and cold starch, but she ate them anyway.

On a gray, rainy day in late March, in the backyard of the kitchen, a chubby, wet rat ran from the top of the compost pile and scurried through a small opening at the bottom of the high wooden fence. Clara went over to the enclosure, set the basket of potato peelings down, and knelt in the mud. The hole was the size of a baseball, the wood around it soggy and jagged. She stood and kicked the planks surrounding the opening, trying to bust the wood, then knelt and broke pieces away with her hands. Splinters gouged her palm but she kept working, breaking away a bowl-sized chunk. She looked through the gap and saw more mud and, several yards away, the stone foundation of another building. She threw the broken wood through the hole, then hid the opening behind a pile of potato and vegetable peelings. The next day, she removed more pieces of the fence. By the end of the week, her palms and fingers were raw, but the opening was nearly big enough to squeeze through.

The next afternoon, she went out to the compost pile, dumped her peelings, and broke away another chunk of wood. She got down on the soggy ground next to the fence, lay on her back so she wouldn't hurt the baby, then shimmied backward until her head and shoulders were through the hole. She dug in her heels and tried to push herself through, but her stomach was too big. The baby was in the way. Just as she was about to work her way out and make the opening bigger, someone grabbed her ankles and yanked her out of the hole, dragging her through the mud.

"You okay?" a man said, panting above her. He wore a plaid wool jacket and filthy overalls, his boots covered with sludge. "You fall?"

Clara sat up. "I . . ." she said, her heart like a train in her chest.

"You tryin' to get out?" He glared at her with one good eye, the other swollen closed.

Clara shook her head and tried to stand. The man reached down to help her up, gesturing toward the fence with one hand. "Won't do no good to get through that fence," he said. "Boiler room is over there. Ain't no way around it."

"How did you get in here?" she said, wiping her hands on her dress. Her hair felt stiff and cold on her neck, the back of her arms and legs wet with mud.

The man spit in the dirt, a string of saliva running from the corner of his mouth. He pointed at the fence near the back wall of the kitchen. "Door's right there," he said. "We got a new passel of hogs. Boss sent me to get some extra scraps. I saw you on the ground and . . ."

Clara squinted at the wooden fence, trying to see the opening. The only sign of an entrance was a slightly wider space between two planks. It was barely noticeable. A shovel and wheelbarrow sat inside the enclosure, tilting sideways next to the compost pile. She trudged through the mud over to the entrance and pushed her nails into the crack, trying to pry open the door. But the crack was too narrow. Her fingers wouldn't fit in far enough to get a grip.

"How do you open it?" she asked the man.

He plodded toward her and stopped in front of the door. "Boss gave me a key to get in," he said. "Showed me a trick to get out." He thumped the end of his fist on the wood and the door popped open. He caught it by the edge and pushed it closed. "See?"

"Can I try?" she said.

He shrugged and stood back. Clara thumped her fist on the same spot. The wood vibrated and bounced, but the door didn't open.

"I told you it was a trick," the man said, grinning.

Clara took a deep breath and hit the wood again, using all her strength. This time, the edge of the door popped away from the fence. She grabbed it and yanked the door open. On the other side, a rutted driveway followed the length of the building, then turned a stone corner and disappeared. Clara bolted out of the enclosure, running as fast as she could, her pulse roaring in her ears. A few yards from the corner, the man grabbed her from behind and lifted her off the ground, his arms clamped around her belly, squeezing so hard she could barely breathe. He carried her back inside the fence, set her down, and slammed the door, panting.

"You played a trick on me," he said, his red face contorted. "Boss said not to let anyone use this door. Ever."

"I'm sorry," Clara said, trying to catch her breath. "It's just that . . . I'm not supposed to be here, you see."

"You can't leave," the man said, shaking his head. "That's breaking the rules. You'll get in a heapload of trouble if you break the rules."

"I know," she said. "It's just . . ." She hesitated, trying to find the right words. "By the way, what's your name?"

"Stanley," he said. "My father named me Stanford, but my mother called me Stanley."

"Are you a patient here, Stanley?" she said, hoping to make him see they were on the same side.

"Twenty years," Stanley said, nodding. "Since I was seventeen."

Clara's stomach tightened. "Why were you sent here?"

"Parents died," he said. "I was nothin' but trouble and gettin' too old for the orphanage."

"Well, I wouldn't want to get you in any more trouble, Stanley," she said. She bit down on the edge of her lip, trying to think of another approach. "When I was growing up I used to live on a farm. I love animals. Do you think you could show me the new hogs?"

"Nope," he said. "Boss wouldn't like that. Boss says no one else is allowed in the pig barn."

"How about just letting me through that door, then?" she said. "No one has to know."

Stanley shook his head, teetering back and forth as if marching in place without taking his toes off the ground. Just then, a growling engine

218

approached from the other side of the fence.

"I gotta get back to work," Stanley said, his good eye blinking. "Boss is coming." He hurried over to the wheelbarrow, pushed it closer to the compost pile, and started filling it with vegetable scraps.

Clara followed him. "When do you normally pick up the compost?" she said. "What time do you usually come?"

Stanley shoved his pitchfork into the kitchen scraps and slung a pile of vegetable peelings into the wheelbarrow. "Before the sun is up," he said, keeping his head down. "When everyone is still sleeping and no one bothers me."

A vehicle stopped outside the fence, gears grinding. A heavy door opened and closed, metal slamming against metal. Then the fence door opened and a man in muddy overalls entered.

"What in blue blazes is taking so long, Stanley?" he said. "You were supposed to meet me out on the road ten minutes ago!"

Stanley kept working, his shoulders hunched. "Sorry, Boss," he said. "This lady was stuck in the fence and I had to help her get out." The man looked at the hole, then considered Clara, his brows knitted.

"What's going on here?" he said.

"Nothing." Clara picked up her basket and headed toward the kitchen. "We were just talking."

The man followed, entering the kitchen behind

her. "You let Stanley be," he said. "You hear me? He's a good worker and stays out of trouble. You might make note of that."

Clara kept walking and Stanley's boss went in the other direction. She looked over her shoulder and watched him make his way between the dishwashers and prep counters. Then he turned left and disappeared. Clara went back to her station and got to work, swallowing the surge of panic that threatened to shut off her breathing. Surely, Stanley's boss was going to turn her in. The other women stared at her, no doubt wondering why her arms and legs were covered with drying mud.

A few minutes later, Stanley's boss and the pudgy kitchen forewoman approached. The hunched-over forewoman trudged toward Clara, her chin jutting out to one side. She had to be at least sixty, and yet her pale, thick arms were corded with muscle.

"What's this I hear about you getting stuck in the fence outside?" she said.

"I fell in the mud," Clara said. "My leg went through a hole. It was an accident."

The forewoman took her by the arm and dragged her outside. Stanley waited by the fence, his wheelbarrow full. He dropped his eyes, fidgeting with the edge of his jacket.

"Did you make that hole?" the forewoman said to Clara.

"No," Clara said. "I told you I fell and . . ."

"Get that boarded up right away," the fore-woman said to Stanley's boss. Then she dragged Clara back inside, led her out of the kitchen, and took her to Dr. Roach's office.

"Where would you have gone if you'd escaped, Clara?" Dr. Roach said. "Willard consists of hundreds of acres, including dense forests. The nearest town is miles away."

"I don't know," she said, her fists in her lap. "All I know is I need to get out of here!"

"What if something happened to you? How would I explain that to your father?"

"I don't care about my father!" she said. "You can tell him anything you want. You and he both know I don't belong here."

Dr. Roach furrowed his brow, clearly taken aback. "I don't know any such thing," he said. "You're here for a reason, Clara. And I want to help you get well."

"Like I told you before," she said. "I'm here because I had a fight with my father. I don't need help!"

"But don't you see?" Dr. Roach said. "Trying to escape just reinforces my opinion that you're not thinking clearly. A woman of your status and frail constitution shouldn't be out hiking alone across the countryside. It's not safe!"

"I'm not as helpless as you think."

221

"You know what kind of hospital Willard is, don't you?"

"Of course I do," she said. "It's an institution for the insane. But I don't hear voices. I don't see hallucinations. I know my father told you I'm insane, but he's lying!"

"Lying?" Dr. Roach said. He gave her a sad smile. "My dear, Clara. Why would he do that?"

"To keep me here."

"Do you really believe that?"

"Yes. I do! At first, I thought he just wanted to teach me a lesson and would eventually let me come home. Now I think he's just glad to be rid of me."

Dr. Roach shook his head, his brow creased. "You're worrying me, Clara," he said. "You continue to believe your father is plotting against you, that we're keeping you here to hurt you somehow."

"Please," she said. "Just let me go. You can tell my father I'm still here. Tell him I've gone completely mad and you had to lock me up for the rest of my life. I don't care. Just release me! He doesn't have to know!"

"You're being irrational, Clara," he said. "I'm a doctor. I took an oath to help people. That's all I'm trying to do."

"I've never been more rational in my life," Clara said. "I'm being kept in an insane asylum against my will. My mind is all I have left and I assure you it's perfectly clear! I'm not like the rest of the patients here, blindly believing everything you say, letting you lock them up like animals. That's not what a doctor is supposed to do. It's criminal."

Dr. Roach frowned, his eyes narrowed. "Perhaps you need a break," he said. "Maybe some time to think will do you good. Trying to escape is a serious offense that usually warrants harsh treatment. But I'm willing to be lenient because I think you're smart enough to learn from your mistakes . . ."

She reached across his desk and grabbed his hands, the dried mud on her elbows smudging the spotless blotter. He recoiled and tried to pull away, a small, startled sound escaping his lips. She tightened her grip.

"How would you feel if I refused to let go?" she said. "I know you don't like people touching you. I have no idea why, but it frightens you. And in case you haven't heard, morally upright men don't cheat on their wives. Perhaps you're the one in need of help, Doctor. Perhaps you're the one who needs to be locked up! How would you like that?"

He stood and yanked his hands from her grasp, his face red, his nostrils flaring. "I don't know what games you're trying to play," he said. "But I won't stand for it." He closed her folder. "We'll talk again at your next appointment. In the meantime, I'm not the enemy, Clara. Perhaps by your next appointment, you'll have a change of heart."

For the next six days, Clara was locked in a foul-smelling, cement-walled room on the isolation ward, the only furniture a toilet and a metal cot bolted to the floor. Twice a day, a tray with dry bread and a tin of broth was shoved under the riveted door through a hinged slot. The only way to distinguish night from day was by a bare bulb on the ceiling, turning on and off. Clinking chains and slamming metal doors echoed in the hall, punctuated by screams and groans. On the sixth day, Nurse Trench unlocked the door to let Clara out, clucking her tongue with disapproval. Too weak to speak, Clara followed the nurse back to the ward without a word.

By mid-April, approximately two months before what Clara estimated was her due date, her belly protruded enough to make her dresses skintight. But she had seen similar-looking stomachs on other female patients—maybe they had been obese before being half-starved at Willard, or carried all their weight in their abdomens—so she knew there was nothing remarkable about a woman with a bulging belly. No one paid attention to the fact that Clara's was getting bigger every day. No one believed or cared that she was indeed going to give birth, and no one had bothered to check to see if she was telling the truth.

On the last day of May, during her second

appointment with Dr. Roach, Clara sat in the chair opposite his desk, the rigid seat pressing hard against her pelvic bones. Her skeleton ached as if she were ninety years old instead of nineteen. She wasn't sure if her body was stiff because she was pregnant and suffering from the lack of proper nutrition, or if it was from the thin, lumpy mattresses she'd been trying to sleep on for the last five months.

Every night, her fitful sleep was filled with nightmares about going into labor in the ward, with no one to help her give birth but the other patients. In the dream, she was screaming on the filthy bed, the other women gathered around, rocking back and forth, drooling, wailing. She sat up, clutching the edges of the mattress, and bared down, her face twisting with exertion. The woman with the tattered doll ripped the newborn from between Clara's legs and ran out of the ward, the bloody umbilical cord trailing behind her.

Now, as she always did, Clara sat with one hand on her belly, waiting to feel the baby move. Her greatest fear was that the fetus had died and she wouldn't know until she gave birth. As usual, she felt nothing. The only time she felt movement was at night. Even then, she worried she had imagined it; so slight was the flutter beneath her hand. For the millionth time she thought that either the baby was abnormally tiny, or something was horribly wrong. The idea made her heart constrict.

From the other side of the desk, Dr. Roach considered her, his pen poised over her chart. She looked at the fancy, carved pen in his hand. How foolish she had been, thinking she would have access to ink and stationery to write letters to Bruno, thinking she would ever get anyone to mail them. No one at Willard cared about why she was there, let alone her previous life. She thought about Nurse Yott. For some reason, the young nurse had been able to tell immediately that Clara was sane. Why was it that no one at Willard could do the same? Clara had to believe that Nurse Yott had either changed her mind about mailing the letter, or had been caught somehow. Otherwise, Bruno would have come to rescue her by now. A dull, empty ache gnawed beneath her ribcage.

"What were you just thinking, Clara?" Dr. Roach said, his voice deep and relaxed.

"I was wondering how you expect to help patients if you never see them," she said.

His brow furrowed. "I'm afraid I don't understand what you mean," he said.

"I've been here five months and this is only my second appointment with you. The only other time I saw you was when I got in trouble."

He sat back in his chair, stroking the edges of his neatly trimmed goatee between his thumb and fingers. "We have over three thousand patients here at Willard," he said. "Male and female. You can't expect special treatment now, can you? This isn't the Long Island Home."

"I'm not asking for special treatment," she said. "But you claim you want to help me. How can you help me if you never see me? I'm beginning to think the only thing Willard is good for is locking people away."

"This institution was founded on the belief that madness can be cured by a firm but humane hand, a safe haven from the stresses of life, rest, and regular work. You're getting all of those things, aren't you, Clara?"

Clara shifted in her seat, her back screaming in pain. "First of all, I'm not mad. Second, this is not a safe haven from the stresses of life. I'm being kept here against my will. Is that supposed to make me feel peaceful and carefree?"

"How can I relieve some of your stress, Clara?"

"Release me. I've been here long enough. I'm sure even my father would agree."

Dr. Roach shook his head. "I'm afraid you're wrong," he said. "Your father is counting on me to cure you. Unfortunately, you haven't said anything to show me that you've made progress."

"What do you want me to say? Tell me, and I'll say it."

"Do you still believe your father sent you here to get rid of you?"

Her shoulders dropped. "That's the tenth time you've asked me that question."

"It's my job to ask questions."

"But you twist my answers around to fit your preconceived notions of who I am. You're convinced that just because I'm here, something is wrong with me!"

"Just answer the question, please."

She took a deep breath and sighed loudly. "My father sent me here, that's all I know. If you send me home, I'll do whatever he wants."

"Are you saying you finally understand your father only wants what's best?"

She bit down on the inside of her cheek and nodded. Right now she'd agree to anything if it meant she would regain her freedom. Whatever happened when she got home would be better than being locked up. Dr. Roach scribbled on her chart, his forehead wrinkled in concentration. Then he looked up.

"Do you ever entertain thoughts of suicide, Clara?"

She shook her head. "Why are you even asking me that? I haven't given you any reason to think . . ."

"I'm not sure if you're aware of it, but suicide can run in families. I just want to make sure . . ."

"No," she said. "Like I said before, all I want is the chance to live a normal life, to be with the man I love, to raise our baby. But I can't do any of that as long as you keep me here."

"I assume you're talking about Bruno."

Clara's breath caught in her chest. "How do you know his name? Did my father tell you?"

Dr. Roach glanced at her file, frowning and rolling his pen between his thumb and fingers. Then he looked up at her, searching her face. "I'm afraid it's time to tell you the truth, Clara."

She sat forward in her seat, her heart thundering in her chest. "The truth about what?" she said.

"You're right about one thing," Dr. Roach said. "Your father told me about Bruno Moretti."

"Yes?" she said, unable to breathe. "What did he tell you?"

Dr. Roach set down his pen and folded his hands on his desk. "Clara," he said, his face etched with pity. "Bruno Moretti doesn't exist."

By the first of June, the spring rains finally stopped. Now that the grounds of Willard were dry, the patients were allowed outside for supervised walks. Each ward was kept in their own group, lined up four across like a confused marching band. Some patients turned left when the group turned right, others fell back, unable to keep up. Females were sent in one direction, males in the other. Squinting beneath the blazing sun, Clara followed the other women on her ward, looking out over the shimmering waters of Seneca Lake.

A tall, slender woman hummed beside Clara, rolling up her sleeves and turning her face toward the sun. Esther had been at Willard six weeks, committed by her husband when he caught her kissing another man. Even without makeup and wearing a plain, blue housedress, she looked like a movie star, with thick blond hair and peaches-and-cream skin. The first time Clara saw her in the cafeteria, looking around at the other patients with fear-filled eyes, Clara knew she didn't belong in Willard any more than she did. Later, in the ward, Clara warned her about the Sun Room, and told her that the only way to escape it was to behave. Since then, they'd struck up a friendship and Clara was beyond grateful to have someone to talk to.

Walking on the other side of Esther was Madeline, a petite woman in her mid-twenties, admitted to Willard over a year ago, after losing two babies and leaving her abusive husband. She and Clara had become friends while working in the kitchen, where Madeline washed dishes.

"The sun was shining just like this when I came to Willard," Madeline said, lifting her chin toward the sky. "The buildings and the lake looked so beautiful that day. I thought someone was finally going to take care of me."

"Ain't no one going to take care of us in this place," Esther said. "When I get out of here, I'm going to find me a sugar daddy and never have to worry about being taken care of again."

"Maybe that's what I should have done," Madeline said, grinning. "I should have found a sugar daddy to pay rent to that miserable old landlady."

"She would have called the cops on you anyway," Esther said. "She probably would have said you were a prostitute or something."

"I thought you were sick in bed when the cops came?" Clara said. "Isn't that why you couldn't work and pay your rent?"

"I wasn't sick," Madeline said. "I'd just come back from asking my no-good husband to give me a little money for food. He beat the tar out of me. Took me a week before I could get out of bed other than to use the bathroom. After the cops took me in, the doctor said I was below normal physically and should go to the hospital. But that damn landlady said I used vulgar language and talked to myself, so they sent me to the loony bin instead."

Clara shook her head. She looked at the other women in line ahead of her, shuffling with their heads down or their shoulders hunched, women who, like her and Esther and Madeline, had believed they would live ordinary, happy lives. Of course some of them were truly sick, with mental issues that prevented them from being normal and productive. But how many were victims of circumstance, women left penniless by husbands who abandoned them or died, women who lost children and needed help coping with unbearable grief, women banished by parents who disapproved

231

of their decisions? How many were at Willard because of a single angry outburst, or because they had grown old and been abandoned by their children, or had lost their parents at a young age and had grown up in an orphanage? How many were sane when they got here, but after months of abuse or overtreatment with ice baths and sedatives, would never be rational again?

A while back, Madeline had told Clara the story of Ruby, an Italian immigrant who had come to America with her husband twelve years ago. Two years after they arrived, Ruby's husband was killed in a construction accident. Starving and homeless, Ruby took to prostitution on the streets of New York, unable to speak more than a few words of English. Eventually, she was arrested and sent to Willard. That was ten years ago. Now, she sat in the Sun Room every day with her head down, silently picking at the skin on her arms.

Being locked up was bad enough, but Clara couldn't imagine the torture of being unable to communicate, of not having the right words to try to explain how she got there, or that she was perfectly sane. Why hadn't the doctors found someone who spoke Ruby's language? What if Ruby had family in Italy, wondering where she was and what happened to her? What if all it had taken was a simple letter to get her out of this hell? Thinking about the injustice of it all, Clara felt a dull, empty ache gnawing inside her chest.

"How are you feeling today?" Esther asked her. "Won't be long now before your daughter is here."

Clara put a protective hand over her stomach, her heart filling with a strange mixture of love and fear. She had told Esther and Madeline everything; about Bruno and her father, about her belief that the baby was a girl. "I'm fine," she said. "A little weak, but other than that . . ."

"What do you think is going to happen after the baby comes?" Esther asked Madeline. "Do you think they'll let Clara go?"

Madeline shrugged. "I don't know," she said. "I've never heard of anyone giving birth here." She turned her face toward the lake, avoiding Clara's eyes.

Clara took a deep breath, trying to ignore the feeling that Madeline wasn't being completely honest. She couldn't fault her for it. If Madeline knew something and wasn't telling, she was only trying to be kind. Madeline understood that if Clara allowed herself to think any further than the day of the baby's birth, she might not find the strength to put one foot in front of the other. For now, Clara had to believe things would change for the better. There was no other choice.

"I hope they're going to let me go," Clara said. "This is no place to raise a baby."

"I think you're right," Esther said, smiling. "They'll let you go."

The group of women followed Willard's main road toward a thick pine grove on the other side of Creek Mears, a long, wide stream that emptied into Seneca Lake. Due to weeks of heavy wind and rain, the grass-banked creek barreled west like a raging river, nearly overflowing, branches and leaves swirling and spinning in the swift, gray water. The women crossed a wooden bridge, the rushing surge drowning out their voices. Clara thought about jumping over the railing, letting the strong current sweep her out to the lake, where a passing boater could pick her up or she could make her way to the opposite shore. But the creek was too deep and powerful, the rough water breaking thick branches on boulders and rocks. Besides, she didn't know how to swim, having done little more than wade and splash on the beach at Coney Island. Even if she wasn't pregnant, the risk of drowning was too high. What good would freedom be, if she were dead?

At the end of the bridge, the women turned right, following a dirt road toward the lake. To their right, between the road and the pine grove, a wide field was filled with row after row of iron markers, each two feet high and a foot wide. In the back row, a man in rubber boots and overalls was digging a hole in the ground. When he saw the women, he stopped and pushed his shovel into a mound of fresh dirt, took off his cap, and waved.

"That's the grave digger, Lawrence Lawrence," Madeline said. "He's been at Willard for over thirty years and can pretty much do whatever he wants. I heard that one summer he started sleeping in that shack over there, by the cedar grove." She pointed toward a small, one-story house nestled at the edge of the woods, its roof littered with pinecones and needles. Clara had no idea how long the dwelling had stood empty, but to her it looked tired; ready to collapse into a dusty heap, years of bone-dry wood and stale attic air released into a thunderous cloud of sawdust and jagged splinters. She couldn't imagine what condition it was inside. "Lawrence asked the doctors if he could stay in the house instead of the men's ward," Madeline continued. "He told them not to worry. He wasn't going anywhere because he doesn't have any place to go."

"He never tries to leave?" Esther said, her eyes wide.

"He says he's happy here."

"He must be crazy," Esther said. "No one could be happy here."

On the left side of the road stood a four-story building with a green-tiled roof that sagged in the middle, as if supporting an invisible burden. At one time, apparently, the brick building had been painted white. Now, the exposed stone looked grainy and pink, with ashy patches of peeling paint clinging under the eaves and around the window casings. Iron bars crisscrossed the grimy windows, like black thread in a mended sock. Beside the structure, a tall, dark tree reached for the sky, its limbs twisted and bent.

In the side yard, two groups of patients trudged along the ragged edge of weed-choked grass, some with their wrists tied together, some in straitjackets or leather mittens with chains, all bound together by ropes around their middles. Males made up one group, females the other. Their white hospital gowns were torn and caked with filth, their legs, arms, and hair encrusted with feces, vomit, and urine. One woman kept falling and being dragged along by the others, until the orderlies stopped the group long enough for her to stand up. Every ten steps or so, the woman fell again. Several of the patients staggered or limped, and some cried out for help. One kept trying to hit everyone around her, and another tried to turn around and walk in the other direction. A male patient in a straitjacket thrust a shoulder forward with every step, first the left, then the right, like a football player practicing his moves. One of the men had a muzzle over his mouth. Several of them cursed at the top of their lungs.

Clara tried to look away, but couldn't. "Who are they?" she asked Esther.

"They're too violent to be put in with the general population," Esther said. "The doctors keep them locked up there, in the Rookie Pest

House. I heard there's no heat and they chain the patients to the beds."

Clara shivered, even though she wasn't cold, and looked out over the lake. A teakwood boat cut a white line through the waves, a string of colored flags from the mast to the bow flapping in the wind. She squinted, trying to see the people sitting in the open area behind the cabin, wondering what they thought when they looked across the water toward Willard. Did they know what this place was? Did they think of the patients as real people, or did they look at them as nonhumans who never stood a chance at a normal existence anyway? Were they happy the patients had been locked away, relieved that they could enjoy their lives unburdened by someone who might have a problem? Did they realize that most of the patients once had hopes and dreams of their own? That some were being kept locked up against their will?

Just then, Clara was pulled from her thoughts by someone shouting. A naked man ran out of the Rookie Pest House, wild eyes above a scraggly beard. He raced toward the lake as fast as his spindly legs would carry him. Two orderlies ran after him. The naked man tripped over a tree trunk and fell, then scrambled back to his feet. The orderlies caught up to him and wrestled him to the ground. Then they yanked him upright and dragged him backward, toward the brick building.

Clara pulled her eyes away, relieved when the orderlies led her group in the other direction, toward the boathouse and dock, away from the Rookie Pest House.

Later, in the kitchen, she couldn't stop thinking about the man from the Rookie Pest House, wondering what horrors he was running from. How could there be a place like Willard, where people are treated like cattle, while everyone else goes on with their lives? She wondered if her father knew how awful Willard was, or if he'd even care. From where she sat peeling potatoes, she could see Madeline at the sink washing dishes, sweat dripping from her brow. The woman in charge of the kitchen didn't allow talking between workers, but Clara was just glad to have Madeline nearby, to exchange a smile or wave, to remind her that she and others at Willard were still sane. The woman sitting on a stool to Clara's left never said a word. She just sat with her head down, peeling potatoes and mumbling to herself.

As if Madeline had heard Clara's thoughts, she turned and raised a soapy hand, her eyes tired, but smiling. Just then the kitchen boss crossed the room, moving between Clara and Madeline, her mouth twisted into a determined scowl. Madeline turned and put a thumb to her nose and stuck out her tongue, making a face at the kitchen boss's back. A wet plate slid from her other hand, shattering into a hundred white shards on the tiled floor.

The kitchen boss stopped in her tracks and spun around to see what happened. Without missing a beat, she rushed toward Madeline. Madeline edged backward until she was trapped in the corner between the wall and the metal sink. The kitchen boss dug her fingers into Madeline's arms, pulled her forward, then shoved her into the counter. The back of Madeline's head collided with the cupboards with a hollow *thump,* rattling the silverware in the strainer. The kitchen boss raised a hand to slap her, yelling something about the cost of supplies. Clara dropped the potato peeler and started toward them.

"Leave her alone!" she shouted. She grabbed the kitchen boss's wrist, trying to pull her away from Madeline. The kitchen boss turned, red-faced and panting, and shoved Clara away with both hands. In what felt like slow motion, Clara flew backward, arms circling, eyes wide. She scrambled to keep her footing, slipped on the wet floor, then fell and hit her head on the tiles with a nauseating thud, a bolt of pain shooting through her skull. She looked up and blinked, black curtains of unconsciousness threatening to close in from every side. Then she felt a warm, wet gush between her legs and passed out.

Clara blinked and opened her eyes, trying to focus on the bright orbs flashing overhead. She was moving forward, feet first, drafts of foul-smelling air gliding across her face and arms. She had no idea where she was. Then she realized the fuzzy lights passing above her were ceiling lamps. She turned her head and saw dimly lit rooms and hospital beds, nurses bending over patients, giving shots, checking pulses, writing in charts. She was on a stretcher, being rushed along the halls of the infirmary. All of a sudden, her stomach muscles twisted and pulled, like a knife stabbing into her lower abdomen. She struggled to sit upright, to pull her knees up and curl into a ball, but a strong hand pushed her back down. Looking up to see who was pushing the stretcher, she saw a nurse she didn't recognize.

The nurse directed the stretcher around a corner and inside an examination room, where a doctor stood waiting. He looked like a toad, short and swollen, his jowls sliding down into his double chin.

"What happened?" the doctor asked the nurse.

"She fell and hit her head," the nurse said, coming around to stand beside the stretcher. "She just woke up."

"How long has she been unconscious?" the doctor said. He bent over and held Clara's eyelids open, looking into her pupils with a tiny, bright light.

"Maybe fifteen minutes?" the nurse said.

"How are you feeling?" he said to Clara in a loud voice. "Are you dizzy?"

Clara shook her head. Another contraction started and she pulled up her knees, trying to stop the ripping, burning pain in her lower abdomen. She felt like she was being torn apart. She bit down on her lip, moaning softly.

"Are you having pain in your head?" the doctor said.

"No," Clara said. "I'm in labor."

The doctor's brows shot up and he looked at the nurse, a question on his face. The nurse shrugged.

"Can you get up and move over to the examination table?" he said to Clara.

Clara pushed herself up on shaky arms, her head pounding in time with her thundering heart. She swung her legs over the mattress and got down from the stretcher, one hand on her belly. Warm liquid ran down the inside of her leg, wetting her leather shoes. The doctor went over to the sink to wash his hands.

"She'll need to remove her bloomers," he said to the nurse.

Clara slipped off her shoes without untying them, the pain in her belly making it impossible to stand up straight. The nurse came over and started lifting Clara's dress, reaching for her underwear. Clara pushed the nurse's hands away and pulled her underwear off herself, trying to step out of them without falling. She climbed onto the examining table, struggling to take slow, deep breaths.

The doctor pulled the foot stirrups out and motioned for Clara to lie back. She did as she was told, her head coming to a rest on a small, lumpy pillow. The doctor guided her feet into the stirrups and she closed her eyes, trying to picture Bruno's face, his dark hair and white smile. When the doctor's hands touched her, she jumped and turned her head, staring at her reflection in the glass of a white cabinet filled with tongue depressors, cotton balls, and shiny, sharp-looking instruments. When the exam was over, the doctor patted her knee and told her to sit up.

"This poor girl is about to have a baby," he said to the nurse. "Let's get her into a room."

The nurse glanced at Clara, her lips pressed together, then picked up a clipboard and handed it to the doctor.

"Who is her physician?" the doctor asked, scribbling something on the chart.

"Dr. Roach," the nurse said. "Should I get a wheelchair?"

"Yes," the doctor said. "And be quick about it." The nurse left the room and the doctor addressed Clara. "Do you know who the father is?"

Clara nodded, unsure that she could answer. The contractions were getting closer and closer together. "My boyfriend, Bruno," she said, gasping.

"And where is Bruno now?"

"I don't know," Clara managed.

"Is he a patient here?" the doctor said.

Clara shook her head, beads of sweat forming on her forehead and upper lip. The nurse came back into the room with a wheelchair and retrieved a hospital gown from a cupboard. Clara climbed down from the table and sat in the wheelchair, doubling over in the seat. Her insides felt like they were coming out, and would soon be a bloody pile in her lap. Suddenly, the urge to stand up overwhelmed her, and she tried pushing herself out of the chair.

"Sit down!" the nurse said, shoving her back into the seat. Before Clara could protest, the nurse started pushing the wheelchair across the room.

"The baby is coming!" Clara screamed.

The doctor threw open the door and the nurse pushed Clara into the hall. She turned right and ran along the corridor, yelling at other nurses and patients to get out of the way. An orderly pushed a wheelchair straight at them, one hand trying to keep the unconscious man in the seat upright. The orderly couldn't turn fast enough and they nearly collided. Finally, the nurse turned down a short hallway and wheeled Clara into a room with a single bed.

"Stand up," the nurse said.

A second nurse helped Clara out of the wheelchair and started stripping off her clothes. "Let's get you into this hospital gown." she said, yanking off Clara's brassiere. "You're about to have a baby. Do you understand that?"

"Yes," Clara said, gasping. "I told Dr. Roach I was pregnant but he didn't care." She slipped her arms into the hospital gown, climbed up on the mattress, and lay back. Another band of pain tightened around her middle and again she felt the overwhelming urge to push.

The first nurse covered Clara with a thin sheet while the second held her legs together at the ankles, telling her not to push until the doctor came. Clara thrashed on the bed, fighting the urge to bear down. Her body felt like it was being ripped in two, sinew and muscle twisting in opposite directions, veins stretching until they burst. Finally the doctor hurried in, instructing the nurses to get blankets, towels, and a basin of hot water.

"We'll need morphine and scopolamine," he said, his voice filled with urgency. The nurses hurried out of the room and he examined Clara again. She pushed herself up on her elbows and looked at the doctor, studying his face for any sign that might convey her baby's condition. Her roaring heart clogged her throat.

If her estimates were right, the baby was two weeks early. And now, because of the sudden onset of labor, she was terrified that, along with everything else, her daughter was coming too soon and wouldn't survive. Then, as suddenly as it had started, the powerful contraction eased. Clara collapsed back on the pillows, panting.

"Is something wrong?" she said.

"Just lie as still as you can now," the doctor said. "I'll take care of you."

The nurses rushed back into the room, their arms laden with towels, a basin, a doctor's bag, and a pitcher of steaming water. Clara's stomach tightened again and another contraction started, every muscle feeling squeezed inside a giant vise. She took a deep breath, put her hands on her knees, and bore down. The baby was crowning; she could feel its wide, damp head forcing its way out of her body and into the world.

Clara started to hyperventilate, her breath coming in quick, shallow gasps. A rush of fluid gushed between her legs. The sting of a needle in her skin made her jump. She turned to see a nurse burying a syringe in her upper arm, her mouth pressed into a thin, hard line. Clara tried to sit up again, but her strength was gone. She looked down at the doctor, his determined scowl the last thing she saw before the world went dark.

CHAPTER 11

IZZY

Willard

In the backseat of Peg and Harry's Mitsubishi, Izzy picked at the edges of her nails, watching the buildings of Willard State roll past the car windows. The sun was shining in a September blue sky filled with anvil-shaped thunderheads, hinting at a possible storm. Out the left side of the vehicle, Seneca Lake shimmered in the distance, shallow waves rippling toward the opposite shore. Treetops swayed in the gentle breeze and seagulls congregated on the sagging, shingled roof of Willard's boathouse.

And yet, the buildings and grounds of Willard looked dead and still. Not a blade of grass moved, not one vine or leaf of ivy stirred. Not one bird flew past the roofs or landed on the chimneys. Against the red brick walls, the ward windows looked burned out and black, as if there had been a fire inside, or it was impossible for sunlight to penetrate the darkness within.

Izzy couldn't believe she was back at the old asylum again, to go inside the abandoned hospital and look at old medical records. She did her best to take deep breaths and push her fears away, concentrating instead on the excitement of finding out more about Clara.

Three nights earlier, after supper and home-work, Izzy had finally admitted to Peg that she had Clara's journal. Peg was disappointed, but she wasn't angry. She understood Izzy's fascination and believed she had every intention of returning it. After thanking her for telling the truth and giving a gently worded lecture about the virtues of honesty, Peg seemed excited about everything Izzy had found out.

"Thank you for not being mad," Izzy said.

"Just do me a favor, will you?" Peg said. "Next time, ask."

Izzy nodded. "I will," she said.

"And since you're so into this project," Peg said, "would you like to go to Willard with us on Saturday? I still can't believe it, but the state has given us permission to search the medical records!"

"Will you be looking at Clara's file?" Izzy said.

"Sorry," Peg said, shaking her head. "But it was pretty simple to piece her life together from the things we found in her trunk. She isn't one of the patients we chose to find out more about. And like you said, her journal explains a lot. But if you want to come with us, you can try to find her records. We're only allowed a few hours inside the hospital, so it will have to be quick."

Now, the closer they got to the abandoned structure, the faster Izzy's heart raced. Harry pulled up a narrow road and parked the car near a four-story brick building. He shut off the engine and got out. Izzy climbed out of the backseat, watching two cars pull up and park beside them. Peg and Harry went around to the back of the Mitsubishi and opened the trunk. Two museum workers got out of the first vehicle while the second car parked on the other side. Izzy couldn't see who was in the front seat, but she knew the second car belonged to Ethan's father because Peg had told her the photographer was coming. The door opened and Peter hoisted himself out, the car roof springing up, the frame squeaking. Izzy held her breath, waiting to see if Ethan would be with him. Peter went around the vehicle and opened the trunk. No one else got out of the car.

In a way, Izzy was relieved. Instead of worrying about trying to avoid Ethan, she would be free to concentrate on looking for Clara's file. It had been four days since the scene in psychology class, and Izzy hadn't heard a word from him. When she passed him and Shannon in the halls, they ignored her. None of the other kids brought up Izzy's mother or made fun of her. Suddenly, it was like she was invisible. The only one who talked to her was Alex. For reasons Izzy couldn't put her finger on, Shannon's indifference felt like the calm before the storm. Even Alex thought it was weird.

Izzy went around to the trunk of the car and was surprised to find Peg and Harry putting hospital scrubs on over their clothes. Peg handed Izzy a flashlight and a set of green scrubs.

"What is all this?" Izzy said.

"This old hospital is contaminated with asbestos and lead paint," Harry said. "It's important for us to wear protection."

Izzy looked over at the other vehicles and saw the museum workers also pulling on protective gear. Peter lumbered toward Peg and Harry's car with a wide grin on his face, his photography equipment slung over one shoulder, the wide strap of what looked like a giant flashlight over the other. Peg and Harry slipped paper masks around their necks and started toward the building, Harry carrying a flashlight and duffel bag, Peg carrying a canvas tote over one shoulder. Izzy and everyone else followed. When they reached a set of chained and padlocked double doors that had been boarded up from the inside, Peg gave each person a pair of protective paper booties to put over their shoes.

"Don't you have something to put over your clothes?" Harry said to Peter.

Peter waved a dismissive hand in the air. "I'll be fine," he said.

"Well, you should at least wear these," Peg said,

holding out a mask and a pair of booties. Peter took the mask and put it on. He leaned over to try putting the booties over his massive shoes but they were too small. He smiled and put them on his ears instead. Everyone laughed.

"No Ethan today?" Peg said to him.

He shook his head. "Basketball practice," he said. Then he smiled at Izzy. "He told me to say hi and he's sorry he's missing this."

Izzy felt blood rise in her cheeks. She bent over and pulled the paper booties on over her sneakers, wondering why Ethan would bother saying hello. If he wasn't man enough to say hi to her in public, what was the point? Was he ashamed to admit they were friends, or was he scared of his girlfriend? She clenched her jaw and straightened, hoping her face wasn't red.

Harry pulled a set of keys out of his pocket, unlocked the padlock, and pulled the chain out from around the brass door handles.

"This is the newer hospital," Peg said. "At first, Chapin Hall housed the medical wards, the operating rooms, and the morgue. Eventually, they moved the patients with infectious diseases into an old farmhouse and built this, the main hospital."

Harry pulled the door open, a sudden swirl of stale air sending a slip of curling paper across the cracked threshold. A slanted rectangle of sunlight reached across the shadowy floor, illuminating layers of dirt and dried mold. Everybody pulled their masks over their faces and filed inside. Weak daylight filtered in through open hallway doors, crisscrossing the long, dark passageway. Harry flicked on his flashlight and looked around. Yellowed papers, pieces of drywall, paint peelings, plastic bottles, and trash littered the floor tiles. A wheeled chair sat against one peeling wall and a broken metal cart sat tipped over in the middle of the hall. Curtains of dust hung in the air, like millions of tiny larva floating in seawater.

"Think we'll have enough light to see what we're doing?" Peg said, her voice muffled by the paper mask.

"Yeah," Harry said. "Peter brought a battery-powered construction light, and there should be some light coming in through the windows. It will be fine. They said the records room is down the hall to the left."

Izzy followed the group down the hallway and shined her flashlight through open doors, plaster and dried paint crunching beneath her sneakers. In a room to her right, a row of sinks lined a mold-covered wall, their porcelain basins filled with broken drywall and dust, rivulets of rust running from scale-covered faucets. A dozen showerheads hung from a long pipe along the ceiling, the metal couplings scaly and green. The next room was stuffed with wheelchairs, except instead of canvas or plastic, the seats were toilet seats without lids.

One room was empty, except for a single, filthy mattress and a wide chunk of moldy plaster hanging from the ceiling. The sounds of dripping water echoed from somewhere down the hall.

Finally, they came to a closed door with a sign that read "Records." Harry tried three keys before he found the right one. He opened the door and everyone followed him inside. Two tall windows on the far wall let in just enough light so they could see. Dust hung in the sluggish air, illuminated by shafts of weak sun.

Peg put a hand over her chest and looked around with wide eyes. The space was filled with an assortment of different-sized tables, filing cabinets, cupboards, and shelves, everything filled and piled high with folders and papers and boxes. Ragged-edged forms spilled out over the floor while others were bundled half a foot high, secured with a dried-out rubber band. X-rays and files littered the floor tiles, scattered around as if someone had thrown them in the room and closed the door.

"How are we ever going to get through all this?" Peg said.

"I don't know," Harry said. "We just have to work fast."

Peter set up the battery-powered construction light in one corner, illuminating the center of the room. He cleared some boxes from the top of a small table, put the table in the center of the floor, and started setting up his equipment. Peg went over to the farthest corner and picked up a thick file. She looked at it for a few seconds then set it back down and picked up another one a few feet away. After looking at a half dozen files, she said, "It looks like there might have been some attempt to keep them in alphabetical order."

"Why don't we each pick a patient name and look for their files?" Harry said.

"Good idea," Peg said. She pulled a paper from her tote, assigned a name to everyone but Izzy and Peter, and then handed out clipboards. "Write down the name of the patient and any information you think we can use. Let Peter take as many pictures of important files as possible. We've only got one chance at this so work fast. Izzy, you can help me."

Everyone scattered in different directions and got to work. Izzy followed Peg to the far side of the room.

"What do you want me to do?" she said.

"The last name of the patient I'm looking for starts with a C, like Clara's," she said. "So maybe you'll find what you're looking for over here."

Peg pulled out a four-inch-thick file and together they looked at the first page. Affixed to the folder were two black-and-white photos; one of a middle-aged woman wearing a blouse with a lace collar. She had bobbed hair, a shy smile, and kind eyes. On the wall behind her head were five digits, black numbers on a white strip. The second picture showed the same woman with gray, wrinkled skin and deep circles under her eyes. She was frowning, her lips sinking into her toothless gums. It was the saddest face Izzy had ever seen.

"Esther Baldwin," Peg said. She closed the chart and put it back. "We're in the Bs." She moved along the wall several feet, picked another file off the top of a medicine cabinet, and opened it. Izzy kept her eyes on Peg, avoiding the photo of another face ravaged by years spent inside an institution.

"Dmitry Cabell," Peg said. "Now we're in the Cs." She returned the file and lowered her voice. "Go ahead and see if you can find Clara's records."

Izzy moved along the wall and took a chart off the shelves. It belonged to someone with the last name Cahill. She put it back and pulled out another chart two shelves down. The woman's last name was Callahan. Izzy took out another file, then another, clenching her jaw at every broken glance and toothless face. It was unthinkable that so many people had been put away, some for the rest of their lives. She wondered how many were like Clara, normal one minute, locked up the next. What would have happened if the patients had been asked what had happened to them instead of what was wrong with them? Most of the files were inches thick, spanning years of institutionalization. Something cold and hard writhed in Izzy's stomach.

She started to wonder why she was putting herself through this, trying to find out more about a woman who was dead and gone. Someone who had never gotten a chance to live the normal life she deserved. Izzy had enough problems of her own. Why was she digging around in someone else's mess?

One of the museum workers took a file to the center of the room, where Peter was snapping pictures of charts and X-rays and papers filled with medical text. Izzy watched for a second, then slid a thick file from beneath a thinner one. She opened the cover and nearly dropped it. Clara looked back at her with frightened eyes, her mouth in a thin, hard line, as if she was trying not to cry. Written beneath her name in bold cursive were the words *Paranoid delusion with hallucinations.*

Izzy swallowed, her eyes growing moist. She sat on a step stool next to the cabinets and pulled out her flashlight, hoping no one was paying attention. She put the thick file in her lap, turned to the first page, and started reading.

January 1, 1930: Patient seems in good physical health. She is clean in her habits and has settled quietly into the ward. She is rather withdrawn and seems to be at a complete loss as to why she was brought here. Dr. Thorn has warned that patient does not believe she is mentally ill. She may be hallucinating and delusional. She is fairly cooperative and eats and sleeps well.

January 2, 1930: Upon examination, no physical cause for patient's maladies. Temperature and pulse normal. Thoracic and skeletal examinations revealed nothing abnormal. She is under the delusion that she is with child, but no signs of pregnancy could be found. She is rather thin. Patient's delusion could be in part due to the growing hallucinogenic manifestations of her illness.

Izzy gasped. Clara thought she was pregnant? Why hadn't she mentioned it in the journal? Could she have been so desperate to escape that she'd started imagining things? Was being torn away from Bruno just too much? Izzy skimmed over the next few pages, reading as fast as possible.

March 5, 1930: Patient attempted escape. She is definitely paranoid in her thinking and continues to express delusions about her commitment and detention here. She was hostile during the interview. Confined to isolation for six days in an attempt to adjust paranoia.

May 31, 1930: Patient continues to be

256

paranoid and delusional. As her father, Henry Cartwright, stated in his letter, she continues to believe she is in love with a man named Bruno. Her father has assured me this man does not exist. Any attempt to force patient to face reality has failed.

June 1, 1930: Patient caused disturbance while working in the kitchen. She was knocked unconscious and later presented with severe stomach pains. Head trauma was not life threatening. Several hours later, patient gave birth to a healthy, albeit underweight, female infant. Father unknown.

Izzy's heart thumped like a boulder in her chest. She could hardly believe what she was reading. Clara and Bruno had a daughter! And Clara's father had told her doctor that Bruno didn't exist! Izzy couldn't imagine a father sending his daughter to an insane asylum because she was in love with someone he didn't approve of. Her mind raced, wondering what had happened to the baby. Was the newborn even strong enough to survive? Were children kept at Willard? She pictured two markers in the Willard cemetery, mother and daughter side by side for eternity, never having the chance to live a normal life. Her eyes flooded. She tried to think of another alternative, but nothing came to her.

Izzy flipped through the pages, looking for something that would tell her more. There were more entries about delusions and paranoia and hallucinations. Eventually, the entries got further and further apart, mainly chronicling Clara's physical health and how she was getting along with the other patients. There were chart entries in a dozen different scripts, medication logs, lists of initials to signify doses given. Izzy flipped to the last pages, looking for a postmortem report or a certificate of death. There were none to be found.

She wondered if Bruno had any idea where Clara was all those years. Did he know he had a daughter? Did he forget about Clara and move on? Then Izzy remembered the envelopes in Clara's trunk, dozens of letters to Bruno that were never mailed. She closed the chart and looked at Clara's picture.

I'll find out what happened to your daughter, Izzy thought. *And if by some miracle she's alive, I'll give her your journal and the pictures of you and Bruno. I'll tell her how much you loved her and that she doesn't have to be afraid. I'll tell her the truth about you.*

CHAPTER 12

CLARA

Chapin Hall Infirmary
September 1930

Outside the infirmary room window, the leaves on the trees were starting to turn and the sun shimmered like a thousand splintered mirrors on Seneca Lake. If Clara's estimates were right, she'd spent nearly four months in the room in Chapin Hall, watching gray sheets of May rain give way to summer days of hazy sunshine, and Willard's vast lawns turn brown due to a long August heat wave. Three times a day her food was brought in, twice a day her chamber pot was emptied, and once a week a nurse accompanied her to the water closet so she could bathe. Other than that, she was being kept prisoner. But it was better than being on the ward.

Now, guessing it was nearing the second week of September and wondering how long she'd be allowed this relatively decent treatment, she sat in a cushioned metal chair in the rectangle of sunlight coming in through the grimy windows. As usual, the radiator sat silent, a cold iron block beneath the brick sills. According to the nurses, it was too early in the season to turn on the heat, even though the high-ceilinged room grew frigid at night and never got warm during the day. Clara had to wear her socks and sweater to bed.

Today, it looked warmer out by the lake than inside the room. She longed to push open the windows and let in some fresh air. She knew what the world outside felt like. The soft autumn breeze was balmy and the day smelled clean, a fertile combination of musty earth and dry leaves. She would have done anything to breathe in the outdoors. The infirmary was filled with the rank aroma of mildewed grout, peeling paint, urine, and disinfectant. Clara was certain she could taste the warm, coppery odor of blood and the bitter tang of death. She imagined her nose and lungs lined with dust and black mold, pink tissue struggling to breathe, airways clogged with infection and disease.

Her eyes flooded and she looked down at her daughter, Beatrice Elizabeth Moretti, sleeping in her arms. An overwhelming feeling of love and the desire to protect her pierced her heart. Would they ever be let out of Willard? To live free, in the sunshine and fresh air? This closed-up, stinking institution was no place to raise an infant. Musty hospital air filled with germs, medicine, and sickness couldn't be good for Beatrice's tiny pink lungs. Again, as it did several times a day, the cold hand of fear clutched Clara's heart and she nearly sobbed out loud.

"I'm so sorry you ended up here," she whispered. "It's my fault. I should have just married James. I could have said you were his and you would have had everything. But I didn't know. I didn't know my father would do this to me. I didn't know he would stop loving me."

Dr. Roach had told Clara he'd informed her parents about the baby, but there had been no reply. Clara imagined that the news she'd given birth to a bastard merely infuriated Henry further. From now on, she had the feeling, she and Beatrice were on their own. If they survived.

On Clara's weekly trip to the washroom, with Beatrice wrapped in a blanket and clutched to her chest, she overheard the doctors and nurses talking about tuberculosis, typhoid fever, cholera, and diphtheria. From what she could gather, the sickest patients were kept on another floor, isolated from the rest of the infirmary. But people were dying here every day, and there was a great deal of concern about controlling the infectious diseases. What would become of her and her child if they got sick? The nurses wanted to bathe and hold Beatrice, but Clara refused. Ever since the day after she gave birth, she wouldn't allow anyone to touch her baby, afraid they might be carrying germs. If anything happened to her daughter, there'd be no need for Clara to leave

Willard because she would, once and for all, lose her mind.

Now, Clara struggled to push her fears away. Hysteria and panic would be of no help. She had to keep her wits about her if she was going to survive. In place of fear, a hard mass of anger swirled in the pit of her stomach, growing bigger and colder with every breath. How could her parents do this to her? How could they just abandon her to doctors and nurses who knew nothing about what kind of person she really was? Was everyone just going to leave her and her daughter in this room, to lose their minds, to get sick, to rot away? She thought about her mother, wondering if it was possible for the maternal instinct to be missing in some women. What kind of mother doesn't care if she never sees or talks to her child again?

She thought about the day Beatrice was born, waking up after giving birth, blinking and becoming aware of bright light and two blurry figures standing over her. When her vision cleared, she saw Dr. Roach and a nurse looking down on her.

"Where's my baby?" she asked, panic plowing through her chest at heart-stopping speed, stealing the breath from her lungs. She tried to sit up and felt a quick pull of sharp pain, deep inside her abdomen. She ignored it, intent on finding out if her daughter was alive.

"Just lie still now," Dr. Roach said.

"Your baby is right here," the nurse said, putting her hand on a wooden crib. "It's a little girl and she's perfectly healthy."

The grip of panic left Clara's body and she exhaled, her thundering heart starting to slow. She pushed herself up on wobbly arms and looked over at her newborn daughter, who was wrapped in a white blanket and sound asleep. When Clara leaned back against the pillows, she winced. It felt like a knife was being plunged into her lower stomach.

"You must stay still," Dr. Roach said "You suffered quite a blow to the head. We think you'll be fine, but you need to stay in bed for the next few days."

"What's wrong with me?" she said, putting her hands over her abdomen.

"Dr. Slade performed a small procedure on you," Dr. Roach said, his voice calm. "It's nothing to worry about. You'll be good as new before you know it."

"What kind of procedure?" she said. "What did he do?"

Dr. Roach went to the end of the bed and lifted her chart from the footboard. "As a doctor," he said, taking a pen out of his lab coat pocket, "it's my responsibility to think of the public as a whole. If society is to prosper, we need to encourage those with good germ plasma to breed and to discourage those with bad germ plasma from having offspring. Sterilization is a common procedure in state asylums. It's our responsibility to keep the unfit from passing along the insanity gene."

A burning lump clogged Clara's throat. She thought of Bruno, how his eyes had sparkled when they talked about getting married and having children, how he wanted two boys and two girls.

"How dare you!" she cried.

Dr. Roach wrote something in her chart, then hung it on the end of her bed. "We'll talk later," he said. "When you've recovered."

"You had no right to make that decision for me!" she said, fighting the urge to get up and strangle him. "There's nothing wrong with me and you know it!"

He turned and started for the door, his polished shoes clacking on the tiled floor. Clara called after him. "This is Bruno's baby," she said, her voice catching. "Bruno exists, no matter what my father told you."

Dr. Roach turned at the door. "Like I said," he said. "We'll talk about this in a few days. At least you won't be getting into any more trouble. For now, you should rest."

Just then, the baby started fussing, mewling and whimpering, getting ready to wail. Dr. Roach left the room, closing the door behind him.

"Hush now," the nurse said to Clara. She went

over to the crib and picked up the newborn. The baby girl's face was bright red, her mouth open and howling. "You need to think about your daughter." The nurse pulled the blanket down to Clara's waist, laid the wailing baby in her arms, and pushed aside her nightgown with rough fingers, exposing Clara's swollen breast. Clara put a hand over her chest, her cheeks flushing with fury and humiliation. For the first time since she woke up, she realized her nipples were sore. While she had been unconscious, someone had been putting her baby to her breast. "She's a good eater," the nurse said.

Clara blinked and looked down at the newborn in her arms, her tiny face a blur through her tears, and forgot all about the nurse standing over her. Her daughter's cheeks were pink and soft, like the underbelly of a lamb, her eyelashes long and dark, sweeping from her lids just like Bruno's. Clara touched her daughter's small, gauzy hand, and the baby wrapped her tiny fingers around hers. The infant whimpered and shuddered, her soft, pink mouth searching for Clara's nipple. Once she found it and latched on, she quieted and closed her puffy eyes. Like the ebb and flow of the tide, Clara's head and stomach ached in powerful waves, cresting and ebbing in perfect rhythm with the pull and swallow on her breast. She kissed her daughter's forehead and hung her head, shoulders convulsing as overwhelming love and sorrow threatened to burst her heart.

Now, sitting in the warm shaft of sunlight coming in through the infirmary room window, Clara pressed her fingers into the thin, hard line on her lower abdomen and a hollow wave of grief washed through her. The stitches had been taken out months ago, but the spot was still tender, her fury over what the doctors had done without her consent, raw and bleeding. She ran her fingertips along Beatrice's soft cheek, trying to ignore the shadows of bars lining her pale skin. Clara thought of her own mother, holding Clara as an infant, and wondered if Ruth had felt the same overwhelming love toward her small, defenseless daughter. She wondered how a woman could give birth to a baby and then, once the baby was grown, not care if they ever spoke again? She wondered how a mother could be indifferent to the fact that her daughter had been locked away, abused and drugged and sterilized. How could a mother not want to find out if her child was cold or hungry or afraid? It was incomprehensible.

Every day, Clara fell in love with Beatrice more and more, her heart bursting with such fierce affection it was almost painful. She couldn't imagine feeling any different. During the long, lonely months inside the dim hospital room, Beatrice had lain beside Clara on the bed, looking up at her with curious eyes as Clara told her about the sparrows and robins perched on the branches outside. Beatrice listened intently, cooing or quiet in the appropriate places, while Clara made up stories about castles and princes and told her about the lake and the grass and trees. Beatrice's chocolate eyes widened as if she understood every word when Clara described Bruno, the first time they met, and what a wonderful father he would be if they were ever released.

To Clara's surprise, and for reasons she didn't understand, Dr. Roach had grown more attentive than ever. He came to Clara's room for weekly sessions, taking time at the end of every visit to ask how the baby was doing and if she seemed healthy and strong. At their last session, Clara had stiffened when Dr. Roach reached into the crib and pulled the edge of the blanket back, as if he wanted to get a better look. Clara picked up her daughter and moved toward the window.

"Please stay away from her," Clara said. "I don't want anyone touching her."

"But I'm her doctor," Dr. Roach said. "There's no need to worry. I only want what's best."

"She doesn't need a doctor!" Clara said. "And if you really want what's best, you'll let us out of this place!"

"I can't, in good conscience, release either of you," he said. "You're not well, Clara. And until I determine otherwise . . ."

"You'll what?" Clara interrupted. "Keep us locked up in this room forever?"

"No," he said. "I'm waiting to hear from your father, and then I'll . . ."

Clara's breath caught in her throat. "My father?" she said. "I thought you hadn't heard from him since you told him about the baby? Did you tell him I wouldn't ask for a penny? That all I want is my freedom?"

Dr. Roach shook his head, his lips pressing together. "No, no," he said, waving a dismissive hand in the air. "I haven't heard anything."

"There's something you're not telling me," she said. "What is it?"

"Your father might need more time to process the fact that he has a grandchild," he said. "I'm sure it came as quite a shock, especially considering we don't know who the father is."

"Bruno is Beatrice's father," she said, her eyes burning. "Just ask my father."

"I did," Dr. Roach said, heading for the door. "And his answer will determine what happens next. If he answers at all."

Every night since, Clara prayed her father would tell Dr. Roach the truth. What reason would he have for wanting her to stay at Willard any longer? Marrying James Gallagher was out of the question now. All her father had to do was tell Dr. Roach that Bruno was real and she would be free. Was that asking too much?

Now, she buried her nose in Beatrice's thick hair—the same chestnut brown and wavy texture as Bruno's—and breathed in her innocent baby smell, willing them both to be strong. Beatrice had been unusually fussy over the last few days, and Clara wondered if it was because she needed to start on solid foods. Growing up, Clara hadn't spent any time around babies, and Ruth certainly hadn't passed down any maternal wisdom. But Clara knew that at some point, breast milk wouldn't be enough. Clara asked the nurses what they thought, but they just shrugged or said they would look into getting something suitable.

To her surprise, her meals in the infirmary were comparable to the provisions at the Long Island Home; eggs and toast for breakfast, ham and cheese sandwiches with fruit for lunch, and either chicken or pork with a roll and a side of beans, corn, or peas for dinner. When she mentioned it to one of the nurses, she was even more surprised to hear that Dr. Roach had ordered the meals so she would have enough milk to nourish the baby. But despite her balanced diet, her breast milk was getting thin. There wasn't enough to keep a growing baby satisfied.

Shortly after Clara gave birth, the nurses had managed to come up with cloth diapers and three infant nightgowns. The nightgowns had been mended and were thin at the elbows, but they were better than the hospital gowns Clara had been using to swaddle Beatrice. Because of that early kindness, Clara held out hope that the nurses would find suitable foods for a growing baby; rice cereal or strained fruits, or, at the very least, cows' milk.

Just then, she heard the key in the infirmary room door. She stood and turned, holding Beatrice in her arms, wondering who would be coming to her room at this hour. It was too early for lunch to be delivered, and she didn't have another appointment with Dr. Roach until the end of the week. Could it be that her father had finally answered Dr. Roach's letter? Clara held her breath, watching the door swing open.

A nurse entered and stepped aside, holding the edge of the door. Clara recognized her as one of the nurses who had brought in baby nightgowns and cloth diapers. She had smiled and cooed at Beatrice, telling Clara she had a beautiful baby. Now, the nurse kept her eyes on the floor, as if avoiding Clara's gaze. Dr. Slade and a woman in civilian clothing walked into the room, their faces set. The woman was wearing a long, wool coat and a green bucket hat, strands of auburn hair peeking out from beneath the low brim. With a pink blanket draped over one arm, she looked around with her mouth pursed, wrinkles lining her upper lip like marks on a ruler. Two orderlies followed Dr. Slade and the woman inside, then closed the door behind them. Clara couldn't understand why Dr. Slade was there. It had been weeks since he'd been in to check on her.

"What's going on?" she said.

"This is Miss Mason," Dr. Slade said, his face void of emotion. He and the woman moved across the room toward Clara. "She's from the Children's Aid Society."

Miss Mason gave Clara a quick nod, and then her eyes fell to Beatrice. The orderlies remained by the entrance, alert and watching. The nurse kept her head down, her hand clasped at her waist as she stared at the floor. Something was wrong. Clara edged backward, Beatrice clutched to her breasts, her heart racing.

"What do you want?" she said.

"This is no place for a baby," Miss Mason said. "I promise I'll find her a good home."

Agony seized Clara's chest, as if a giant hand had reached into her rib cage and yanked out her heart. Her breath came in short, shallow gasps and her stomach twisted in on itself, a writhing coil of pain nearly bending her over.

"No!" she cried. "She's mine! You can't take her!" She moved backward until she hit the wall next to the window, her legs like water, her arms like ice. She started to gag, certain she was going to throw up.

Dr. Slade and Miss Mason came around the bed, moving closer and closer. Dr. Slade reached for Clara's arm. Miss Mason draped the blanket over the footboard and reached for Beatrice.

"No!" Clara shouted. She darted sideways and

escaped their grasp, hurrying toward the far corner of the room. The orderlies left their post and started toward her, their mouths set. Dr. Slade and Miss Mason followed Clara and herded her into a corner, their arms outstretched as if they were closing in on a wild animal.

"Just give us the baby," Miss Mason said. "You don't want to drop her, do you?"

"Get away from us!" Clara screamed. "I won't let you take her!"

Dr. Slade leapt forward and grabbed Clara by the arm with both hands, grunting with the effort. Miss Mason reached for Beatrice, her rough hands trying to pry the baby from Clara's grasp. Clara shoved her away and Miss Mason stumbled backward, arms circling, eyes wide. Beatrice woke up and started to wail, her face crumpled and red. Miss Mason recovered and moved forward again, her hands up. Clara twisted and turned, trying to escape Dr. Slade's strong grasp. She kicked him in the shins. He cursed and tightened his grip, pushing his thick fingers into her muscles. Before Clara knew what was happening, the orderlies were on top of her, one behind holding her upper arms, the other in front so she wouldn't drop the baby. Miss Mason forced her hands beneath Beatrice.

Clara pulled her arm free and punched Miss Mason in the mouth. Miss Mason touched her lower lip and drew her hand away, wide eyes staring at the blood on her fingertips. The orderlies yanked Clara's arm behind her back. Miss Mason glared at her and wiped her mouth, smearing blood across her chin. Clara held Beatrice to her chest with one hand, thrashing and writhing, trying to break free. It was no use. The orderlies were too strong.

"No!" she screamed, her throat raw. "Please! You can't take my baby!"

"We can and we will," Miss Mason said. With the help of Dr. Slade, Miss Mason pulled Beatrice from Clara's grasp, a smug smile on her face. With every ounce of strength she had left, Clara launched forward and broke free of the orderlies. She dug her fingernails in Miss Mason's cheeks and reached for her daughter. Miss Mason screamed, splayed fingers flying to her face. Clara clutched Beatrice to her chest and turned to make a run for it, but the orderlies grabbed her by the shoulders. Dr. Slade pried Beatrice from Clara's arms, his face twisting with determination.

"No," Clara said, sobbing. "Please. Don't take her."

"I'm sorry," Dr. Slade said. "Someday you'll realize it's for the best."

The nurse used a towel to blot Miss Mason's cheek, her eyes brimming. Miss Mason snatched the towel out of the nurse's hand and wiped her face, then picked up the blanket and spread it out over the bed. Dr. Slade handed Beatrice to Miss

Mason, supporting her small, dark-haired head with one hand. Miss Mason laid Beatrice on the bed, wrapped the blanket around her kicking legs, then lifted her up, cradling the wailing baby in her arms.

"Clearly you've made the right decision," she said to Dr. Slade. "This woman is not fit to be a mother." Dr. Slade nodded, still trying to catch his breath.

"Nooooo!" Clara screamed until she tasted blood in the back of her throat. She thrashed and kicked, fighting to break free from the orderlies with everything she had. Miss Mason started toward the door and Clara sagged to the floor, every muscle and bone aching with agony and grief. The orderlies pushed her down all the way, her cheek hitting the cold tiles with a bone-jarring thud. She felt a sting on her arm and turned her head toward the exit. The last thing she saw was Miss Mason walking out the door with her daughter in her arms, the pink blanket hanging down one side of her wool coat. Beatrice was screaming.

Clara turned her head on the stiff pillow, the gray light of early morning filtering in through a barred window. She could see a stand of cedar trees, and a man in rubber boots walking along a road with a shovel thrown over his shoulder. Then Clara heard someone scream. She sat up and looked around the room. Half a dozen women sat on filthy metal beds, their legs chained to the footboards. Clara looked down. There was a chain around her ankle. She was in the Rookie Pest House.

CHAPTER 13

IZZY

On a cool, clear Saturday night in early October, the full moon hung in a cobalt sky, a blue-speckled globe surrounded by a billion pinpricks of light. Wearing jeans, sneakers, and hoodie, Izzy rode in the leather passenger seat of Alex's Beamer, trying not to feel guilty about lying to Peg and Harry again. First, she didn't tell them that Ethan was the one who took the journal, and now this. Granted, it was only a little white lie; that she was staying at Alex's when she was really camping with seniors from Lakeshore and nearby Romulus Central. But even that small fib made her feel awful. Peg and Harry had been so good to her.

Alex drummed her fingers on the steering wheel, singing along with "You Oughta Know" by Alanis Morissette blaring from the radio. When Alex turned off the two-lane highway onto a narrow dirt road, Izzy's chest tightened. She still wasn't sure this was a good idea. Alex slowed the car on the potholed road, turning the radio down when they entered a dark, leafy tunnel formed by low trees, ducking in her seat when a branch scraped along the car roof. The headlights bounced along the rutted gravel, catching small, glowing eyes in the underbrush.

"Are you sure this is the right way?" Izzy asked.

"Yeah," Alex said. "We have parties down here all the time. No one ever checks this area. It's state land, part of the old Willard Asylum."

Izzy swallowed. This most definitely was a mistake. "I don't think I should have come," she said, peering into the woods. "With what happened with Shannon and everything. I don't want there to be any trouble."

"There's going to be so many people here you won't even know she's around. Just ignore her."

"What if she doesn't ignore me?"

"You'll be with me and my friends from Romulus. They won't put up with Shannon's shit either. You'll be fine."

"I don't know . . ."

"Will you relax and live a little? This is your senior year! You gotta get crazy while you can!"

No thanks, Izzy thought. *That's exactly what I'm trying NOT to do.* At the end of the dirt road they came to a grassy clearing full of cars and trucks and motorcycles. Izzy bit down on her lip.

Through the trees on the other side of the parking area she could see a group of kids drinking and smoking and dancing around a huge bonfire on the shore. Red sparks shot into the night sky, like fireflies spinning out of control. In the background, Seneca Lake loomed like a giant black bowl, the full moon reflecting off its surface in a wide, wavering stripe. Izzy remembered reading somewhere that the word "lunatic" originated from the idea that the rays of the moon could adversely affect people's minds. Hopefully, that wouldn't be the case tonight.

Alex parked and they got out of the Beamer, pulling their duffel bags, blankets, and tent from the backseat. The thumping bass of loud music beat like someone else's heart inside Izzy's chest. A cool breeze carried the not unpleasant smell of fire and burning wood, decaying fish and wet weeds, cold water in an iron cup.

Izzy grabbed her extra jacket, threw her duffel bag over her shoulder, and followed Alex toward the other side of the parking area. They made their way along a wooden boardwalk over a wet, marshy swamp, then followed a winding path through gangly saplings and thin stretches of sand until they came to the shoreline. Dozens of kids gathered on the beach, standing or sitting in camp chairs around the bonfire, setting up tents, congregating on blankets, eating pizza and chips, smoking pot and drinking beer. One group sat around a hookah while another played volleyball and another passed around a bottle of Jack Daniel's. Someone had pulled their Pontiac Sunfire onto the sand and opened the trunk, the thumping stereo speakers vibrating the entire car. The party had started at three in the afternoon, but Izzy and Alex were late because they'd had to work.

"Let's set up over there," Alex said, pointing to an empty spot near the sloping edge of a grass-covered dune. Izzy followed Alex through the crowd, searching faces for people she recognized, wondering if anyone would ask what the hell she was doing there. She saw a guy doing a handstand while Luke and Josh held him up by his legs and poured beer into a funnel, a hose running into the guy's mouth. A crowd gathered, chanting, "Go, go, go!" while the upside-down guy tried his best to swallow the beer without spilling it.

Izzy noticed a few couples sitting near the fire, holding hands and making out. When she saw Ethan and Shannon wrapped in a blanket, talking and laughing with Crystal and her boyfriend, Dave, she looked away.

"I guess the rumors aren't true, after all," Alex said, dropping her bag on the sand. "Not yet, anyway."

"What rumors?"

Alex nodded toward Ethan and Shannon. "Everyone's saying Ethan is going to break up with Shannon so he can ask you out," she said.

Izzy felt blood rush to her cheeks. "That's not going to happen."

"What? He's not going to break up with her, or he's not going to ask you out?"

"Neither."

"Are you telling me you're not interested?" Alex said, grinning. She knelt down to unroll their tent.

"I'm not. Least of all because I don't need the school bully coming after me."

"So if it wasn't for Shannon, you'd be interested?"

"That's not what I said."

"Oh, I get it. You've still got a boyfriend from your old school."

Izzy shook her head. "I'm just concentrating on getting through this year, that's all. I need to figure out what I'm doing after I turn eighteen. I don't need some stupid relationship messing up my life."

"Uh-huh," Alex said.

Just then, a group of girls and guys came over carrying blankets, a tent, duffel bags, and a cooler. The guys set down the cooler and went to work pitching the tent while the girls hugged Alex. Alex made introductions to Izzy. "This is Kim and Jackie from Lakeshore." She gestured toward the boys. "Chris is from Lakeshore, and Fin and Turtle are from Romulus."

"Hey," Izzy said, smiling. Jackie reached into the cooler and handed Izzy and Alex a wine cooler. She was tall and slender, her sandy hair in long braids, her skin smooth and tanned. She looked straight out of a Coppertone commercial. Kim was short and chubby, with auburn hair and thick glasses. The guys stopped working, grabbed some beer, and joined the girls.

"Did Alex tell you why they call Turtle 'Turtle'?" Fin asked Izzy.

Izzy shook her head and Turtle smacked Fin on the arm. "Shut the hell up!" he said.

Fin pointed to his crotch. "Because it looks like a baby turtle head poking out."

Everyone laughed and Turtle jumped on Fin's back, trying to wrestle him to the sand.

"Don't pay any attention to them," Jackie said to Izzy. "They're idiots."

"Uh-oh," Alex said. She was looking past Izzy, toward the bonfire. Jackie and Kim followed Alex's gaze, their brows lifting in surprise. Izzy turned to look and her heart started doing double-time. Ethan, Shannon, Josh, Crystal, and Dave were headed toward them. Izzy looked at Alex, wondering what to do. Alex shrugged. When Ethan and the others reached them, the guys mock-punched each other, held up their beers, and said cheers. Izzy kept her eyes on the ground.

Shannon and Crystal said hi to the group, their words practically dripping with sugar. Alex rolled her eyes. Jackie, Kim, and the guys welcomed everyone into the circle, offering beer and wine coolers. The guys started talking about cars and football while the girls talked about how many pillows they brought and lying out in the sun the next morning. Izzy kept her eyes on Alex, Kim, and Jackie. Then someone touched her arm and she jumped. It was Shannon.

"Can I talk to you?" she said, her voice syrupy. "Alone?"

Izzy took a long swallow of her wine cooler and glanced at Alex, who was watching and frowning. Shannon looked at Izzy with sad eyes, her lower lip nearly curling under.

"What do you want to talk to her about?" Alex said in a loud voice.

Ethan stopped joking with Fin and Dave and looked over to see what was going on. He moved closer, his face filled with concern. "Everything okay?" he said. Shannon took his hand. Crystal tugged on Dave's sweatshirt and told him to be quiet. One by one, everyone stopped talking. Izzy had the unsettling feeling that they were getting ready to perform a ritual on the beach and she was about to become the sacrifice.

"Okay, fine," Shannon said, rolling her eyes. "I'll just say it right here, in front of everyone."

"This should be interesting," Alex muttered.

"I know I've been a bitch and I'm sorry," Shannon said. "Really. I mean it. This is our senior year and I want to make good memories, not bad ones. I was going to start by apologizing to Izzy. But I know I need to apologize to you too, Alex."

Alex laughed. "You really think it's going to be that easy?" she said. "You've been a lot worse than a bitch to me, and to a lot of other people too."

"Why don't you just listen to what she has to say?" Crystal snarled.

"I'm listening, aren't I?" Alex said.

"It's okay, Crystal," Shannon said. Then, as if suddenly chilled, she rubbed her arms and moved closer to Ethan. Ethan took off his jacket and wrapped it around her. She smiled and kissed him on the cheek, then glanced at Alex and Izzy, her chin trembling. It felt like a show, put on for everyone's benefit.

"This is hard for me to say," Shannon said. "But Alex is right. I've been worse than a bitch. I've been a mean, self-centered, horrible person. I've treated people like shit and I'm sorry. There's no excuse."

"So," Alex said, her voice filled with doubt. "After years of being terrorized by you, we're supposed to believe you've suddenly seen the error of your ways? We're supposed to just swallow your shit and say, 'mmm, good cook'?"

Shannon stared at her, color mounting in her cheeks. "I know it's a lot to ask," she said. "But all these years, hearing what everyone was saying about my father and my mother." She dropped her eyes. "I know you think my heart is made of stone. But it's not. Hearing people talk about my family hurts. I guess I just . . . I don't know. I wanted to lash out and hurt people back. I know it was wrong."

Izzy heard words coming out of her mouth before she could stop them. "People are going to talk," she said. "There's really nothing you can do about it. Just ignore them."

Shannon tilted her head and smiled at Izzy, like a little girl seeing a puppy in a pet shop window. "See," she said. "I knew Izzy would understand. I'm sorry about telling the class your mother is in jail." Izzy winced and glanced at Alex's friends, waiting for their reaction.

"Oh my God, you just did it again!" Alex said, her voice high. "Izzy just met my friends and you just blurt shit out in front of everyone!"

Shannon put a hand over her mouth. "Oops," she said. "I didn't do it on purpose! Not this time, really!"

Alex shook her head. "I don't know," she said. "It seems like you used this opportunity to embarrass Izzy again."

"No," Shannon said. "I didn't. Really. Come on. You have to give me a chance. It's going to take time to change. I'm really sorry, Izzy."

Shannon stared at Izzy with brimming eyes. Beside her, Ethan studied the beer in his hand, the sand, Fin and Turtle, anything but Izzy. Shannon's words, the tone of her voice, her posture, the way her lip trembled when she talked, all of it seemed genuine. And yet, Izzy could have sworn she saw the hot flash of fury still dancing in Shannon's eyes. But for tonight at least, she decided to play along.

"I can't speak for everyone," she said. "But I'm willing to give you another chance." In truth, she was relieved. Even if Shannon returned to her evil ways when they went back to school on Monday, maybe for one night, Izzy could relax, enjoy herself, and make some new friends.

"Seriously?" Alex said to Izzy. "You're going to forgive her, just like that?"

"It's okay, Alex," Shannon said. "I know I've treated you worse than anyone. You have every reason never to speak to me again. You don't have to forgive me if you can't find it in your heart. But I hope we can at least be civil to each other until graduation."

Everyone stared at Alex, waiting for her reaction. Izzy shrugged, hoping Alex wasn't pissed at her for giving in so easily.

Finally, Alex rolled her eyes. "Whatever," she said. "I'm going to give you another chance because I'm sick of all the fighting and back-stabbing. But I'm warning you, don't make a fool out of me. I won't forgive you again."

"I won't!" Shannon said. She started toward Alex, arms outstretched, but Alex stepped back, holding up a hand. Shannon stopped short. "It's okay," she said, smiling. "I get it. We're not there yet." She held her wine cooler out at arm's length. "Can we at least drink to starting over?"

"Sure," Alex said, briefly raising her wine cooler.

After everyone took a drink, Shannon said, "Our tent is over by that stand of birch trees. After you get settled in, why don't you come over?"

"We'll see," Alex said.

Shannon looked at Izzy. "Will you come hang out for a little while?" she said.

Izzy shrugged. "Sure," she said.

"Great!" Shannon said, smiling. "Josh brought firecrackers. We'll wait for you before we light them off!" She kissed Ethan and pulled him away, little clouds of sand flicking from the back of her flip-flops as she hurried toward the bonfire. Halfway there, she lifted her drink in the air and shouted, "Let's paaaarty!"

Fin and the guys went back to setting up their tents while Jackie and Kim set up chairs and blankets. Izzy knelt in the sand to help Alex with their tent.

"What the hell was that all about?" she said in a low voice, so the others couldn't hear.

"I have no idea," Alex said. "But you know that old saying, keep your friends close but keep your enemies closer?"

"You think that's what she's trying to do?" Izzy said.

"Most definitely," Alex said. "Which means you need to be extra careful."

"Me?" Izzy said. "Why?"

"Because that, my naïve friend, was the first time she's apologized to anyone. Ever. It just about killed her. She must be really threatened by you."

Izzy's stomach dropped. She'd hoped Shannon's apology was sincere, that she really was going to turn over a new leaf. Izzy should have known better. Nothing was ever that easy.

By midnight, about half the seniors were passed out in the sand, in their tents, or sitting around discussing politics and religion, their voices loud, their words slurring. Alex, Izzy, Jackie, and about a dozen others, including Shannon and Ethan, were sitting on pieces of driftwood around the dying bonfire. Izzy poked the orange, pulsating embers with the end of a long stick, breaking charred bits and pieces off the burning logs while Alex and Fin had a heated debate about global warming. The night had gone better than Izzy had hoped. She'd actually relaxed and laughed; throwing firecrackers into the bonfire and watching some of the guys and girls play chicken in the lake. She was just getting ready to tell Alex that she was going back to the tent when Josh stood and lumbered around the bonfire toward her. She still marveled at his gigantic size and his tiny voice. He was the star linebacker on the football team and she couldn't help chuckling when she thought about him cheering, "Go, team!" out on the field.

"Hey, want some company?" he said, looking down at her. He was barefoot and shirtless, his broad chest covered with ginger-colored hair.

Izzy swore under her breath. "Actually, I'm getting ready to turn in," she said.

He ignored her and folded his thick legs beneath him, like a giant bullfrog, perching himself beside her on the log. His hip touched hers and she scooted sideways.

"So how do you like living on the beautiful shores of Seneca Lake?" he said. He sat on the driftwood with his arms resting on his knees, a beer bottle in one beefy, freckled hand.

Izzy kept her eyes on the glowing embers. "It's okay."

"I'm sure things will be easier now that you and Shannon are friends."

She looked at him. His eyes were glazed and his face was crimson, flushed red from too much sun and alcohol. But he didn't appear drunk. Izzy imagined he could drink a case of beer and never feel a thing. "Let's hope so," she said. "How long have you and Shannon been friends?"

Josh's brow creased, a quick flash of uncertainty passing over his features. Then the confusion was gone and he smiled. "Oh, she and I go way back," he said. "We've been best friends since kindergarten. We used to kiss behind the piano."

"Does Ethan know you used to make out with his girlfriend?" Izzy said. It was a lame attempt at being funny, but she couldn't think of anything else to say. Then again, maybe she was just trying to find out more about Ethan and Shannon.

Josh made a *pshaw* motion with one hand. "Ethan and me are buddies. He knows me and Shannon used to be best friends."

"Used to be?"

Josh skewed his thick lips to one side, as if rethinking what he'd said. "She's dating Ethan now. He's her best friend. We're still friends though."

"Oh," Izzy said. Suddenly she felt Josh's heavy arm on her shoulders. Her nostrils filled with the bitter odor of sweat and beer.

"Maybe you and me can be best friends," he said.

"Um," Izzy said. She shrugged his arm from her shoulders and stood. "I think I'm going to hit the hay."

Josh grabbed her arm, his giant hand like a warm, sweaty muff around her wrist. "Sit back down," he said, tugging. "Can't we just talk for a few minutes? Get to know each other a little better?"

She pulled away. "Sorry," she said. "But I'm tired and going to bed."

Just then, Dave stood, went over to the car, and turned off the stereo. "Hey, everybody!" he shouted, coming back to the dying fire. "It's midnight! You know what that means!"

Josh stood and pumped his fist in the air. "Yes!" he shouted. "Let's do this!" A couple dozen other kids jumped to their feet, talking excitedly and grabbing flashlights and beer. On the other side of the dying fire, Ethan stood and tested his flashlight. Shannon and Crystal put on their hoodies and waited with excited smiles, legs wiggling in anticipation.

"Let's do what?" Izzy asked him.

"We're going to check out Willard State!" Josh said. He finished the rest of his beer and threw the bottle in the embers. "Come on! I brought some extra flashlights."

Izzy's stomach started to churn. Beside her, Fin and Alex stood, folding the blanket they had wrapped around their shoulders.

"You're not going, are you?" Izzy asked Alex.

"Hell yes!" Alex said, her eyes shining. "I love ghosts and séances and all that shit. It's going to be awesome! We used to follow the shoreline over to Willard to go inside the old boathouse. It was creepy as hell but we never saw anything. Now we can explore *all* the buildings!"

"Well, you have fun," Izzy said. "I'm going to stay here and get some sleep."

"Oh, come on," Alex said. "Don't be a party pooper! It's only about a mile-and-a-half walk."

"I'm not worried about the walk," Izzy said.

Alex tilted her head. "Come on. If it gets to be too much we'll come back. I promise."

"If she doesn't want to go," Josh said, "she doesn't have to. I'll stay here and keep her company." He put his arm around Izzy again, pulling her toward his plump, sweaty body. Izzy peeled his fingers from her upper arm and pulled out of his grasp.

"On second thought," she said to Alex. "Maybe the walk will do me good."

Everyone put on shoes and shirts and the seniors made their way along the shoreline, flashlights bobbing, illuminating rocks and sky and sand and forest. The full moon reflected off the lake, giving the water a bluish, otherworldly glow. Luke and Josh led the way, picking the easiest route around overturned trees and car-sized boulders, carrying some of the girls over marshy areas so their feet wouldn't get wet. When Willard's boathouse and dock came into view, Luke stopped and turned to face everyone.

"Let's split up into groups," he said. "That way we can cover more territory. If anyone sees anything, we'll regroup and check it out together. A couple of my friends went down in the tunnels below Chapin Hall and found the morgue. They saw what looked like a woman near the vault where they used to keep bodies."

Crystal and one of her friends squealed and hugged each other, giggling. Luke put a hand in the air to quiet them. "The woman's face was bloated and black," he said. "Like she'd been underwater or something. She opened her mouth, like she was screaming, and then she vanished."

"Oh my God!" one of the girls cried.

"Be quiet!" someone said.

"The doctors used to do electric shock therapy in the basement of Chapin Hall," Luke said. "In the forties there was a huge flood and a bunch of patients drowned down there. About fifty people, I guess. We think the woman was one of them."

"Bullshit!" one of the guys shouted.

"You can let me know how it goes," Jackie said to Alex. "I'm going back."

"Oh, come on," Alex said. "It's just for fun."

Jackie shook her head. "It's way too intense for me."

"I'll go with you," Izzy said.

"You both can't leave me!" Alex said. "Come on, Izzy. Please? You've got to stay."

Izzy groaned inside. "Okay," she said. If nothing else, maybe she could find something that would tell her more about Clara and her daughter.

"If anybody wants to go back," Josh said, "go ahead. The rest of us are going in. Now let's get this show on the road. Me, Bryan, Paul, and Ethan will be the team leaders. One group will go into the wards, one into the morgue below Chapin Hall, one into Hadley Hall, and one into the Rookie Pest House. Luke and Dave, how about we check out the morgue?"

"We're in," Dave said. He put his arm around Crystal, who grinned and nodded in agreement.

"Me too," Luke said.

"Awesome!" Josh said. He looked at Alex and Izzy. "You guys want to be in our group?"

Alex looked at Izzy. "It would be amazing to check out the morgue," she said.

Izzy shrugged. "I don't care which group I'm in," she said.

"Looks like we're in," Alex said to Josh.

"Got my group!" Josh announced.

Izzy clenched her jaw. Going inside Willard during the day was bad enough, but going into the morgue below Chapin Hall at night? And with some of Shannon's friends? It sounded like a really bad idea. But what was she supposed to do? If she tried to go back, Josh would probably offer to go with her. And she wasn't about to admit she was afraid. At least there was safety in numbers. The best thing to do was get it over with.

"Everyone, turn off your flashlights until we get up to the buildings," Josh said.

They trudged up the grassy incline toward the shuttered buildings of Willard State, moonlight and shadows sweeping across the vast grounds. When they reached Chapin Hall, everyone stopped and stared, shining their flashlights over barred windows and dark dormers. The huge Victorian looked ten times scarier at night. Izzy felt the first flicker of anxiety fluttering across her chest.

How the hell did she find herself here for the third time? And about to go into a morgue after midnight, no less?

"Oh my God," Crystal said. "That's the creepiest building I've ever seen!"

"I bet the morgue is creepier," Alex said, grinning.

Crystal gripped Dave's hand in hers. "Eek!" she said, bouncing from one foot to the other. "I'm so scared I feel like I'm going to pee my pants!"

On the decaying, potholed road in front of Chapin Hall, the teams split up, Ethan's team headed to the patient wards, Bryan's team headed to the Rookie Pest House, Paul's team headed to Hadley Hall, and Josh's team headed to the morgue.

Josh led the group around the wards to the back of Chapin Hall, the brick, two-story buildings going on for blocks, with numerous wings, extensions, and rooftop additions making it look like a hodgepodge of smaller buildings had been added as an afterthought. Piles of dead leaves slumped in the corners of the foundations and old birds' nests hung from the high eaves.

Behind Chapin Hall, Josh stopped at the bottom of a rusted fire escape. Like the fire escapes on the patient wards, the second floor exit and the steps leading to the ground were inside a wire cage. Izzy hadn't noticed before, but at the bottom of the stairs was another cage, large enough to hold a dozen or more people, with a wire door padlocked from the outside. If there had been a fire, the people inside could have gone out the door and down the steps, but they'd have to wait inside the cage for someone to let them out. Izzy shivered, realizing it was a preventive measure against escape.

Josh handed his flashlight to Izzy, telling her to shine it on the cage at the bottom of the fire escape. A vertical line had been cut along one edge of the steel-framed pen. "This is where my friends got in," he said.

He hooked his massive fingers through the diamond-shaped holes in the wire, peeled it open, and crawled inside. Everyone but Izzy followed. Luke, Dave, and Crystal hurried up the iron steps to the second-floor landing, their sneakers clanging on the metal, while Alex waited for Izzy. Josh knelt in the cage and reached out to help Izzy up. She ignored his outstretched hand and scrambled inside.

Dave swept his flashlight over the exit at the top of the fire escape. A piece of plywood covered the upper half of the door. "How do we get in?" he said.

"Hold on!" Josh said. "I've got this!"

Alex and Izzy waited at the bottom of the stairs while Josh hurried up the steps. He grabbed the bottom of the plywood and yanked it off the door, nails screeching. Behind the plywood was an empty window frame.

"Your huge ass won't fit through there!" Dave said, laughing.

"You want to make a bet?" Josh said. He turned sideways and shoved the upper half of his body through the opening, his feet flying in the air. Dave laughed, thinking Josh was stuck. Then Josh's hips and legs disappeared and there was a loud *thump-thump*. Then nothing.

Dave edged closer to the door, shining his flashlight in the window. "You okay, big guy?" he said, snickering.

Just then, Josh jumped up in the dark hall, his face contorted, his hands clawing at the air. "Let me ooouut!" he screamed. Everyone jumped.

Dave scrambled toward the opening, his face red, his nostrils flaring. "I'm gonna kill you!" he said, pushing himself inside.

One by one, everyone crawled through the opening. When everyone was through, Dave and Josh led them down a hall, moving slowly and shining their flashlights along the walls and floor. The rest of the group followed close behind, paint chips and plaster crunching beneath their feet. The high ceilings made it feel as if there was nothing above their heads, like the roof was gone, leaving a dark hole of black space. Grayish-green paint hung from the walls in ragged flaps, like crustaceans clinging to underwater wreckage. Moldy papers, plastic jugs, and pieces of cardboard littered the floor. The sound of water dripping echoed along the passageway.

Izzy looked at each closed doorway, hoping to

find a file or records room, trying to ignore the feeling that the doors were slowly opening after she passed. Alex walked beside her, her hand clamped on Izzy's elbow in a death grip. Up ahead, at the end of the hall, a tall doorway topped by a large archway led into a dark abyss.

"Oh my God!" Crystal screeched. "What is that?"

Everyone stopped. "What?" Josh said, his head whirling around.

"Up there!" Crystal said, pointing toward the end of the hall. Josh turned his flashlight on the doorway. On the other side, a seat and what looked like part of a wheel sat in the passageway, tilted to one side like a deformed dwarf.

"It's just a wheelchair!" Alex said.

"Jesus!" Dave said. "Don't do that again!"

Crystal exhaled. "Sorry," she said.

They started moving again. Then Dave and Josh stopped.

"What is it?" Luke said. "Why are we stopping?"

"I just heard something," Dave said.

"Me too," Josh said.

"What was it?" Crystal said.

"I don't know," Dave said. "It sounded like something moving in the next room. Like rustling or something."

"There's no door on the next room," Dave said.

"So?" Alex said.

"You go first," Josh said to her, gesturing with

his flashlight toward the black, empty entrance to his left.

Alex grabbed the flashlight, took a deep breath, and stepped in front of the entrance, shining the beam into the room. "Gross," she said, and went through the opening. Everyone followed.

Moonlight streamed in through the barred, filthy windows, casting long, striped shadows on the tile floor. Giant hunks of plaster hung down from the ceiling, exposing old lath and thick clots of black mold. Beneath the windows, the outer bricks showed through jagged holes above piles of dust and plasterboard. In the center of the room, a thick metal pole came out of the floor, a curved rod sprouting from one side in an elongated *S*. At the end of the curved rod, a blue plastic seat and buckle hung in the air like a carnival swing. Izzy's stomach twisted, thinking of the hundreds of tortured souls who had sat in that very chair and had who knows what done to them. To the left, a rusty pipeline and a half dozen porcelain tubs lined one enamel wall. The tubs were surrounded by metal frames and all but one were covered with a dirty, ripped canvas. The canvases were riveted to the metal frames, with a reinforced hole for the patient's head yawning on one end like an open mouth. Izzy shivered, wishing she'd tried harder to get out of coming.

"What the hell is this?" Luke said, sitting in the plastic seat attached to the pole. He pushed his feet on the floor and the seat spun around.

"I have no idea," Alex said. "But these tubs were used for ice water baths. They used to plunge the patients into freezing water and keep them there until they lost consciousness."

"Come on," Josh said. "I thought we came in here to find the morgue."

"Yeah," Dave said. "Let's go."

Izzy followed the group out the door, relieved to get out of the depressing room. At the end of the hall, they took a right, threading their way around wheelchairs, rolling carts, wooden crates marked Willard State, stained mattresses, and rusted gurneys. Eventually, they came to the top of a stairway. Izzy pulled the sleeve of her hoodie over her hand, grabbed the railing, and followed Alex down the steps. She didn't want to touch the railing, but it was better than falling, landing face-first at the bottom of the stairs on who knows what.

The first-floor halls were cluttered with broken wheelchairs, small tables, and vinyl-covered seats with belts and wheeled legs. Signs above doorways read Chronic Block, Acute Block, Epileptic Block, Sick and Infirm Block. The farther the group went inside the maze of halls, the more patient-room doors were missing. Izzy swung her flashlight into the dark entrances, illuminating metal beds, moldy boxes, plastic containers marked Soiled Linen, carts piled high with EKG machines, examining tables with stirrups. Izzy scanned the junk-filled spaces for filing cabinets, but didn't see any. She wondered if Clara had given birth to her daughter in one of these rooms. How horrible it must have been to deliver a small, innocent baby in this awful place.

At last, they found a sign that said Basement, with an arrow pointing to the right. They followed a short hallway to a service elevator and a set of double doors below a green sign that read Morgue. Josh pulled the doors open, a blast of cold air rushing past him, and started down the steps. Izzy, Luke, and Alex followed, with Dave and Crystal bringing up the rear. At the bottom, the group stopped. Izzy swallowed.

Wide cement tunnels led off in all directions, left, right, and straight ahead. Crusty, dripping pipes of various sizes traveled along the length of the ceilings, next to metal conduit used to house electrical wires. Every ten feet, a stone archway lined each passageway, making the tunnels look like corridors beneath a medieval castle. Izzy had the illusion she was standing between two mirrors, the reflection of the archway reflected a thousand times in every direction. She imagined getting lost and never finding her way out. On the archway straight ahead, a sign said Electroshock Treatment. On the archway to the left, a sign read Morgue. To the right of the staircase, a wide service elevator stood open, the rusty brass grate partly closed. A hospital bed with a broken wheel and a grungy, ripped sheet tilted against one elevator wall.

"That must be how they brought the bodies down," Alex said.

"Ewww," Crystal said.

Josh started down the hallway toward the morgue, his giant form nearly blocking out the flashlight beam that bounced along the floor in front of him. "This way," he said. Dave and Crystal followed.

"Wait!" Alex said. "Let's check out the room where they did shock treatments!"

Josh stopped and turned. "There's nothing down there," he said.

"Come on!" Dave said. "We're going to the morgue!" He sounded irritated. Izzy wondered why he was in such a hurry. Maybe he was using anger to hide his fear.

"I'm going to check it out," Alex said.

Josh grunted and lumbered toward them, reluctantly rejoining the group. "Let's make it quick," he said.

To the left of the tunnel after the fourth arch, they found the electroshock treatment room. The low-ceilinged space was filled with examination tables, rusty carts, and riveted metal boxes that looked like giant batteries, with black dials and wires coming out. Along the far wall, peeling medicine cabinets stood with half-open drawers spilling out wire coils, rubber mouth guards, and what looked like joysticks for a video game. Izzy walked along the walls, looking for filing cabinets or anything that seemed like it might hold paperwork. There was nothing.

"They must have shocked more than one person at a time," Dave said. "Kind of like a herd of cattle getting branded."

"Sure looks that way," Alex said. "You said there was a flood and people died in here?"

"Yeah," Josh said, rummaging through a drawer. He turned to look at her, shining his flashlight in her face.

Alex put up her hand, shielding her eyes. "Dude," she said. "You're blinding me!"

The flashlight beam fell. "Sorry," Josh said.

"This is so gross," Crystal said.

"I wonder if they did lobotomies here," Alex said.

"Come on," Dave said. "We're supposed to be exploring the morgue, not wasting time in here."

"Yeah," Izzy said. She felt like throwing up. "Let's get out of here."

As they made their way toward the morgue, the air grew even more damp and cold. Izzy shoved her hands in the pockets of her sweatshirt and pulled up her hood. Beside her, Crystal swatted the empty space above her head, terrified that a spiderweb would snag her hair or whisper across her face. Without warning, Josh came to a sudden halt, shining his flashlight into an open door on his left. Dave kept walking, then stopped and turned.

"Come on," he said. "We're almost there!"

Josh edged toward the open doorway. "What the hell is this?" he said, his voice filled with disgust.

Dave joined him. "Holy shit," he said. The two of them disappeared inside the room. Everyone followed.

The walls of the stone room were lined with iron cages made of two-inch thick metal, the bars riveted together in a crisscross pattern, like a loose basket weave. Inside the cages, metal cots were bolted to the floor and chains and cuffs hung from the wall.

"What is this place?" Crystal said.

"They kept people in these cages!" Josh said, laughing nervously.

"Maybe this is where they kept the violent patients," Alex said.

"It might be where they kept patients with tuberculosis or typhoid," Izzy said.

"This is so creepy!" Alex said. "No wonder Willard is haunted."

"Can we just go to the morgue and get this over with?" Izzy said, trying to keep her voice steady.

"Yeah," Josh said. "Let's go. We can come back here some other time."

The group filed out of the room and turned left. Finally, they saw a set of double doors with a faded metal sign that read Morgue in green letters. At the end of a tunnel, they could see another entryway, with broken windows in the upper half of the double doors. Muted moonlight filtered in through the grime-covered glass, like glowing blue eyes. Stack after stack of homemade coffins clambered up the walls near the doors, like piles of oversized books.

"Oh my God," Crystal said. "That is so gross!"

They edged through the double doors into the morgue, moving slowly as if afraid something waited on the other side. Dave and Josh shined their flashlights around the room. Along the farthest wall was a deep, three-basin sink, its porcelain counter filled with yellowed plastic jugs and filmy bottles. Garbage cans and moldy boxes littered the stained cement floor, along with a corroded necropsy tool cart and several broken folding chairs. Industrial lighting hung from the peeling ceiling over a stainless steel autopsy table. On both sides of the table, near the middle, were square drain holes, and on one end was a small basin with a black hose. Next to the table sat a large, wheeled vat with a rubber hose coming from the top. The metal side read Embalming Fluid.

In the far corner, a wooden body storage vault with six doors filled nearly a quarter of the room, its hinges and handles rusty and tarnished. Next to the vault sat a black, corroded motor used to power the refrigerated storage chamber. The top two doors of the vault looked relatively spotless, their wooden planks reflecting the beams of the flashlights. The four doors below were stained and streaked with what looked like black tar, as if something inside the top doors had rotted and melted, leaking down the front of the unit. A faint odor of formaldehyde, mold, and something that smelled like warm pennies hung in the air.

Izzy put her hand over her mouth, fighting the urge to run out of the room and outside, toward fresh air. Then she saw a two-drawer filing cabinet in the corner. She hurried over to it and pulled open the top drawer, shining her flashlight inside. A stack of folders slumped toward the back of the drawer, nearly gray beneath a thick layer of dust and spiderwebs. Alex came over to see what she was doing.

"What is it?" she said. "What did you find?"

Izzy handed her the flashlight. "Hold this," she said. Alex directed the light inside the cabinet while Izzy riffled through the folders, holding her breath. They were all empty. She opened the bottom drawer and found a haphazard stack of yellowed papers. Izzy picked up the top sheet and took the flashlight from Alex. It was a blank New York State Death Certificate.

"What are you looking for?" Alex said.

"We're working on a Willard project at the museum," Izzy said. "I'm just trying to see if I can find anything that will help."

"How would you explain that to your foster mom?" Alex said.

"I'll worry about that later," Izzy said.

Just then, Crystal appeared. "Come on," she said, taking Alex's arm and pulling her toward the autopsy table. "Let's see if we can get that lady to show up again. Everybody, get in a circle and we'll ask if she's here."

Izzy looked through the rest of the papers. The entire stack was nothing but blank death certificates.

"Hurry up," Alex said to her.

Izzy rolled her eyes and closed the cabinet.

"Everybody, get over here," Crystal said. "We're going to have a séance!"

"Awesome!" Dave said, hurrying over to Crystal's side. "Good idea, babe."

Luke pushed a soggy cardboard box from the autopsy table and said, "Hey, Josh, come over here and lie down. We'll give you a massage you'll never forget!"

Josh laughed and moved toward the storage vault. He opened one of the middle doors and shined his flashlight inside. The interior of the vault was pockmarked and full of mold. "I'll lie down on that," he said. "Right after you lie down in here." He rolled out a rusted slab, filling the room with the sound of screeching metal.

"How much will you give me?" Luke said.

"Five bucks," Josh said.

"I'll give you ten if you let us push you in and close the door," Dave said.

"Will you guys quit messing around!" Crystal said. "I thought we came here to see if this place was haunted!"

Josh came over to the table, leaving the door to the vault partway open. "Okay, okay," he said. "Don't get your panties in a bunch."

"Shut up, will you?" Crystal said. "This is serious." She pulled a small, fat candle from her jacket pocket, asked Dave for his lighter, and lit the short wick. Then she placed the candle in the center of the autopsy table, moving slowly and carefully so the flame wouldn't go out and her fingers wouldn't touch the stained surface. "Okay, come on," she said in a soft voice. "Everyone, stand around the table. And shut off your flashlights."

Everyone shut off their flashlights and edged closer. Izzy stood between Dave and Josh, her back toward the vault, her flashlight under her arm, her fists shoved in the pockets of her hoodie. Crystal took Dave's hand and reached for Alex's, the flickering flame casting dark shadows beneath her eyes.

"We have to be quiet," Crystal said. "And we have to hold hands." Alex bit her lip and took Crystal's and Luke's hands. Dave and Josh reached for Izzy's hands at the same time. For a second, she kept her hands in her pockets, then decided to play along. The sooner they got this silly séance over with, the sooner she could get out of here. Josh's hand felt like a soggy baseball glove. Her stomach turned. Then Luke and Josh realized they were next to each other.

"I'm not holding hands with a dude," Luke said.

"Me either," said Josh.

"Just do it!" Crystal said, glaring at them. "This won't work unless we take it seriously!"

"She's right," Alex said. "We have to hold hands."

"Why?" Izzy said. "What does it mean?"

"In case any of the spirits we bring forth are evil," Alex said. "If we're touching each other, the evil spirit can't attach itself to anyone."

"See?" Crystal said, grinning. "I told you. Now let's get this show on the road."

Josh rolled his eyes and held a hand out to Luke, who reluctantly touched the edges of Josh's fingers.

"If I hear any rumors going around about this, I'll—" Luke said.

"Our lips are sealed," Dave said, pretending to blow kisses in his direction.

Crystal stomped on Dave's foot. "Did you forget what we came here for?" she said.

Dave's face contorted in pain. "Jesus!" he said. "Okay, okay!"

"Everyone ready?" Crystal said, directing her attention particularly to Josh and Luke. Josh and

Luke nodded, doing their best to stop smirking. Crystal waited another second or two, then closed her eyes. "Is there anyone here with us?" she said, her voice hushed and reverent. One of the guys made a small, snorting sound, as if trying to suppress his laughter. "We're not here to cause you harm," Crystal continued.

"If there is anyone here with us," Alex said, "can you give us a sign?"

Izzy opened her eyes to look at Alex, surprised to hear her speaking. Her eyes were closed, her head down. Beside her, Luke stood with his shoulders hunched, his face in knots as if he expected to be hit or touched at any second. Izzy closed her eyes again. She wondered what would happen if they called Clara's name. She thought about suggesting it, then changed her mind. Everyone would ask questions about how she knew a patient's name. Right now, she just wanted to get this over with.

"We invite you to move among us," Crystal said. "You can touch our hair, knock on the walls, anything to let us know you're here."

"If someone touches me, I'm outta here!" Luke said.

"Shhh!" Crystal said. She took a long, deep breath, then let it out slowly, waiting. Then she said, "Please give us a sign that you're with us. We want to understand why you're still here, trapped inside this asylum."

"We can help you find peace," Alex said. "To move on from this place and join your loved ones who have already crossed over."

Just then, a soft *thud-thud* sounded behind Izzy. Alex made a high-pitched squeak, as if trying to suppress a scream.

"Shhh . . ." Crystal whispered. "It's okay. Just relax. If that was you, can you make that noise again?"

Thud-thud.

Josh's sweaty hand tightened around Izzy's. She wiggled her fingers, trying to loosen his grip. It was no use.

"We hear you," Crystal said.

"Were you a patient here?" Alex said. "Were you locked up in this horrible place?"

Thud-thud. Thud-thud.

Izzy's heartbeat quickened. *Is this for real?* She'd come in this awful place to humor Alex, not to get scared shitless. The only thing worse than being in an old insane asylum would be seeing the ghosts of former patients.

"Are you here alone?" Alex said. "Are there others with you?"

"Can you make a different noise?" Crystal said. "Something to let us know it's really you?"

Just then, Izzy heard three knocks behind her, as if a person was rapping their knuckles on the inside of the wooden vault. The hair on her arms stood up. All at once, the air felt heavy and hot, as if someone had turned on the furnace. Despite her doubts, she pulled her shoulders inward to make herself smaller, squeezing Dave's and Josh's hands.

"Can you make that knocking sound again?" Alex said.

Knock, knock, knock, knock.

"We're here to help you," Crystal called out. "Can you tell us your name?"

Knock, knock, knock, knock, knock, knock, knock, knock.

Alex screamed. Izzy opened her eyes and let go of Josh's and Dave's hands. She dropped her flashlight. Just then, the candle went out, pitching the morgue into blackness. Alex started shouting. "Get off me! Leave me alone! What are you doing?" Then she was mumbling, as if someone had a hand over her mouth.

Izzy rushed toward the door, slamming face-first into Josh. To her surprise, he grabbed her and spun her around. For a split second, she thought her sense of direction was off and Josh was trying to help her escape. Maybe the door was to her right, not her left. The room filled with the sounds of people shuffling and fighting. Then Josh wrapped his arms around Izzy's chest and picked her up, his beer-soaked breath coming hot and fast in her ear. She thought he was going to carry her out of the room, toward safety, but then someone grabbed her ankles and lifted her legs off the floor.

"What the hell are you doing?" Izzy yelled, kicking. One foot collided with someone's head, setting that leg free, and she heard someone cuss. It was Dave. She twisted and turned, trying to fight her way out of Josh's grasp. It was no use. Dave grabbed her ankle again, and they carried her across the room. "Let me go!"

Metal screeched against metal. It was the sound of the vault slab being rolled out. Then Izzy was dropped onto the cold block and held down, the back of her head thumping against the steel. Strong hands held her down. Metal screeched again and she moved forward, as if slipping along a horizontal slide, except the slide was moving with her. She was shoved inside the vault, the slab slamming into the back wall with a vibrating thud. She raised her arms to stop the door from closing, her elbows and wrists scraping along the rough interior of the chamber. Her forearms caught in the door, crushing her muscles and tearing at her skin. She screamed. Rough hands pushed her arms inside. Then the door slammed closed, plunging her into total darkness.

CHAPTER 14

CLARA

The Rookie Pest House

As the leaves curled around the edges and fell one by one from the oak trees outside the Rookie Pest House windows, Clara sat on her filthy bed and watched Lawrence Lawrence push a wheelbarrow between the rows of iron markers in the cemetery across the road. He worked in the graveyard at least three times a week and his routine was always the same. First, he stopped at the chosen location, unbuttoned his coat, and took off his newsboy cap, smoothing his hands over his gray hair, once on each side, then four times down the middle. Then he made the sign of the cross over his chest and bowed his head, his cap clutched over his heart. After a long minute, he looked up at the sky, put his cap back on, pulled his shovel out of the wheelbarrow and started digging, stopping only long enough to lift a rock over the edge of the hole or switch from a shovel to a pick. He didn't stop until the hole was dug and the pile of dirt beside it was free of roots and stones. When the job was finished, he took off his cap, smoothed his hair again, wiped his brow, and put his cap back on. Even on the days when he raked leaves or cut the grass, he worked nonstop until the job was complete.

While the weeks passed and Clara felt herself giving up and growing weaker, she marveled at the gravedigger's stamina. Even as winter's snow weighed down the cedar trees and built up between the bars outside the windows, the gravedigger shoveled paths through the cemetery to dig a patient's final resting place. Near the end of December, he finally gave up trying to break open the frozen earth, but only for a short time. A few weeks later, after an unseasonably long January thaw, when Clara could see the white banks of Creek Mears nearly overflowing with icy water, Lawrence Lawrence got back to work.

Every night, she prayed the gravedigger would soon be digging a grave for her. Other than mealtime and being taken to use the bathroom two times a day, she spent her days and nights chained to her bed, sleeping or staring out the dirt-covered windows. Like most of the women in the Pest House, her bodily functions didn't always correspond with the bathroom schedule. As a result, her hospital gown was encrusted with dried urine, blood, and feces, her sheets and thin blanket soiled and rank. When her monthly cycle came, she was given rags to put in her undergarments, to be rinsed out when she used the bathroom. If she was lucky, she was given a fresh nightgown after her weekly ice bath. More often than not, there weren't enough clean ones to go around.

Shouting and screaming often came from elsewhere inside the building, but other than the sounds of weeping, coughing, and women talking to themselves, Clara's room was relatively quiet. The Pest House workers were nothing more than untrained guards, and a daily, evening dose of laudanum kept most patients drifting between a state of unconsciousness and a groggy, dreamlike stupor.

Clara grew to love the bitter taste of the laudanum. It tasted like black licorice rolled in sugar and dirt, but the numbness on her tongue meant the ignorance of unconsciousness was soon to follow and she would no longer be subject to the black mass of grief that sat like a house on her chest, making it nearly impossible to take the next breath. Despite the medicine, she had the same nightmare every night. In it, Beatrice was thin and wailing in a filthy nightgown, her metal crib in the center of a ward with hundreds of other cribs, each filled with another screaming, emaciated baby.

Every morning, when the medicine wore off and Clara opened her eyes, tears already blurring her vision, the memory of Beatrice being taken away made something foul and vile churn in her stomach. She lay there, wishing to die, crushing grief turning her blood to lead, her heart to stone, her muscles to granite. She closed her eyes and tried to go under again, but sorrow always pulled her back to reality, as if she deserved to be punished. Agony nearly swallowed her.

During her first few days in the Rookie Pest House, she had tried reasoning with the orderlies, begging them to let her out so she could find her daughter before it was too late, before Beatrice was so far away she would be lost forever. Numb to patients' pleas, the orderlies ignored her, their faces blank, prodding her along the hallway, wrestling her into bed, roughly clamping the ankle iron around her leg. Once, after being taken to use the bathroom, she shoved an orderly to the floor and ran down the hall, only to find a locked door and a group of orderlies waiting to carry her back to her room.

A week later, she tried to stop eating. But the orderlies noticed and stood over her, ordering her to eat the gruel already drying in her bowl. When she refused, they lifted her from her stool and slapped her hard, across the face, warning that if she didn't do as she was told, things would only get worse. With her lip split and bleeding, she took a spoonful and nearly choked. Afterward, she cursed herself for not being strong enough to let them punish her further. Beatrice was gone and she was locked away in a mental institution. There was no reason to live.

Then, near the end of February, she dreamed of

seeing Beatrice as a grown woman, her dark hair like satin against the shoulders of a yellow dress. Beatrice entered what looked like a hospital room, then kneeled and smiled up at her, tears glistening in her eyes. The next morning, the mass in Clara's chest had loosened. It was still there, heavy and painful, but it no longer felt like her heart was being crushed. The dream was so vivid Clara could almost smell Beatrice's perfume and feel her soft cheek. It had to mean something. And she'd never find out if she spent the rest of her life locked away in the Rookie Pest House.

That night, Clara held her dose of laudanum in her mouth instead of swallowing it. The nurse moved on to the next patient and Clara put her blanket to her lips, spitting the narcotic into the stained fabric. Over the next few weeks, she kept up the drugged mannerisms of the other women so she wouldn't draw attention to herself. Then, on the first of March, when Dr. Roach finally came to the Pest House to make rounds, she looked him in the eye and agreed that Beatrice was better off being raised by someone else.

CHAPTER 15

Izzy

Chapin Hall

Trying to catch her breath, Izzy struggled to turn over on the metal slab inside the morgue vault. It was no use. There wasn't enough room inside the narrow compartment to bend her knees and push her body over. She kicked at the low ceiling and pounded on the walls.

"Let me out of here!" she screamed.

Thuds and muffled laughter filtered in through the insulated, wooden walls. The morgue doors banged open then squeaked back and forth, swinging briefly on their hinges. And then there was nothing.

"Help!" Izzy shouted.

She reached above her head and pounded on the door, the rough wood tearing at her knuckles. After a few seconds, she forced herself to lie still, trying to hear over her own labored breathing. She closed her eyes and counted to ten, struggling against the panic that threatened to overwhelm her. *They'll come back,* she thought. *They're just out in the hall having a laugh. They'll be right back.* Then, suddenly, the heavy, cloying stench of decay and formaldehyde filled her nostrils. She pressed her lips together and tried not to take deep breaths. The lack of oxygen made her dizzy.

"Okay, the joke's over!" she yelled. "Let me out of here! Alex? Josh?"

Still nothing. Maybe this wasn't a joke. Then she remembered Alex yelling at someone to let her go, her muffled cries. Did they put her in one of the vaults too?

"Alex?" she cried. "Are you in here?"

Still nothing. What the hell was going on? Maybe Alex had been dragged out of the room against her will. Then she remembered Alex's warning; she needed to be even more careful after Shannon apologized. Loathing welled like bile from Izzy's stomach. Could Shannon have put Josh, Crystal, and Dave up to the whole thing? Then she had another thought and the cold fingers of fear clutched her throat. If they dragged Alex through the basement, up the stairs and back outside, Alex wouldn't realize Izzy was missing until they let her go. Alex had no idea Izzy was locked inside the vault!

She took deep breaths, trying to recall how the groups were formed, how it was decided that her group would investigate the morgue. Had she been so preoccupied with not wanting to go inside Willard she'd missed the signs that she was being set up?

She clenched her fists, suddenly shaking and gasping for air, fighting the flood of horror that made her feel as though she might pass out. Tears of anger and fear spilled from her eyes. "Let me out of here!!" she screamed at the top of her lungs. And then, from the vault below her . . .

Knock, knock, knock, knock.

She pressed her hands over her ears, her heartbeat thundering in her chest. *What the hell is going on?*

Knock, knock, knock, knock.

"If somebody doesn't let me out of here right now, you're going to be sorry!" she shouted, knowing her threats meant nothing. What could she do, turn them in to the principal? She kicked the walls as hard as she could, banging her ankles and jamming her toes. "Dave and Josh! I know you put me in here!"

She thought about telling the person doing the knocking to stop, that she knew it was part of the hoax. It had to be. Instead, she decided to ignore it. Then again, what if it wasn't a person down there? An image came to her: a dirt-brown skeleton lying in the vault below her, its lipless mouth opening and closing, its bare bone knuckles rapping on the damp wood. She imagined a rotting hospital gown hanging off the skeleton's arms, jagged pieces of decayed cloth and rotted flesh hanging from its ribs. She crossed her arms and pushed the image from her mind, keeping her eyes closed, trying to ignore the noise and the fact that she was trapped inside a morgue vault. *What if no one comes back? What if they leave me here? I could die and no one would know what happened. No one will know where I am. No. Alex won't let it happen. Once she gets away from Luke and Crystal, once she realizes I'm missing, she'll ask where I am. She'll come back for me.*

Suddenly, a hazy childhood memory came to her, or maybe it was a forgotten nightmare, she couldn't be sure. She was in bed, her My Little Pony night-light glowing pink in one corner of the dark room. The click of her bedroom door pulled her from the warm, fuzzy weight of near sleep. She blinked and started to sit up. Then someone, a man, was lying beside her, the smell of sweat and whiskey wafting through the air like a mist. At first she couldn't see the man's features, but then he smiled and his face morphed into a snarling demon, his blood-filled eyes swelling until they reached his hairline, his pointy teeth jagged and black. She opened her mouth to scream but couldn't. The demon was holding her down.

Izzy bit her lip, her hands clenching and unclenching, her nostrils flaring as she tried to catch her breath. The air felt hot and dry in her throat. The first memory of her recurring childhood nightmare came to her now, no doubt brought to the surface by being locked in the vault. Now, she remembered being so terrified she couldn't move, unable to tell her mother until hours later, when she finally came out of what felt like a trance. Her parents would allow her to crawl in bed with them until morning, her mother telling her over and over again that she had no reason to be afraid, that monsters weren't real and besides, she would always protect her. Then, suddenly, the nightmares just stopped. She remembered her mother apologizing, for what, she wasn't sure.

Now, somehow, she pushed the terrifying image away. But the feeling of being trapped, of being suffocated, bore down on her like an oncoming train. She tore the zipper down on her hoodie and pulled at the collar of her T-shirt. Sweat broke out on her forehead and upper lip. She pushed up her sleeves and dug her nails into her arms, trying to break the skin. If Shannon wanted to drive her crazy, it was working. *No,* she thought, *I can't let her win.* She tried willing her body to relax, imagining the muscles in her toes, her feet, her legs, going loose. The trick worked for a few seconds, but then panic seized her all over again. She took a deep breath and started over.

Finally, she willed herself into something that resembled self-control. The knocking below her had stopped and she wondered if the perpetrator had fallen asleep. Whoever it was, they must really want Shannon's approval. Thinking about Shannon, she clenched her jaw. What if Izzy had been so scared she had a heart attack or a nervous breakdown? What if she ran out of oxygen before someone came back for her? Did Shannon hate her so much that she was willing to risk something happening to her? And what about Ethan, was he in on this horrible trick?

No. He couldn't be. He might be naïve enough to make excuses for Shannon's mean school pranks, but he would never go along with this. It had to be Shannon, Josh, Crystal, and Dave.

Eventually, the sweat of panic began to evaporate, cold air drifting around her wrists and ankles, like the icy fingers of ghosts touching her skin. She zipped up her hoodie and pulled the hood over her head, hugging herself to try to stay warm. Her teeth chattered. She envisioned herself trapped in the vault while fall turned to winter, growing thinner and weaker, starving to death. She reached up and wiped her hands over her face. Her skin felt like wax; cold, dead skin on the outside, pulsing and hot on the inside. She remembered hearing stories of people being buried alive, scratching and clawing the wooden lids of their coffins, fighting to get out. She imagined their bloody fingers, nails scraped to the quick until there was nothing left but bone.

No, she reminded herself. *You're not in a coffin. You're in a vault, with a door. There is a way out. You just have to wait until someone comes and opens it.* She pushed the image away and tried to concentrate on something else. Her jaw ached from gritting her teeth and she was getting a headache, a sharp stab of pain thumping at both temples.

Finally, she heard muffled voices, heavy footsteps running down the hall, the double doors swinging open.

"Izzy?" someone shouted. "Where are you?" It was Alex.

"I'm in here!" Izzy yelled. She banged on the side of the vault.

"Holy shit," a male voice said.

"We're going to get you out of there!" Alex said. "Just hang on!"

Their voices sounded low and muffled, as if she were listening through a door with a drinking glass.

"Which one is she in?" the male voice said. Izzy's heart raced. It sounded like Ethan.

"I don't know," Alex said. "Just open the doors!"

Izzy pounded on the wood above her head. "I'm in this one!" The lower left-hand vault opened. Then the one directly below her.

"What the hell?" Ethan said. "What are you doing in there?" Metal screeched against metal and then there were several loud thumps, as if someone was struggling to stand, or wrestling. Something heavy scraped along the floor, then hit the door above her head. The vault shook. "Where is Izzy?" Ethan snarled. His voice sounded right outside the door and Izzy pictured him pushing

323

someone against the vault, his face contorted in anger.

"It wasn't my idea!" a male voice said. "They paid me!"

"Who paid you?" Ethan said, thumping the person against the vault again.

"Never mind about him!" Alex said. "We've got to find Izzy!"

"I'll deal with you later!" Ethan said.

Izzy sensed rather than felt a person being yanked away from the vault. A metallic bang echoed in the room, as if someone had fallen over the vat of embalming fluid. The swinging door squeaked.

At last, the thick door above her head wrenched open and beams of light sliced through the dark interior. She gasped for air and pushed on the sides of the vault, trying to force herself out of the chamber. Then someone yanked out the slab. She blinked and covered her eyes with one shaking hand, suddenly blinded by lights. The bright beams dropped and Alex stood holding two flashlights, staring at Izzy, her face pale, her eyes wide.

"Oh my God!" Alex said. "Are you all right?"

"I think so," Izzy said, pushing herself up on her elbows. She swung her legs over the edge of the slab, sat up too fast and immediately felt dizzy. She took a deep breath and closed her eyes, trying to regain her equilibrium. A warm hand touched her back and she turned to see Ethan, his brow furrowed, his lips pressed together in a hard, thin line. He came around in front of her, offering to help her down. Unable to stop shaking, she grasped his upper arm for support and moved to the thick edge of the metal slab. Ethan put his hands around her waist and lifted her up, then gently set her down on the floor. The world turned gray and teetered away from her as she swayed and tried to keep herself upright. Ethan grabbed her shoulders and held on.

"Are you sure you're all right?" he said, bending down to look in her eyes.

Izzy nodded. Despite the overwhelming relief of being rescued, she wondered what he was doing here. She wanted to ask him where Shannon was, if he knew what his girlfriend had been planning. But first, she wanted to get the hell out of Willard.

"I'm so sorry!" Alex said. "I had no idea what was going on! When they dragged me out of here, I thought they were dragging you out too. I couldn't see anything and tried to get away but . . ." She was crying now, her words coming in short, shallow gasps. "I didn't know you were missing until we were back outside!"

"It's okay," Izzy said. "It's not your fault. Just get me out of here."

"They took off with the flashlights and just left me outside the building," Alex said. "It took forever to find someone to help."

"Come on," Ethan said, putting an arm around Izzy's waist. "Let's go."

She walked toward the exit on elastic legs, holding on to Ethan's arm to keep her balance. She shivered, her teeth chattering, partly from cold and exhaustion and relief, partly from anger.

"It must have been Shannon!" Alex said, her words rattled by fury. "She put them up to it!"

"Yeah," Izzy said. "That's what I thought too."

Ethan stopped in the hall, unzipped his sweatshirt, and held it out for Izzy. She pushed her arms into the sleeves and wrapped the too-big garment around herself. The inside of the sweatshirt was dry and warm, the familiar smell of Ethan's cologne wafting out of the collar. She wanted to pull the edge of the sweatshirt over her face, to block out the wet, rotten smell of the basement, but she resisted. She started walking again, moving along the cement corridor as fast as she could, eager to fill her lungs with fresh air.

"Who put you in the vault?" Ethan said. "Do you know?"

"Josh and Dave," Izzy said. "I'm sure of it."

"I'm really sorry about this," he said. "I can't believe she would do that to you. To anyone."

"Your girlfriend is one messed-up bitch," Alex said. "She's out there, acting all concerned about Izzy, wondering what happened. Izzy should press charges!"

At the end of the hall, Izzy grabbed the banister

and pulled herself up the stairs. "She can't be too happy with you right now," she said to Ethan. "If she knows you came looking for me." He shrugged. "Where is she now?"

"Everyone is waiting down by the boathouse," Alex said.

"Take me there," Izzy said.

Flashlight beams bobbed and crossed, yellow shafts of light lining the black lawn and briefly illuminating the decaying shingles of the old boathouse. Groups of kids milled about, pacing and jumping up and down to stay warm, waiting to hear what happened. When Crystal saw Izzy coming down the hill, she hurried toward her, running across the grass. Izzy felt her chest and face grow hot.

"Are you all right?" Crystal said, her voice filled with feigned pity. She reached out to Izzy, as if to embrace her. Izzy brushed past her and kept going, her eyes searching the crowd for Shannon.

Finally, Izzy saw her, talking and laughing with Josh and Luke, a beer in one hand, a cigarette in the other. Izzy pushed her way through the crowd, ignoring the fact that everyone was staring. The closer she got to Shannon, the more her fury grew, swelling up inside her like a balloon being filled with hot air. Normally, she would have pushed the feelings of anger out of her mind as soon as they appeared. But this time her fury was too big, too massive, consuming all thought. She wouldn't hit Shannon, but she wouldn't let her get away with this either. She marched toward her, taking long, even strides, her body tense, her hands clenched into fists.

In slow motion, she saw Shannon's head turn toward her, her eyes glazed over with alcohol and lack of sleep. Her smile disappeared when she saw Izzy coming toward her. Shannon opened her mouth to speak, but Josh stepped between them, blocking Izzy.

"What the hell happened back there?" he said to Izzy. "Are you okay?"

"You know perfectly well what happened," Izzy said.

She skirted around him and made her way toward Shannon. Shannon stared at her, her lips working as she tried to decide if she should smile or frown, no doubt wondering if her deceit had been discovered. But having been in this position a thousand times, Shannon instinctively knew what to do. She smiled, a look of artificial relief washing over her face.

"Oh my God!" she said. "Are you all right?"

For a split second, Izzy almost stopped in her tracks and turned away, knowing Shannon wasn't worth it. But then something dark gave way in her brain and she rushed forward, grabbing Shannon by the collar with both hands. She shoved her face into hers.

"If you mess with me again," she snarled, "you'll be sorry!" Spittle flew from her lips, landing on Shannon's perfectly tanned cheek. Shannon blanched and pulled backward. She tore at Izzy's fingers, trying to break free.

"Get your hands off me!" she yelled.

"Say you're sorry!" Izzy said, her words rattled by fury.

"I didn't do anything!" Shannon cried.

"Say you're sorry or I'll pound you to a pulp!" Izzy shouted.

Before Izzy knew what was happening, Josh pulled her away, one hand gripping her hoodie, the other around Shannon's upper arm, forcing them apart.

"Leave her alone!" he said, holding Izzy back. "I don't know what happened back there, but she didn't have anything to do with it."

Izzy yanked herself from Josh's grasp. "Bullshit!" she said. She shoved a finger in his face. "You know exactly what happened! You put me in a vault and left me there! And she put you up to it!"

"Me?" Josh said, raising his eyebrows. "I don't know what you've been smoking, but I didn't touch you! Alex started screaming and we all ran out. I thought you were right behind us!"

"You're lying!" Izzy said.

"You weren't with us!" Alex said to Josh. "You didn't come outside until a couple minutes later, after Luke and Crystal let me go!"

Shannon stood next to Josh, arms crossed over her chest. "I can't believe this," she said. "I apologize for everything and ask for another chance, and this is the thanks I get. I don't know if you're trying to get revenge or what, but saying I put Josh up to locking you in a vault is a pretty serious accusation. I would never do anything so terrible."

Izzy started toward Shannon again. Josh stepped between them and pushed her away. Then Ethan appeared, his back to Izzy. He cocked his fist and punched Josh in the face, grunting with the effort. When Ethan straightened, Josh staggered backward and fell to the ground, his hand up, his nose bloody.

"Stay the hell away from Izzy!" Ethan snarled.

Dave appeared, eyes blinking as he looked at Josh, then Ethan. "What the hell are you doing, Ethan?" he said. Ethan pulled back his fist, ready to deliver another blow, this time to Dave, but Izzy grabbed his arm.

"Don't," she said. "They're not worth it."

Ethan wiped his forearm across his mouth, panting and staring. He put a hand on Izzy's shoulder. "You okay?" he said. Izzy nodded. Dave helped Josh up and they stared at Ethan, shaking their heads.

"What's wrong with you?" Dave said.

"What's wrong with me?" Ethan said. "When are you going to grow up and start thinking about the consequences of your actions? What would you have done if something happened to Izzy? What if she got hurt or we didn't find her?"

"What the hell, Ethan?" Shannon said. "Why are you sticking up for her? *I'm* your girlfriend, remember?"

Ethan stared at the ground for a minute, then looked Shannon in the eye. "Not anymore," he said, scowling as if he'd tasted something rancid.

"What?" Shannon said, her voice high. "What did you just say?"

Ethan took a deep breath, holding Shannon's gaze. "I'm breaking up with you. I can't date someone who enjoys hurting other people. I don't know what's happened to you lately, but you took it too far this time."

"I took it too far?" Shannon said, her voice breaking. "You're just going to take her word for it?"

"I found your buddy Bryan in the vault," Ethan said. "He said you paid him."

"That's not true," Josh said, his words wet and muffled. He held his nose, his plank-thick hand covered with dark blood. "She didn't have anything to do with it."

"You can stop trying to impress her now, Josh," Ethan said. "She's all yours."

Ethan took Izzy by the arm and turned, making his way toward the shoreline. Alex followed.

"Do you want to go to the ER?" Ethan asked Izzy.

"No," she said. "I'll be okay."

"Come on," Ethan said to Alex. "Let's take her home."

CHAPTER 16

CLARA

March 1931

A week after her release from the Rookie Pest House, Clara was allowed back in the general population. She was sent to a different ward and given a job at the laundry, sorting, starching, and ironing. The work was hot and exhausting, but she was relieved to be out of the Rookie Pest House, grateful for the chance to stand up and perform labor, to use her body and stretch her muscles. More than anything, she was grateful not to be chained to a bed twenty-four hours a day.

The women in the laundry kept to themselves, except for Matilda, an older woman who talked to everyone. Matilda spoke with a thick European accent and wore her gray hair in long braids. Head and shoulders taller than most of the other women, she had thick, muscular arms and incredibly wide fingers. Matilda delivered the freshly washed sheets and pillowcases to the starch baths by lifting the tubs full of wet laundry up on one shoulder and carrying them in slow motion across the room. When she wasn't lifting impossibly heavy tubs of wet laundry in the air, Matilda pushed wagons of torn and ripped clothing into the sewing room across the hall. At every stop, she hugged every woman and recited the same words.

"I don't hear voices. I don't see visions. I'm not crazy. I am nervous."

Normally, the patients weren't allowed to touch each other, but no one tried to stop Matilda from doling out her daily hugs. Clara found herself looking forward to seeing Matilda every day, feeling her strong, warm arms around her. It felt like forever since she'd been hugged, so she held on a little longer every time. When Clara thanked her, Matilda grinned and said she was sweet. It became a bright spot in Clara's day, a tiny demonstration of kindness in a cold, heartless place.

After two weeks, Clara was allowed to go to the recreation room for an hour every afternoon. The room was long and narrow, with striped wall-paper, brocade curtains, and Victorian chandeliers. Patients sat on cushioned sofas or cane-bottom chairs, talking, staring, or playing cards and board games at oak tables. In one corner, a patient cranked the handle on a Victrola, playing a scratchy rendition of "America The Beautiful" over and over. Decorated to look and feel homey in an attempt to make the patients relax, the room had the opposite effect on Clara. To her, it felt like a mockery, an attempt to placate patients into thinking their needs were being met while years and months slipped by. Their lives were disappearing and no one was making an attempt to help get them back. Behind the fancy curtains and comfortable furnishings, the windows were still covered with bars, the doors were still locked, the orderlies still watched with vigilant eyes.

Clara threaded her way through the chairs and tables, trying to find a quiet spot where she would be left alone. Then her heart leapt in her chest. Esther and Madeline were sitting together in front of a bookshelf, Madeline leaning forward and reading to Esther, who was sitting in an over-stuffed chair with her head back and her eyes closed. Clara hadn't seen Madeline since the day in the kitchen, when Clara hit her head and went into labor. And the last time she saw Esther was on their daily walk, when they went past the Rookie Pest House. Clara rushed over and knelt next to Esther's chair.

"I'm so happy to see you two!" she whispered.

Madeline dropped the book in her lap, her eyes wide and staring. "Clara!" she said. "Where have you been?"

Clara glanced at Esther to see her reaction, but

she was asleep. Up close, Esther's face looked paler than Clara remembered, dark circles lining the wrinkled skin under her eyes. She looked like she'd aged ten years, her movie-star features stolen by grief and stress. All because she kissed another man. Clara swallowed, trying to find her voice.

"I went into labor that day in the kitchen," she said. "They kept me and the baby in the infirmary for a few months. But then . . ." Her voice caught, trying to speak around the burning lump in her throat.

"Where's your baby?" Madeline said in a small voice. Her eyes grew glassy and she gripped the edge of the book, her knuckles turning white.

"They took her," Clara managed. "A woman came and took her away from me." It was the first time she'd said the words out loud. All of a sudden, she felt dizzy and nauseous. She stood and pulled up a chair, wiping tears from her cheeks.

"Oh no," Madeline said. "I was hoping you'd been released, or your parents came to get you after your fall. That's what I told myself anyway. I wouldn't have been able to bear it if something bad had happened to you because you were defending me. But now, they've taken your baby. . . ." She lowered her head and sniffed, fat, swift tears falling from the tip of her nose.

Clara squeezed Madeline's hand. "It's all right,"

she said. "I'm going to see my daughter again someday. I don't know when or how, but I am. For now, I just have to hold on to that and do what I'm told. And somehow, I've got to convince Dr. Roach that I'm cured."

Madeline lifted her head. She bit her lip and starting picking at the skin around her thumb.

"What is it?" Clara said. "What's wrong?"

Madeline glanced at Esther. "Be careful," she said. "Dr. Roach did that to her."

Clara turned to look at Esther. "Did what?" she said. "What's wrong with her? I thought she was sleeping."

"She is," Madeline said. "Because that's all she does now. Before this, Dr. Roach kept asking her for details about her affair. Her husband said she was acting like a common whore and Dr. Roach said the only way he could cure her was if she told him everything. He wanted every detail. At first she refused, but Dr. Roach said she'd never be released if she didn't cooperate. Then, when she finally agreed and told him everything, he wanted her to act out what she had done with her lover. He tried to get her to have sex with him."

Clara clenched her jaw, a hot coil of anger building up beneath her ribcage. "Did he hurt her?"

Madeline shook her head. "He tried to force himself on her and she kicked him," she said. She pointed toward her crotch. "You know where. A week later, she disappeared. When she finally came back to the ward, Nurse Trench said she had been in an insulin-induced coma. Esther was fine, but really, really tired. They let her stay in bed for a while. But then something happened. She says a man came into the ward. I think it frightened her."

Clara frowned. "A man came into the female ward? How is that possible?"

"He was with the carpenters. They were fixing a leak in the ceiling or putting up a new door. I'm not sure."

"He didn't hurt her, did he?"

"No," Madeline said. "I don't think so. But, after it happened, Esther kept asking where you were. She wouldn't stop. She kept saying, 'Where's Clara? Where's Clara?' over and over again."

Clara sat up, startled. "Me?" she said. "Why would she be asking about me?"

Madeline shook her head. "I don't know," she said. "We both wondered where you were, but this was different. She was frantic. Like her life depended on finding you. She asked everyone where you were. After it happened, Dr. Roach put her on some kind of medication that makes her want to sleep all the time. And when she sleeps, it's like the dead. When she wakes up long enough to talk, she won't tell me anything. She's afraid she'll forget if she tells me. That was over two months ago."

Clara looked at Esther. "Will she talk if we wake her up?"

"She might," Madeline said. "Sometimes she does, sometimes she doesn't. It depends on the time of day."

Clara put a hand on Esther's arm and gently shook it. "Esther?" she said. "Esther, can you hear me?"

Esther moved her head ever so slightly. Madeline sat forward in her chair, looking around the room to make sure no one was watching. The orderly in charge of the recreation room was sitting at a desk reading a magazine. Madeline took Esther's hands and gently pulled her forward.

"Esther," she said. "Wake up. Clara is here and she wants to talk to you." Esther's upper body started bending forward, but her head lolled backward and her eyes remained closed. Madeline stopped pulling and let Esther sink back into the cushion. "Did you hear me, Esther? Clara is here. She's right beside you."

"Esther," Clara said, fighting the urge to shout. She moved closer and leaned over the arm of the overstuffed chair, getting close to Esther's ear. "It's me, Clara. Madeline said you want to talk to me. What is it? What do you want to tell me?"

Esther's eyelids fluttered and she lifted her head from the cushion.

"That's it," Madeline said. "Wake up, Esther. Clara is here. Remember Clara?"

Finally, Esther blinked and opened her eyes. She looked at Madeline and squinted, then put her hands over her face and took a deep breath.

"Esther," Clara said. "Why did you ask Dr. Roach where I was? Do you want to tell me something?"

Esther dropped her hands in her lap and slowly turned toward Clara, a thin line of drool trailing from her lower lip. "Where's Clara?" she said, her speech slow, her words slurred.

"I'm right here," Clara said. "Open your eyes and look at me. I'm right here."

Esther forced her lids open, trying to focus on Clara's face. The whites of Esther's eyes were bloodshot, her irises dull. "Clara," she said. "A man came into the ward."

"Yes," Clara said. "Madeline told me."

"I was sleeping and he woke me up."

"What happened?" Clara said. "Did he do something to you? Did he hurt you?"

Esther shook her head. "He shook my shoulder and it scared me. But then he asked about you. He asked if I knew you."

Clara's heart thundered like a train in her chest. She dug her nails into her palms. "What did he look like?" she said. "Did he tell you his name?"

"Dark hair. Brown eyes." Esther closed her eyes and for a second, Clara was afraid she was falling asleep again. Then a faint smile played across Esther's lips. "Very handsome."

Clara could barely breathe. "Esther," she said. "What did the man say to you?"

Esther swallowed and blinked. "Tell Clara I'm working with the carpentry crew. Tell her I came to get her."

"Who?" Clara said, the hairs on her arms standing up. "Who came to get me? What was his name, Esther?"

"Bruno," Esther said. "Bruno came to get you."

CHAPTER 17

IZZY

The morning after being locked in the vault, Izzy crawled out of her sleeping bag and staggered into Alex's bathroom, her joints stiff and her muscles tight, as if she'd been in a brawl. She rinsed her face and squinted in the bathroom mirror. Her eyes were blurry, her hair disheveled. She sat on the toilet to pee and, for the first time, noticed her knees were scraped and bruised. Dark blue blotches covered her elbows and forearms, and the skin on her knuckles was torn and bloody. Even her toes were purple. All of a sudden, the feeling of being trapped came over her again. She pushed the sensation away, got up from the toilet, and went to the window. Outside, the day was gray and rainy, mirroring her sour mood.

At least they had decided to go back to Alex's house instead of staying at the lake last night. They would have gotten soaked, not to mention the ensuing drama that would have occurred when Shannon caught up to them. Besides, Izzy hadn't been able to stop shaking since they pulled her out of the vault. Her thin sleeping bag wouldn't have been enough to warm her. On the way back to town, she'd cranked the heat in Alex's Beamer until Alex and Ethan complained.

After a quick breakfast of orange juice and Rice Krispies, Alex dropped Izzy off at the end of her foster parents' driveway, promising to come back later to watch a movie. Despite her dark mood, Izzy was grateful for Alex's attempts to get her mind off what happened at Willard. She hunched her shoulders against the rain and hurried along the paved drive, sidestepping the growing puddles. She could still picture Ethan standing on the curb when they dropped him off at his house last night, leaning in through the open passenger window. At first, she thought he was trying to kiss her and she backed away. Then she realized he was just saying good-bye and her face flushed with embarrassment. He asked her for the hundredth time if she was all right and insisted she keep his sweatshirt until school on Monday, but she refused. Everything was moving too fast and she didn't want him to think that, just because he was done with Shannon, she was ready to be his girlfriend. Actually, she didn't think she'd ever be ready to be his girlfriend. She still wasn't sure she could trust someone who used to go along with Shannon's mean tricks. And yet, she kept the Green Day pin she'd found inside his sweatshirt pocket. Now, she rubbed her thumb over it, taking a deep breath before opening the door leading into Peg's kitchen.

Normally, on Sunday mornings, Harry made pancakes and the three of them sat around in their pajamas, reading the comics and doing the crossword puzzles until noon. It was Izzy's favorite day of the week. Those few hours when they laughed and talked, and Peg and Harry helped with her homework, made her feel like she was part of a real family. Now, her stomach growled thinking about the crisp bacon and fluffy buttermilk pancakes covered with sticky maple syrup. But when she entered the kitchen, Peg and Harry were dressed and sitting at the table, coffee mugs in their hands, the Sunday paper folded neatly between the placemats. Peg looked up, startled, her lips in a grim, hard line. Harry turned in his chair and considered Izzy, his eyes serious.

Izzy's heart dropped. Somehow, they'd found out about the party on the beach. She had lied to them about staying at Alex's and now they were going to tell her she had to leave. She just knew it.

She let her duffel bag slip off her shoulder and sat down, holding her breath as she waited, staring at the picture of President Clinton and Monica Lewinski on the front page of the newspaper.

"Did you have a good time last night?" Peg said, attempting to smile.

"It was okay," Izzy said, wondering if this was a test. She decided to come clean. "But I—"

"We have something to tell you," Harry interrupted. He pushed his glasses up on his nose and wiped his hands on his pants. Peg shifted in her chair, her knuckles turning white as she tightened her grip on her coffee mug.

"First, we have some good news," Peg said. Her voice shook and she cleared her throat. Izzy stared at her, a hot lump threatening to cut off her breathing. What could Peg possibly say to soften the blow? "I found a nurse who used to work at Willard. We think she might have taken care of Clara. We can go talk to her, if you'd like."

Izzy nodded, her heartbeat picking up speed. "Do you think she knows what happened to Clara?" she managed. "Or her daughter?"

"I don't know," Peg said. "But we'll ask her. If she doesn't know, we'll try to find out together. I promise."

Together. Izzy's eyes filled. Peg said they would try to find out together. They weren't sending her away after all. She took a deep breath and exhaled, waves of relief washing through her. But then Harry glanced at Peg, as if for reinforcement.

"There's something else," he said, his brows knitted. "It's your mother."

Izzy stiffened. Harry and Peg rarely mentioned her mother. Whatever Harry was about to tell her, it was bad. Really bad. She could see it in his face.

"What about her?" Izzy said, her stomach knotting. Peg put a gentle hand over Izzy's. Izzy felt something move in her head, as if her brain was shoring up, preparing for shock.

"She had a stroke last night," Harry said. "She was in her cell and no one knew anything was wrong until this morning."

Izzy swallowed.

"I'm sorry," Peg said, her eyes brimming with tears. "But she's in a coma. They don't think she's going to pull through."

Izzy stared at Peg, trying to form words. Her tongue felt like lead, her lips heavy and useless over her teeth. Peg rubbed Izzy's hand, her soft fingers catching on Izzy's torn knuckles. She looked down and gasped.

"What happened?" she said.

Izzy pulled her hand away, clenching it into a fist on her lap. "Nothing," she said. "I fell trying out Alex's Rollerblades." Somewhere in the back of her mind, she was surprised at how easily the lie came. What had changed between yesterday and today? She reached for her duffel bag and stood, pushing her chair under the table.

"Are you okay?" Harry said. "Do you want to know what the doctors are saying?"

Izzy shook her head, her body numb. "Um . . . not right now," she said.

"We can take you to see her after school tomorrow," Peg said. "If you want."

Izzy dug her nails into the back of her chair. *What good will that do?* she thought. "I'm really tired," she said. "If it's okay with you, I'm going to take a shower and a nap."

"Can I get you something to eat first?" Peg said.

"I'll make pancakes if you're hungry," Harry said.

Izzy shook her head and left the room, her legs like elastic beneath her. Halfway up the staircase, she slowed and grabbed the banister, her heart booming as she pulled herself upward. At the top step, the hallway teetered in front of her. She gripped the newel post, waiting to regain her sense of balance. After a long minute, she went to her room, dropped her duffel bag on the floor, and hurried into the bathroom.

She opened the toilet and threw up the Rice Krispies she'd eaten at Alex's, dry heaving until it felt like her esophagus would come spilling out, slithering into a bloody coil in the bottom of the toilet bowl. Eventually, she was able to take a breath without gagging. She spit into the toilet over and over, then wiped her mouth and straightened. Half a can of Coke sat on the edge of the sink. She drank the rest of the flat soda, hoping the caramel-flavored liquid would wash the sour taste from her mouth.

Still dizzy, she stumbled into her bedroom and fell on the bed, lying on her side and gripping her pillow against her chest. She squeezed her eyes shut, trying to stanch her tears, but it was no use. For ten years, she'd been too afraid to visit her mother in jail. Too afraid her mother would look and act crazy, or wouldn't know who she was. Now, there was nothing she wanted more. Somewhere in the back of her mind, she'd hoped the day would come when her mother would be cured, or released from all charges. Maybe, by some miracle, it would be discovered that her father's murder was a big misunderstanding. Maybe a burglar had shot him. And Izzy's mother, having witnessed her husband's violent death, had temporarily lost her mind. When the truth came out, her mother would be set free and she and Izzy could be a family again. Over the years, a hundred different scenarios played over in Izzy's mind, but she always pushed them away, certain they were nothing more than the impossible imaginings of a lost little girl. Now, it was final. None of those things would ever come true. Izzy was going to be an orphan. The chance of ever having a real mother again, no matter how infinitesimal, was gone.

Izzy's shoulders convulsed and she bit down on the pillow, surprised by the depth of her emotions.

She'd kept her head high and held herself together for so long that she'd convinced herself she was invincible. Now, it all came crashing down. She knew someday things would change. But not yet, not now, not like this. She blinked against her tears, then lifted her head and looked at the dresser. Her mother's cards and letters were still there, stuffed in a manila envelope behind her socks and underwear.

She sat up and wiped her eyes, her heart slogging in her chest. Reading the letters could make things better, or make things worse. She thought about the envelopes in Clara's trunk. Clara's life might have turned out differently if they had been mailed, if Bruno had had a chance to read them. Maybe he would have gotten Clara out of the Long Island Home before she was sent to Willard. Maybe they would have gotten married, raised a family together, and lived happily ever after.

Now, Izzy wondered if things would have been different if she'd read her mother's words. Maybe the answers she'd been looking for had been right there all along. Her stomach churned. Regardless of what the letters said, it was too late for things to change. And yet, she needed to know the truth. Either her mother's letters would paint a picture of the woman she used to be, full of love and adoration, or reveal once and for all that she really was a lunatic.

Izzy stood and retrieved the letters from the back of the top drawer, then sat cross-legged on her bed, the bulging envelope on the comforter in front of her. She undid the metal clip, opened the flap, and let the cards and letters spill out. The tilting pile of differently sized and colored envelopes reminded her of Valentine's Day in elementary school, when everyone got cards from their classmates. She always wondered if she'd get as many Valentines as the rest of the kids, eager to see how they were signed on the back. Would there be just a name, or would it include the initials BFF, best friends forever, or even BF, best friends?

One by one, she turned her mother's envelopes right side up, checking the postmark and putting them in chronological order. She would read them year by year, starting with the first months after her mother's incarceration. At first, there had been a letter a month. Then, as time went on, the frequency dwindled to three or four times a year. Izzy guessed that, along with the regular letters, there were birthday and Christmas cards. All had the same return address: Bedford State Prison.

She took a deep breath, picked up the first letter, postmarked July 1986, the month after her mother was sentenced to prison, and ripped open the envelope. It was now or never. She put her fingers over her trembling lips and began to read.

Hi, baby girl,

How are you? I hope you're doing okay. I miss you so much! I want you to know that I'm so sorry about what happened to your father. I know you don't understand what's going on right now, but someday you will, I promise. I'm sorry I was sick for so long and wasn't able to be there for you. By the time I got better, it was too late. I know you're sad and confused, baby. And I'm sorry about that. Please come and see me. I miss you so much my heart hurts. Please be a good girl for your Gramma. I'll see you soon.

Love you to the moon and back,
Mommy OXOXOX

Izzy's eyes burned. *Love you to the moon and back.* Her mother had said that every night after tucking her in, before turning off the light and slipping into the hall. Somehow, Izzy had forgotten. She ripped open the next envelope. It was a birthday card.

The front of the card read "Birthday Wishes for a Sweet Eight-Year-Old." Inside, her mother had signed, "Miss and love you to the moon and back!" *Where does an inmate go shopping for a birthday card?* Izzy wondered. The next letter was more of the same; a letter to an eight-year-old girl whose life had been turned upside down. More apologies and requests for a visit. Eventually, in the letters, her mother stopped asking Izzy to come, instead saying all the things she wished she could say in person, all the advice she wanted to impart to her only daughter. Izzy had to remind herself to breathe, waiting to read that one sentence, that one group of words that would confirm her mother's mental illness. So far, she hadn't found it. The other thing she hadn't found was any further mention of her father. It was as if he never existed.

Izzy felt cold shards of regret forming in her chest. Could she have been wrong all along? Had she wasted years being afraid? On paper, her mother sounded normal. The more Izzy read, the more it felt like losing her all over again. And yet, she was no closer to understanding what happened than she was ten years ago.

By three o'clock, Izzy had read nearly forty letters. Peg had come up several times, softly knocking on the door and asking if Izzy was okay, if she could get her something to eat or drink. Each time, Izzy refused, saying she needed to be alone and thanking Peg for the offer. In truth, Izzy couldn't have eaten anything if she'd tried. Her stomach felt sour, like it was boiling.

An hour later, the words were getting fuzzy and it was getting harder and harder for Izzy to keep her eyes open. The letter in her hand had been folded inside her thirteenth birthday card, the creases making it even harder to read. She decided to finish one last letter, then shower and take a nap. But in the next instant, her breath caught in her throat and she sat up. She read the words again.

I shot your father because I caught him in your room, doing things a father shouldn't be doing to his daughter. I'm sorry for not telling you sooner, but I wanted to wait until you were old enough to understand what goes on between a man and a woman. Don't worry, sweetheart. I stopped him before he went too far.

Izzy dropped the letter and clamped her hands over her mouth, acid rising in the back of her throat. No, it couldn't be. It was just a bad dream! Who tells their daughter on her thirteenth birthday that her father had been molesting her? Her mother had to be lying! She was crazy after all! Izzy's father would never do anything so horrible, would he? Shaking, Izzy curled into a fetal position and stared at a single rose on the bedroom wallpaper, her blurred vision filling with pulsing red petals, like an animated drawing of her broken, bleeding heart.

Then her nightmare came back to her full force, the demon's sweaty hand between her legs, his heavy arm holding her down. The demon sat up and grinned, a strange mixture of disgust and ecstasy twisting his features into a terrifying mask. Then the mask morphed into a human face and Izzy recognized the demon. It was her father.

Izzy scrambled out of bed, ran to the bathroom, and fell to her knees in front of the toilet, her chest and stomach aching as she dry heaved again and again. Finally she caught her breath and leaned against the tub, pushing the heels of her hands into her eyes. Hot waves of panic lit up her neck and chest, pulsating around her heart like an electric charge, making every inch of her skin prickle with goose bumps, every muscle in her arms and legs jitter. She tried taking deep breaths and exhaling slowly, her head spinning as she came to realize that everything she'd believed was a lie. A lie she'd fabricated entirely on her own.

Her mother had given up her life, her freedom, to protect her. All these years, Izzy had thought her mother was a lunatic, her father a loving man who paid the ultimate price for his wife's insanity. All these years, wasted because she'd never been brave enough to ask her mother's side of the story!

Then something clicked in Izzy's brain, like a giant puzzle piece finally dropping into place. Suddenly, it all made sense. Her mother had always been over-overprotective, the slightest infraction in her perfect plan to protect Izzy sending her into panic mode. Once, while grocery shopping, Izzy had let go of the cart while her mother was examining cantaloupes. Izzy had only moved a few feet away, around the end of the aisle to look at a toy display. But when her mother couldn't see her, she screamed Izzy's name over and over, loud enough to make the store manager come running. Izzy hurried back to the produce aisle and touched her mother's elbow, looking up with fear-filled eyes, afraid her mother had lost her mind. Her mother fell to her knees and sobbed, telling Izzy to never, ever leave her side again.

Seeing her husband violate her little girl would have easily put Izzy's mother over the edge. It would for most mothers. Granted, most mothers would have called the police, not shot her husband in the head with his hunting rifle. But at least Izzy understood what happened now.

In the letter, Izzy's mother admitted shooting her husband was wrong, that she had lost her mind for just a little while. She knew why she was being punished. Her lawyer couldn't convince the judge to offer leniency because he had no proof Izzy's father had done anything wrong. Izzy's mother refused to put Izzy through a physical examination, choosing instead to give up her own freedom. She believed she'd get out on parole someday and they'd be reunited.

Izzy bit down on her lip. All these years, the truth had been right there, waiting for her to open an envelope and read it, written in black and white. But she'd been too stubborn to see it. And now her mother was in a coma! Izzy would never be able to tell her she finally understood. She'd never be able to apologize for not coming to see her.

She thought about Shannon, whose mother had ignored what her husband was doing. How could Shannon live with her mother day after day, knowing she hadn't protected her? It had to be the worst feeling in the world. Despite the horrible things Shannon had done, Izzy's heart ached for her. If only Shannon's mother had done something to stop her husband, Shannon's life might have turned out differently. How could Shannon face her mother every day? How could she ever forgive her?

Izzy put her hands over her face. Unlike Shannon's mother, her mother had spent all these years alone, thinking her daughter would never forgive her, thinking she was no longer loved. Then Izzy remembered reading that comatose people could sometimes hear their loved ones speaking. Her mother was on life support, she wasn't dead. There was still time to see her, to say good-bye. She would ask Peg to take her to Bedford tomorrow. And maybe, just maybe, her mother would hear her apology.

When Izzy thought she could trust her vibrating legs to hold her upright, she stood and peeled off her clothes. Her knees, elbows, and feet were still sore from pounding on the inside of the vault and now her head throbbed too. She climbed into the empty tub, the cold, hard porcelain like tombstone against her skin, and struggled to push the stopper closed and turn on the hot water, her hands shaking like a hundred-year-old woman's. As the tub filled, she stared into the blackness of the overflow drain, her mind blank, aware of nothing but cold and the beginning of heat as hot water pooled around her feet. When the water was to her waist, she filled a washcloth with shower gel and lathered up her skin, scrubbing it back and forth with more pressure than necessary, watching in a trance as white bubbles formed over her arms and legs. She looked at the thin scars on her arms, wondering now if she'd been cutting herself to repress the horrible memories of what her father had done. She turned off the faucet and lay back in the soap-clouded water, soaking without moving, a slow, steady drip echoing like an underwater clock in her ears.

After a few minutes, she ran her hands over her body, brushing her fingers over her breasts, the fine, fluffy hair between her legs. How many times had she thought about having sex, about having a man kiss her bare breasts and warm skin, having him touch her in all her tender, private places? How many times had she thought about Ethan making love to her? Countless. Thankfully, she didn't have any real memories of her father violating her. But would anyone be able to tell what he'd done? The thought filled her stomach with greasy nausea. She washed between her legs a second time, then stood and rinsed off under the shower, letting the hot stream loosen her neck and shoulders. Finally, she turned off the water and emptied the tub. She toweled off and put on clean pajamas, then went to her room and crawled under the covers.

I won't let my past define my future, she thought. *I was a different person back then. And I'm not going to spend the rest of my life paying for my father's sins. I won't and I can't.*

CHAPTER 18

CLARA

After talking to Madeline and Esther, Clara spent the next few weeks trying to figure out where Bruno might be working. At night she couldn't sleep and during the day she was distracted. At her job in the laundry she mixed up the sheets with the towels, the hospital gowns with the aprons. When the foreman saw her mistake, he put her to work in the sewing room across the hall, making and repairing shirts and trousers and nightgowns. She sat on a stool making tiny, precise stitches, trying to think of new ways to find Bruno. So far, nothing had worked.

The day after Esther told Clara what happened, Clara thought about asking to see Dr. Roach to convince him once and for all that Bruno did exist. Somehow, she would insist he bring the construction crew into his office one by one. Bruno would be among them and he would recognize Clara, proving she'd been telling the truth all along. Then she remembered Madeline saying Dr. Roach had put Esther on medication because she was frantic, acting as if her life depended on finding Clara. Why would he medicate her, other than to keep her quiet? Was he afraid Clara would find out Bruno was at Willard? And if so, why? Before she went to Dr. Roach, she needed to ask more questions. That afternoon, in the recreation room, she sat across from Esther, gently shaking her awake.

"I need to ask you something," Clara said, leaning forward and keeping her voice down.

Esther blinked and lifted her head, giving Clara a thin smile. "Did you find Bruno?" she said, her words slurring.

"Shhh," Clara whispered. "I don't want anyone to hear."

Esther exhaled. "Okay," she whispered.

"Just shake your head yes or no, all right?"

Esther nodded, her wet lips parting, her eyelids half closed.

"Did you tell Dr. Roach the name of the man who came into the ward?" Clara whispered.

Esther nodded.

"Did you tell him Bruno was looking for me?"

Esther nodded again.

Clara's heart started racing. "What did Dr. Roach say?"

Esther's mouth contorted in disgust. "He said I was hallucinating."

"Is that it? Is that why he put you on medication?"

Esther shook her head. "I asked about you. He said you were very ill. Then I asked about your baby. I said Bruno was the father."

"And?" Clara said, holding her breath.

"He was surprised I knew about the baby."

"Did he tell you they took her?"

"No," Esther said, her chin quivering. "He said I should mind my own business."

Clara's face and chest felt on fire. She couldn't imagine why Dr. Roach refused to believe Esther's story. Esther had nothing to gain by saying Bruno was real. And why wouldn't Dr. Roach look into it, to find out if Clara had been telling the truth all along? Had he gone too far— keeping Clara locked up, taking her baby away— to admit he'd made a mistake? Or was her father behind it all, pulling Dr. Roach's strings?

Suddenly, Esther's face twisted in anguish. "I'm sorry," she said, dissolving into tears. "It's all my fault."

"What?" Clara said, her stomach tightening.

"I shouldn't have told Dr. Roach about Bruno," she said, her voice catching.

"It's all right," Clara said. "You were just trying to help."

"But what if Dr. Roach got rid of him?" Esther said.

Clara felt the blood drain from her face. The room started to spin. She hadn't thought of that. Dr. Roach could easily have Bruno fired and banned from the property. What then?

A few days later, she stole a pair of pants and a boiled shirt from the sewing room, wet her hair down and slicked it back from her face, then went into the laundry to try to sneak out with the male patients picking up the clean linens. The foreman caught her and pulled her aside, earning her a week in isolation before she was allowed to come back to work. She asked the other patients if they'd seen the construction crew, and if so, where. They all said no, shaking their heads with worried eyes, just wanting to be left alone. She thought about sharing Esther's story with Nurse Trench, hoping she would feel sorry for her, but decided it was too big a risk. At times, finding Bruno seemed impossible. But she had to try. There was no other choice.

The wee hours after midnight were the worst. That was when she worried Bruno had been fired and wouldn't find another way to rescue her. She worried he'd get discouraged and stop looking. She worried Esther had been dreaming. After all, Clara had told Esther and Madeline everything, that she and Bruno were in love, that her parents had disapproved, that her father had sent her away, that she was expecting a baby. Maybe being locked up in Willard and being put into a coma had sent poor Esther around the bend. Maybe she had imagined the entire thing! The thought pressed against Clara's chest like a slab of cold granite.

For nights on end, doubts and questions kept Clara awake. Every time she was finally on the edge of sleep due to pure exhaustion, the horrible idea that Bruno wasn't at Willard made her sit up in bed, breathless and sweaty, her legs tangled in the grimy sheets. Afterward, she'd curl up and cry herself to sleep, wondering if she would ever be free.

Then, one day in the sewing room, while sitting on a hard stool with her back to the window and a basket of freshly starched shirts at her feet, Clara watched the forewoman climb a ladder to change a lightbulb. The forewoman was a petite, older woman who limped around the sewing room, her long, full skirt rustling along the plank floors. She called the female patients "dearie" and made sure they kept their heads down, their eyes on their work. Sometimes, she used a cane to get around, complaining about the weather making her bones ache, frequently stopping to massage her gimpy leg. Lately, due to the damp spring, she used the cane every day.

Watching the forewoman on the high ladder, Clara cringed when she teetered and nearly fell. Clara had no idea what was wrong with the forewoman's leg, but she wondered why she'd risk climbing a ladder to change a lightbulb. There were three blown bulbs in the sewing room, including the one above where Clara was sitting. But the ceilings were twelve feet high, the light fixtures nearly ten feet from the floor. Surely, Willard had men to do jobs like that.

Then, like a jolt, an idea came to her.

If she couldn't go to Bruno, maybe she would find a way to get Bruno to come to her. Esther said he was working with the carpentry crew. Madeline said they were fixing a leak in the ceiling or putting up a new door. Clara looked around the sewing room, trying to figure out what she could break. After a minute, her heart sank. The doors were too thick, the moldings too wide. The walls were lined with open cupboards used for storing folded cloth and linens, and there were dozens of wooden stools, sorting tables, and high-back chairs, but nearly all the furniture was made out of solid oak or maple. The room's support beams were bigger around than Clara's head. Then she realized that, unlike the windows on the wards, which were covered by protective mesh, the insides of the sewing room windows were exposed. The panes were separated by thin, wooden grids and could be easily broken.

With her heart in her throat, Clara got up from her stool and went over to the ladder, where the forewoman was climbing down. On the last rung, the forewoman lost her balance and nearly fell. Clara grabbed her arm.

"Can I help you?" she said.

The forewoman exhaled in relief, then straightened her skirts, her face red, her gnarled hands shaking. "Thank you, dearie," she said. "I hate climbing ladders."

Clara and the forewoman moved the ladder across the floor, positioning it beneath the next light fixture. Clara climbed up and changed the bulb without incident. Then they dragged the ladder beneath the next bulb, near the windows where Clara had been sitting. Clara took a deep breath and climbed the ladder, trying to keep her knees from shaking. There was no other choice. She had to get out of Willard. She had to find Bruno and Beatrice. And she had to do something drastic right now, before she lost her nerve.

Clara reached for the lightbulb and purposefully leaned too far, tilting the ladder toward the windows. She pretended to lose her balance and pulled the ladder over, crashing the top step into the windowpanes, sending glass shards and splintered wood across the room. At the last second, she let go, falling to the wooden floor with a bone-jarring thud. Then the ladder fell sideways, tipping over a cupboard, stacks of white shirts and brown trousers sliding from the shelves in what seemed like slow motion. The top shelf cracked in half, and the ladder fell to the ground with a loud clatter.

"Oh lord in heaven!" the forewoman cried. "Are you all right, dearie?"

Two orderlies rushed into the sewing room, hurrying over to help Clara up. Several patients stared with frightened eyes, while others shrugged and whispered. Most sat watching, their pasty faces blank. Clara stood on shaky legs, brushing off her dress.

"I'm fine," she said, rubbing her elbow. Her hip screamed in agony and her shoulder felt like it had been wrenched from its socket, but she wasn't about to complain and get sent to the infirmary.

Flustered and red-faced, the forewoman ordered everyone back to work. The women found their stools and resumed their sewing, some crying, some mumbling, others whispering behind trembling hands. The forewoman got the broom and held it out to Clara, panting and leaning on her cane as if she was the one who had just fallen off a ladder.

"I'm sorry," Clara said, taking the broom. "I was just trying to help."

"Don't you never mind about that, dearie," the

forewoman said. "Just sweep up this mess, then find another stool and get back to work." She gripped her cane with both hands and looked around the room, clucking her tongue. "I suppose I better get someone over here to fix all this."

"When?" Clara said.

The forewoman furrowed her brow. "As soon as I can," she said, her voice flat. "Although I have no idea why that makes any difference to you, dearie."

After breakfast the next morning, Clara hurried through the sewing-room door with her heart in her throat. Her eyes flew toward the broken window and cracked cupboard, hoping to see men working there. But the window was boarded up and the broken cupboard was gone. Her shoulders dropped. If the carpenters had been here, she'd missed them. She went across the room and found a stool among the other women, baskets of sheets and nightgowns at their feet. She could barely push the end of her thread through a needle, the world a blur through her tears.

How stupid and foolish of me, she thought, biting down hard on her lip. *Even if the carpenters had come while I was here, there was no guarantee Bruno would be among them. Like Esther said, Dr. Roach could have gotten rid of him, or maybe there's more than one carpentry crew.* The hard toast and dried prunes from breakfast churned in her stomach and she nearly gagged. One of the patients started singing "Bye, Bye, Blackbird" in a high, off-key voice. Another started humming along, her thin, white fingers floating in the air as if she were conducting an invisible orchestra. It was all Clara could do not to yell at them to stop. Then the forewoman came in to make her rounds, and Clara was grateful when the woman stopped singing.

She plucked a torn nightgown from her basket, then lowered her head and got to work, accidently sticking the needle in her fingertip. She ignored it and kept working, stitching a ripped shoulder closed. The forewoman limped past, her cane tapping on the wooden floorboards. A red blotch bloomed on the nightgown in Clara's hands, bleeding into yellowed stains. Clara put her finger in her mouth, got off her stool, and shoved the nightgown to the bottom of the basket, swearing under her breath. The woman next to her watched, her mouth pinched in disapproval.

Just then, Clara heard a male voice in the hallway. Her head snapped toward the sound, her heart racing in her chest. A man was moving backward through the sewing-room door, his shoulders hunched as if he were lifting something heavy. The ceiling lights reflected off his bald head and his torso was short and thick, as if his body was that of a dwarf despite his limbs being long and lean. Sawdust coated his overalls like a fine layer of yellow fuzz. The bald man shuffled backward into the room, one end of a window frame in his hands, trying not to scrape the wide sash along the doorframe. Clara held her breath as she watched the window inch through the entrance, thinking she might pass out before she saw who was holding the other end.

Then her shoulders sagged. The man carrying the other end of the repaired window was pale and lanky, with short blond hair. Clara sat down hard on her stool, blinking against her tears. The men carried the window past her and set it up against the wall, next to the boarded-up window.

"When are you fixing the cupboard?" the forewoman asked the bald man.

"Here it is now," the bald man said, turning toward the door.

Clara swallowed, following the bald man's gaze. Another worker backed into the doorway, one end of a wooden cupboard in his hands. He was square shouldered and sturdy looking, his black hair slicked close to his head. Clara gasped. She dropped the nightgown and got to her feet. It seemed to take forever for the rest of the cupboard to come through the door. Clara glanced at the man on the other end. He had gray hair and glasses. Her eyes snapped back to the dark-haired man. Finally the cupboard was all the way in the room. The men set it down and, in what looked like slow motion, the dark-haired man turned. He took off his gloves and glanced around the room, as if looking for someone. His hair was longer than Clara remembered and there was a fresh scar above his eye, but Clara knew that face.

It was Bruno.

A cry of joy burst from her throat. "Bruno!" she cried, her voice breaking. She started toward him.

Bruno's eyes went wide and his mouth fell open. He dropped his gloves and started toward her.

"Stop right there!" the forewoman shouted. "Orderlies!"

"Do as they say," Bruno said.

The orderlies rushed into the room and Clara stopped in her tracks, fighting the urge to run into Bruno's arms. But he was right: Getting into trouble wouldn't help their situation. Bruno moved backward, his hands up in surrender. The forewoman glared at Clara.

"What do you think you're doing?" she said, scowling. She limped across the room and grabbed Clara's chin with hard fingers. "You been doing something you're not supposed to be doing? You just wait 'til Dr. Roach hears about this. There's a special ward for women like you, dearie."

"She's my wife!" Bruno said, his voice strong.

The forewoman glared at him. She let go of Clara's chin and looked him up and down, her lips pressed into a rigid line. Then she lifted her cane, pointing the end of it at the bald man. "You have any idea what's going on here?" she said.

He shook his head.

The forewoman jerked her head toward the door. "Take them to see Dr. Roach," she said to the orderlies.

Clara and Bruno sat on opposite ends of Dr. Roach's office, an orderly on both sides of their chairs. Dr. Roach sat at his desk while Nurse Trench stood behind his shoulder, worried eyes darting back and forth between Clara and Bruno. She held a patient chart against her ample chest, a straitjacket draped over her arm like a serving towel. Nurse May entered from the hallway, handed Dr. Roach a folder, then obediently stood at one end of his desk. Dr. Roach opened the folder, laid it on the blotter and scanned the papers, clenching and unclenching his jaw. Clara could barely breathe, waiting for him to say something. Finally, he looked up.

"I'm not sure I understand what's going on here," he said. "Would you care to enlighten me, Clara?"

"This is Bruno!" Clara said. "The man you said doesn't exist! I told you I wasn't insane! He's . . ." She swallowed the sudden lump in her throat and stared at Bruno, tears flooding her eyes. There was no other way to tell him. "He's the father of my baby. The little girl you took away from me."

Bruno stiffened, his face turning crimson. He closed his eyes and hung his head, his fingers digging into the arms of the chair, his temples working in and out.

"Maybe he'd care to explain why his employee chart says Joseph Russo," Dr. Roach said. "Not Bruno Moretti."

Bruno looked up and cleared his throat, his eyes glassy. "Joseph is my father's first name," he said, his words hard and forced, as if he could barely control his anger. "Russo is my mother's maiden name."

"Why didn't you use your real name when you applied for the carpentry job?" Dr. Roach said.

"Because Clara warned me in a letter that the doctors at the Long Island Home knew about me," Bruno said. "Her father had ordered them to keep me away from her, going as far as intercepting her earlier letters so I wouldn't find out where she was. I used a different name because I figured you'd been given the same instructions."

"So you took a job at Willard to find your girlfriend?" Dr. Roach said.

"Yes," Bruno said. "I knew you wouldn't listen if I came to the front door and demanded you release her. Henry Cartwright is a powerful man. I know she's being held here under his orders. And just to be clear, she's not my girlfriend. She's my wife."

"Henry Cartwright cares about his daughter's well-being," Dr. Roach said. "He sent her to Willard because she's not well."

"Bullshit!" Bruno said, the veins in his fore-head standing out. "He sent her here to keep her away from me! There's nothing wrong with her!"

"I'm afraid you're not qualified to judge her mental state," Dr. Roach said. "Whereas I, on the other hand, am." He directed his gaze at Clara. "Would you care to explain why you never mentioned being married?"

Clara glanced at Bruno, unsure of what to say. But he was glaring at Dr. Roach, clearly fighting the urge to launch himself across the desk and strangle him. Then, sensing Clara's hesitation, he looked at her, his forehead furrowed, as if trying to convey she should play along. He reached into his back pocket and retrieved a folded piece of paper from his wallet.

"Here's our marriage certificate," he said, holding it out to Dr. Roach. Nurse May came around the desk, took the paper, and laid it on the open folder. Dr. Roach scanned the certificate.

"How did you two meet?" he said.

"At the Cotton Club," Clara said. "My father had no idea that I used to go there with my girlfriends. One night, Bruno was—"

Dr. Roach waved a hand in the air. "No, no," he said. "I don't want to hear any more stories. I want to know how you met here, at Willard. Clearly, our system of keeping outside help from mingling with patients has some serious flaws."

"It's not a story!" Clara said. "We—"

"Clara was working in the sewing room," Bruno interrupted, his voice strained. He moved to the edge of the seat, as if getting ready to stand. The orderly grabbed his shoulder and urged him to stay down. Bruno shot him a dirty look before resuming. "I was helping deliver a cupboard from the woodshop. It was the first time I saw her here, even though I've been searching for months."

"So you didn't start a relationship with Clara while she was a patient here?" Dr. Roach said.

"No," Bruno said, holding Dr. Roach's gaze. "We met two years ago at the Cotton Club, just like she said."

"Why won't you believe anything we're telling you?" Clara said. "All along I've said my father sent me here to keep me away from the man I love. Now he's right here in front of you and you're still not listening!"

"You've been delusional since you arrived," Dr. Roach said. "This man is trying to take advantage of your illness by telling you he's someone he's not."

"That's not true!" Clara said, pounding a fist on her leg. "How do you explain the names on the marriage certificate?"

Dr. Roach lit his pipe, took a long drag, then looked at the certificate again, smoke rolling from his lips. "This doesn't prove anything," he said. "It could be forged for all I know."

"What about Beatrice?" Clara said, panic tightening her chest. "If Bruno isn't the father, who is?"

Dr. Roach shook his head. "I'm sure I don't know," he said. "But your father made me aware that you were being rather, how shall I say, free with yourself before you were sent to the Long Island Home. He said it was unlike you and that's when he started to suspect something was wrong." Dr. Roach gave a nod to Nurse May and she left the office, exiting through the examining room door.

"That's a lie!" Clara cried. "I was with Bruno, that's why my parents sent me here! Don't you see? It all makes perfect sense!"

"Where's our daughter?" Bruno said, grinding the words out between clenched teeth. "I demand you give her back to us." He took a deep breath and held it, clearly trying to maintain self-control.

"I'm sorry," Dr. Roach said to Bruno, his voice flat. "I know you think you're helping Clara, but she's unfit to be a mother. Trust me when I tell that her daughter has been placed in a loving home and is being well taken care of."

Just then, Nurse May reappeared with a hypodermic needle on a tray. Clara's heart hammered in her chest. Bruno looked at the tray with a furrowed brow, then stood, his hands in fists. The orderlies grabbed him by the arms.

"This can't be legal!" Bruno said, his voice

rattled by fury. "You can't just lock people up and do whatever you want with their children!"

"Clara's father has trusted me with her care," Dr. Roach said. "I'm only doing what's best for everyone."

"I'll go to the police!" Bruno shouted. "I'll tell them you kidnapped our baby! I'll bring them back here and demand you return my daughter and let Clara go!"

Dr. Roach considered Bruno for a long moment, as if trying to decide whether or not he was bluffing. Bruno glared at him, his chest heaving in and out.

"Where's my daughter?" Bruno said again, his eyes burning with rage. "If you don't tell me, I'll find someone who will. And then I'll have you arrested!"

Dr. Roach put his pipe in an ashtray. He shifted in his seat, then wrote something in Bruno's folder, perspiration breaking out on his forehead.

Clara stood. "Why are you so nervous?" she said. "Has my father been paying you to keep me here? Did he tell you to give my baby away?" The orderlies shoved her back into the chair.

Dr. Roach ignored her and turned to Nurse Trench, his hand out. She bit her lower lip and gave him the chart she'd been holding. Dr. Roach opened it, turned to the last page, and scribbled something at the bottom. Then he closed the folders and made a small gesture, as if shooing away a fly. The orderlies shoved Bruno back into the chair. Bruno struggled and tried to stand. It was no use.

"What the hell do you think you're doing?" Bruno shouted. "You have no authority over me! I'm not one of your patients!" Dr. Roach stood, reached for the coat on the back of his chair, and pushed his arms into it. He directed his attention to Nurse Trench.

"Insulin therapy for Clara," he said, buttoning his jacket. Nurse Trench nodded, her eyes growing moist. Then Dr. Roach looked at Bruno, his face flat. "I'm recommending you be admitted for evaluation, Joseph or Bruno or whoever you are."

Bruno struggled to stand, his hands in fists, his mouth twisting in contempt. "That's it?" he bellowed. "You're just going to decide we're lying, or insane, or whatever you want to call it? You're just going to lock us up?"

"I'm doing my job," Dr. Roach said. "I'm trying to help Clara. Now I'll try to help you."

"The hell you are!" Bruno shouted. "What are you afraid of? What are you trying to hide?"

Clara slumped in her chair, certain she was going to throw up. One of the orderlies grabbed her under the arm and yanked her to her feet. Finally, Bruno pulled out of the orderlies' grasp. He flew across the room, grabbed Clara, and dragged her toward the door.

"Stop them!" Dr. Roach shouted.

An orderly caught Clara by the waist and carried her backward, her feet coming off the floor. She clawed at the orderly's arms, breaking his skin, but it was no use. The orderly wouldn't let go. Clara watched, suspended in midair, as the other orderlies wrestled Bruno to the floor and held him there. Dr. Roach rushed over with a straitjacket and the orderlies yanked Bruno to his feet. Bruno thrashed and bucked, trying to escape, but the orderlies twisted his arms backward, pulling them up behind his shoulder blades. Bruno doubled over in pain, his eyes bulging. He lifted his head to look at Clara.

"Don't worry," he said, his voice strained. "I'll find a way to get you out of here!"

Dr. Roach buried a syringe in Bruno's upper arm, then stepped back, watching the orderlies wrestle Bruno into the straitjacket. Clara squeezed her eyes shut. She couldn't watch.

CHAPTER 19

Izzy

Bedford State Prison

The October wind whipped Izzy's hair across her face as she stood looking up at the two-story metal gate outside Bedford Hills Correctional Facility. She turned her back to the icy gusts and gathered her coat beneath her chin, trembling and waiting for the guard to let her in. Behind the gate, the hodgepodge collection of brick buildings, barred windows, and clusters of chimneys reminded her of Willard State. The only differences between the asylum and the prison were the watchtowers and the curling barbed wired above the metal fences.

She glanced across the road toward the parking lot, where Peg sat in the driver's seat of her car, watching from behind the windshield. Peg had called ahead to arrange the visit and offered to go in, but Izzy insisted on saying good-bye to her mother alone. Now, her stomach started doing flip-flops and she wondered if it was too late to change her mind. Just as she made the decision that she really wanted Peg to come with her, a guard ambled through the inside gate to let her in.

He scuffed his heels along the pavement and looked around as if bored, his expression indifferent.

"Visitor's pass?" he said when he reached her.

"No," Izzy said. "I . . . um. I've never been here before. My mother is in the infirmary. My foster mother called and talked to the warden. He said I could visit."

"What's your name?"

"Isabelle Stone," she said.

"Hang on," he said. He opened a black box on a pole next to the gate, dialed a number, and told whoever was on the other end about the situation. "Yeah," he said. "Isa . . . what's your name again?"

"Isabelle Stone," she said.

"Isabelle Stone," the guard repeated. "Yup. Okay." He hung up the phone and looked at her. "You got some ID?"

She reached into her purse and pulled out her birth certificate and school ID. He examined them, glancing up at her to compare the pictures, then unlocked the gate.

"You have to go to the visitors' entrance and get a pass," he said. She shoved her IDs back in her purse, glanced over her shoulder and gave Peg a quick wave, then entered the prison grounds. The guard pointed toward the brick buildings to his right. "See that blue sign over there? The one that says All Visitors?"

"Yes," she said.

"Follow the sidewalk to the lobby entrance, then press the intercom and tell them what you told me."

"Okay," she said. She dropped her head and walked into the wind, putting her hands on her dress to hold it down, berating herself for wearing it in the first place. When she was little, her mother had insisted on making her wear homemade dresses, curling her hair and tying it back with pink ribbons. At six years old, Izzy started rebelling against the frilly clothes, begging her mother to let her wear T-shirts and jeans like her friends, as if that was the most important thing in the world. Her mother had relented, but Izzy never forgot the sad look in her mother's eyes when she realized her little girl was growing up. Today, wearing a dress felt like the least Izzy could do. Now, with the wind whipping against her bare legs, she realized how foolish it was. After all, her mother wouldn't know the difference.

With her heart in her throat, Izzy pushed the buzzer on the outer door of the visitors' lobby and was let inside. Sitting behind a sliding window and keeping her eyes on her work, a receptionist handed Izzy three forms, instructing her to fill them out. Izzy took the clipboard over to a chair and sat down, trying not to stare at the children playing and reading at the kid-sized tables in the center of the room. They were school-age children, toddlers and babies, girls and boys around ten to twelve years old, smiling and laughing, as if playing in a prison lobby was the most natural thing in the world.

At first, Izzy was confused, wondering why children would be hanging out in a jail. But then she realized they were there to see their mothers. Their mothers, who were locked up in prison. She bit down on her lip. *Had the older ones ever refused to visit?* she wondered. *Or were they always loyal, visiting their moms no matter what?* She filled out the paperwork, a sour mass of guilt twisting in her stomach.

Finally, a female guard came to lead her to the infirmary. Izzy followed the guard through a riveted metal door into a short cement passageway that smelled like damp stone, iron, urine, and something that reminded her of curry. Long, barred windows ran along one wall and three open doors lined the other. The guard stopped and motioned Izzy through the first doorway. She did as she was told. Inside a small room, another guard waited beside a white table.

"I need to search your bag," the guard said.

Izzy slid her purse from her shoulder and handed it over. The guard dumped the contents on the table.

"Lift your arms and stand with your feet apart," the first guard said.

Izzy swallowed the lump in her throat and raised

her hands. The guard patted her down, feeling between her legs and beneath her breasts. Finally, the search was over and the first guard took her back into the passageway. At the end of the hall, they came to a door made of iron bars. Izzy stood behind the guard, waiting for her to unlock it, her knees jerking up and down. The only sound she heard was her racing heart, roaring in her ears. It was bad enough being inside a prison for the first time, but the closer she got to seeing her mother, the harder it was to put one foot in front of the other.

She followed the guard through the bars into a concrete hallway with caged ceiling lights, then through another locked metal door into a small lobby. The guard instructed her to take a seat and wait for someone to come get her. She did as she was told, sitting on her hands, trying to take deep, calming breaths. The guard left, exiting through another doorway.

A nurse sat on the other side of a glass partition, an open door behind her leading into another room. *Maybe this is a mistake,* Izzy thought, blinking back tears. The image of her mother sprawled on the bed in the mental ward jerked into her mind and she nearly cried out loud. Not only did she wonder what her mother was going to look like now, after ten years of being locked up in prison, but when she thought of seeing her mother in a coma, her stomach churned and she felt like she was going to be sick. The last image she had of her mother had haunted her dreams for years. What horrible picture would be painted in her mind today?

She remembered a book by Stephen King called *The Dead Zone*, where a man injured in a car accident spent five years in a coma. She pictured the main character waking up and grabbing someone's hand, unable to let go until he'd made a prediction about the person's future. After reading the novel, Izzy hadn't been able to sleep for weeks. Being in a coma seemed like the worst possible thing that could happen to anyone. And now she was about to see her mother in that condition. Between the guilt she felt for refusing to visit all these years, the sorrow about the prospect of being an orphan, and the fear of seeing her mother on life support, Izzy felt like screaming. But she had to apologize and say good-bye. She had to tell her mother that she'd never stopped loving her. She owed her at least that.

When one of the lobby doorways opened, Izzy jumped. A female guard called her name and held the door open. Izzy went through it and stood in the hall, her fingernails buried in her palms. A dark-haired nurse in scrubs appeared and led her down a long, green hallway, her shoes squeaking on the tiled floor. The nurse stopped outside a set of double doors and, to Izzy's surprise, smiled at her.

"You okay?" she said.

Izzy nodded. It felt more like a spasm.

"Just so you know," the nurse said. "We rarely allow family members in the infirmary. Normally, someone in your mother's condition would be sent to the public hospital. I hate to be blunt, but we don't think she'd survive the trip. Your foster mother begged us to keep her here until you could come see her. You're only going to have a few minutes."

Izzy nodded and tried to thank her, but her mouth had gone dry.

"Don't worry," the nurse said, putting a hand on Izzy's shoulder. "She just looks like she's sleeping." The nurse opened the door and led Izzy inside. A dozen metal beds lined the white walls of the vast room, a female prisoner lying on each one, some sleeping, some talking to the prisoner next to them, some reading. A guard sat at a desk beside the door. The prisoners stopped what they were doing and looked up, eyes widening in surprise, brows wrinkling in confusion. The nurse led Izzy to the first patient, pulled a curtain between the beds, brought over a metal chair, and then stood with her hand on the bed railing. Beside the bed, monitors beeped, ventilation machines squeaked and wheezed.

"Your daughter is here to see you, Joyce," the nurse said to the woman lying in the bed.

Izzy steeled herself, her stomach clenching. Her

lungs felt like they were wavering inside her chest, as if at any second her organs were going to spasm once and shut down forever, leaving her dead on the floor. She edged over to the railing, her fingers over her trembling lips, and looked down at the woman on the bed.

When she saw her mother's familiar features, her high cheeks and straight nose, the little scar above her right eyebrow from the time she fell on ice in the driveway, Izzy's breath caught in her chest. Wrinkles lined the skin around her mother's eyes, and streaks of silver lined her black hair, but other than the ventilation tube taped over her mouth, she looked unchanged. When Izzy was little, she thought her mother was the most beautiful woman in the world. Over the years, she'd come to wonder if every little girl thought her mother was beautiful, if the picture she had in her head had been enhanced by time. Now, she realized she was right. Her mother was stunning. She dropped her purse in the chair and moved closer.

"Is there any chance at all she might wake up?" she asked the nurse.

The nurse shook her head. "No, honey," she said. "By the time they found her, the damage was done." She came around the bed and put a hand on Izzy's arm. "I'm so sorry. Is there anything I can do for you? Would you like a glass of water, or a soda?"

"No," Izzy said, her voice tight. "Thank you. I just need a few minutes alone with . . ."

"Are you all right? You look a little pale."

Izzy nodded and the nurse patted her shoulder. "Okay," the nurse said. "I'll leave the two of you alone for a minute." She jerked her chin toward the guard at the door. "Just behave yourself, okay?"

Izzy tried to smile and the nurse finally left. Trying to figure out where to begin, Izzy held the bed railing to keep from falling over. Bolted to the bed's metal footboard, a heavy chain traveled beneath the blanket near her mother's feet. The absurdity of chaining a comatose patient to a bed briefly crossed Izzy's mind. Barring a miracle, her mother wasn't going anywhere. She lay still as a stone, her pale arms at her sides, her palms down, her long, slender fingers like ivory against the blue blanket. Piano-playing hands, Izzy's grandmother used to call them. Izzy thought about reaching down to hold her mother's hand, but she couldn't bring herself to do it. Besides the fact that she didn't know if touching an inmate was allowed, she was afraid to touch her mother's skin. She hated herself for feeling that way, but it was true. Just like touching the contents of the Willard suitcases made her legs feel rubbery, so did the thought of touching someone in a coma. Even her own mother.

She wiped her cheeks and took a deep breath.

"I'm so sorry," she whispered. "I made a mistake. I didn't read your letters until it was too late." She swallowed her sobs, struggling to speak. One second she felt like crying hysterically, the next she wanted to punch something, angry that life had turned out this way. For a split second, she wondered if the other inmates could hear her. Then she decided she didn't care. "Please forgive me for not coming to see you, Mommy. I was stupid and stubborn and scared. I thought there was something wrong with you. I forgot what Daddy did. Now I know the truth. I know you sacrificed your life for mine." She hung her head, wiping her nose on her sleeve. "I just want you to know I never stopped loving you."

It was too much. She fell into the chair, shoulders convulsing. If only she'd read her mother's letters sooner. If only she'd visited, she might have realized her mother wasn't crazy. All these years, she would have had someone to talk to, someone who loved her, even if that someone was behind bars. The one time Izzy tried asking her grandmother what happened, her grandmother started crying. And seven-year-old Izzy, not wanting to upset the only person she had left, never brought it up again. Three short years later, her grandmother was gone.

Then Izzy remembered Clara's daughter. If she survived, she'd probably gone through life thinking the same thing—her mother was locked away because she was crazy. Izzy stood. If Clara's daughter was alive, she deserved to know the truth; she had to read Clara's journal. Now, more than ever, Izzy was determined to find out what happened to her, and if possible, let her know her mother wasn't crazy.

Now all Izzy had to do was say good-bye to her own mother. More than anything, she wanted to feel her mother's arms around her, hugging her tight, letting her know she was loved no matter what. But that wasn't going to happen. Izzy glanced at the guard to see if she was watching. The guard was leaning back in her chair, reading a magazine. Izzy took a deep breath, kissed her fingers, then gently pressed them to her mother's cheek.

"I want you to know that I'm going to be okay," she said. "I'm strong and I have people who care about me. I love you, Mommy. I always did and always will. I'm sorry I didn't tell you sooner." She tried to think of something else to say, but her organs felt like they were swelling, looking for an escape, like an overheated boiler ready to burst. Just then, the nurse entered the room, wiggling her finger to let Izzy know her time was up. There was only one other thing to say. "Good-bye, Mommy."

CHAPTER 20

CLARA

Willard
Valentine's Day, 1932

Spiraling white streamers and red paper hearts hung from the ceiling in Hadley Hall, stirring slightly as patients shuffled and swayed beneath them. The final, scratchy melodies of "All Alone" filled the air while Nurse May stood next to the phonograph, rocking and singing to herself, keeping a watchful eye on the dancing couples. Several dozen patients watched from the sidelines, strapped to wooden chairs with attached tables, slumped in wheelchairs, leaning on crutches and canes. Nurse Trench threaded her way through the patients on the dance floor, making sure they stayed the required distance apart. Orderlies sat around the perimeter of the room in folding chairs, near the windows and doors, ready to step in if anyone got out of line. The patients, orderlies, and nurses wore red tissue paper boutonnières and corsages, made by the patients during arts and crafts.

Clara sat on a bench at the foot of the stage,

glancing at the main entrance again and again, hoping and praying more male patients would show up and Bruno would be among them. It had only been a month since she'd earned extra privileges—now she could participate in arts and crafts, and attend concerts and movies in Hadley Hall—but this was the first time she'd been to an event for both male and female patients. Now, she dared hope against hope that she would see Bruno again. She had to believe he had done his best to cooperate, to earn and maintain what little freedom Willard patients were allowed. If not, the chances of them finding each other and escaping were slim to none.

The only thing that kept her going during the last ten months, the only thought that kept her from becoming truly insane, was remembering that Bruno was somewhere at Willard. It seemed reasonable to believe that, by now, he had been put to work in the rail yard or blacksmith's shop, in the orchards or the hayfields, the stables or dairy, or one of the shops that manufactured shoes, brooms, or soap. Hopefully, his job involved working outside. If she could return to her job in the kitchen, they could meet at the compost pile. He could open the gate and they could run into the woods.

During every walk, on every trip to the bathroom, the cafeteria, the sewing room, at every chance to look out a window, she searched for him. When she saw a group of male patients walking along the lakeshore, working by the dock, or hauling supplies from the trains, she scanned every figure, hoping she would recognize the way one of them walked, or a familiar head of dark hair. So far, she hadn't seen him, but she had to believe the day would come. Otherwise, what was the point?

She had given up hope a long time ago that her father would release her. Seven months earlier, Dr. Roach had indicated he and Henry were in agreement; she might never be ready to return to society. After that, her sessions with Dr. Roach stopped completely. Nevertheless, she refused to believe she'd spend the rest of her life locked up inside Willard, day after day spent among the insane, nothing more than a number among the throngs of thrown-away wives, mothers, sisters, and daughters. Bruno had promised they would find a way out and she had to believe it. She had to. There was no alternative. And yet, there were times when she wanted to give up and give in. She wanted to stop thinking rationally, to let herself fall into a deep pit of despair so she wouldn't have to feel anymore. But she couldn't do that. She owed it to Beatrice and Bruno to keep her wits about her.

She shuddered to think what might have happened if Bruno hadn't gotten her letter, if he hadn't tried to rescue her. Surely, she would have lost her mind by now. On one hand, she was beyond grateful. On the other, the guilt that he was locked up in an institution because of her was almost too much to bear. Every time the thought crossed her mind that something horrible might have happened to him—maybe he had died from tuberculosis or been chained to a bed inside the Rookie Pest House—her chest felt hollow and cold, as if her lungs and heart were gone and she would drop dead at any second.

She had no idea what happened to him after that horrible day in Dr. Roach's office, but she prayed it was no worse than what had happened to her. She had been taken to a special ward, where, every day for two months, she was given repeated insulin injections until she fell into a coma. She remembered sweating profusely, twitching and moaning, drooling until she lost consciousness. Eventually, the nurses brought her out of the coma with intravenous glucose, then occupied her with board games and map reading in an attempt to prevent hypoglycemic shock. At the end of two months, she was sent to the infirmary to recover.

Three weeks later, she returned to her job in the sewing room. At times, her vision was still fuzzy, her thoughts confused. She had trouble concentrating. Taking the nurse's advice to get rid of the aftereffects of insulin by using her brain as much as possible, she sang childhood songs in her head until her mind cleared.

Now, she watched Esther waltzing with a heavyset man wearing high pants and suspenders, both of them looking down at their feet. Esther was wearing her flowered housedress, and it looked like she was leading. Eight months earlier, Dr. Roach had determined Esther was free of her tendency toward "hostility" and had given her extra privileges. Because Esther had told Clara the men were always seated on opposite sides of Hadley Hall during concerts and movies, Clara was shocked when she realized males and females were allowed to dance together on special occasions.

On the other side of the room, Madeline stood near the refreshment table, putting her hands in the punch bowl. A nurse slapped Madeline's wrist, telling her to stop. According to Esther, Madeline's great uncle had offered to take Madeline in, and she had been released from Willard while Clara was receiving insulin treatment. A few weeks later, Madeline was back at Willard, unable to remember her name or where she was from. She had stopped talking, apart from crying for her lost babies. As Clara watched, a limping male patient pulled Madeline onto the dance floor. Madeline wrapped her arms around his shoulders and pulled him close, burying her face in his neck. Nurse Trench hurried over to separate them.

Clara gripped the edge of the bench, digging her

nails into the wood while Gene Austin sang "My Blue Heaven." *This isn't heaven,* Clara thought. *This is hell.* Granted, after being locked in a ward she was relieved to have privileges. But this was the first holiday party she had attended, and it was almost more than she could bear. Seeing the patients of Willard dancing and celebrating as if they were living normal lives, as if they had a real chance at finding true love or happiness, made her want to run out the door screaming.

For every smiling patient on the dance floor, two more looked on with blank faces. Some hobbled and jerked, unable to sway in time to the music. The number of patients in wheelchairs out-numbered those on their feet by three to one. Most gazed around the room with open, drooling mouths, their wrists bent toward their chests, their hands hanging limp and useless. Somehow, this was what their lives had become. What her life had become. It was enough to drive her mad.

She was just about to get up and go over to the refreshment table when someone tapped her on the shoulder. She stiffened. It would be the third request to dance, two by the same man. She smiled and turned, steeling herself to say no again. But then, her breath caught in her chest.

The man had a thick mustache and dark beard, a few gray strands lining the hair above his ears. His nose was slightly crooked, as if it had been broken several times. He looked like a mountain man, wild and disheveled. Clara's heart fluttered in fear. He reached out to take her hand, and she stood and started walking away. Then he spoke.

"Hello, Bella Clara," he said, his accented voice deep.

She spun around, biting her lip to stifle a cry, then rushed toward Bruno, hands outstretched.

"Don't," he said. "They'll wonder what's going on and come over."

She dropped her arms and tried to breathe normally, glancing around to see if anyone had noticed. Nurse Trench was separating two women trying to dance together, her red face contorted. Nurse May was looking through the gramophone records, trying to decide what to play next. She slid a black disc from its paper casing, placed it on the phonograph, and set the needle on the edge. Ethel Waters's voice filled the room, singing "Am I Blue?" Clara's heart beat so fast she could barely speak. "What if they recognize you?" she managed.

"They won't," he said. "I've been sitting across the room the entire time."

"Are you sure?" she said.

"Yes," he said, taking her hand. "I waited awhile to approach you so they wouldn't get suspicious. Like all patients, I'm invisible unless I start trouble."

He led her out to the dance floor and, keeping the required distance between them, put a hand on the side of her waist, his palm like a hot iron pressing through her cotton dress. Just being near him she felt herself growing warm, after months of feeling so cold and alone her skeleton felt shriveled. She lifted her eyes to his, forcing her quivering lips into a smile.

"I've been looking for you," she said, blinking back tears. "Every day." She searched his face, drinking in his familiar chestnut eyes, his long, dark lashes. He gazed over her shoulder, watching the nurses and orderlies.

"Don't look at me," he said in a quiet voice. "You don't know me, remember?"

She pulled her eyes from his and looked at the walls, the other patients, the orderlies. Everything was out of focus. "I'm sorry," she said. "It's just . . ."

"I know." He squeezed her hand. "I'm happy to see you too."

"What happened to you?" she said. "You know, after they took you out of Dr. Roach's office?"

"I was in isolation for three months," he said.

"Oh my God," she said. She pressed her lips together and hung her head. "I'm so sorry."

"It doesn't matter," he said. "What matters is here and now. You and me. And what we're going to do to get out of here."

"When?" she said, lifting her eyes to his. She couldn't help it. She had to look at him. All of a sudden, she felt light-headed.

"Soon," he said. He gave her side a quick squeeze, as if he could feel her tensing. "Relax and listen to me. I'm working with the grave-digger, building coffins and forging grave markers. We've got access to the tunnels beneath Chapin Hall. That's where they keep the coffins, in a storage area next to the morgue. Once we decide when we're going to do this, you need to find a way to get down to those tunnels. There's a sign—"

"How am I supposed to do that?" she said, panic tightening her throat.

"I don't know," he said. "For now, just listen. Let me tell you everything first. Then we'll figure out your side of the plan. Once you're in the tunnels, follow the signs to the morgue. The storage room is across the hall. Hide inside one of the coffins. Lawrence and I will carry you out."

"The gravedigger?"

"Yes."

They moved around the dance floor, turning in slow circles, the blur of faces behind Bruno's head making her dizzy.

"He won't tell on us?" she said, gripping his shoulder tighter.

"No," he said. Just then, Nurse Trench strolled past, her red lips in a determined line. Clara dropped her chin, certain Nurse Trench would read the truth in her eyes. Beads of sweat broke out on her forehead and her knees started jerking up and down. Nurse Trench checked the space between them, put a plank-thick hand on their shoulders, and pushed them farther apart.

"Too close," she said.

When Nurse Trench turned to move on to the next couple, Clara thought she might not fall into a heap on the floor after all. Then Nurse Trench stopped and stood in one spot for what seemed like eternity, narrowed eyes darting back and forth between their faces. Clara felt her bowels turn to water. Nurse Trench had recognized Bruno. For a split second, everything went black. Then Clara swallowed, forcing herself to look at Nurse Trench.

"Happy Valentine's Day," she said, her lips twitching as she tried to smile. "Thank you for throwing this lovely party."

Frowning, Nurse Trench stared at Bruno, studying his face. Bruno took on the expression of someone in a trance, swaying and staring at a paper heart above Clara's head.

"Humph," Nurse Trench said, pursing her red lips. Then she gave Clara a stern look, nodded once, and moved on. "Just watch yourselves," she said as she left.

Clara let out a trembling sigh, her legs nearly buckling beneath her.

"Are you all right?" Bruno said.

Clara tried to find her voice. "She recognized you!" she whispered.

Bruno shook his head. "She would have called the orderlies over."

Clara tried to breathe normally, watching Nurse Trench stop beside the next couple. "I don't know," she said. "It seemed like . . . like she was warning us to be careful or something."

"She was warning us to stay apart while we danced," Bruno said. "That's all. Now listen to me. I need to finish telling you the plan."

Clara took a deep breath and let it out slowly. Maybe Bruno was right. Nurse Trench would have called the orderlies or taken her and Bruno to Dr. Roach. Instead, she continued checking the dancing couples, acting as if nothing was wrong. "Okay," Clara said, trying to stop shaking. "I'm listening."

"Lawrence lives in an old shack on the other side of the cedar grove."

She nodded. "I've seen it," she said.

"We'll hide there until nightfall, then sneak down to the lake, where a boat will be waiting."

"A boat?"

"Yes. A few years ago, Lawrence found an old rowboat in the cedar grove. It was half rotten and covered with a layer of pine needles and leaves. But I've patched up the hull and fashioned some oars out of the wood we use to make coffins."

"Is it safe?"

"We'll find out, won't we?"

Clara nodded. Then she remembered it was

February and her stomach dropped. The lake was frozen. They'd have to wait until spring. But now that the chance to escape had been planted in her mind, she didn't think she could wait that long. She couldn't stand another day of being locked up inside Willard, let alone two more months. Given the chance, she'd try to escape this very minute. If she and Bruno had to wait until spring, if they had to hold out until the lake thawed, she might go crazy with apprehension. And besides, what if something happened between now and then? What if one of them got sick, or thrown into isolation? What then?

"When?" she said, holding her breath.

"Soon," he said.

"But the lake is frozen!"

"The ice is thin right now," Bruno said. "The last two weeks have been unusually warm. We should be able to break right through it."

Clara's stomach started doing flip-flops. She took a deep breath, lifted her chin, and stood up a little straighter. This was their chance. Finally. Their chance to be free, to be together, to find Beatrice. But first, she had to figure out a way to get down to the tunnels beneath the infirmary. It seemed nearly impossible, given the fact that her daily schedule never brought her anywhere near Chapin Hall. Then she had an idea.

"Tomorrow," she said. "We have to do it tomorrow."

Bruno furrowed his brow. "Why?" he said.

"Just trust me, all right?"

"What are you going to do?" he said.

"I'm going to get myself taken over to the infirmary," she said. "Then I'll find a way down to the tunnels before nightfall. Can you get in the tunnels on a Sunday?"

"Yes," he said. "Lawrence buries patients on Sundays too. We've got one to bury tomorrow as a matter of fact."

"All right," she said. "Tomorrow it is."

Just then, "Am I Blue?" ended and Nurse May changed the record. Gertrude Lawrence began singing "Someone to Watch Over Me" and Clara's throat constricted, remembering the first time she and Bruno danced at the Cotton Club. Now, they were dancing to the same song while locked up inside an insane asylum. The thought nearly brought Clara to her knees.

On Sunday afternoon, after making baskets with Esther and Madeline in the recreation room, Clara asked one of the nurses if she could return to the ward earlier than usual. Complaining her stomach hurt, she said she needed to lie down. The nurse instructed an orderly to take Clara back to the ward, her face indifferent. Clara glanced over her shoulder at Esther and Madeline, her heart squeezing in her chest. They were sitting together on a bench, working with their heads down. Clara had made the decision not to share her plan of escape, hoping what they didn't know couldn't hurt them. Besides, it was too big a risk. Who knows what they might reveal if threatened with isolation, an induced coma, or being locked up in the Rookie Pest House. Instead of saying good-bye, she sent a silent prayer, hoping Esther and Madeline would get out of Willard someday too.

Half an hour later, right before the nurses were scheduled to return the other patients to the ward, Clara took the saturated sanitary pad from between her legs and smeared menstrual blood across the grimy bed sheets, and the inside of her thighs. She hadn't changed the pad all day and, since it was the second day of her period, when her flow was always heaviest, the blood was plentiful and dark. With her heart in her throat, she curled up on the bed, waiting. When she heard the keys in the door, she started moaning and crying, her hands wrapped around her middle. The patients filed in and gathered around her bed, staring, whispering, rocking back and forth. One of the women started petting Clara's forehead, gently brushing hair from Clara's eyes. A nurse ordered the patients out of the way.

"What's the matter with you?" she said.

Clara grimaced and drew up her legs. "I don't know," she said, her voice straining.

"Turn over and let me see," the nurse said.

Clara groaned and rolled onto her back, her knees bent, her eyes squeezed shut. The nurse pulled Clara's hand away and palpated her abdomen. Clara howled and rolled over again, holding her breath so her face would turn red.

"Get a wheelchair," the nurse said to one of the other nurses. "And take her to the infirmary."

Twenty minutes later, Clara lay on an examining table in Dr. Slade's office while he felt her stomach, his forehead creased. A nurse had helped Clara get cleaned up, giving her a fresh sanitary pad and a clean nightgown. Now, the nurse looked on with little interest.

"I don't feel anything abnormal," Dr. Slade said. "Can you be more specific about where it hurts? Show me where your pain is coming from."

Clara put her fingers near her hipbone. "Right here," she said.

"And has this been more painful than your normal monthly discomfort?"

"Yes," Clara said. "But I think it's starting to feel better now."

"Send for Dr. King," he said to the nurse. "The patient needs a gynecological exam."

Clara shook her head and sat up. "I'm all right," she said. "I think I just need to walk a little bit." She slid down from the examining table and stood bent over, her hand on her lower abdomen.

"What are you doing?" Dr. Slade said. "I didn't tell you to get up."

"I need to move around," she said. "It's getting better."

Dr. Slade glared at her over the top of his spectacles. "Are you telling me you made a fuss over a bad case of gas?"

Clara shrugged. "I don't know," she said. "You're the doctor, not me." She put both hands over her abdomen and winced. "There it goes again."

"Lie back down and we'll see what happens." He looked at the nurse, frowning. "I'm not going to order more exams or X-rays if she's just having a bad case of gas or a painful cycle."

"Please," Clara said. "I just need to walk. If that doesn't help, I'll do whatever you say."

Dr. Slade considered her, then shook his head, motioning toward the door with a disgusted look. "Take her to the end of the hall and back," he said to the nurse.

Clara followed the nurse out of the examination room, her heart racing in her chest. She checked both ways to see if there was a stairway leading down to the basement, knowing in the back of her mind it wouldn't be that easy, yet hoping, for once, things would go her way. On both ends of the corridor, the hallway connected to other hallways, leading left or right. Her stomach dropped. She shuffled along the wall behind the nurse, one hand on her abdomen, the other gripping the wall railing. She wondered if she'd find a stairway right away, or if, somehow, she'd have to get herself committed to the infirmary. If she couldn't find a way down to the tunnels now, she'd have to find a way to sneak out of her room later. It would be nearly impossible.

When they reached the end of the hallway, the nurse did a U-turn, starting back toward Dr. Slade's examination room. Clara stopped, gripped the railing tighter, and looked down the hall to her left. The wide passageway was lined with patients strapped to chairs, leather belts tightened around their waists, some crying and moaning, others staring off into space. The hallway to her right was practically clear, apart from an empty wheelchair and a metal cart full of glass medicine bottles. The patient room doors on both sides of the hallway were closed. At the end of the corridor, a service elevator stood open next to a set of double doors below a green sign that read Basement. Beads of sweat broke out on Clara's forehead. She turned right, toward the stairs.

"Where are you going?" the nurse said. "Turn around!"

Clare kept moving, fighting the urge to run. "I just need to walk a little bit longer," she said. "I think it's helping."

"You should do as I say," the nurse shouted. "Dr. Slade is waiting!"

Clara ignored her and kept going. The nurse sighed, her shoes squeaking as she hurried after her. Clara glanced over her shoulder. "Just to the end of this hall," she said. "Then I'll go back."

The nurse marched past, her lips pursed, her arms pumping. Clara slowed, letting the nurse get ahead, trying not to hyperventilate. This had to work. It just had to. When they turned around in front of the set of double doors, Clara collapsed on the floor, her limbs jerking in stiff, violent movements. She rolled her eyes back and stuck out her tongue, twisting and thrashing on the cold tiles. The nurse spun around and gasped, eyes wide. She knelt and put her hands on Clara's shoulders. Clara kept thrashing, pretending to gag. The nurse stood and ran for help. As soon as the nurse was gone, Clara scrambled to her feet, ran through the double doors, and scurried down the stairway toward the cellar beneath Chapin Hall.

She stopped at the bottom of the stairs, trying to determine which way to run. Long cement tunnels led off in all directions, left, right, and straight ahead. The air was filled with the cavelike odor of mold and wet stone. Dripping pipes of various sizes traveled the length of the ceilings, and caged lights emitted a weak, jittery glow, their yellowed bulbs encrusted with dirt and dried cobwebs. Every ten feet, a bulky archway lined each passageway, like cloisters below a medieval fortress. On the archway to the left, a sign read Morgue.

Behind Clara, shouting voices traveled down the stairway and the elevator motor roared to life, grinding gears echoing in the rusty shaft. Clara hurried left toward the morgue, thankful that the cellar was one enormous maze. Whoever came looking for her would have no idea which way she went. And she prayed that, because it was Sunday, no one else would be down there.

Her footsteps echoed in the empty tunnel, her hard-soled shoes banging on the stone floor. She stopped and took them off, then froze, certain she heard talking up ahead. A male voice drifted down the passageway, followed by what sounded like moaning and crying. She edged forward, keeping close to the wall, ready to turn and run. But the more she listened, the more it sounded like the voice was repeating the same phrase over and over. Metal struck metal, and chains dragged across stone. Up ahead, on the opposite wall, was a door made of thick iron mesh, the handle chained and padlocked. She crossed the tunnel and moved closer, her shoes clutched to her chest.

The closer she got to the door, the stronger the rank smell of urine and feces grew. She clamped a hand over her mouth and peeked through the edge of the iron mesh door, her heart booming in her chest. The stone room was lined with iron cages filled with patients, some naked, some in filthy hospital gowns, most chained to the wall, sitting on cots or lying on the floor. Clara stifled a gasp, her eyes burning. Why were these patients being kept in the cellar in cages? It was bad enough being locked up in Willard, but this? This was barbaric. How did the doctors get away with it? She vowed then and there that after she got out of Willard and went to the authorities to tell them about Beatrice, she'd inform the police about the mistreatment here. Wiping her cheeks and saying a silent prayer, she hurried down the tunnel, determined to find someone who would put a stop to this.

Finally, she saw a sign that said Morgue above two swinging metal doors. Farther down the hallway, a set of wooden doors marked the end of the tunnel, weak sunlight coming in through the grimy windows in the upper half of each panel. For a split second, she thought about running to the end of the tunnel and trying the door handles. Maybe she could get outside. Then she remembered the orderlies and nurses were already looking for her. Even if the doors were unlocked, she'd have no idea which direction to go. And what if they were already searching for her outside? It was best to stick to Bruno's plan.

She pushed on the storage room door across from the morgue, the hinges screeching like a wailing cat. She stopped the door to silence it, then moved through the narrow opening, slipping sideways into the dark room. The smell of tree sap and sawdust filled the air, and long, rectangular shapes lined the walls. She put on her shoes and moved forward inch by inch, feeling her way in the dark. When she banged a shin on something hard, she reached down, her fingers brushing raw wood and what felt like the thick, sanded edge of a coffin. She pushed the lid to the side, stepped into the coffin, then lay down and pulled the cover closed, her heartbeat thumping like a train in her ears. Once inside, she pushed the cover up with her fingers, then let it down and felt along the edges, making sure there were no openings.

Satisfied that no one would see her if they came in and turned on the light, she closed her eyes, her breath coming hard and fast, her head pulsing against the bottom of the wooden coffin. After only a few seconds, it was nearly impossible to resist pushing off the lid and standing up, running out of the room and down the tunnel toward sunlight. It was all she could do not to bend her knees and elbows, to move and stretch and sit up. Every so often, distant shouts and banging doors echoed through the cellar halls. Who would find her first, Bruno or one of the orderlies?

The sound of close movement in the tunnel made her freeze. A heavy door opened and closed, then muffled scrapes and a *thump* outside the storage room. Keys turned in a lock. Then the door to the storage room screeched open. Clara held her breath. What would be the punishment for trying to escape? Isolation? Insulin coma? The Rookie Pest House? The door thumped closed. A switch clicked. Slivers of light filtered in through the edges of the coffin lid. Heavy footsteps plodded across the room. She squeezed her eyes shut.

"Are we waiting here 'til she shows up?" a male voice said.

"That's the plan, remember?" another man said. The hair stood up on Clara's arms. It sounded like Bruno. But she had to be sure. She waited, trying not to breathe, certain she would pass out before he spoke again. And then, after what seemed like an eternity, the same voice said, "Did you lock the morgue?"

"Uh-huh," the first voice said. "I locked the morgue, I did." It sounded like an older male. His voice was deep and raspy, his words careful and slow.

"And if someone comes?" the first voice said.

"We are burying Miss Annie Blumberg today," the second voice said.

Clara drew in a sharp breath. It was Bruno and the gravedigger. She started to push up on the coffin lid, then heard heavy footsteps running in the tunnel. She froze. The door to the storage room screeched open.

"You seen anyone down here?" a man said, panting.

"We are burying Miss Annie Blumberg today," the gravedigger said. "She is going to heaven to be with Jesus."

"I didn't ask what you were doin', Lawrence,"

the man said, irritated. "I asked if you've seen anyone down here in the tunnels. We're missing a female patient."

"We haven't seen anyone," Bruno said. His voice was louder than it had been a minute ago, as if he were standing over the coffin.

"I'm not asking you," the man said. "I'm asking Lawrence here. You seen anyone or not, Lawrence?"

An eternity passed before Lawrence answered. Clara thought she would scream before he said anything. "No," Lawrence said. "I have not seen a female patient down here in the tunnels. We are burying Miss Annie Blumberg today. She is going to heaven to be with Jesus."

"Well," the man said. "You make sure and let us know if you see anyone. You understand me, Lawrence?"

"Yes," Lawrence said. "I will tell you if I see a woman who is not Miss Annie Blumberg."

The door screeched shut and Clara exhaled, her limbs shuddering in relief. Her first instinct was to push open the coffin and get out, but she had to wait. She had to make sure the orderly was gone for good. She dug her nails into her palms.

"You in here, Clara?" Bruno hissed. He sounded farther away.

Clara swallowed and tried to speak around the burning lump in her throat. Nothing came out.

"Clara?" Bruno said again.

"Here," Clara finally managed. She rapped her knuckles on the wood. "I'm in here."

A loud *thump* on the coffin made her jump and the coffin shuddered, as if someone had kicked it. Then the lid slid to one side. First, she saw fingers, then a slice of Bruno's face. He removed the lid and looked down on her, his face etched with concern. She started to sit up.

"Don't move," he whispered. "And don't say anything." She lay back down. "You all right?"

She nodded, forcing herself to smile. It felt like a spasm.

"We're going to get you out of here," Bruno said, still whispering. "And we're going to escape tonight. Lawrence is here to help."

The gravedigger's long, bristled face appeared above her. He took off his cap, ran a hand over his gray, disheveled hair, and gave her a quick nod. The skin around his eyes was thin with age, giving his lids a pinkish tone, and the creases around his neck were lined with grime.

"It's not right what they did," Lawrence said, shaking his head. "It's not right that they took your baby."

Clara's eyes filled. She took a deep breath and nodded, smiling weakly at Lawrence. But then Bruno's face went dark and she started shaking again. Something was wrong.

"We have to carry you out of the tunnel," he whispered. "We have to take the coffin up the steps, load it on a wagon, and take it over to the cemetery. We took Annie's body out early this morning and hid her in the cedar grove near Lawrence's shack. We're going to make the switch in the woods, but we have to hurry. There's still a couple hours of daylight left and when they can't find you in the infirmary, they'll start searching the grounds." He straightened and scratched the back of his neck, avoiding her eyes. Then he sighed and directed his gaze at her again, searching her face. "We have to nail the coffin shut, Clara. We won't put in all the nails, but we have to nail it shut in case someone stops us on our way to the cemetery."

She nodded and tried to smile, a cold, hollow feeling making her shiver. Bruno knelt and reached into the coffin, wrapping his warm hands around the back of her head. He bent over and kissed her, hard, on the mouth.

"I promise I won't let anything happen to you," he whispered, his eyes glassy. "You're going to be all right."

He released her and reached for the coffin lid, his face white as bone. Then he slid the lid into place, locking eyes with her until the last second, until the coffin was closed all the way. Again, Clara was pitched into darkness. She closed her eyes and clenched her fists, trying to breathe normally. Then she heard what sounded like someone rummaging around inside a bag of nails. A soft *thump* hit the lid.

"Here's the first nail," Bruno said.

Despite the warning, the loud bang made Clara jump. Then there was a pause, as if Bruno was letting her get used to the sound, then *bang, bang, bang, bang.* She winced with each report, tears sliding down her temples, then slid her hands up her chest and pushed her fingers into her ears, the sharp metal whacks piercing her brain. She bit her lip, her stomach churning, and tried not to think about what would happen if, somehow, Bruno was prevented from letting her out of the coffin. Finally, Bruno spoke again.

"That was the last nail," he said, his voice tight. "We're going to take you outside now. Try not to move."

The coffin rocked slightly, then was lifted in the air in one swift upward movement. For a second, Clara couldn't feel her body weight. Her head started spinning and she pressed her hands against the wooden sides, tiny splinters digging into her skin. Bruno and Lawrence carried her into the tunnel, up the steps, and onto a waiting wagon, her body shifting inside the coffin like a rolled rug, no matter how hard she tried to stay still. It was all she could do not to scream.

Near the back of the cemetery, Bruno and Lawrence unloaded the coffin from the wagon and carried it into the cedar grove, hiding it within a dense stand of trees. Bruno used a crow bar to pry open the lid, careful not to break the wood so they could reuse the coffin for Annie Blumberg. Waiting to be free, Clara took slow, shaky breaths, fighting the urge to push her way out. Then, finally, Bruno pulled the cover off. Clara bolted upright and scrambled out of the coffin, taking deep gulps of fresh air, like a woman rescued from drowning. Bruno stood and crushed her to his chest, his face buried in her neck, his warm, jagged breath on her skin. She pressed herself into him, soaking in his warmth, trying to stop shivering. It felt like an eternity since she'd felt his arms around her. She didn't want him to let go. Bruno took her face in his hands and kissed her with a hungry, open mouth. Then he drew back and looked at her, his eyes glassy.

"I've missed you so much," he said.

"I've missed you too," she said, teeth chattering. "I don't know what would have happened to me if you hadn't—"

He put a finger to her lips. "Shhh . . ." he said. "Everything's all right now. We're going to get out of here and find our daughter." He kissed her again, once on the lips. "But right now, you need to run. Hide under Lawrence's bed until I come for you."

She nodded and threw her arms around him one more time, pressing her head to his chest. "I love you," she said.

"I love you too," he said. "Now go!"

Clara turned and ran, her breath pluming out in the cold air. She glanced over her shoulder and slowed, pausing to watch Bruno and Lawrence pull layers of evergreen boughs off Annie Blumberg's sheet-wrapped body. They lifted her up and laid her in the coffin, then replaced the lid. Clara said a silent prayer of thanks to the woman for giving her a chance to escape, then ducked beneath the trees and ran without looking back.

When she reached Lawrence's shack, she hurried across the crooked front porch and yanked open the sagging door, her heart racing in her chest. Inside, she clamped a hand over her nose and mouth, overcome by the rank smell of feces and decomposing rodents. The stench burned her eyes and she could hardly breathe without gagging. She was afraid she'd have to hide outside, lying on the roof or crouched inside a concealed nook behind the house. But no, she couldn't risk being seen. She had to follow the plan. Looking around, she tried to get her bearings.

The disintegrating structure consisted of two small rooms—a kitchen/living area and a bed-room. The living area floor was made of shale, and a crumbling brick fireplace dominated one timbered wall. A painted cupboard sat beneath a filthy window with a ripped paisley valance, its wooden countertop outfitted with a water pump and a rusted sink. In the center of the room, a cane back chair sat on three legs, the fourth leg replaced by a stack of broken bricks. A dining table had been fashioned out of an old door, its entire surface covered with empty cans and old newspapers. A pot-bellied stove crouched in one corner, licks of orange fire crackling behind its iron grate.

Fighting the urge to sit by the woodstove and get warm, Clara hurried across the living room into the dirt-floored bedroom, where a wooden bed with a horsehair mattress was pushed up against one wall, and a lopsided chest of drawers squatted like a deformed dwarf beneath a partially boarded-up window. The upper windowpanes allowed the waning daylight to filter across a threadbare rug in front of the dresser. It was a Persian throw rug, the geometric design reminding Clara of the carpet outside her father's study.

Pushing the image of her father from her mind, Clara scrambled beneath the bed, her knees and elbows scraping the earth floor. She pushed herself under as far as she could, until her back was against the timbered wall, then peered out from beneath the low bed rails, trying to take shallow breaths. The stench of feces was nearly unbearable. A metal bucket sat in the corner near the dresser, grainy splashes and brown trails caked to its sides. She pulled one corner of a wool blanket down from the bed, blocking her view of Lawrence's makeshift toilet. Dusty cobwebs clung to her wrist. She brushed them away and waited, trying to ignore the cold radiating from the dirt floor.

Wondering how long it would be before Bruno came to get her, she tried remembering how much time it took Lawrence to bury someone when she watched from the Rookie Pest House. But she had been consumed by grief and laudanum then, and couldn't remember. Hopefully, he and Bruno would hurry and, between the two of them, the job would take only half as long. It was already getting dark outside, the light in the shack growing gray and thin.

After what seemed like an eternity, the front door opened. Clara started out from beneath the bed, hardly able to see in the darkening room. Then she shrank back, suddenly realizing it might not be Bruno and Lawrence. Even if it was, they might not be alone. She froze and listened, trying not to breathe. Out in the living area, someone struck a match. Something hissed and ignited. A pair of mud-covered boots came through the doorway, a yellowish glow lighting up the bedroom. The rubber boots scuffed across the dirt and stopped near the opposite wall. A rusty oil lantern was set on the floor. The owner of the boots slipped them off, exposing filthy bare feet. A jacket fell in a heap on the dirt. It looked like Lawrence's.

Why would Lawrence be here without Bruno?

she wondered. *Did he turn Bruno in? Was he waiting for the orderlies to come get her? What if Bruno was sent back to the ward because a patient was missing? Had Lawrence forgotten she was hiding under his bed? Then again, maybe the man in the shack wasn't Lawrence.*

The filthy feet padded over to the bucket. Suspenders stretched and snapped, and trousers fell around the man's ankles. A stream of urine hit the walls of the bucket. The man groaned and waited a moment before pulling up his pants, then turned and headed in her direction. At the edge of the bed, he got down on his hands and knees, gnarled white fingers digging into the dirt. Clara held her breath and pushed her back against the wall, her heart about to burst. Then Lawrence's wrinkled face appeared, pink-lidded eyes squinting. She exhaled.

"They are searching for you," Lawrence said.

"I know," she said, trying to rein in her galloping heart. "Where's Bruno?"

"He is burying Miss Annie Blumberg," he said. "He said to say I am sick when they come to my house."

Clara swallowed. "When is he coming to get me?"

"When it is safe," he said. "When it is safe you and Bruno will be able to go find your little baby. But I must hide you in a better place."

Clara felt blood drain from her cheeks. "Where?" she said.

Lawrence grinned, his crooked teeth like kernels of corn between his chapped lips. He motioned for her to come out, then scrambled to his feet. She dragged herself across the earth floor, clambered out from beneath the bed and stood, brushing dirt and cobwebs from her elbows and knees. Lawrence hurried toward the dresser, bent over, and drew aside the throw rug, revealing a small trapdoor. He grabbed the iron ring and pulled the door open. A set of rickety steps disappeared into what looked like a bottomless pit. Lawrence gestured for her to climb down.

"Do you have a candle or another lantern?" Clara said, trying to breathe normally. "So it won't be dark down there? If I hear someone coming, I'll put it out."

Lawrence twisted his mouth and looked down at his feet, scratching behind his ear. Then he hurried into the kitchen. She followed and stood in the doorway, keeping an eye on the front window in case someone came across the porch. Outside, the sky was nearly dark, the shadowy silhouettes of trees growing murky. Lawrence went over to the makeshift table and picked up tin can after tin can, looking into each one before dropping it to the rock floor with a clatter. Bugs and maggots moved in the bottoms of the tipped-over cans, squirming in a blackish-gray mass. Clara clamped a hand over her mouth. Finally, Lawrence found what he was looking for. He headed to the woodpile next to the cast-iron stove, broke up several pieces of kindling, shoved the snapped sticks inside the tin, then retrieved a box of matches from the windowsill above the sink.

Back in the bedroom, Lawrence held Clara's hand as she climbed into the old root cellar, then handed the tin can and matches down to her. She knelt, set the can on the earth floor, and lit the kindling. The flame caught and burned, flickering along the rock walls, illuminating layers of dried dragonflies and praying mantises tied to strings and hanging from nails stuck between crevasses like a giant bug collection. At first, Clara recoiled, then she realized what she thought were bugs were actually tiny crosses made of wood and twine. There were thousands of them, covering every square inch of the cellar walls.

She looked up at Lawrence. "What is all this?" she said.

"It is wrong," Lawrence said.

Clara shook her head, confused. "What's wrong?"

Lawrence grimaced, struggling to keep his emotions in check. "The people," he said. "It is wrong to mark their graves with only a number."

Clara held the light closer to the stone walls, peering at the tiny crosses. Three initials and a number had been carved into every one, the writing so small she could barely read it. Her eyes misted over. How did someone as kind and thoughtful as Lawrence get locked away in

Willard for the rest of his life? It wasn't fair. She put a hand over her heart and gazed up at him.

"You are a good man, Lawrence," she said.

Lawrence smiled, his eyes glassy, and gave her a quick nod, blood rising in his wrinkled cheeks. "I should close the door now," he said.

"Yes," Clara said. "Thank you, Lawrence."

Trying to ignore the returning grip of claustrophobia, Clara sat on the cold dirt floor, her legs folded beneath the skirt of her dress. Lawrence closed the trapdoor and again she was engulfed in darkness. The flame inside the tin can cast trembling shadows over the crosses, giving the illusion that the sticks had suddenly sprouted wings, shuddering as they tried to break free.

Above her, the rug slid over the trapdoor and the wooden bed frame creaked. Within minutes, Lawrence was snoring. Clara bit down on her lip and squeezed her eyes shut, trying not to cry. *It will be getting dark soon,* she thought. *Then Bruno will come and get me. I just have to hold on a little bit longer.* Then she had another thought, one that made her blood run cold. How was Bruno going to get to the shack after dark?

Normally, the patients were back in the wards by nightfall. Granted, Bruno held an unusual position, but wouldn't someone wonder where he was? And who was responsible for bringing him back on time? Or was he, like Lawrence, given more freedoms than most? Her heart started racing, hot fingers of panic lighting up her chest. Then the front door to the shack opened. She blew out the flame in the can and held her breath.

"Lawrence!" a man yelled. Clara stiffened.

It wasn't Bruno.

"Lawrence!" the man shouted again.

Heavy footsteps crossed the stone floor and plodded across the dirt bedroom. The bed started creaking, as if someone was shaking the frame.

"Wake up!" a second man shouted. "Get the hell out of bed!"

Lawrence snorted and the bed creaked again, as if he were rolling over or sitting up.

"What are you doing?" the first voice said. "Don't you have work to do?"

"I am sick," Lawrence said. "Bruno buried Miss Annie Blumberg."

"You don't look sick," the second man said. "You look lazy."

"I am sick. Bruno buried Miss Annie Blumberg."

Clara cringed, worried the men would suspect something if Lawrence kept repeating himself.

"How long have you been sleeping?" the second man said.

"I don't know," Lawrence said.

"Come on," the first man said. "We're wasting our time here. We're not going to get anywhere with this retard."

"Have you seen anyone roaming around, Lawrence?" the second man said. "Did a female patient come here? Has anyone knocked on your door or looked in your windows?"

"I am sick," Lawrence said. "I have been sleeping while Bruno buried Miss Annie Blumberg."

"Let's go," the second man said.

"Wait," the first man said. "What's that?"

"What the hell?" the second man said.

"There's smoke coming from beneath that rug!"

Clara's stomach dropped. She clamped a hand over the can, biting down on her lip as the hot tin burned her palm. It was too late. Above her, the rug swished across the trapdoor. She crawled into a corner, her heart pounding so fast she could barely breathe. Someone fumbled with the iron ring and started lifting the trapdoor. A slice of light pierced the dark cellar. Then the door fell shut. Something heavy slammed into it. It sounded like a body.

A man shouted and the bedroom filled with the sounds of fighting—heavy breathing, fists meeting muscle and bone, grunting, wood splintering and cracking, furniture crashing to the floor. Then, muffled voices, and what sounded like something heavy being pulled off the trapdoor. Someone grabbed the iron ring and the door flew open. Clara gasped.

It was Bruno.

She wilted in relief, one hand over her roaring heart.

"Are you okay?" he said.

She nodded, scrambled to her feet, and bolted up the stairs on shaky legs. Lawrence was sitting on the bed, a trembling hand held to his bleeding lip. Two orderlies lay on the floor, one on his stomach, the other on his back, their eyes closed.

"Are they dead?" Clara said, her breath rasping in her chest.

"No," Bruno said. "Come on! We have to get out of here!"

She went over to Lawrence. "Are you all right?" she said.

He nodded and stood, then retrieved his jacket and held it out for Clara. "It will be very cold on the lake," he said.

At first, she hesitated, but then she slid her arms into it, turned, and gave Lawrence a hug. "Thank you for helping us," she said.

Lawrence grinned, still holding his lip. "I hope you will find your baby soon," he said, his eyes brimming.

"Come on," Bruno said again, his voice tight. "We've got to go!"

The three of them hurried out of the shack and fled into the dark forest, Lawrence leading the way. The rising moon gave the night a bluish glow, providing just enough light so they could see where they were going. Clara held Bruno's hand as she ran, dodging beneath branches, hurrying around trees and bushes. In the distance, lanterns bobbed around the dark monolith of

Chapin Hall and oil lamps flickered along the patient wards, casting long, human-shaped shadows over the brick walls and barred windows. Flashlight beams swung across the lawn, while shadowy figures crept near the boathouse and dock. It had started to snow; thick, slow flakes drifting down from the sky. For some strange reason, the scene made Clara think of caroling with her family, and she nearly laughed out loud with the madness of it. Distracted, she tripped over a stick in her path.

"Careful," Bruno whispered, catching her.

She stopped to catch her breath. "How are we going to get down to the water without being seen?" she said.

"The rowboat is hidden onshore," Bruno said. "On the other side of a road at the end of these woods. No one will see us, but we've got to hurry."

She nodded and they started running again.

When they reached the end of the woods, they stopped to check the road. The road was empty. Lawrence scurried to the other side, climbed a rocky embankment, and disappeared. Then his head popped up, and he motioned for Bruno and Clara to follow. They looked both ways, darted across the road, then scrambled up the embankment and down to the rocky shoreline below.

Lawrence and Bruno pulled the rowboat out from under a cluster of honeysuckle bushes and dragged it across the shore, the wooden keel scraping across the rocks. Once the boat was in the clear, the men pushed the bow into the water, backs bent over the stern. Clara looked out at the lake, the silver moonlight reflecting off the softly rolling waves, the snow falling silently through the cold night air. The ice had broken up days ago, and now small pieces floated here and there, jostling against each other in the water, thin layers cracking and clinking, like distant glass chimes. She took a lungful of air and held it, certain she could taste the cool, clean breath of freedom.

"Come on!" Bruno said, looking over his shoulder at her. "Get in!"

Waves lapped against the hull, rocking the boat up and down like a cradle. Lawrence held on to the stern while Bruno helped Clara step off a rock and climb in. She took a seat near the bow and waited, her breath shallow and fast. The men walked into the water up to their thighs, their shoulders hunching at the cold. Bruno lifted himself over the back of the boat and started to climb in. Just then, Clara saw lights at the top of the embankment. Dr. Roach and two orderlies appeared, their lanterns held high. One of the orderlies blew a whistle and they both scrambled down to the shoreline. Bruno let himself back in the water and tried to help Lawrence get in the boat, while still hanging on to the stern. Lawrence shook his head, resisting.

"You've got to come with us," Bruno said. "They'll lock you up!"

"No," Lawrence said, vigorously shaking his head. "I don't go in boats."

"Please," Clara said. "Get in! We have to go!"

"No," Lawrence said, turning and trying to lift Bruno into the boat. "I am staying here."

"Stop right there!" Dr. Roach shouted. He stumbled down the rocky embankment, slipping and nearly falling before he reached the bottom.

The orderlies charged across the rocks and rushed into the water, slogging through the waves as fast as possible, their arms swinging in the air. One grabbed Lawrence by the head and pushed him down, holding him underwater. Bruno let go of the boat and punched the orderly in the face, trying to get him to release Lawrence. The second orderly wrapped his arms around Bruno's shoulders, pulling him away from the first. The boat started drifting away. Clara stood, scrambled over the middle seat, and put the oars in the water. She pulled the oar handles toward her, moving the boat farther from shore. Trying not to panic, she dipped the oars in the water again and pushed. This time, the rowboat moved toward the men.

A third orderly appeared and scrambled down the embankment into the water. He hit Bruno over the head with a truncheon, his face contorting with the effort. The second orderly let go and Bruno disappeared beneath the surface. The orderly reached down, his shoulders nearly submerged, and pulled Bruno up. Bruno's eyes were closed, his face red with blood, his hair plastered to his forehead like wet seaweed. The orderly dragged him to the shoreline and left him on the rocks, Bruno's lower half still in the water, then hurried back into the lake. One of the orderlies grabbed the boat and tried lifting himself over the transom. Clara stood, pulled an oar from its rowlock and hit the orderly over the head. He fell back in the water, his head lolling. Then he recovered and reached blindly for the boat again, rivers of blood running into his eyes. She lifted the oar a second time, ready to bring it down with all her strength.

A gunshot rang through the air. She froze and looked up, the oar wavering above her head. Dr. Roach stood at the edge of the shoreline with a smoking pistol in his hand, his arm stretched toward the sky.

"I said stop right there!" he shouted.

Clara dropped the oar, the wood clattering on the rowboat seats. Three more orderlies appeared at the top of the embankment, straitjackets and chains in their hands. The orderly holding Lawrence underwater pulled him up. Lawrence's eyes were closed, his mouth hanging open. The orderly dragged him back to the shoreline and dropped him beside Bruno. Clara jumped out of the boat and slogged through the icy water toward shore, her legs like stone, the cold air like knives in her lungs. She fell to her knees on the rocks between Lawrence and Bruno, fear filling her throat like oil. She shook their shoulders, trying to get them to wake up. It was no use.

Lawrence lay on his back with his head to one side, his skin colorless, his lips purple. He wasn't breathing. Clara pushed Bruno onto his back, moved his wet hair away from his eyes, and held his bloody face in her trembling hands, shouting his name over and over. His skin was ice cold, his white hands limp. She put her ear to his chest, holding her breath to hear his heartbeat. The only heartbeat she heard was her own. She screamed and slumped over his body, her limbs vibrating out of control, her shoulders convulsing. One after the other, before she could catch her next mouthful of air, violent sobs burst from her throat, wrenching the air from her lungs. A pair of galoshes appeared in front of her. With what little strength she had left, Clara looked up.

"Now look what you've done," Dr. Roach said, gazing down at her.

CHAPTER 21

IZZY

Shivering despite her winter coat, Izzy sat on Peg and Harry's deck, her hood pulled up, her fists in her pockets. The sky spit snow and a bitter wind made her eyes water. But she didn't care. She needed to be outside. Earlier, she and Peg had gone to the Geneva funeral home to sort out the details of her mother's interment, the dim chandeliers, heavy damask curtains, and hint of formaldehyde reminding her of her father's wake. Sitting in front of the funeral director's desk, she felt seven years old again, lost in a sea of black jackets and dresses, searching for her grandmother, begging to go home. It had taken all her strength to pick out her mother's casket, decide on a grave liner, and explain why there wouldn't be a service. What she really wanted to do was jump out of the Queen Anne chair, throw open a window, and ask why the place had to look and feel so damn depressing.

Now, she couldn't get enough fresh air. She imagined her mother, lying on a metal slab inside a cold vault in the funeral home, her muscles stiff, her eyes sewn shut. All of a sudden, Izzy couldn't breathe. She stood and trudged across the lawn, trying to fill her lungs, the frozen grass crunching beneath her feet. *So this is what it feels like to be an orphan,* she thought, her throat and eyes burning. *From now on, there will never be at least one person in the world thinking of me every day, loving me unconditionally. I am finally, truly alone.*

For years, she'd told herself that after being on her own for so long, her mother's death wouldn't affect her as badly as if she'd seen her every day. But she was wrong. When Peg told her the news, Izzy fell to the floor, violent sobs stealing the air from her lungs. With tears in her eyes, Peg knelt on the rug and held Izzy, letting her cry, a gentle hand stroking her head. Nearly an hour went by before Izzy trusted her legs enough to stand.

Now, between her mother's passing, worrying about turning eighteen, and the incident at Willard, the urge to cut herself grew by the hour. So far, she hadn't given in, but she couldn't stop imagining breaking the compact in her purse and using the shattered mirror to slice through the thin skin on her arms. Over and over, she reminded herself that the relief would only last a minute, and physical pain wouldn't bring her mother back. She had to learn to be an adult, to find her way in the world without giving in to self-pity and misery. Her mother had sacrificed her life for her. The least Izzy could do was make the best of it.

Luckily, after the incident at Willard, Shannon and her friends had left Izzy alone. When they passed in the hallways at school, Shannon dropped her eyes. Izzy wondered if Shannon was afraid she was going to press charges. Shannon and Ethan weren't together anymore, but Izzy ignored Ethan's attempts to talk. He'd sent a note through Alex, apologizing for everything and begging to come over. Izzy threw the letter in the trash. When Ethan called the house, she instructed Peg and Harry to say she was in the shower or out with friends. She needed time to sort out her life and figure out what to do next. With everything else, the last thing she wanted was more heartache. Besides, who would want to date a girl with no family and an uncertain future?

"Izzy?" Peg called from the kitchen door. "Why don't you come inside? Dinner will be ready soon."

Izzy sighed, wiped her eyes, and turned toward the house, her stomach churning. She didn't think she could eat anything, but Peg and Harry had been incredibly kind through everything. The least she could do was be polite. In the kitchen, Harry stood at the island counter, chopping lettuce.

"I'm making tacos," he said, smiling at her. "They're your favorite, right?"

Izzy nodded, fresh tears forming in her eyes. She couldn't remember the last time anyone knew what her favorite food was, let alone taking the time to make it. But Peg and Harry had gone above and beyond making Izzy's favorite dinner. They had paid for Izzy's mother's casket and burial, saving her from an eternity spent in a prison cemetery. She would be buried next to her parents in Geneva. Izzy had never known anyone to be so generous. She was still trying to think of an adequate way to say thank you. But every time the words formed in her mind, her throat closed and she couldn't speak.

Izzy hung up her jacket and stood at the island counter, still shivering. Peg got the milk out of the refrigerator, poured some in a saucepan, and placed it on the stove.

"I'm going to make you some hot chocolate," she said to Izzy. "And you're going to drink it. You haven't had anything since this morning."

"Thanks," Izzy said, managing a thin smile.

Just then, the doorbell rang. Harry put down his knife and hurried to answer it, wiping his hands on a dishcloth. A minute later, he came back, Alex and Ethan at his side. Despite Izzy's decision to keep her distance from Ethan, her heart leapt at the sight of him. He was wearing work boots, a black jacket and black jeans, his cheeks ruddy from the cold. Izzy chewed on her bottom lip, fighting the urge to run into his arms. Alex hurried toward Izzy, her eyes wet.

"Are you all right?" she said.

Izzy nodded and let Alex hug her, blinking back

tears. When Izzy drew away, Ethan wrapped his arms around her. He smelled like winter and spiced cologne, his cool cheek pressing against her temple. It was all she could do not to bury her face in his neck.

"I'm so sorry about your mother," he said.

"Thanks," Izzy said. She gave him a quick hug and pulled away, unable to look him in the eye. But he held on, his strong arms drawing her closer.

"I'm here for you," he whispered in her ear. "Whether you like it or not."

Izzy squeezed her eyes shut, trying not to cry. It was no use. Hot tears spilled down her cheeks.

"Why don't you guys stay for dinner?" Peg said. "Harry is making tacos. He always cooks enough for an army, so there's plenty."

Ethan leaned back and wiped Izzy's cheek with his thumb. "I love tacos," he said, grinning.

"Me too," Alex said, rubbing Izzy's shoulder.

Izzy smiled, her heart swelling. Maybe she wasn't alone after all.

CHAPTER 22

CLARA

March 1946

Due to a continuous downpour over the last seven days, muddy water flowed in the drainage ditches along the tunnel walls below Chapin Hall, making the stone floors wet with condensation. Clara stood in line behind Esther at the bottom of the basement stairs, wondering if anyone would notice if she slipped out of line and hurried down the tunnel toward the morgue, toward the double doors that led outside, toward the green lawn. If she broke the window and squeezed through the pane, then ran as fast as she could toward the lake, she could make it into the water before anyone caught her. She could put an end to this.

She could put an end to sleeping on a hard bed in a cold, filthy ward, listening to women mumble and weep. She could put an end to eternal mornings when it took all her strength to pull herself out of bed and face another day of watching women staring out windows, banging their heads against walls, wailing that they just want to go home. She could put an end to a life spent sewing and playing checkers and eating tasteless food. She could put an end to watching people being mistreated and drugged. She could put an end to the black ache in her chest, every beat of her broken heart like a knife between her ribs.

She looked down at her hands, at the tiny cracks in her fingertips, worn into the skin from years of pulling thread, and the indent on the top of her middle finger left by hundreds of thimbles. Her nails were chewed to the quick, her skin dry and calloused; the hands of an old woman. She thought of her mother's hands; soft and manicured, her nails polished and red, her skin smelling of lavender. She tried to picture her mother now, with gray hair and a wrinkled face, sipping tea from imported china while sitting on a velvet settee. She wondered if her father was still alive, if the two of them were happily living out their years, safe and warm in their mansion. Did they ever think of her? Did they ever wonder if she was all right, if she was still alive? Did they ever think about coming to Willard and begging her forgiveness, or telling the doctors to allow her to go free? Or were they so heartless that they never gave her a second thought? Did they ever doubt their decision to dispose of their daughter like a piece of rubbish?

Now, in the tunnel, the cold iron smell of wet cement reminded Clara of the night she and Bruno tried to escape. After all these years, she could still picture Bruno looking down at her above the coffin, his eyes sad as he slid the cover closed to nail it shut. If she'd known back then what she knew now, she might have asked Bruno and Lawrence to go ahead and bury her instead of Miss Annie Blumberg.

Her eyes began to burn and, as she'd done countless times over the years, she pushed the painful memories from her mind and tried to think of something else. She lifted her chin, remembering it was movie night in Hadley Hall and the annual Fourth of July picnic was coming soon. They were small distractions, but it was something different to look forward to. Something to keep her from going insane. Every day, she reminded herself it was never too late for a miracle to happen; someday she could be let free. If she gave in to self-pity, she would surely go mad. And she couldn't let that happen. She had to keep her wits about her if she was going to survive, if she was going to find Beatrice someday.

The line moved forward and finally, she could see down the tunnel in front of her.

"What do they call this new treatment again?" she asked Esther.

"Electroshock therapy," Esther said. "But I overheard the orderlies calling it 'The Blitz.'"

"What does it mean?" Clara said.

Esther shrugged. Clara leaned sideways, trying

to see around the line of women. Just then, two orderlies carried an unconscious woman on a stretcher out of the treatment room, a sheet draped across her body. The sheet slipped off and fell to the cement floor, revealing that the woman was naked. The orderlies took her into a room across the hall. A nurse picked up the sheet and followed them, her mouth pinched. The orderlies returned to the treatment room. A minute later, they brought another woman out, holding her upright as she stumbled toward one of the chairs along the tunnel wall. The woman behind Clara started whimpering. Clara wanted her to stop. The line moved forward again.

Dr. Roach came into the tunnel and strolled along the line, writing the patients' names on a clipboard. Just before Dr. Roach reached Esther, the orderlies rushed out of the treatment room carrying another woman strapped to a stretcher. She writhed and screamed in pain, her hands clawing the air. Behind the orderlies, Nurse Trench raced toward Dr. Roach, her red face contorted.

"Dr. Roach!" she shouted. "I think her back is broken!"

Dr. Roach put the clipboard under his arm and hurried toward the patient. The orderlies stopped so he could examine her. He ran a rubber-gloved hand along the woman's spine, pulled the clipboard from beneath his arm, and gestured toward the service elevator.

"Take her up to the infirmary," he said.

The orderlies carried the stretcher toward the service elevator, struggling to keep it level while the woman thrashed and twisted. Nurse Trench stared at Dr. Roach, her lips pursed. "I told you it was too high," she said.

Dr. Roach grabbed her arm and led her toward the treatment room, grumbling something in her ear. Clara clenched her jaw, her breath coming faster and faster. What were they doing in that room? She looked behind her, down the tunnel, wondering if she should make a run for it. Maybe she could reach the double doors leading outside before anyone noticed she was gone. Then she reminded herself what happened the last time she tried to escape. She started to shiver, remembering the ten months spent in isolation. She couldn't do that again. She couldn't. It had nearly killed her.

The line moved forward. Clara looked at the woman sitting in the chair. She was leaning back, her head against the tunnel wall, her eyes closed as if she were sleeping. Two more women were led out to sit beside her. Maybe the treatment wasn't so bad. Maybe it was just bad for certain people, people with other problems. Then, before she knew it, an orderly led her and Esther by the arm into the treatment room.

Inside, Nurse May and seven other nurses stood waiting. Four beds lined the middle of the room, each mattress covered with a fresh sheet. Beside the beds, four wooden boxes sat on metal carts, each box filled with some kind of machine, dials and gages and wires coming out in all directions. The machines looked like giant batteries, plugged into wall outlets with thick, black wires. Two more wires connected each machine to handheld paddles. The orderlies led Esther and Clara to the beds, where the nurses instructed them to lie down.

Clara did as she was told, her arms and legs trembling, a slick sheen of sweat breaking out on her forehead and upper lip. Nurse Trench put her fingers on Clara's chin and pushed down, forcing Clara's lips open. She put a round piece of wood in Clara's mouth. The thick, wet wood smelled like tooth decay and vomit. Nurse May appeared at the head of the bed and held the mouthpiece in place, telling Clara to bite down. Clara breathed through her nose, trying not to gag, her heart racing in her chest. Nurse Trench strapped Clara's wrists and ankles to the bed. Dr. Roach held up the paddles connected to the machine.

"You're about to receive electroshock therapy," he said. "I'm going to put these paddles on the sides of your head and then you'll feel a little shock. There's nothing to be afraid of. My colleagues assure me they've had positive results with patients suffering from schizophrenia and delusions. This is going to help you, Clara."

Two nurses held Clara's shoulders down. All at

once, Clara was overcome with the absolute certainty that she had to get out of the bed. She couldn't let them do this to her, couldn't let them shock her brain with electricity. She thrashed and twisted, trying to break free, struggling to push the wood out of her mouth with her tongue. Nurse May pushed down on the wood, making Clara gag. Just then, there was a commotion in the hall. Something rumbled, like distant thunder, and there was another sound, like splashing water.

Women bolted into the room, screaming and knocking each other over in their haste, trampling those who had fallen. Some tried shutting the door, piling against the entrance, while others tried pushing their way inside. Someone yelled, "Flood!" and the door flew open, slamming against the wall and tossing the women to the floor. A knee-high wall of brown water blasted into the room, knocking patients and nurses and orderlies off their feet. Clara gaped at Dr. Roach and Nurse May, silently begging to be untied. Nurse May stared at the door, frozen, still holding the mouthpiece in place. Clara thrashed her head back and forth. Nurse May finally let go. Clara spit the wooden plug out of her mouth and sat up.

"Untie me!" she screamed.

Nurse May disappeared, swept off her feet by the incoming flood. Dr. Roach watched her fall, his face contorted in fear. But instead of helping her, he went in the other direction, slogging through the water toward the back of the room, pushing aside nurses and orderlies. He climbed on top of a cabinet, took off his shoe and reached up, toward a high cellar window. The water filled the room, getting higher and higher. Nurse May's head reappeared at the end of Clara's bed, her wet hair clinging to her face, her nurses' cap crumpled and wet, hanging on by a single black bobby pin. She lifted herself up and clamped one arm over the mattress, reaching out to Dr. Roach with the other.

"Victor," she said, coughing. "Help me! My foot is caught!"

Dr. Roach glanced at her briefly, then turned and broke the window with his shoe. Without looking back, he hoisted himself up and crawled out. Clara held her breath and Nurse May went under, her pale hands clawing at the mattress, trying to hold on. But the water was rushing into the room too fast, creating a powerful current. It came over the edges of the stretcher and climbed up Clara's legs, icy fingers turning her skin numb. She pulled on the wrist straps with all her strength, the veins in her forehead bulging. It was no use. The leather was too thick. The water climbed to her waist.

Nurse Trench surfaced to Clara's right, rising out of the depths like a breaching whale. She gasped for air, spitting and pushing her wet hair from her eyes, and tried to keep her footing. She looked around the room, then leaned forward and slogged toward Clara, swinging her arms back and forth, grunting with the effort. Finally, she reached the bed, the water up to her chest, and undid the straps around Clara's ankles and wrists, feeling her way underwater. Clara held her breath, the water at her chin, her mouth, her upper lip, waiting for the last strap to be unbuckled. Then Nurse Trench disappeared, forced sideways by the strong current. The lights flickered and went out, and Clara was lifted, the last strap coming loose just in time. Her head touched the ceiling. Then the water was up to her neck, her nose, her eyes, filling her nostrils and ears.

She held her breath and swam underwater toward the broken window, feeling her way through bodies and sheets and pillows, her pulse booming in her ears. Suddenly, she was disoriented, unable to tell if she was moving in the right direction. She opened her eyes and saw a faint glimmer of daylight, wavering beneath the water like a mirage of the sun. Then something dark moved in front of the mirage, blocking it out like a sudden eclipse. She tried to get around the obstacle, but someone grabbed her arm, pulling her in the other direction. Struggling to break free, she accidently inhaled, swallowing a mouthful of water. Someone grabbed her shoulders, as if trying to climb on top of her to reach the surface. Then she was floating, her pain gone.

CHAPTER 23

Izzy

Two days after her mother's burial, Izzy stood beside Peg on the front porch of a pea green Victorian, her heart thundering in her chest. After a long hesitation, she took a deep breath, pushed the doorbell, and stepped back. On the other side of the door, footsteps hurried along a hard floor. A lace curtain drew sideways in the transom window, then sprang back into place. Someone fumbled with the doorknob. The door opened and a young woman with glasses and short brown hair smiled at them. Izzy wondered if they had the right house.

"May I help you?" the woman said.

"Is this the home of Miss Rita Trench?" Peg said, smiling.

"Yes," the woman said. "And you are?"

"This is my foster daughter, Isabelle," Peg said. "I'm Peg Barrows, curator at the state museum. I called earlier, asking if Miss Trench would be willing to answer a few questions about her time at Willard State?"

"Oh yes," the woman said. She smiled and extended a hand. "I'm Renee, Rita's nurse. Please come in." Renee let them in, closed the door, and offered to take their coats. A swarm of multi-colored cats wound around her ankles, meowing and stretching, their claws kneading a braided doormat. Curled-up cats dotted the stairs and slept on the foyer settee. "I hope you're not allergic!" Renee said.

Peg and Izzy smiled and shook their heads, then followed Renee down a narrow hallway toward the back of the house. On either side of the hall, open doors led into a dining room and living room, both filled with antique furniture. Every shelf and flat surface was filled with ceramic vases, glass figurines, curio clocks, porcelain teacups, and more books than Izzy had ever seen in one house. Every wall was covered by oil paintings, black-and-white portraits, and gilded mirrors. Everything was covered, everything held something. Even the lamps were draped with ribbons and scarves.

"Does Miss Trench live alone?" Peg said.

Renee stopped and turned to face them. "Yes," she said, her voice hushed. "She's always lived alone. She doesn't have any family. It's very sad. But don't let her age fool you. At ninety-five she's sharp as a tack!"

"Does she remember her time at Willard?" Izzy said.

"Oh yes," Renee said. She continued down the hall. "A lot of people come here asking about their relatives who spent time at Willard. She nearly always remembers who they're talking about."

Peg smiled at Izzy. Izzy's heart beat faster. They entered a wide room at the rear of the house, with a kitchen on one side and living area on the other. Sunlight came in through three patio doors, reflecting off the white walls, filling the room with a bright, airy light. A gray-haired woman lay in a chaise lounge, a white blanket and white cat on her lap. Her slippered feet hung over the end of the chaise, and her shoulders took up the width of the backrest. Her heavily jowled face looked like it belonged to an old football player or heavy-weight wrestler. Izzy had never seen such a large old woman. Apparently, shrinking with age didn't apply to Miss Trench.

Miss Trench smiled and sat up, offering them a seat. "Welcome," she said. "Would you like some coffee or tea?"

Peg and Izzy sat on a cream-colored couch opposite the chaise lounge. "No, thank you," Peg said. "We're fine."

"Oh, come now," Miss Trench said. "I don't get many visitors. Humor an old woman and have a cup of tea. Renee, do we have any more of that chocolate cake?"

"I'm afraid not," Renee said, grinning. "You ate the last piece for breakfast this morning."

"Oh dammit!" Miss Trench said. She laughed and swung her feet over the side of the lounge, setting the cat beside her. "Well, we can still have tea, can't we? Now, what can I do for you young ladies?"

"We're hoping you remember a patient from Willard," Peg said.

"I might," Miss Trench said. "What's the name?"

Peg nudged Izzy with her elbow. Izzy swallowed and sat forward.

"Clara Elizabeth Cartwright," Izzy said.

Miss Trench leaned back, her brow knitted. "You related to her?" she said, directing her milky gaze at Izzy.

Izzy shook her head. "No," she said, feeling blood rise in her cheeks. What if Miss Trench wouldn't help? What then? "But we have Clara's steamer trunk, the one she had with her when she checked into Willard."

"It's part of a museum project," Peg said. "We're trying to re-create the lives of several Willard patients. The state only allowed limited access to the patients' records because they're sealed, even to family members. Clara is one of the patients we'd like to investigate further. But there are a few things missing from her file. For instance, we couldn't find her death certificate."

Miss Trench snorted and closed her eyes, nodding. "I'm sure there are a lot of things missing from her file," she said. She pulled the cat onto her lap again, stroking its fur with a large, gnarled hand. Her head dipped and her hand moved slower and slower until stopping on the cat's neck. For a second, Izzy feared the old woman had fallen asleep. But then Miss Trench looked up, her eyes glassy.

"I remember Clara," she said. "Pretty young thing."

Izzy took a deep breath and held it. Renee appeared with the tea, setting a silver tray on the coffee table. She poured the tea, handed everyone a porcelain cup, then sat in a wingback chair beside Miss Trench. "Help yourself to lemon and sugar," she said.

Peg dropped two sugar cubes into her tea, then did the same for Izzy. Izzy's hand shook as she took the dainty cup and saucer. She took a sip to be polite, then set the tea on the serving tray and put her fists in her lap.

"Clara's file says she gave birth to a daughter while she was at Willard," Izzy said. "Do you know anything about that?"

Miss Trench nodded, her mouth set. "Yes," she said in a small voice. "I remember Clara being very distraught after they took her daughter away."

Izzy stiffened, something cold and hard pressing against her chest. Poor Clara. Not only did she lose her freedom and the love of her life, but she lost her daughter too. How could anyone survive such heartache?

"So Clara's daughter was put up for adoption?" Peg said.

A thousand thoughts ran through Izzy's mind. If Clara's daughter was adopted, had she been brought up in a happy home, or was she sent from foster family to foster family? Had she grown up believing she was an orphan, or that her mother didn't care? Did she even know who her mother was? And if she knew, was her life forever marred by the knowledge that her mother was in a mental institution? Did she ever think about going to visit her? Or did she block all thoughts of her mother from her mind, choosing instead to ignore her existence completely? Had she gone through her life with the same fears as Izzy, that she would find herself in the same boat as her mother, the genes of insanity running amok in her brain, with nothing she could do to prevent them from taking over?

Miss Trench shook her head. "Most babies born at Willard were sent to family members if they were willing to take them," she said. "Or they were put up for adoption. But not Clara's daughter."

Izzy swallowed, a burning lump growing in her throat.

"Why not?" Peg said, frowning. "What happened to her?"

Miss Trench sighed, rolling a tuft of cat hair between her boney fingers. "Why are you asking me about Clara's baby?" she said. "I thought you wanted to know about Clara?"

With trembling hands, Izzy pulled Clara's journal from her purse. "Because we found Clara's journal in her suitcase," she said, holding it out so Miss Trench could see it. "It's about her life before she came to Willard. I want to find Clara's daughter so I can give it to her. If she's still alive, I want her to know the truth about what happened to her mother."

Miss Trench looked at Renee, her face somehow paler than it'd been seconds ago. "I'm going to need something stronger than tea for this one, sweetie," she said. "Fetch me the brandy, would you?"

"It's too early," Renee said. "You haven't even had lunch yet."

"I don't give a damn what time it is!" Miss Trench said, slapping a blue-veined hand on her leg. "I need a little sip, that's all. Now do what I'm paying you for!"

Renee shook her head. "All right," she said. She stood and went toward the kitchen. "But when your doctor finds out about this, he won't be happy!"

"He won't be finding out nothing if you don't tell him!" Miss Trench shouted, her voice raspy. When Renee disappeared into the other room, Miss Trench smiled thinly at Peg and Izzy.

"Clara's baby wasn't put up for adoption because she was special," Miss Trench said.

"What do you mean by special?" Peg said.

"She was born to a healthy mother," Miss Trench said. "The doctor in charge knew the baby would grow into a healthy child. The odds were extremely high that she would not show any symptoms of mental illness."

"So you're saying Clara wasn't sick," Peg said, her eyes dark. "That she didn't belong in a mental institution."

"That's right," Miss Trench said.

"And the doctor in charge knew she didn't belong there," Peg said.

Miss Trench nodded.

"Then why keep her there?" Izzy said. "Why didn't the doctor release her?"

"Things were different back then," Miss Trench said. "There were a lot of folks who didn't deserve to be locked up in an institution, especially women. But we didn't know any better."

"But you just said the doctor in charge knew Clara wasn't sick," Peg said.

"At first, he thought she was," Miss Trench said. "We all did. But there were other things, other people, involved. By the time Dr. Roach realized Clara was just a troubled young woman with a difficult home life, it was too late. Her fate had been sealed."

"Why?" Izzy said, surprised by her anger.

"Dr. Roach's wife couldn't have children," Miss Trench said. "They tried, but the poor dear kept losing babies."

Izzy put a hand over her stomach. She felt like she was going to be sick.

"Are you saying the doctor took Clara's baby?" Peg said. Just then, Renee returned with the bottle of brandy. She poured a little into Miss Trench's tea, then set the bottle on the coffee table. Miss Trench took a long, noisy sip.

"That's right," Miss Trench said. "Dr. Roach took her home and raised her as his own."

"Do you know where the doctor is now?" Peg said.

"Yes," Miss Trench said. "He's buried in the Ithaca cemetery next to his wife." She gazed at the coffee table, her eyes unseeing. "I never understood why she stayed married to him."

"And Clara's daughter?" Izzy said. "Where is she?"

"Last I heard, she lived in Ithaca," Miss Trench said. "She was a teacher. Kindergarten, I believe."

Izzy's stomach tightened. "Was?" she said.

"I would imagine she's retired now," Miss Trench said. "She's in her sixties, after all."

Izzy sighed in relief. "Do you know her name?" she said.

Miss Trench nodded. "Susan," she said. "Dr. Roach's wife brought her to Willard to visit him once. Think Susan must have been around four years old at the time. Dr. Roach wasn't too happy about that. Told his wife to never do it again. I just about keeled over when I realized who Susan was."

451

"Did you say anything?" Izzy said. "Did you tell Dr. Roach you knew the truth?"

Miss Trench shook her head, frowning. "It wouldn't have changed anything."

"Did they tell Susan she was adopted?" Peg said. She put a hand on Izzy's knee, searching her face with kind eyes. "I know you want to do the right thing and give Susan the journal," she said to her. "But if she doesn't know she's adopted, it might be best to keep it that way."

"Oh, she knows," Miss Trench said. "Dr. Roach's wife was a lovely woman. When she introduced me to Susan, she said she never wanted her to find out she was adopted by mistake, the way she did. She wanted Susan to grow up understanding that God had decided she could pick her daughter, and she chose her."

"How often did you see Susan after they took her?" Peg said.

"Just that one time," Miss Trench said. "She was a beautiful little girl, just like her mother, but with dark hair and brown eyes." The old nurse wiped her cheeks.

"Like her father, Bruno," Izzy said.

"That's right," Miss Trench said.

Izzy straightened. "Wait a minute," she said. "How do you know about Bruno?"

Miss Trench pressed her lips together, then took another long swig of tea and brandy. When she leaned forward to set the cup and saucer on the table, her hands shook and she nearly dropped it. Renee took the tea and set it on the serving tray.

"Maybe we should take a break," Renee said. "This seems to be upsetting her."

Miss Trench waved a blue-veined hand in the air, shaking her head. "No, no," she said. "I've kept quiet for far too long. I need to get this off my chest before I die!" She took a deep breath and let it out slowly. "Bruno came to Willard to rescue Clara."

Izzy gasped, her face growing hot. "Did he get her out?" she said.

"No," Miss Trench said, her eyes welling up again. "Dr. Roach locked Bruno up too."

A chill slithered up Izzy's spine, tracing her neck with an icy finger. She swallowed the burning lump in her throat, unable to believe what she was hearing.

"Are you sure?" Peg said, her eyes wide.

"'Course I am," Miss Trench said. "I was there the day he was admitted."

"Was that before or after Susan was born?" Peg asked.

"After," Miss Trench said.

"So Dr. Roach had already taken the baby," Izzy said, something hard and cold writing in her stomach.

Miss Trench nodded, her lips pressed together. "I didn't know where the baby was at the time. I thought she'd been sent to the Children's Aid Society to be put up for adoption."

"Did Clara and Bruno see each other after he was admitted?" Izzy said.

Miss Trench nodded. "It was nearly a year later. I'll never forget the two of them dancing on Valentine's Day. I could tell they belonged together. They didn't think anyone knew they'd found each other, but I knew."

"Why didn't you say something?" Izzy said. "Why didn't you try to help them?"

"It wouldn't have done any good," Miss Trench said. "I didn't have any authority at Willard. Besides, neither Clara nor Bruno had family who cared. Who was I supposed to tell? If Dr. Roach found out, he would have made it impossible for them to see each other again. I knew they'd be together on holidays and special patient events, when male and female patients were allowed to mingle. I figured I'd give them a chance to carve out a life at Willard, sad as it was."

"Did anyone tell Susan about her parents?" Izzy said. "Does she know they were both at Willard?"

Miss Trench dropped her eyes. "She knows her mother was at Willard," she said. "But Dr. Roach told his wife that Clara died during childbirth. I'm sure Susan was told the same story."

"So Susan thought her mother was dead," Izzy said, her voice flat. "And crazy."

Miss Trench shrugged. "I guess so," she said.

"Don't you think she had a right to know that her mother didn't need to be locked up?" Izzy said, unable to hide her anger.

Miss Trench shook her head. She pulled a wrinkled tissue out of her sleeve, her thin fingers shaking. "I told you, I only saw Susan that one time. I kept tabs on her, but I didn't think it was my place to get involved."

"Do you know what her last name is now?" Izzy said. "Did she ever marry?"

"I don't know," Miss Trench said, shaking her head. "I'm sorry."

"Do you know her middle name?" Izzy said.

Miss Trench nodded. "It's Clara," she said. "Dr. Roach's wife insisted she have something from her mother."

"So what happened after Bruno and Clara found each other on Valentine's Day?" Izzy said. "Did they spend the rest of their lives at Willard? Did they find ways to be together, like you said?"

Miss Trench wiped her nose with the tissue. "Well," she said. "It might be best if you ask Clara about that. Her death certificate is missing from her file because she's still alive."

CHAPTER 24

IZZY

A week after meeting Miss Trench, Izzy sat opposite Peg in the fluorescent-flooded Ithaca Diner, jiggling her knee beneath the booth's Formica table. It was noon and the eatery was crowded with college students, elderly couples, and families with young children. Waitresses called out orders, hurrying back and forth with trays full of patty melts, apple pie, root beer floats, and coffee. The bell over the entrance chimed and, for the hundredth time, Izzy craned her neck to look over the customers in the next booth, trying to see who was coming in the door. It was a short, old man wearing a blue veteran's cap, and a woman in a yellow coat waddling into the diner like an overweight duck. Izzy sighed and picked up the saltshaker, turning it around and around in her fingers.

"Have you ever heard the expression 'a watched pot never boils'?" Peg said. She sat forward and grinned.

"Maybe she changed her mind," Izzy said.

"I doubt it," Peg said. She looked at her watch. "I told her between noon and twelve-thirty. It's only twelve ten."

Just then, the waitress appeared, flushed and out of breath. She was young, maybe a couple years older than Izzy, her blond hair pulled into a ponytail. She pushed a stray bang behind her ear, took her pad out of her apron and smiled.

"What can I get 'cha?" she said.

"We're waiting for someone," Peg said. "We'll just order our drinks for now, if that's okay."

The waitress glanced over her shoulder. "Okay, but is your friend going to be here soon? My boss doesn't like it when people tie up the tables too long."

Peg smiled. "She should be here any minute," she said. "But I tell you what, the next time you come around, even if she's not here yet, we'll order."

"Okay," the waitress said. "What can I get 'cha to drink?"

Peg and Izzy ordered coffee and a Coke, waiting silently while the waitress wrote the simple order down. Finally, the waitress left, her ponytail bouncing. Izzy opened her mouth to say she thought it was rude of the owner to expect customers to hurry, when an elderly woman appeared at their table. She was tall and slender, with ebony eyes and a stylish bob of silver hair. Her long black coat and leather boots gave her an air of sophistication, and the lavender scarf around her neck matched the hint of eye shadow on her upper lids. Izzy's breath caught in her chest. The woman was the split image of Clara, but with dark eyes and light caramel skin.

"Peg?" the woman said, her perfectly shaped brows arched.

Peg slid out of the booth and shook the woman's hand. "Yes," she said, smiling. "And you must be Susan. Thank you for coming." She gestured toward the empty seat. "Please, sit down. I'll sit over here with Izzy."

Susan slid into the booth and loosened her scarf. "So you're Isabelle?" she said, smiling.

Izzy nodded and shook Susan's hand. "It's nice to meet you," she said, a nervous quiver in her voice. She touched her purse sitting on the cushion beside her, picturing Clara's journal safely tucked inside. Her heartbeat picked up speed.

"So what's this all about, Isabelle?" Susan said. "Your mother said you have something you want to show me. Something that has to do with where my father worked, Willard State?"

Izzy swallowed and sat up. "Yes, I . . ."

Just then, the bouncy waitress reappeared with Izzy's and Peg's drinks. She placed the drinks on the table and looked at Susan. "Can I get you something to drink while you look over the menu?" she said.

"Sure," Susan said. "I'll have a cup of hot tea, please. With lemon?"

"Comin' right up," the waitress said and left.

"Is it okay if I say a few things before we get

started?" Peg asked Susan. "Maybe ask a couple questions. Just so there's no misunderstanding?"

Susan smiled. "Certainly," she said.

Peg cleared her throat. "I'm Isabelle's foster mother," she said. "Did I mention that?"

Susan's brow furrowed and she looked confused. But then her face cleared and she said, "Yes, you told me that on the phone."

"Unfortunately, Izzy recently lost her real mother."

"Oh no," Susan said, frowning. "I'm so sorry." She considered Izzy, as if to reassure her. "I lost my mother too, right after I was born."

"I know," Izzy said. "And then you were adopted." Peg cringed and gave Izzy a wide-eyed look. It was too soon. But Izzy couldn't help it. The need to tell Susan the truth about Clara and Bruno made her feel like she was holding her finger in a light socket. She wiped her palms on her lap and sat on her hands.

"How could you know that?" Susan said. She gazed at Peg, her mouth in a thin line. "What's going on here?"

"I'm sorry," Peg said. "Izzy is a little anxious. But as I'd hoped, by telling you about Izzy's mother, you confirmed the loss of your own."

"Why didn't you just ask?" Susan said. "I thought you wanted to know more about Willard and my father, Dr. Roach."

"We'll explain everything," Peg said. "I

promise. I just need to know a few things first."

Susan sighed. "All right," she said. "What do you want to know?"

"How much do you know about your biological mother?"

"Just what my adopted mother told me, that she was a patient at Willard."

"That's it?" Peg said.

"My father refused to let us talk about it," Susan said. "My biological mother was one of his patients and she died giving birth to me, that's all I know. About fifteen years ago, after my adoptive mother died, I tried to find my real mother's records, even though I don't know her full name. But I was denied access even though I'm a descendant of a former patient." Susan shook her head, her forehead creased. "It just doesn't make any sense to me. They won't even tell me which grave my mother is in, so I can visit her."

Izzy sat forward, her stomach fluttering. "Did you get along with your adoptive father?" she said.

"What does that have to do with anything?" Susan said, cocking her head.

Peg patted the table in front of Izzy, as if to tell her to hold on. "I think I know what Izzy's getting at," she said. "But let's back up a bit." She shot Izzy another *be patient!* glance, then continued on. "So you've always wanted to know more about your real mother?"

Susan shrugged. "Of course," she said. "Doesn't everyone want to know where they came from?" She clasped her manicured hands together on the edge of the table and sighed. "I'll admit that when I was younger, I didn't want to know anything about my real mother. The thought of her being mentally ill scared the heck out of me. As I got older, I realized how much that fear influenced my life decisions. My adoptive mother never understood why I didn't want to get married and have children. But I didn't know how to explain to her that it was because I was worried . . ."

"You'd pass along your mother's genes," Izzy said.

"That's exactly right," Susan said, her voice incredulous. "I have no idea what kind of DNA is in my bloodline. And I was afraid to ask my father. For the most part, he was very caring, but he had a short fuse sometimes. When I was old enough to ask questions, he flew into a rage, warning me not to ask about my real mother again. And I couldn't ask my adoptive mother because she always obeyed him. Besides, I didn't want to upset her, or hurt her feelings. She was always very fragile, physically and emotionally."

"Do you still want to know about your real mother?" Peg said. "Even if it doesn't exactly match what your father told you?"

Susan's face went pale, her eyes locked on Peg's. Just then, the waitress appeared with

Susan's tea, setting a white mug, a miniature silver teapot, and a dish full of lemon slices on the table, then digging around inside her apron for her pad and pen. Izzy groaned inside.

"Can we get just a few more minutes, please?" Peg said.

The waitress rolled her eyes and walked away.

"I don't understand," Susan said. "How could you know anything about my mother?"

Peg went on to explain her position at the museum, describing the Willard project and Izzy's job cataloging the contents of the suitcases and steamer trunks. When Peg said they were given access to the patients' records, Susan's eyes went wide. She sat forward, hanging on to every word.

"Izzy knows a lot about your mother," Peg said. "Even more than I do. She felt compelled to meet with you, to tell you the truth about what happened to your parents."

Susan's face dropped and she leaned back. "My parents?" she said, frowning. "My father didn't know who my biological father was."

Izzy took a deep breath. "I'm sorry," she said. "But that's not true. Dr. Roach knew everything."

"What do you mean, everything?" Susan said. "Please, just tell me what you know."

"First," Peg said. "I want you to know that I don't think your adoptive father intended to cause you or your biological mother any harm. Treatment of the insane was different back then, along with the definition of what it meant to be mentally ill. He was just doing what was expected of him at the time. As far as his reasons for admitting your real father to the asylum, we can't be sure."

"Are you telling me my real father was in Willard too?" Susan said, her chin quivering. She pressed her lips together, blinking back tears. "Thank God I listened to my instincts and never had children!"

"No," Izzy said, shaking her head. "It's not like that." She reached across the table and laid her hand over Susan's, surprised by the need to comfort someone she barely knew. With her other hand, she pulled a photo from her purse. "Let me show you something." She slid the black-and-white snapshot across the table. "This is Clara Elizabeth Cartwright and Bruno Moretti," she said, her voice catching. "Your parents. And trust me, they were *not* insane."

Susan leaned forward and picked up the photo with shaking fingers. "They're beautiful," she said, her voice filled with awe. She put a trembling hand to her lips.

"You look just like them," Peg said.

"Bruno tried to get Clara out of Willard," Izzy said. "That's when they locked him up."

"Why would they do that?" Susan said.

Peg glanced at Izzy. They had decided to hold off telling Susan their theory, that Dr. Roach admitted Bruno to prevent him from finding out he had taken Susan. It was too much, too soon. Besides, it was just a theory. "We're not sure," Peg said.

"Was he ever released?"

"We're not sure what happened because we didn't realize he was a patient," Izzy said. "Otherwise, when we had access to the records, we would have looked for his too."

"We might be allowed more time with the files," Peg said. "But I highly doubt it."

"Cartwright," Susan said, tapping her chin. "I remember hearing that name. Henry Cartwright and his wife were killed in the Holland Tunnel fire. I was twenty at the time, but it was all over the news because he was a famous banker."

"They were your grandparents," Izzy said.

Susan's brows shot up. "How could you know that?" she said.

Izzy took a deep breath, pulled the journal from her purse, and slid it across the table. "Because it's all in here," she said. "This is your mother's diary."

Susan gasped and touched the green leather with gentle fingers. She opened the journal to the first page, scanning the opening lines.

"We'd like you to have it," Peg said.

After a long moment, Susan picked up the journal and held it to her chest. "Thank you so much," she said, smiling through her tears. "I don't know how I'll ever repay you." She picked up the picture again, her lips trembling.

Izzy cleared her throat. "There's one more thing," she said, her heart ready to burst. "Your mother didn't die giving birth to you. When Willard closed last year, she was transferred to a nursing home, right here in Ithaca."

Susan dropped the picture and clamped a hand over her mouth, her eyes like saucers.

"And after you read her journal," Izzy said, "we were wondering if you'd like to go see her."

CHAPTER 25

IZZY AND CLARA

Orange turkeys and black-hatted pilgrims decorated the windows and walls of the Ithaca nursing home, even though Thanksgiving was over three weeks away. Izzy followed Peg and Susan through the oven-warm halls, parading behind a young nurse in pink scrubs. Beads of sweat broke out on Izzy's forehead. She took off her coat and threw it over one arm, wishing she'd worn a thinner shirt. The air was thick with the stale aroma of chicken soup, boiled potatoes, disinfectant, and urine. An old man shuffled toward them, his gnarled hands gripping two four-legged canes, his age-spotted head shaking above his thin-skinned neck. Izzy kept her eyes straight ahead, trying to ignore the hospital beds and metal walkers inside the rooms, the white-haired women sitting in wheelchairs, their eyes locked on blaring TVs.

She cursed under her breath, frustrated that the nursing home reminded her of her mother lying in the prison hospital. She licked her lips, discovering they were salty from perspiration. The world was full of broken people, and all the hospitals and institutions and jails could never mend their fractured hearts, wounded minds, and trampled spirits. Izzy took a deep breath and pushed the thought from her head, deciding instead to concentrate on Clara and Susan. At the very least, she could be happy and proud of herself for trying to right this wrong, for trying to heal one broken heart.

If the woman they were about to see was really Clara Elizabeth Cartwright.

Until earlier, in the nursing home parking lot, when Susan confided she wasn't entirely convinced the woman was her mother, Izzy had been certain Miss Trench knew what she was talking about. Now, she was starting to have doubts. Like Susan said, over the years, mistakes could have been made. Like other large institutions, Willard's files could have gotten mixed up, names could have been misspelled. Just because a former nurse said this woman was Clara Elizabeth Cartwright didn't make it true. Thousands of women had passed through Willard during the last sixty years, and there was always the chance that one of them had the same last name. There were too many possibilities of mistaken identity to just assume they'd found Susan's mother. Susan said she was struggling, trying not to get her hopes up. And she wanted to be sure before they told anyone, even the nursing home staff.

Finally, the young nurse stopped outside a doorway and turned to face them, her pink scrubs like neon beneath the fluorescent lights. Pulling at the collar of her shirt, Izzy felt on the verge of suffocation.

"Clara is a sweet soul," the nurse said. "And I'm sure she'll be happy and surprised to have company. But I have to warn you. Sometimes her memory goes in and out and she can get moody when she gets confused. The doctors believe she's in the beginning stages of Alzheimer's. I know you're here to ask her about her time at Willard, but if it gets to be too much for her, I'll ask you to leave. If she tells you she has a daughter, just agree with her. She gets pretty upset if anyone tries to tell her any different."

Susan gasped softly, her hand flying to her chest. The young nurse smiled and led them through the open door.

Inside the small, airless room, two hospital beds sat opposite wall-mounted televisions. The televisions were off, their screens black. An old woman slept in the first bed, her mouth open, strands of stringy, gray hair lying across her weathered face. The nurse walked past the first bed and stopped at the foot of the second, directing their attention toward a shriveled woman in a chair, facing the window.

The woman's pink-lidded eyes were closed, her head back, her fine hair like mist in the shaft of sunlight coming in through the glass. Her crooked fingers curled around the ends of the armrests, the fan of thin bones in her age-spotted hands sticking out like ribs. A red blanket covered her legs, despite the room being thick with heat.

"Is she asleep?" Peg whispered.

The nurse shook her head. "No," she said. "She's just a little hard of hearing." She raised her voice. "Clara, look! You have visitors!"

Clara blinked and opened her eyes. She leaned forward and turned to look, holding the arm of the chair with both hands to stay steady. Her lips disappeared into her mouth, her pale skin wizened by decades of pain and heartache. She considered their faces one by one, her petite head wavering ever so slightly.

The nurse hurried toward her. "Let's turn your chair around so you can talk with these nice ladies," she said in a loud voice. She picked up a set of false teeth and handed them to Clara, who pushed them into her mouth, making her lips reappear. "They want to ask you about Willard. Isn't that nice? You remember Willard, don't you?"

Clara gathered the blanket in her spindly arms and pushed herself into a standing position. Wearing a pink housecoat and red slippers with knee-high stockings, she shuffled out of the nurse's way, waiting for the chair to be turned. When she sat down again, she rearranged the blanket over her legs, then gazed at Izzy, Susan, and Peg, her milky eyes lingering on Susan's face just a heartbeat longer. Susan dropped her eyes and fumbled with her scarf, struggling to remove it, her cheeks flushed. The nurse closed the curtain between the beds.

"I'll leave you alone for now," she said in a cheerful voice. "But I'll check back shortly. Is there anything else I can do for you?"

"No," Peg said. "We're fine, thank you."

When the nurse was gone, Susan sank into a chair pushed in the corner. Izzy set her backpack on the floor and touched Susan's shoulder.

"Are you okay?" she whispered.

Susan rubbed her forehead, her temples working in and out. "I'm all right," she said, her voice weak.

"Are you sure you want to go through with this?" Peg whispered. "Maybe it's too soon."

Susan nodded. "I'm okay, really."

Peg went over and knelt in front of Clara, who was watching with curious eyes. "Hello, Clara," she said in a loud voice. "How are you?"

Clara smiled thinly. "I'm as well as can be expected, I guess," she said. To Izzy's surprise,

Clara's voice was low and raspy. For some reason, she'd expected it to be high, like a young girl's.

Peg stood. "I'm Peg," she said. "This is my foster daughter Isabelle, and our friend, Susan. We'd like to talk to you about your time at Willard, if that's all right."

Clara nodded. "That's all right," she said.

"We went to Willard for a museum project and found some old suitcases while we were there," Peg said. She motioned for Izzy to get her backpack. "Among the luggage, there was a huge steamer trunk. We believe it belonged to you." Clara stared at Peg, her face like stone. "Do you understand what I'm telling you?"

Clara nodded.

"We'd like to show you a few of the items we found inside the trunk to see if you recognize anything," Peg said. "Would that be all right?"

Clara nodded again and clasped her hands in her lap, one gnarled thumb rubbing the knuckle of the other.

Izzy reached into her backpack, pulled out a yellowed page of sheet music and held it out to Clara. Hand-drawn hearts surrounded the title, "Someone to Watch Over Me," their red ink faded. Clara lifted her chin to look at it, then gasped. She reached for the paper with shaky hands and put it in her lap, hunched over and studying it with her head down.

"This is mine," Clara said, looking up with wet

eyes. "Someone very special gave it to me. I always wanted to learn how to play the piano, but my father wouldn't allow it."

From the corner, Susan watched with wide eyes, her fingers pressed over her lips.

"How about this?" Izzy said, holding out a postcard from Paris.

Clara smiled and took it. "This is from a trip to Paris when I was sixteen," she said. She chuckled softly. "I was going to mail it to a girlfriend but I kept it as a souvenir instead."

Izzy took a deep breath and held out the picture of Clara and Bruno. Clara stared at it, her pale cheeks turning pink.

"Oh yes," she said. "Weren't we beautiful?" She reached out to take the photo, then put her hands to her trembling chin, as if afraid to touch the picture. She bit her lip, her eyes brimming with tears.

"Do you remember who that is?" Peg said.

Clara sniffed, wiping her nose. "Of course I do," she said, her voice breaking. "It's been a long time since I've seen that photo. A long, long time." Finally, she took the picture and held it to her chest. Then she took a deep breath and looked at it again. "Thank you so much for bringing this to me."

With her heart in her throat, Izzy took the journal out of her backpack and knelt in front of Clara. She placed the journal on Clara's lap. "I'm sorry," she said. "But I read this. I didn't know you were still alive or I never would have . . ." She stopped and swallowed. "But that's why we're here. That's how we found you."

Clara ran shaky fingers over the green leather. For a few moments, she didn't say anything. Then her hand stopped moving and she sat back in her chair and sighed. "So you know everything," she said. "You know my father sent me away."

"Yes," Izzy said. "I do. And I'm so sorry he did that to you."

In what seemed like slow motion, Clara patted Izzy's hand, picked up the photo and put it inside the journal, then set the journal on the table beside her chair. She pushed the blanket off her lap and put her hands on the armrests, preparing to get up. Izzy straightened and stepped back, her heart roaring in her chest. She was afraid Clara was going to tell them to get out, to go away and leave her alone. Clara pushed herself out of the chair and stood, her frail body swaying slightly. She brushed off the front of her house coat, raked her fingers through her thin hair and took a deep breath. Then she looked at Susan.

"And you're my daughter," she said. "Aren't you?"

Susan stood, tears running down her cheeks. "I think so," she said. Clara clamped her hands over her mouth, her face falling in on itself. She edged toward Susan, holding out her arms. Susan closed the distance between them and they wrapped their arms around each other, smiling and crying at the same time.

"I knew who you were the second I saw you," Clara said. "I recognized Bruno's eyes and my nose."

Susan laughed. "Are you sure?" she said.

"In my head, I wasn't sure," Clara said. "But in my heart, I knew."

After a long minute, Clara released Susan and wiped her face. She moved back to her chair, her slippers shuffling across the tiles. "Come and sit with me," she said to Susan.

Susan pulled a chair next to Clara's, taking her hand. "I tried to find out more about you," she said, sniffing. "But it was next to impossible. I had no idea you were still alive or I . . ."

Clara touched Susan's cheek, wiping away her tears with papery fingers. "There, there," she said. "We're together now. That's all that matters. I knew this day would come. It's the only thing that kept me going all these years."

"And my father?" Susan said. "Is he still alive?"

Clara shook her head, her eyes brimming. "Bruno tried to rescue me," she said. "We had a plan to escape and we were going to look for you. We almost made it, but they caught us right before we got away. Bruno went back to try to save the man who helped us, and an orderly hit him over the head. He . . . he didn't make it."

"I'm so sorry," Susan said, her voice catching.

"No," Clara said, swallowing her sobs. "I'm the one who should apologize. If I had just gone along with what my parents wanted, Bruno wouldn't have been killed and you and I could have been together all these years."

Susan squeezed Clara's hand. "It's all right," she said. "You couldn't have known how things would turn out."

"I want you to know that if it had been within my power," Clara said, "I would have kept you. But they . . ." She paused, her chin trembling, her thin lips quivering in grief. "Willard was no place for a baby. But I thought about you every day. I kept thinking, someday I'll get out. Somehow, I'll find you. I never would have stopped looking. I would have searched the earth . . ." She hung her head, tears dripping from her nose.

Susan wrapped her arms around Clara. "I know," she said, rubbing her mother's back. "It wasn't your fault. Now that we're together, we can make up for lost time. We'll just look forward."

Clara sniffed and wiped her nose. "Yes," she said, her voice catching. "You're right." Then Clara drew away, searching her daughter's face. "But I have to know. Were you adopted? Have you had a happy life?"

Susan nodded, smiling through her tears. "Yes," she said. "I was adopted. And for the most part, I've been very happy." She glanced at Peg.

Earlier, she'd told Peg and Izzy that, if indeed the woman in the nursing home was her mother, she didn't want to tell her about Dr. Roach. There was no point in rehashing the past. It would be too upsetting and Clara had suffered enough.

"And they called you Susan," Clara said.

"Susan Clara," Susan said.

"I named you Beatrice," Clara said, smiling. "Beatrice Elizabeth Moretti."

"I love it," Susan said.

Clara looked at Izzy. "How can I ever thank you for bringing my daughter to me?"

Izzy smiled and shrugged. "It was just something I needed to do," she said.

"You must be awfully proud of her," Clara said to Peg.

Peg put her arm around Izzy. "I am," she said.

Just then, the nurse came into the room and looked at Clara, her forehead furrowed with concern. "What's going on?" she said. "Are you all right, Clara?"

"I'm fine," Clara said. "Better than I've been in a long, long time. Nurse Jennie, I'd like you to meet my daughter, Susan." The nurse's mouth dropped open, her eyes like saucers.

Susan stood and shook her hand. "Nice to meet you."

"I told you I had a daughter," Clara said. "But no one ever listens to me. It's the story of my life." She chuckled, her eyes shining.

While Izzy gave Clara the rest of her photos and the letters to Bruno, Susan asked the nurse about Clara's health. After a few minutes, she knelt next to Clara.

"Nurse Jennie says you're fairly healthy," she said.

"I suppose I am," Clara said. "Except for being old and stiff and a little forgetful every now and then."

"Well," Susan said. "How would you feel about coming to stay with me? I've got a big old house not far from here, with a huge garden and two dogs. It's nothing elaborate, but it's home."

Clara's lips trembled. "I haven't had a home in sixty-six years," she said in a small voice.

"Well then," Susan said. "My home is your home if you'd like it to be. And I'm retired now, so I'll always be there to watch over you."

Clara smiled, her eyes glistening. "I would love that more than anything in this world," she said.

CHAPTER 26

Izzy

Hurrying into the kitchen after school on Thursday, Izzy's mouth watered, picturing Harry's famous chocolate chip cookies stacked beneath a glass cover on the island counter. She could hardly wait to pour a big glass of milk and gobble up three or four. Harry made the cookies every other week, and she couldn't remember tasting anything so delicious. She dropped her books on the back door bench, hung up her coat, and stopped dead in her tracks. Somehow, with everything going on over the past two weeks— her mother's burial, talking to Miss Trench, going on her first date with Ethan, finding Clara and her daughter—she'd forgotten what day it was.

Peg and Harry were standing at the kitchen island, wide smiles stretched across their faces. Instead of cookies, a chocolate cake covered with pink and white roses sat on the counter, eighteen burning candles reflected in Peg's and Harry's eyes. Dozens of pink and purple balloons floated near the ceiling, their curling strings like pastel rain. Peg and Harry started singing "Happy Birthday" and Izzy choked back tears. She couldn't remember the last time anyone had thrown her a party, let alone sang "Happy Birthday" to her. How ironic that this was the birthday she'd been dreading.

"Make a wish!" Peg said.

"Okay," Izzy said, her face flushing. She held back her hair and blew out the candles.

"I told Peg we should wait until after dinner to sing to you," Harry said. "But she couldn't wait. She wanted to surprise you."

"Thank you," Izzy said. "You didn't have to get a cake for me."

"Yes we did!" Peg said. She hurried around the island and gave Izzy a hug. "And we have more surprises too." She went to the table and pulled out a chair. "But first, can you sit down so we can talk about something?"

Izzy sat down, her heartbeat picking up speed. Peg folded her hands on the kitchen table, took a deep breath and let it out slowly. She cleared her throat and swallowed, as if she didn't know where to begin. An icy coil of sadness twisted in Izzy's chest. *Here we go,* she thought. *She's going to tell me it's time to leave because they can't afford to keep me here. She's going to apologize and say they wanted to give me a birthday party so I'd have something to remember them by.*

"I know it's probably too soon after your mother's passing," Peg said. "But Harry and I have been talking about it for a while now. We've already got the papers in order, and . . . well . . . it's up to you . . . but . . ." She looked at Harry for reinforcement. Harry came around the kitchen island, wiping his hands on his pants.

"We realize you're an adult as of today," he said. "So you might not think this is a good idea. But we . . ." He sat down and took Peg's hand. "We'd like to adopt you, Izzy. We know you probably think you don't need . . . what I'm trying to say is, we'd really like to be your parents."

Izzy's mouth dropped open. Words escaped her. Peg took her hands in hers.

"We love you and want to be here for you," Peg said, her voice shaking. "You've still got a lot of decisions to make in your life, decisions that are too hard to make alone. We'd like to help you, and see you go to college to find your full potential, whatever that may be. And when you get married . . ." Peg's eyes brimmed with tears and she squeezed Izzy's hand. "Harry would be honored to walk you down the aisle. And we would love to be grandparents someday."

Izzy pressed her lips together, her chin trembling. She opened her mouth to say yes, to tell them she'd love to be their daughter more than anything in the world, but her throat closed.

"What do you say, kiddo?" Harry said.

Izzy nodded, smiling. Peg squealed and put her hands over her mouth. They all stood and hugged each other. Izzy closed her flooding eyes, wondering how it was possible that her heart could be bursting with so much joy after being filled with so much sorrow. She hugged Peg and Harry tighter, letting their strong arms chase away her worries and fears.

"You've made us so happy," Peg said, sniffing.

Just then, someone knocked on the kitchen door. "Come on in!" Harry said.

Alex and Ethan entered the room, their arms laden with presents. "Happy Birthday!" they said at the same time. Behind them, Clara and Susan entered arm in arm, both of them beaming.

AUTHOR'S NOTE

During the writing of *What She Left Behind*, I relied on the following books: *The Lives They Left Behind: Suitcases from a State Hospital Attic*, by Darby Penney and Peter Stastny; *Ten Days in a Mad-House*, by Nellie Bly; and *Women of the Asylum: Voices from Behind the Walls 1840–1945*, by Jeffery L. Geller and Maxine Harris.

Although the above books helped a great deal in imagining what conditions must have been like inside insane asylums, my novel is not a historical work and has no intention of being one. It is my interpretation of what it might have been like to be committed against one's will. The characters in this novel are entirely fictitious. But several of the places described, including the Long Island Home and Willard State, are real. Chapin Hall, and its attached wards and outbuildings, existed. At Willard there were also detached patient wards: the Pines, the Maples, Sunnycroft, and the Edgemere, each with its own dining room, kitchen, supervisor's office, apartments, and boiler house. It is also important to note that for purpose of plot, patient treatments and therapies were portrayed as being in use either earlier or later than was actually the case. The Utica Crib, a locked wooden cage, was put out of use in 1887.

Insulin shock therapy was put into use in 1935. Electroshock therapy was put into use in 1938. And, finally, psychologists were not used in most state asylums until 1960.

Q&A with Ellen Marie Wiseman

What was the inspiration for *What She Left Behind*?

I've always been curious about insane asylums, especially the way patients were treated for mental illness in the past, and how our understanding and treatment has evolved over the years. I've often wondered what it would be like to be committed to an institution and kept against my will. When I read about the Willard Suitcase Exhibit, a collection of patient suitcases found in the attic of the shuttered Willard asylum, I was immediately intrigued. That's how I learned about *The Lives They Left Behind: Suitcases from a State Hospital Attic*, by Darby Penney and Peter Stastny. The authors' mission was to examine the contents of the luggage in an attempt to re-create the lives of those patients who had checked into the institution but never checked out. The book is fascinating and haunting because the pictures and stories are so easy to identify with. After reading it, I knew I wanted to write about finding the suitcases, and what it might have been like being a patient.

How did researching asylums make you feel?

It was difficult reading about people in the past being institutionalized, in many cases for the rest of their lives, because of emotional or economic distress. While some patients were truly ill, many were sent to asylums under circumstances we view differently today: poverty, homelessness, depression, homosexuality, alcoholism, and emotional distress due to divorce, family disputes, abusive relationships, and the loss of children. A person could be committed for something as simple as being unable to find work, or for a single angry public outburst. In the late 1800s, Dr. Judson B. Andrews wrote a paper entitled *Early Indications of Insanity*—suggesting families take note of "morbid dreams, sleep impairments, constant headaches, emotional exaggerations, excessive religious scruples, and changes in habits of dress and cleanliness."

Women were especially vulnerable to being institutionalized for the long term. Husbands could commit their "troublesome" wives, while male doctors were more than willing to oblige. Many women also worked as domestics and were in close contact with their employers; any bad behavior or dispute could be contrived as mental illness. By the end of its first year of operation, Willard housed four times as many women as men. In one case, a woman sent to Willard because of depression spent the remaining seventy-five years of her life there, until she died at the age of one hundred and one. Immigrants with few community connections were sometimes sent to asylums while their families in the old country had no idea where they were. Many "mad" patients were sent to public asylums from other state hospitals, arriving in groups of a hundred or more, crammed into trains or buses, unaware of where they were being taken. Nearly half of the 54,000 individuals who entered Willard died there.

What surprised you most during your research?

What surprised me the most was that forced sterilization was a common practice in state mental hospitals from about 1910 to the end of WWII, when it was largely stopped because of embarrassing comparisons to Nazi policies. In some southern states it continued into the 1960s. This led to my discovery that the United States was the first country to concertedly undertake compulsory sterilization programs for the purpose of eugenics (a science that deals with the improvement of hereditary qualities of a race or breed, usually through selective breeding and sterilization), the principle targets being the mentally ill. Between 1907 and 1963, over 64,000 individuals (including others who were not mentally ill) were forcibly sterilized under eugenic legislation in the United States. According to Edwin Black, award-winning author of *War Against the Weak: Eugenics and America's Campaign to Create a Master Race*, one method commonly suggested to get rid of "inferior" populations was euthanasia. A 1911 Carnegie Institute report mentioned euthanasia as one of its recommended "solutions" to the problem of cleansing society of unfit genetic attributes. The most commonly suggested method was to set up local gas chambers. However, many in the eugenics movement did not believe that Americans were ready to implement a large-scale euthanasia program, so many doctors had to find clever ways of subtly implementing eugenic euthanasia in various medical institutions. For example, one mental institution fed its incoming patients milk infected with tuberculosis (reasoning that genetically fit individuals would be resistant), resulting in 30 to 40 percent annual death rates. Other doctors practiced eugenicide through various forms of lethal neglect.

What did you learn about patient treatment in insane asylums?

Because psychotropic drugs weren't discovered until the mid-1950s, the only drugs available to treat patients were sedatives. Patients with psychiatric symptoms as a result of syphilis were treated with arsenic and infected with malaria! At Willard, psychologists weren't available until the 1960s, and patients rarely met with a medical doctor. According to Darby Penney, coauthor of *The Lives They Left Behind*, some patients were not seen by a doctor for decades. In the 1930s, the time period of Clara's story, treatment included ice baths, arts and crafts, and exercise. Years later, treatment also included insulin therapy and electroshock therapy. In my research I found no evidence that lobotomies were performed at Willard. Able-bodied patients who were not dangerous or actively delusional were required to work, which was considered therapeutic.

What else can you tell us about Willard Asylum?

Like most state-run mental institutions, Willard was dependent on unpaid patient labor to sustain its operation. Willard had over six hundred acres of farmland, a greenhouse, a dairy, stables, chicken houses, piggeries, and barns where nearly all the facility's food was raised and processed. Industrial shops produced clothing, shoes, brooms, baskets, soap, and caskets. There were laundries, bakeries, kitchens, a slaughterhouse, woodworking shops, brickworks, a blacksmith's shop, and a coal-fired power plant whose boilers were fed by patients hauling coal by wheel-barrows from the hospital's rail yard. The facilities were overseen by paid labor but most of the work was done by patients, who worked on the grounds crews, excavated for new construction, cleaned the wards and offices, served the food, and staffed the luxurious home of the super-intendent.

Your first novel, *The Plum Tree*, is loosely based on your mother's experiences growing up in Germany, and follows a young woman through the chaos of WWII as she tries to save the love of her life, a Jewish man. How was writing *What She Left Behind* different?

The biggest difference was the dual timeline. I basically had to write two stories and blend them together in a way that worked. It was harder than I thought!

Are there any similar themes in *The Plum Tree* and *What She Left Behind*?

Yes, in the case of Christine (of *The Plum Tree*) and Clara, both are young women being denied a normal life during a time of great social change. Christine suffered as a result of poor economic times, war, and her government's intolerance of certain individuals. Clara suffered because of the stock market crash, her father's and society's expectations of women, and, once she was labeled mentally ill, also because of her government's intolerance of certain individuals. It's very likely that, before Clara was sent away, she, like Christine, saw posters advocating for the "removal" of certain individuals deemed unfit for society. A 1926 U.S. Eugenics poster claimed "Some people are born to be a burden on the rest," and reminded people that every sixteen seconds a person is born and one hundred dollars of their money goes toward the care of persons with bad heredity, such as the insane, feeble-minded, criminals, and other defectives. Both women were forbidden to marry the man they loved, Isaac because he was Jewish, and Bruno because he was a poor immigrant. Both rebelled against doing what they were told, Christine against the Gestapo, and Clara against her father and the doctors at Willard. Both endured terrible hardship at the hands of institutional captors who showed little regard for human dignity, Christine in Dachau, and Clara in Willard. Both women refused to give up hope, and did whatever they could to improve their situations.

Discussion Questions

1. When Izzy first arrives at Willard, she's afraid to go inside the old buildings because they remind her of visiting her mother in the psychiatric ward. She also has a difficult time handling the contents of the old suitcases because they remind her of the dead and dying. Some people would find the abandoned asylum fascinating, while others would stay away. Would you want to go inside the buildings? Would you want to go through the old suitcases?

2. Before coming to live with Peg and Harry, Izzy cut herself to deal with her emotions. Self-harm is most common in adolescence and young adulthood, usually appearing between the ages of twelve and twenty-four. Have you ever heard of self-injury as a way of dealing with emotional pain, anger, and frustration? Why do you think some people hurt themselves as a way of coping? What do you think would have happened to Izzy if she had lived during Clara's time?

3. Displaying opposite ends of the spectrum when it comes to a mother's protective

instinct, Izzy's mother shoots her father to protect her, while Shannon's and Clara's mothers do nothing to protect them. Discuss the maternal instinct. Do you think it's stronger in some women than in others? Do you think the difference is due to circumstances, as in the way women are brought up, or do you think the difference is due to genetics?

4. Clara tries everything she can think of to get out of Willard. Is there anything else she could have tried?

5. New York State has sealed the medical records of former mental patients, even denying access to the descendents. Why do you think they remain sealed? Do you think this law should be changed?

6. How do you think Izzy changed over the course of the novel? How did Clara change? What were the most important events that facilitated those changes?

7. At first, Dr. Roach truly believes Clara needs help, partly because of Clara's father's stories, and partly due to the era, when emotional outbursts were often seen as a sign of mental illness. Why do you think Dr. Roach refused

to release Clara even though Bruno confirmed the truth about why she was there? Why do you think Dr. Roach committed Bruno to the asylum? Do you think Dr. Roach was more worried about his reputation and his job, or concealing the fact that he took Clara's child?

8. Izzy refused to visit her mother in prison because she was afraid. Do you think she was angry with her mother, or just sad and scared?

9. Clara refused to go along with the arranged marriage to James because she was in love with Bruno. She had no idea her father would send her to an insane asylum. Hindsight is always 20/20 and, in Clara's time, women were still subject to the whims of their husbands and fathers, but what would you have done in that situation? Would you have obeyed your parents' wishes and married James? Would you have continued seeing Bruno?

10. Bruno had no idea Clara was at the Long Island Home because he never received her letters. Izzy couldn't understand why her mother shot her father until she read her mother's letters. Can you think of an instance in your life that would have turned out differently if you'd had more information?

Do you think most people jump to conclusions, or that they try to find out all sides of a story?

11. Nurse Trench presented a tough exterior while hiding a soft interior. How did you feel about her when you first met her? How did you feel about her when she was an old woman? Do you think Nurse Trench could have tried harder to help Clara while she was at Willard? What could she have done?

12. Izzy feels like nothing will ever change when it comes to bullying. What do you think? What can be done to make those changes? Do you think we've made progress when it comes to bullying, or do you think things have gotten worse?

13. Clara is sterilized after she gives birth, because Dr. Roach felt it was his duty to keep her from passing along "inferior" genes. Do you think it was right for doctors to make that decision for patients who were considered mentally ill? Do you think the government should have a say in who can and cannot reproduce? How far do you think we've come when it comes to a woman's reproductive rights and the right to choose?

14. Bruno had to nail Clara inside a coffin for them to have a chance to escape. Would you have been able to stand being nailed inside a coffin if it meant a chance to be free?

15. During the flood in the electroshock therapy room, someone grabs Clara underwater. Who do you think it was?

16. Do you think reuniting Clara with her daughter helped Izzy heal? In what way? How do you think Clara felt when she saw her daughter?

17. *What She Left Behind* is composed of two interweaving story lines—Clara's in the past and Izzy's quest in present day. Discuss the structure of each narrative. Did you enjoy the alternating stories and time frames? What are the strengths and drawbacks of this format?

18. Which "voice" did you prefer, Izzy's or Clara's? Is one more or less authentic than the other? If you could meet one of the two characters, which one would you choose?

19. How are Clara and Izzy the same? How are they different?

20. What do you think Izzy's future looks like? What about Clara and her daughter's future?

Center Point Large Print
600 Brooks Road / PO Box 1
Thorndike ME 04986-0001 USA

(207) 568-3717

**US & Canada:
1 800 929-9108**
www.centerpointlargeprint.com